THE

A P P A R I T I O N :

A ROMANCE.

" As to a belief in apparitions, sir," said the Doctor, " there are thousands who deny it
with their tongues, but confess it with their fears."—JOHNSON.

LONDON:
PUBLISHED BY EDWARD LLOYD, 12, SALISBURY SQUARE,
FLEET STREET.

——

1846.

PREFACE.

In concluding this work, the author has but little to say to his readers, further than that he has been gratified, but not surprised, at the sale it has attained ; fer the subject of spectral appearances is altogether one, which, from the very earliest ages, has excited so much of the curiosity of mankind that those relations of facts, or presumed facts, which have borne upon the popular belief, have always been perused with interest.

Probably, in the whole range of literature, there is nothing which so fixes upon the imagination as a narrative that takes us from actual, every day existence into that unreal world of shadows, of which we know so little, but of which we conjecture so much.

The various tales that from time to time have appeared, bearing upon the subject of spectral appearances, have always been sufficient to keep the world acutely alive to a desire of investigating the truths concerning which we, in the year 1846, are just as far off knowing as the limited population of the year 1, with their limited scientific acquirements.

As regards the tales of the wild and the wonderful which are in the pages of this work, we can only say that they have been carefully collected from the most authentic sources, as narratives of the supernatural, which had never been presented to the public in any shape or guise whatever ; and if our ghosts have amused the leisure hours of any of our readers, without attracting injuriously that quality of imagination which takes so large an interest in such matters, we shall not regret the toil of their concoction.

As regards ourselves, we must confess that the spirits have, by the great patron-
age which this work has received, assumed a tangible shape of the most gratifying
character, having a pleasant jingle with them—ringing soft music on the ears, and,
take them for all in all, being such rare spirits that we have no objection to live a
long life in their sweet society.

These are the kind of spirits with which we hope all our readers will be continually haunted ; and with such a hope we, with such an accumulation of
thanks as one who has deserved well of the public feels that he ought to return to
it, the author of the " Apparition," for the present, bids farewell to his readers.

THE APPARITION.

A Romance of the Imagination.

BY THE AUTHOR OF "NEWGATE."

See p. 7.

INTRODUCTION.

ONE, two, three, four, five, six, seven, eight, nine, ten, eleven, and twelve. Midnight! that witching hour, when disembodied spirits burst from the thr of the tomb; when millions of inert existences become endowed with a and a terrible principle of life; when those who have walked the earth in the

No. 1.

pride of their youth and their beauty again revisit it by the glimpses of the pale moon, making the night hideous.

Midnight! a still and solemn time, when the watchful think back upon the events, perchance, of a long and embittered career; when the wise, the truthful, and the just feel sweet fancies of the future creeping over them, as if their trammelled souls were for a time wafted a little nearer Heaven than earth's mists ordinarily permit.

Midnight! a time when the guilty wretch—he who has oppressed the widow and the fatherless—he who has caused tears of affliction to dim the lustrous eyes of beauty and of innocence, trembles, and looks aghast, as the mind daguerreotypes to him the past but too faithfully, with all its points of aggravation, cutting him off from that species of imaginative flattery which, in the broad daylight, he may have hugged to his heart as a consolation against the whisperings of conscience.

Midnight! when the honest man seeks his happy home, when the thief, owl-like, slinks forth from the den in which he has slept the live-long day, to wage war against the social institutions of that society of which he is an unhallowed member.

Yes, it is midnight; and the teeming fancy overpowers the judgment, running riot in the brain. Strange thoughts, unsanctioned by the soberer judgment, hold high revel in the chambers of the mind. The very air seems loaded with vapoury shapes, and through the mists of darkness we may fancy dreamy shapes of the uncouth and the terrific.

It is a time when human nature shrinks, as it were, with a consciousness of a contact with the invisible world; a time when a shuddering kind of conviction comes across the boldest, that there are more things in Heaven and in earth than are dreamt of in their philosophy.

Is it nature, or is it education, which makes men shudder as instinctively they feel their better energies depressed, and scarcely dare assert a disbelief in that which, although repugnant to their reason, seems but too familiar with their imagination?

There are soldiers who have marched unflinching to the deadly breach, and these same men would shrink with trembling apprehension, and turn pale if they were but to traverse, at the midnight hour, the lonely aisle of some crumbling cathedral, sacred to Heaven and to the dead.

There are skilful rhetoricians, subtle, special pleaders and splitters of hairs in logical controversy, men who would circumvent Heaven itself, and so confuse the ordinary perceptions of simple-minded mortals, that no longer can they trust their senses, but they will shrink to believe that what they fancy they see is the unreal, and what they see they fancy the possibly tangible. But take these men—place them among the tombs, strip them of the admiring throng that hang upon their honeyed sentences, let them feel convinced that they are alone, and that the only witness to their fears is Heaven, then will they not shrink—will not the proud heart tremble—will not the haughty eye quail?

Yes; and the materialist, the man who has discussed so largely and so learnedly of mind, of matter, fate, pre-knowledge, and the thousand and one philosophies that have from the world's creation disturbed mankind, will tremble at the shadow cast by the pale moonlight across his path.

And is all this as nothing? Is this but what we call fancy in its unbridled moments? Is there not one of these touches of nature that make the whole world kin in this community of feeling as regards the capacity of the dead once again to glide the living likenesses of themselves among the living portion of mankind?

From the highest to the lowest, from barbarism to civilization, among the ignorant, and among the most refined and highly educated, shall we find the same hankering after the unreal, the same professed denial, but the same trembling conviction that the spirit, when it has shuffled off its mortal coil, may yet, in form and shape as palpable as when encompassed in its earthly tabernacle, it walked the earth, appear again to warn, to promise, to threaten, and always to terrify.

The painted savage, in the wildest haunts of nature—where the rank vegetation of a thousand years has accumulated, until such a natural temple is erected beneath the thickly clustered leafy boughs that only in small glimpses, dappling the green sward beneath with light and shade, can the sweet sunshine peep down upon the verdant earth—feels, and knows, or at least believes—that the dim shades of those who have preceded him stalk around his lonely hut, showing their shadowy forms in the forest glades, floating like things of air down foaming cataracts, and peopling the depths of nature with solemnity, if not with fear.

A monarch awakens at the midnight hour; the gaudy and glittering emblazonry of all his state and dignity meets his eyes. He knows that around him are careful watchers, while slumbering lightly within his slightest call are armed men. He knows—he feels that he is safe within that very penetralia of his palace; but all is still, and it is midnight. Some thought of the dead flits across his awakened imagination. Why does he look around him with suspicion and a scrutinizing glance? Why does he breathe short and thick, and draw the silken curtains of his couch closer about him? What need has he to assure himself that he is quite alone, and that the fear which is creeping momentarily across his heart is a something far beneath his dignity to feel?

Is all this fancy? Are these similar effects in different stations but freaks of unbridled imagination? Is there no dim reality—no tangible something to be deduced from all this, which we may safely put down in our catalogue of facts, and banish from the shadowy list of our mere surmises?

Surely yes, there must be—the very universality of the feeling goes far in proof of the veracity of the idea from whence it springs.

That circle of philosophers who doubt, and who deny all that they do not understand, is rapidly decreasing its dimensions. There are more wonderful things of daily occurrence beneath our ordinary nature than the re-appearance upon the earth again of the disembodied spirit of some one who has played a part in the busy drama of existence.

We shudder to believe, and yet to disbelieve were arrogance; but peradventure the following pages may do more to place before the thinking portion of mankind all the evidences for and against a belief in the subject of spectral appearances than any work which has yet issued from the press; and if, while we beguile the tedium of some lone watcher, we likewise impart to him materials for thinking upon a subject most interesting to the whole human race, the labour of years which has been expended in the following narratives, full of the terrific and the wonderful as they are, will not in vain have furrowed the brow, or whitened the locks of him who has devoted a lifetime to the task.

*   *   *   *   *   *   *

One, two, three, four, five, six, seven, eight, nine, ten, eleven, and twelve. Midnight! There is a vault, situate far below the surface of the earth, and beneath a cumbrous pile of masonry, reared to the worship of the one God. We will not particularize the structure by name, for we have made a solemn promise not to point the finger of curiosity to the ancient cathedral, whose dreary and desolate subterranean abodes became the locality in which such strange adventures were narrated.

The vault is large and arched; a tomb of black marble is in its centre, on which reposes the effigy of a knight in armour, with the hands crossed, indicative of a pilgrimage to the Holy Land having been made by the rotting form that sleeps beneath.

All around are niches for the dead; a lamp of bronze hangs from the groined ceiling; the ground is thickly strewed with the dust from some odoriferous wood, mingled with rushes, so that the pressure of any foot must needs be noiseless in that place of sepulchre.

Some coffins have been dragged from their niches—God knows by whom—and most singularly are they arranged around this tomb, which occupies the centre of the vault.

The midnight hour has struck—a death-like stillness for about five minutes pervades the solemn place. Hush! a footstep! There is a low, arched door; it creaks upon its hinges; a current of air sweeps moaning in! The step again!—It is a human form! A man enters—he bears a taper—his face his pale—his eyes look wistfully around him, and his feet tremble as he walks.

He utters no word, but he comes into the centre of the vault, and, by the aid of the taper that he carries, he lights the lamp of bronze that, by a massive chain, hangs far down from the ceiling.

There again!—another step and another!—what can this mean?—what assemblage is this, meeting in a place sacred to the repose of the dead?

There is a silent and a quiet greeting between these men, as slowly, one by one, they walk into the vault. Be their object and their purpose what it may, they respect the sanctity of the place in which they meet.

The lamp sheds a dull and a sickly glare over their faces; the air of the vault is not favourable to combustion, and, after all, it is but a dim and uncertain kind of twilight in which they meet.

How strange an assembly!—and mostly are they clad in dim and sombre looking garments. And now the door of the vault is closed, and a heavy stone is placed across it in the inside, indicative of their being all assembled.

There are twelve of them, and they stand in a silent group around that tomb in the centre, while one steps forward from among the rest, and, in a low and earnest voice, he speaks as follows:—

"My friends, it is well known to you all that the object of our meeting here is of the most deeply interesting character that can engage the attention of any human beings. We are mortal, and yet we yearn for immortality; and we wish, while yet we linger in this world, to endeavour better to establish those relations between it and the world which is to come, than they have yet been established or defined."

A murmur of assent ran through the assemblage, and then several of them sat down upon the coffins, which had been dragged from their niches; and then, after a slight pause, he who seemed by general consent to be appointed spokesman of the party, said—

"We are all searchers after knowledge; not that ordinary knowledge which schoolmen teach—not that knowledge of the real, the tangible, and the defined, which those who look but with a casual glance upon the world may register in the tablets of their brain, and feel that they possess; but we are searchers after that knowledge which is only to be acquired by patient and by attentive reflection. We wish to know if it be really true that the spirits of another world can, under any possible circumstances, make themselves visible to earthly eyes, and exercise an influence, benign or otherwise, upon mundane affairs."

The eleven persons who heard him inclined their heads in token of assent.

"My friends," he added, "it is quite impossible that any human being could have lived so long as we have each of us, without being able to add something to a common stock of information regarding subjects of the most intensely interesting character that can, by any possibility, engage individual attention. I propose that each man among us shall relate his individual experience, and such facts connected with ghostly interpositions in human affairs as shall come within the sphere of his own knowledge."

The eleven looked at each other, and then one spoke, saying—

"But it may be possible that some one among us, from timidity—from want of tact in expatiating upon that which he knows, or from a want of knowing any particular circumstance worthy the narration—may not be able, when his turn shall come, to add to the general stock of knowledge which it is the purpose of our meetings to acquire."

"There must be a penalty for non-compliance," said another.—"Ay," exclaimed a third; "it must not be that any one among us is to be permitted to be a mere listener to what is going on, without of himself adding to the general stock of information."

"A penalty, a penalty," cried several; "there must be a penalty."—"Be it so," remarked he who may be called the president of this most singular society; "be it so; let there be a penalty; and I am certain that none here present will shrink from it. But it shall be such a penalty, that in its onerous consequences it shall be so fearful that even the most timid should shrink from encountering it, and come forward with his narration of the wild and of the wonderful, rather than submit to its conditions."

The others looked at each other, and then at the president, for it was evident he had something in his mind to propose, to which these remarks were but a sort of preface. He saw that he was expected to continue; so, adopting a more solemn tone than he had even before spoken in, and looking keenly in the countenances of those around him, he said—

"Since the onus of making such a proposition, by general consent falls upon me, I do not hesitate to say that I have considered it, and it is as follows."

There was a death-like silence, and every one looked in his face as he spoke.

"I propose, then, that he who shrinks, at any one night of our meeting, from taking his turn in the relation of some moving incident connected with the supernatural, shall be placed in one of those old leaden coffins, and, supplied with a certain quantity of bread and water, left in the vault until our next night of meeting; and if, when we come again, in that interval, he have not something to tell us, the experiment be repeated."—"Good God!" said one of them.

"Yes, sir," said the president; "and, to escape so heavy a penalty, you have only to narrate something which has either come under your own personal observation, or that you have arrived at the knowledge of in some way which enables us to give credence to the narrative."

No one else spoke, and after two or three minutes' pause, the president said,—

"Are we all agreed then, gentlemen, upon this being the penalty?"—"Agreed—agreed," they said.

"Then our compact is complete; once in each week will we meet in this dreary vault—a fit place, my friends, in which to hold such solemn congregations. The very atmosphere of this abode of the dead will be suggestive of scenes and events which otherwise might escape the memory, or, at all events, if brought before us, be couched too much in the language of the every-day world to transfix our attention; but here we shall leave, as it were, the earth behind us, and, hovering upon the confines of immortality, we shall feel, while in discourse of the dead, a kind of affinity with them, and that we are so closely allied to the crumbling remains of those who have gone before us, that we are better qualified to converse of their feelings and their attributes. I, myself, have had dreadful experiences, which go far to prove that disembodied spirits may, for good or for evil, yet revisit this world which they were supposed to have left for ever."—"And I," said another.

"And I," said a third.—"And I—and I," said several in a breath.

Then one man arose, and, in a trembling voice, said,—

"If it's all the same to you, gentlemen, I'd rather go home; my wife expects me; and, as I never saw a ghost in all my life, and hope I never shall, I rather think I'd better not belong to this society, though I said I would, out of curiosity, you see, gentlemen; and so I'm your very humble servant, Good night."—"Hold," said the president; "you have joined us, sir, and it appears to me, that since you have expressed reluctance, we ought to commence with you."

"With me! Oh! no—oh! no."—"Yes—and therefore I propose that you be placed in the leaden coffin at once, and kept there till this night week, with a gallon of water and four quartern loaves."

"I'll see you all d——d first," said the individual alluded to. "I'm not in the habit of telling stories, and I'm not going to begin. I tell you I don't like it. I only came to oblige a friend of mine who told me it would be deeply interesting; and, as my wife believes in ghosts, I thought it would be a good thing to join the society, so as to be able to tell her all that I heard."

" And was that," said the president, " the vile motive that induced you, sir, to come amongst us? Was it merely to gratify the morbid curiosity of your wife, sir ?"—" Well, I don't mind confessing that it was something of that sort; and, if you don't feel inclined to have me among you, I'm quite willing to go."

" Sir," said another one, rising, " I'm quite certain that, notwithstanding the modesty of our friend here, Mr. Pentwhistle, he is just the man, of all others, to be of great advantage to us in the investigation which we are about to institute."—" Indeed, sir," said the president.

" No—no—no !" cried Mr. Pentwhistle ; " it's quite a mistake ; I don't know anything about ghosts, and never did."—" However rude it may sound," continued the other speaker, " I feel that I must contradict my friend, and assert that no man knows more upon such subjects than he does."

" Then," said the president, " we will insist upon his remaining in the society ; and I shall consider it as carried by acclamation that he continues one of us."

It was in vain that Mr. Pentwhistle protested, and finally resumed his seat, on finding that nothing he said was at all attended to. Then an individual arose, who presented a remarkable contrast to that gentleman. He had all the aspect of a man of acute and lively imagination ; and any one, to have beheld him for a moment, would have at once said that he was, of all others, just the individual to become an active member of such an association for such purposes.

" Mr. President and gentlemen," he said, " I rise to propose to you a resolution, in which I hope and trust we shall all most cordially agree. It is one so strictly in accordance with the views which have induced our meeting, that I am certain no gentleman here present can, with any degree of consistency, object to it."

He paused a moment, and all was hushed around him in mute curiosity, to hear what was the nature of the proposition he had to submit.

" Gentlemen," he continued, " it is just possible, as human life is so uncertain, that at some period or another, during the continuance of our ghostly researches, some one among us may shake off the trammels of humanity, and getting rid of that dusty tabernacle in which his spirit is confined, he may be in a position to discover, beyond all cavil and dispute, the grand secret which we are all striving after, and, as a disembodied spirit himself, to know the power and the capabilities of such mysterious beings."

Expectation sat upon every countenance, and, after pausing sufficiently to allow his words to have free effect, the orator continued,—

" Gentlemen, then what I propose is this, that, should any one of our fraternity expire, he will, if he have the power, set at rest the question as to the appearance of supernatural beings, by visiting the whole of us when here assembled, or, gliding into the chamber of some individual among us, enable him to inform the remainder of the particulars of the ghostly visitant."

There was a look of dismay upon several countenances, and two or three of those who were assembled evidently shrank aghast from this proposition, which was of too practical a nature to please them. Others, however, again seemed to like it ; while, upon every countenance, there was rather an expression of eager curiosity to know what he who made the proposition next would say.

The individual who had thus drawn universal attention upon himself, appeared to derive some pleasure from the notoriety he was acquiring.

" Gentlemen," he said, " do not suppose for one moment, that in making this proposition to you, I am endeavouring to do something which may have a tendency to render our proceedings unpalatable to any persons here assembled ; but the cause in which we have embarked is one of deep interest to ourselves, as well as of great importance to the human race ; therefore, for one, I distinctly say, that if I should die, I will most certainly take an opportunity of visiting every individual member of this society ; and not only, gentlemen, will I visit you, but I will come accompanied with such aggravations and such horrors as any ghostly personage may be presumed to collect about him, so that while the warm blood curdles in your veins, and you feel yourselves trembling upon the brink of madness, you will have no excuse for a nonbelief in the existence of supernatural beings."

"Sir!" exclaimed one, starting to his feet, "Mr. President, I move that gentleman be forthwith expelled from this society, so that his ghost may have no possible excuse for visiting any of us. I consider, Mr. President, that the idea he has given utterance to, is a most diabolical one."

There was a great deal of confusion—two or three voices seconded the motion, and the president in vain for some moments attempted to make himself heard. When he did, however, succeed in doing so, his voice had all the effect of oil upon the troubled waters, for he said,—

"Gentlemen, I do not perceive that there can be any difficulty in meeting the proposition of our learned friend; but let such an argument be a private one, and not one belonging to the society. Let any gentleman who is curious to see that learned individual's ghost, make an agreement with him to that effect."—"Hear—hear—hear—hear!" echoed through the vault, and the gentleman who had made the proposition sat down, with a sardonic smile upon his countenance, as if he viewed with great contempt the unmanly being which had, to his mind, dictated this compromise of one of the most important matters connected with the proceedings of the society.

But it was evident that the majority rejoiced in the escape from the infliction of his ghostly appearance, and now the storm of discord being hushed, and so much of the preliminary business being settled, the chairman spoke again, saying,—

"Gentlemen, I presume that it's quite understood how we are to carry on the proceedings of this association. It is expected that each member in his turn shall narrate to us some ghostly episode, some tale of an apparition, which he shall vouch for on his own credit, to having actually occurred, and at the end of each of these episodes of reality, or the imagination, those of us who have listened to the narration can make what remarks we may think proper with regard to the probability attending upon it."

This was assented to, and now a general crying arose as to who was to commence the narrations, which were to come under the consideration of the club. All eyes were turned upon the president, as being the most fit and proper person to do so; but he hung back for a time, and he was observed to change colour, a circumstance which only more vividly impressed upon the minds of his compeers that he must have something of a dreadful character to disclose—something, the thoughts of which were almost too much even for him; and which, although probably he felt it to be his duty to make those who were associated with him acquainted, he yet shrunk from putting into appropriate language, or recalling from the depth of his memory, where it lay enshrouded.

This, though, only stimulated the curiosity, which, perhaps, he intended to repress, and by general consent it was agreed that the president should commence the proceedings of the society by some narration of an apparition, the correctness of which he could vouch for. But still he held back.

"No, gentlemen—no, gentlemen," he said; "let us act fairly towards each other in this matter. I cannot help owning that there is a something upon my mind which I have not yet communicated to mortal man; the only other individual who knew it besides myself, is now himself among the dead; but what I propose is, that we should draw lots which is to commence. Here is a skull; let the names of the persons present be written on small scraps of paper, and placed within this hollow orifice, where, perchance, once dwelt a glorious intellect; thus, although the orifice is small, one of us, with his wetted finger, can dip for one of the papers, and the name of the individual that is upon it shall be he who is to commence our proceedings."

This was a disappointment to those assembled; and yet it was too reasonable to object to, so it was agreed that it should be so, though with not the best grace in the world. The skull was produced, and a few minutes sufficed to complete the preparations, and when all was in readiness, the president held forth the ghastly receptacle of the names, saying,—

" What gentleman will oblige me by drawing forth one of these papers?   The remainder can remain in the skull until they are wanted."

All shrunk back but he who had proposed the ghostly visitation, and, without hesitation, he plunged his finger through that circular jagged orifice left at the base of the occiput where the vertebra column inserts itself, and drew forth, adhering to his finger, one of the scraps of paper.

The name was read aloud, and those assembled looked at each other with surprise, not unmingled with gratification, for it was that of the president himself. There was a pause of some moments' duration, and then, with rather a sorrowing aspect, he said,—

" Gentlemen, I perceive that fate has declared it to be my duty to commence the proceedings of this club, and therefore I shall no longer shrink from the fiat of destiny.   That narration which I have alluded to as one which moved me strongly at the time, although years have now elapsed since it occurred, you shall hear from my lips.   At the same time, I shall beg your indulgence for such faults of style I shall be guilty of."

There was a murmur of assent, and then he continued, as he laid his watch before him,—

" I shall conceal nothing from you, and I shall beseech you to take my word that I shall add nothing to the actual and bona fide circumstances which I shall place before you.   It is now one o'clock, and it will be necessary, to avoid observation and ungracious comment from persons not so interested as we are in the discovery of truth, that we should separate

" ' Before the early cock gives salutation to the morn.'

I do not think that in one night I shall be able to give to you the whole of the tale which it is my purpose to lay before you, but I will compress those portions which may not be so interesting to you, as far as possible, and I must throw myself completely upon your indulgence to bear with me if I have to occupy the next, and even the next night of meeting after that again, before I arrive at the conclusion of a set of circumstances which I shall never forget, and which I have no doubt will make some impression upon yourselves."

There was a dead silence, and the eleven members of the club disposed themselves in various attitudes in order that they might listen with greater ease to the communication which was about to be submitted to them.   All looked anxious, and full of interest; there could be no doubt that they expected something of a more than ordinary character from the president.

And he, too, looked agitated, and was evidently endeavouring to inspire himself with something like nervous energy before he should commence the narration which had produced so great an effect upon his own mind, and which, no doubt, he fully expected would similarly affect his hearers.

He sighed deeply, and passed his hand across his brow as though memory was travelling back to painful scenes of bygone years, and then suddenly his voice rose loud and clear, and then he said,—

" I shall call the narrative to which I shall call your special attention, simply by a name which, while beforehand you will say expresses but little, you will afterwards admit has a strong relation to the subject matter of the narrative; you will hear from me a narrative which you may call

THE DEATH FACE.

I HAD a friend of the name of Franklin, and I lost sight of him for many years. We had been early juvenile intimates ; so much so, indeed, that one scarcely stirred anywhere without the other, and almost all our feelings and opinions were in common.

But, as is most frequently the case with regard to these early associations, time and circumstances separated us, and we only met occasionally in the busy world to exchange a few friendly expressions, or an affectionate pressure of the hand, an then we were apart again, each struggling in the huge Babel-like confusion of society for that which man may never know—contentment. And still, whenever I met my ancient friend, it was a pleasant thing, for days and days to come, to think about; for memory would fly back to those happier times when ambition was more restricted in its views, and when the romance of life had not yet been crushed by the sad realities that too soon teach us we had but dreamt of the world as it might be, but, alas! awaken to find it widely different from all that we had pictured it to the glowing fancy of our early days.

I never made a friend such as I made of Franklin; the world taught me distrust and caution—the first gush of youthful feeling and of confidence soon passed away, and I, in common with all others who think at all, soon found the sad necessity of acting apart, instead of being as nature really made me.

You may judge, then, that it was a pleasant thing to meet this intimate of my early boyhood—this man to whom I thought I could be natural—if it were but for a fleeting moment.

But sometimes more than a year would elapse, and I saw him not, until at length once I missed him for nearly three years, and then one day I met him in the street. I thought I knew him—but I only thought so, and I paused and looked upon him with a dreamy and doubtful expression upon my countenance, he was so changed.

"Franklin," I said, "can it be possible, Franklin?"—"You know me," he said; "my mother would not; look upon me again."

"Yes, Franklin," I said, "I do know you, but how strangely altered you are; why, you are quite a different man to what you were a few years since."—"A different man!" he said, and he laughed bitterly. "Yes, I was a different man three years since; I was poor, dependent, lowly, and compelled to live humble; I am now rich, and may be haughty, if I choose. I have my mansion, my horses, my carriage, my dogs, and my servants—more fawning and sycophantic than the meanest of the breed. I have wealth, Mortimer—wealth; I can command every luxury of life from the four quarters of the globe. There is nothing so costly but at a wish I can see it placed before me. And yet, Mortimer, a word in your ear, it is—it is a secret—I am wretched."

"Wretched," I said, "you surely dream!"—"Oh, would I could!" he replied. "Or if I thought, Mortimer, that you, by killing me, could consign me for ever, body and soul, to the oblivion of corruption, I would implore you, by a remembrance of all those ties of early friendship that linked our hearts together, to do the deed. I would bid you remember how we promised each other that no wish should go ungratified. How, hand in hand, we have looked in each other's faces, and uttered, in deep sincerity of soul, that word, friendship. Mortimer, Mortimer—friend of my boyhood, dear companion of my earliest days, I would beg of you to kill me, but there is a dread of that world beyond the tomb—that undiscovered country, from whence no traveller returns, that makes me rather bear the ills I know, than rush on others that I know not of."

"Good Heavens! Franklin," I said, "is this a mood of madness, or can there be any reality in this desperate state of feeling? My old friend Franklin, rouse yourself; you know not what you say, and there sits an expression upon your face ——"

"Face! face! what face? Hold me, Mortimer; where are we now? Look, look how the eyes are bent upon me! The pale lips, too, except where spots of gore belie their whiteness! Mortimer, Mortimer, the dead face! the dead face!"

"The what?" I said; "Franklin, compose yourself. You're in the open streets, recollect; come, come, step aside. Franklin, my old friend, do not tremble thus; why, you clutch my arm with a vice-like energy. There, there, you are better, now; walk with me awhile; something has disturbed you."

"Hush!" he said; "did you see it?"—"See what?"

"I—I thought you spoke of the face; you might have seen it. I do not know but that to you, with whom I have often held such sweet communion of soul; you who could once sound so easily the depths of this heart, gathering, without an effort, all its various emotions—I thought it possible that to you it might have shown itself,

No. 2.

for a passing moment."—"Now really, Franklin, you must be labouring under some most strange delusion. What do you mean by the face—and the dead face? Come home with me, and explain to me, at your leisure, with that same confidence in each other's friendship that we had of old—a confidence which it is a charm to me to think is now unbroken—what it is that stirs your nature to such an extent, and fills you with the very agony of fear. Come, Franklin, come—come home with me."

He paused, and looked me in the face. A visible emotion disturbed his features, and then, by a great effort, I saw that he composed himself to speak with some degree of calmness.

"No, Mortimer, no," he said; "we have not met for three long years. God send that we may never meet again. I have still sufficient feeling left to implore you now, and for ever, to repudiate the wretch whom you once knew, and called by the endearing name of friend. Shun me, Mortimer, shun me—ask nothing concerning me. Avoid me, if you see me in your path—forget me, forget me."

He would have turned away, but I held him by the arm.

"No, Franklin," I said; "no. In our recent meetings we have but exchanged words of sympathetic kindness, and then separated; but now, I feel certain that something must have occurred, which calls loudly upon early friendship to succour you. I cannot now part with you as we have lately parted. Let me know, I implore you, where you are to be found, and tell me that the remembrance of early days still sufficiently clings to me, to make me feel unhappy in your unhappiness, and that it is a sacred duty to aid you in every possible way that lies within the compass of my power."

He did not speak for some moments, but he looked wistfully in my face, and then he said, as if rather communing with himself than addressing me,—

"Shall I—dare I? No, no, no."

Before I could be aware of his intention, he turned abruptly from me, and at a rapid pace, which set pursuit almost at defiance, he fled, and I lost sight of him completely.

This meeting with Franklin was anything but productive of the pleasant feelings which my former encounters with him in the public streets had always produced in me. I felt extremely uncomfortable to know what it was that so much affected his intellect, and I much blamed myself for allowing him to go so easily, and not positively insisting, which the right of early friendship gave me a title to, upon knowing what it was that so disturbed him.

But I was now helpless, for I had no clue to his whereabouts, and except I might chance again to meet him, I could entertain no hope of arriving at a solution of the mystery connected with his singular behaviour.

I was much engaged during the whole of that day, and yet I may safely say, that a consideration of my friend's singular behaviour occupied my mind more completely than any business of my own; and even when I retired to rest, I could not forget it, but indulged in a thousand conjectures, not one of which, probably, was near the truth, though all might have been plausible.

What, however, was my agreeable surprise, to find upon my breakfast-table on the following morning, a card, on which was the following name and address :—"Ernest Franklin, Bellenden Lodge, Suffolk."

I rang instantly for my servant, and inquired how the card came there.

"Why, sir," was the reply, "it came by hand. A boy left it, who said there was no answer, but that it was to be placed before you as soon as you arose."

"What can this mean?" I said to myself. "Is this an invitation thus mutely conveyed to me? Has my old friend repented, and thought that at last he would take my advice, and consult me upon the fearful subject of his apprehensions, be they of what character they may? Bellenden Lodge, Suffolk. I never heard of the place, but no doubt it is in existence, and I dare say there will be very little difficulty in finding it. Shall I seek him, or shall I not? Yes. At the sacred call of friendship which it pleases me to translate this to be, I will sacrifice a portion of my time."

I fear, gentlemen, that I must plead guilty to not being quite so disinterested as my language would imply. If I were to analyse my feelings properly, I dare say it would be found that no small share of personal curiosity assisted me in coming to a conclusion, that to go to Bellenden Lodge as soon as possible, would be the very best way to serve my friend Franklin.

There was something so utterly inexplicable in his conduct, that while it awakened a perfect maze of conjecture, it left me, notwithstanding the ingenuity, however, of some of my conjectures, just where I was, let me spend what time I would upon the inquiry.

I felt that from his own lips only could I hope for a solution of the mystery which his conduct clearly indicated existed. But yet my business arrangements would not permit me immediately to respond to the implied invitation, and I knew that it would be nearly a week before I could consider myself free to proceed to the county of Suffolk, in search of Bellenden Lodge.

And I fretted all this time, because I was extremely anxious to see Franklin, and ascertain what it was that so much afflicted him, and how he, in the possession, as he avowed himself to be, of all that could render life desirable, could possibly feel such an amount of affliction, such as that which his language and manner bespoke.

More than once I told myself that it must be some species of hypochondriasis under which he laboured, and that probably, when I came fairly to examine that which he would tell me when I reached his home, I should have the gratification of discovering that his terrors were only those of the imagination.

I had frequently heard of cases where the sudden acquisition of wealth had created so many new and strange desires, that the mind became wearied, and the fancy, acquiring a preternatural activity, was apt, in the absence of great evils, to imagine artificial ones, which assumed a worse aspect the more they were committed to the reflection of a fevered fancy.

I say, I hoped this, and yet there was something terrifically real in the fear that was manifest in my friend Franklin's countenance.

My impatience to proceed to Bellenden Lodge was so great, that I managed to start upon the journey earlier than I had thought it possible to get rid of the numerous professional engagements which were pressing upon my attention; a day less than a week had elapsed since my receipt of Franklin's card, and then I bade adieu to London for a time, and set out for my solitary journey.

I had taken the precaution, before my departure, to consult one of the best compiled road-books I could find, and in it, to my great satisfaction, I found Bellenden Lodge mentioned, as being an ancient edifice of the Tudor style of architecture, and situated about half a mile from the village of Bellenden, and distant five miles from the market town of Haverford.

This information was sufficiently precise for me to go upon, and finding, upon inquiry, that a mail passed through the town of Haverford, I took my place on a somewhat raw and cold evening, and was rattled along at good speed in the direction to which friendship called me.

From the inquiries which I made of the coachman, for I enjoy that place of honour, the box-seat, I found that it was twelve hours journey at the mail rate of travelling, admitting for changing horses, and so on, before we could reach Haverford, the distance being somewhere about one hundred and ten miles, therefore I should arrive in the immediate vicinity of Bellenden Lodge at rather an early hour in the morning, starting, as I did, from St. Martin's-le-grand at half-past eight o'clock in the evening.

It was a long and dreary thing that night journey. Occasionally I fell into a doze, but was sure to be startled up again by the change of horses, which, to my imagination, seemed to be a process gone through extremely often; but when I remarked as much to the coachman, he replied,—

"Yes, it's all very well for you to think so, but if you was a hoss, you wouldn't; besides, you goes to sleep while we're a driving on, and you only wakes up when you doesn't hear the sound of the wheels; and, besides, at the pace we goes ——"

—"That will do," said I; "the reasons are quite enough. Don't elaborate."

" No, sir," said the coachman. " I've been on this ere road a matter of eighteen years, and nobody catched me never laboring. I know, sir, it's French for running again a wagging."

I felt completely used up by the coachman's amount of information, and after merely saying, just so, I rolled myself up like a hedgehog, in the large cloak I had brought with me, and endeavoured to snatch an hour's repose.

I must have slept a considerable time, for when I awakened the grey light of morning was shining gently upon the tree tops, and we were going through an exquisitely beautiful valley, in a state of high cultivation, beyond anything I had ever seen before. Always, as I have been, an admirer of Nature, it is not to be wondered at that I was soon wide awake to the charms of that delightful scene through which I was whirled, and it presented so pleasing and delightful a contrast to the city life which I had been leading, that for the moment I completely forgot Franklin and all the object of my journey, thinking myself amply repaid for all my trouble by the beautiful scenery around me, which, while it presented to my eyes the most beautiful autumn tints, seemed at the same time to be teeming with life, as thousands of forest birds carolled forth their early lays, and flew from tree to tree, in all the happy exultation of early freedom.

" This is a sweet spot," I exclaimed.—" Oh, this ere valley," said the coachman. " Yes, sir ; it would be werry well, but what I always says is this—there wants a public-house here ; it's a matter of five mile now since we passed the old Bugle Inn, and it'll be two mile more afore we comes to the Green Cat and Winegar Cruet."

How my dreams of romance vanished at this matter-of-fact statement. I seemed to see in my mind's eye that confounded Green Cat and Vinegar Cruet, with its abominable sign, demolishing all the beauty of the landscape. Really that coach-man was a most impracticable subject. I gave him up, determined to say no more to him. Not that I had much opportunity of doing so had I felt inclined, for we were near, or at least I was near my journey's end.

" Here we is," said the coachman, as we came up the long straggling high street of a country town. " Here we is at Haverford. I believe you gets down here, sir. You'd better go to the Spectacles and Grasshopper, there you'll find good accommodation. Remember the coachman."

I gave him the expected gratuity, and alighted from the vehicle, soon finding myself the centre of an admiring throng of boys, who, upon my inquiring for the Grass-hopper and Spectacles, preceded me to that establishment in a body, as if I had been some great conqueror or a wild beast, and perhaps they are much the same.

I was glad to get housed, for it is no pleasant thing for a man who has lived in London and been accustomed to lose, as it were, his personal identity in the throng surrounding him, to find himself all at once the centre of an admiring host and an object of great attraction.

The inn fully bore out the landlord's recommendation of it. It was comfortable and cleanly, and the landlord obliging, and more obliging still was he when he found I had no objection to engaging a post-chaise to the village of Bellenden, and paying all the proper charges thereupon. I, moreover, ordered a breakfast which completely won his heart, so that we soon became upon the very best of terms, which was just what I wished, for I had a notion of inquiring of my host as quietly and insidiously as possible, if he knew anything of Mr. Franklin who resided at Bellenden Lodge.

You may safely a hundred miles from London make such an inquiry, for everybody makes it his or her business to know everything about everybody else, and the moment I mentioned Mr. Franklin, the landlord gave me a pretty accurate description of his person, and asked me if that was the gentleman.

" Yes," I said, " you are right, that is he. I have come from London on purpose to visit him."—" Why, sir, in a manner of speaking, we know, and we don't know anything about him. Bellenden Lodge and the estate around it came to him, they say, in a very odd sort of way."

" Indeed, how was that?"—" Why, I can't tell you the rights of the story, sir, and what I can tell you, I don't know if it's quite the thing. They say he married somebody as died in about half an hour afterwards, and then that he came into possession of Bellenden Lodge, because it was left to her, whoever she was, and he claimed it as heir-at-law.".

" I never heard that he was married."—" That's the story they tell, sir, and an odd sort of life he seems to lead in the lodge. Of course it's very odd, but they do say it, that not a servant will remain in the place on account of its being so frightfully haunted."

" Haunted! that must be some idle superstition."—" So I should say, sir ; howsomever he never has a servant there above a few weeks, though he gives more wages than any gentleman in the county, and lets them do just as they like. I have heard them say that they wouldn't live with him for love or money ; and more than ever, every servant has left him excepting one there they call old Joe, who has been a soldier in his time, and who don't care for the devil himself. Excuse me, sir, for naming the devil to you."

" Oh, don't name it," I said. " And now, whenever you can get the post-chaise ready, I'll proceed to the lodge. I don't know how long I remain, but you may depend upon it, that be it for a long or a short time, I shall do myself the pleasure of paying you another visit when I leave it."

In the course of an hour a ricketty and most abominable post-chaise, which I am quite certain could not have been turned out for twelve months before, made its appearance at the inn door, and a very venerable post-boy touched his cap to me, as I walked and took my seat in the faded vehicle.

" Will you ride to the lodge, sir," he said, " or only to the village?"—" To the lodge, by all means," I said.

" Oh, oh, I suppose near hand 'll do, sir ?"—" What do you mean? I suppose I can be driven where I please."

" Oh, yes, sir, in course, in course, sir ; only of the two, sir, I'd rather not go nearer Bellenden Lodge than I can help. You may, or you mayn't know it, sir—of course it isn't for me to say, but it's haunted, and I wouldn't sleep in it one night—no—no ; not to be made landlord of the Spectacles and Grasshopper, I wouldn't."—" Nevertheless," said I, " you must drive me to Bellenden Lodge," and I sprang into the vehicle.

It took three-quarters of an hour to accomplish the distance of five miles, and notwithstanding we passed through some of the most delightful scenery, I was positively wearied at this slow rate of locomotion, before we arrived at our place of destination. Suddenly, however, the vehicle stopped, for I did not know where we were exactly, and it was with a feeling of pleasurable surprise that I found the door opened, and the elderly post-boy touching his hat, said,—

" This is the place, sir, and if you go through the iron gates up the avenue, you'll come to the lodge."

I alighted and dismissed him with a gratuity, and found myself close to a pair of high, massy, iron gates, most profusely ornamented, and wrought with singular beauty. They were supported on each side by massive square brick turrets, with white dressings, and many parts of the iron arch of the gates showed that they had been at one time gilt, particularly the centres, which represented the coat of arms of the family whose original abiding place that ancient structure had been.

A little within those gates, I could perceive a thatched building with latticed windows, which I conjectured to be a porter's lodge, and, doubtless, inhabited by some one, who would act as my guide to the house, of which, as yet, by-the-bye, I could see no trace whatever.

Upon a closer investigation of the locality, I saw that a massive bell hung at the top of the iron gates, but in my minutest investigations could discover no means of awakening its iron tongue ; and I stood for nearly ten minutes wondering how people got into Bellenden Lodge, when there seemed no means of signifying their presence. Then I did what I might have done at first, and succeeded in, that is, tried to open the massive gates without assistance.

They yielded at a touch ; and, after a moment's hesitation, I passed through them, closing them behind me, and expecting each moment to be challenged by some one for intruding on the domain. I walked on with that timid, cautious

step, which involuntarily a person uses when he feels that he is somewhere un-
authorised, and only as yet permitted because unchallenged.

Oh, what a delicious avenue of trees—meeting over head, and forming one of
the most natural of canopies that ever I beheld, was that in which I   Nothing could be finer in its way, or more majestic, and the autumnal   which
pervaded the foliage lent a gentle and a dignified charm to the scene, which at
no other season of the year could it have possessed.

Millions of leaves had already fallen, and my footsteps were perfectly noiseless
as I trod upon that soft, yielding mass of fading vegetation. There was a chaste
and sentimental serenity about the place which pleased me much ; and when
after a short distance I came upon the statue of some sylvan deity, half obscured
by the rich foliage that around it sprung in rich luxuriance, I asked myself,—

"Is this neglect or is it the very perfection of the art ? If it be the former it is
a happy accident; if the latter, he who has planned it must have a soul full of
sentiment and poetry."

I passed on, still pacing up that majestic avenue. Nothing disturbed the
solemn stillness that reigned around, except now and then the low whistle of
some bird calling to its mate, or the caw of a rook as it left its aerial home, to
take a wide circlet through the neighbouring plantations. It was a place to
spend a long summer's day in—busy with one's own thoughts, and yet to know
no weariness.

And now I came upon a gentle turn, and a dozen paces more opened to my
enraptured eyes a sight, which, probably, owed much of its charm, for the moment, to its being so utterly unexpected.

The avenue seemed suddenly to expand, and I stood almost upon the threshold of one of the sweetest green swards the eye of man ever rested on.

Such a perfect velvet carpeting of turf I never before beheld. It extended before me for three or four hundred feet in length, and there was nothing to break its
continuity of beauty, except one cedar tree, whose dark and magnificent foliage
took nothing from the beauty of the bright green from which it sprung, but, on
the contrary, wonderfully aided its effect.

It was one of those trees into the very centre of which you can walk, for its
spreading, graceful, fan-like branches, commenced not twelve inches from the
verdant turf, out of which it seemed to spring; and thus I saw the mansion
through the intersstices of that noble tree, which towered far above its topmost
pinnacles. I saw the rich, red brick, of which the building was composed,
glancing warmly in the soft beams of the morning sun. I saw the windows,
looking as if studded with molten gold. It was a noble sight, and all was so still,
too—so full of the very majesty of solitude, that I could have stood with folded
arms, looking upon that ancient house, even as in the dreams of early imagination we look upon some distant fancied dwelling, which we fear to attempt a
nearer approach to, lest the romance of its beauty should vanish, giving place
to a colder and a sterner reality.

And this was the house of the man who had told me me that he knew no peace ;
that he shrunk from the sound of his own voice, and whose whole appearance
denoted the agony of disturbed passions, and a mind ill at ease with itself.

Oh, Heaven ! what glorious capacities of enjoyment, what rich material have
you not given to your creatures to turn to the most beautiful uses, and yet how
is it all marred by the storm of human passions, which will not let the calmness
of beauty sleep upon the face of nature, but with its own wild and evil aspirations,
wars with the very divinity of beauty, and will not have so much of heaven in
its keeping as yet lingers on the green earth.

There wanted but one charm to invest this scene with the very perfection of
beauty, and that, even as if with the thought I had invoked it, came.

From among the branches of the cedar there slowly emerged two stately
antlered deer. It was nature's grouping that made them stand in such bold and
beautiful relief against the black green boughs behind them, and then, as if they
scented the presence of a stranger in that soft, balmy air, that played around the

favour...hid&not, they with arched necks and graceful movements bounded off, and were...w in a wilderness of wood to the right of the mansion.

"It is...strange," I thought, "that as yet no living being challenges an intruder's rig...) tread in such a scene as this."

It took me an effort to shake off a feeling of awe and fear that had crept over me, and then I slowly paced up that green sward, feeling as I did so that it was a sort of profanation to tread upon such beautiful and springing verdure.

I gained the tree. I passed beneath its drooping canopy of boughs, and then I stood in front of the old mansion, with its numberless windows, its painted roofs, its turrets, and all its irregular beauties of architecture, forming to my mind a delightful retrospection of the past, and pregnant with the richest associations, domestic and historical.

Still no one came to me, and a feeling of superstition crept over my heart as I stood upon the threshold. There was a massive knocker, formed of some fancied design, embodying a fabulous monster, half fish, half dragon. I raised it in my hand, and struck a heavy blow upon the oaken door.

The sound echoed through the place, but the echo of the knock I gave was not the only answer to the summons. I heard a wild, a strange, and hideous shriek—a shriek that made the scalp of my head feel cold, and sent a creeping shudder through my veins. The door's flung open, and a tall, weather-beaten, ancient-looking man, stood before me. A gaunt-looking hound was at his heels, and he regarded me in silence from beneath his shaggy brows. This man seemed determined that I should speak first; and, as I was the intruder, I considered that he was perfectly entitled to insist upon so much.

"Is Mr. Franklin within?" I said.—"No," was the reply; "are you Mortimer?"

"My name is Mortimer, certainly."—"Ah, well, he said you'd come. What made you knock? he can't abide knocks; walk in—left face, right shoulder forward—you'll come upon the great staircase—second door to the right—walk in."

With this laconic sort of address, he put his hands in his pockets and walked off in another direction, followed by the gaunt-looking hound, who gave me a look askance, and a parting growl, as if he would have said, "I am forced to endure you here, it appears, but I'm none the less indignant for all that."

The direction, although given not in the most courteous manner, was precise enough; so I followed it, and ascended an open staircase, the balustrades of which were beautifully carved. The staircase terminated in a corridor of great length, from which a number of apartments seemed to open. I paused, according to the direction I had received, at the second door on my right hand; and at that door I tapped twice before I received any answer. Then a voice, which I guessed to be that of Franklin, shouted from within,—

"No, no, no, no, no!—oh, God! no; spare me! spare me!"

Not doubting, then, for a moment, but that he mistook my summons for admission to be something of a fearful character, I thought it best at once to open the door and walk in; and I shall not easily forget my first impression upon entering that stately apartment, for such indeed it was.

It was one of those rooms such as one rarely sees in reality, but which lovers of the picturesque and the beautiful are fond of painting to the imagination. It was as different from what might be called modern splendour as anything could well be. Indeed, the furnishing was mostly done by the architect, for of moveable articles, such as might be added by a tenant of that house, there were few.

The oaken floor was but partially covered by a Turkey carpet, the sombre magnificence of which well accorded with the panelled walls and the ornamented ceiling of the place.

Huge, cumbrous-looking chairs, with heavy *fauteuilles*, were scattered here and there, while the centre of the room was occupied by a table, no way remarkable in itself, but gorgeously beautiful on account of a tapestried covering that completely concealed it, and trailed its heavy bullion fringe upon the floor.

A wood fire blazed and crackled upon the hearth, and a huge screen of many leaves, and covered with some gorgeous fabric, the nature of which I could not at first ascertain, but which I afterwards found to be of a rare description of figured velvet, enclosed an arm-chair, in which sat my friend Franklin.

But before I quit a description of this apartment, let me do justice to the costly draperies which half concealed the bay windows. They were of the most massive and exquisite material; not looped up in that clever, housewife sort of style which characterises our modern curtains, but reposing upon the floor in well-draped and picturesque masses, while the long, ample folds gave great richness of design to the whole fabric.

And portraits, too, around the panelled walls—portraits of ancient worthies, some in doublet and trunk hose, and some clad in complete steel, while here and there those grim and warlike personages were agreeably diversified by some sweet female face, surmounting the antique dress of a period long gone by, with a grace that lent even to it a charm to my modern conceptions.

Let not my auditors suppose that I took leisure at the moment of my entrance to this apartment to note these objects. No; they became matter for more careful investigation during the course of the next few hours; but as I wish to convey as exact an impression of Bellenden Lodge as possible, I exercise a discretionary power in presenting you with what I think proper first.

And now to Franklin. He was seated in the chair that I have spoken of, with the fire-light glancing upon his face; but scarcely had I taken two steps into the apartment, when he rose, clutching the arms of the seat as he did so, and, in a half-shrieking voice, he cried,—

"Who's that—who's that?—who comes here? Am I to have no peace?"—" 'Tis I," I replied. "Do you not know me, Franklin?"

"Yes, yes. I think I sent for you; did I not? I sent for you to make a dreadful confidence with you, with the hope that, after that, I should not suffer quite so much. The hope may be a delusion, and Heaven help me if it be!"

"Franklin," I said, as I moved one of the heavy chairs up to the fireside, and sat down by him—"Franklin, such a hope is never a delusion. There is nothing so bad but that the imagination may make it much worse, and, probably, if you submit that which torments you to the more sober judgment of myself, I shall be able to reason you into a more rational train of thought, and perhaps to show you that some of your fears are groundless, and that, after all, there is greater room for hope in your position, be it what it may, than you yourself think; and likewise you can have the advantage of being well aware that the confidence you repose in me is one which will not be afterwards attended with any regrets."

"Yes, yes," he said; "I know that—I know that. Do you think—are you sure that we are quite alone? Will you—will you look behind the screen? I have not seen it for an hour, and it must be hiding somewhere—somewhere among the folds of the cumbrous drapery in this apartment, or in some obscure nook or corner of its architecture, but to give me such a respite as will enable it again to loom upon my affrighted senses with aggravated horrors. But I will not forget; I will not for one moment be seduced to forget. Look behind the screen, I pray you!"

"Now, Franklin," I said, "this is madness. What is it you dread?"—"The dead face!" he cried—"the dead face!" and then bursting into a sort of scream of terror, he rose from his chair, and pointing with both fingers just past my head, he shouted, in a voice that actually terrified me,—"There it is—there—there it is! God have mercy upon me! Do you not see it, how it mocks me with its tenderness, and that reproachful smile, enough to hurl a soul to perdition? There needs no other accuser before the judgment throne of God than that face. It looks upon me, and I am condemned. Mercy—mercy! Do you not see it—do you not see it? There it floats past me—nearer—nearer—oh, save me Heaven!"

He turned and sank down by the chair, resting his face upon its velvet cushion, and trembling so that I felt convinced many such occasions of nervousness must soon consign him to the grave.

But was it nervousness? That was a question that I even trembled to ask myself, and, I must confess, that when he pointed in that strange, significant manner past my face, that I felt the blood retreat to my heart with a cold kind of gush, and, turning slowly, I cast my eyes round the vast extent of that apartment, with something like an expectation that they would rest upon a shadowy existence—a something not of this world, and yet mingling strangely with its inhabitants.

I thought it at the time imagination, but truth compels me to admit that, although my outward senses were not cognizant of the presence of any spectral form, I yet seemed, in a manner of speaking, to shrink within myself, and I thought that a soft and gentle sort of air went through the apartment, as if its atmosphere were disturbed with the presence of something not sufficiently substantial for mortal eyes to define, and yet having a tangible existence in the great scheme of the universe.

I made an effort, and I shook off the tremor that had seized me. I advanced to Franklin, and, by main force, lifted him from off his knees.

"This will kill you," I said; "this is the very frenzy of imagination. Shake it off, I pray you. If you do not, I will predicate its end for you."—"You need not," he said, faintly. "It's end is death or insanity. Did you see nothing?"

"Nothing whatever."—"No, no; it is only for me to look upon that dreadful sight—dreadful even in its seraphic beauty. Oh, Heaven! surely—surely I have now suffered enough for what, at the best, was an involuntary crime. I have erred, and erred grievously; but I have erred through passion given to me by the great God that made us all; and how grievously am I punished."

"You should not dwell upon such thoughts," I said; "but remember your promise to tell me all."—"I will—I will. But can it be possible you saw it not? Did you feel no consciousness of the presence of a something not of this world? Did those invisible senses which are superior in their subtlety to those which we are in the habit of ordinarily appealing to, not tell you that you stood, even for a moment, in the presence of a soul that had shaken off the trammels of its earthly state —a wandering spirit from the starry paths that light the way from earth to heaven— a being of another world, with just sufficient of its earthly trammels clinging to it, to soil its pure pinions with the dull heavy mists of earth on a mission of retribution?"

"I hear you," I said, "and it is with grief I hear you—great grief that you should have adopted such opinions and sentiments. Look around you, Franklin— we're alone."—"Yes, we are now. I can feel that the weight is lifted off my heart for a brief space; and while I may, while yet sufficient reason is left to me, I would fain tell you all."

"Do so; and be assured that in the relation you will find great relief. With us the unburdening our bosoms of some calamitous secret, and clothing it in fit and appropriate language, has as pleasant and mollifying an effect as the tears of the gentle sex have upon their griefs. Our sterner natures forbid us an indulgence in such soft emotions, but be assured that you will find yourself far the better for an unreserved communication to me."

"I know it, and I believe it. I am better now. At times a whole day will pass, and such a paroxysm of dread as crept over me awhile ago will not recur. Sometimes the sweet sunshine will stream in at those old latticed windows, and serve to chase away all sad and gloomy thoughts. Some pitying angel then takes mercy upon me, and stays the vision on its earthward progress. I do not see it always, but there will come times when, for many hours, I can feel it close to me, destroying me by its very glance—cursing me even by a forgiving look."

"Well, well—well, well; you shall tell me more at large."—"Will you stay here to-night?"

"Yes, and to-morrow night—and the next night, too, if it will give you pleasure."—"Do not be hasty in such a promise. I had another friend; he came here a bold and fearless man."

"Well—well."—"While day-light lasted it was well—but when the mists of night closed in—when all was calm and still, a change crept over him. He slept in the purple room."

"The what room?"—"A room called the purple room on account of the character of its hangings—a choice apartment for a man of iron nerves."

No. 3.

"Then that room," said I, "I beg you will allot to me to-night, for, without boasting iron nerves, I, at all events, claim exception from superstition."

"You do?"—"I do, indeed. But tell me what became of your other friend."

"He came, as you might come, to comfort and console me. He came boldly—he laughed at my fears—he told me that I was the creature of a disordered fancy, and in the morning he left me an altered man."

"Indeed! do you mean to say that he had seen something?"—"He had, indeed. The night had changed his sentiments, and taught him to believe that there was more in Heaven and on earth than in his philosophy he had dreamt of."

"Well," said I, "I will risk all that; I'm not superstitious, but, at the same time, I'm no infidel in matters which I don't comprehend, and I'm never disposed to deny any natural phenomenon because it don't happen to accord with what I know by previous experience with the general laws of nature."—"Be it so."

"One thing, however, I ask of you, which is, that before I retire to rest, you will relate to me the episode in your life which has produced the state of mind under which I find you labouring. It is needless for me to say, that it is no idle curiosity that prompts the request; but I do hope the journey I have undertaken will have the effect of rescuing you from the mental thraldom in which you are held."

"Oh," he cried, "if I could but hope so too! but, in the terrors that beset my brain, I am forgetting that you are my guest, and that you have ridden far. This is what you may call one of my lucid intervals, an interval in which I am able to be a little rational. I will order you refreshment."

"Which will not be unwelcome," I said; "and then I hope you will make a commencement of your narrative; for, if you have not inflamed my fears, I must confess that you have awakened my curiosity."

He ordered some refreshment, which was brought in sulkily enough by the man who had encountered me with the dog at the door of the lodge; but that did not spoil my appetite, and I did ample justice to the good cheer, notwithstanding the manner in which it was placed before me.

My friend Franklin eat and drank but sparingly, and occasionally I was afraid of a paroxysm of his fears, for he looked round him now and then in a suspicious manner, as if he saw something, or fancied he was about to see something, of a spectral nature. Whenever, however, I observed such symptoms, I did all I could to divert his mind to some other channel, and always began to talk upon indifferent subjects.

The greatest impression that I succeeded in making upon him was when I recalled to his mind the scene of our early acquaintance, and then, as he assisted me in some of my recollections of the past, he seemed, for a moment or two, to forget the pervading care which sat so gloomily upon him ordinarily, and the whole aspect of his countenance, such as I had known it to wear in happier days, would return, so that I began to entertain a hope that I might be instrumental in recovering him greatly from the state of despondency into which he had fallen.

With this view I thought it prudent not to press him too earnestly to recount the proceedings of the past; and hence it was, that as we sat and talked upon subjects which I called unconnected with his mania, the twilight stole gently upon us.

The objects in the apartment in which we sat became dimmer and dimmer, until at last, in the further extremity of it, all was gloom and darkness.—To be sure, the fire occasionally sent out a ruddy glare, which danced upon the faces of the old portraits upon the panels, giving them an aspect of reality, to me most pleasing and novel.

"This, to my mind," said I, "is a pleasant time. I like to sit thus between lights, as people call it, when it is not quite dark enough to justify us in excluding altogether the last lingering reflected rays of the sun, and yet so dark as to make me feel that in-doors is the proper place to enjoy just such a confidential chit-chat as that which we have been engaged in."

I glanced around me as I spoke, and he did the same; but he by no means participated in my relish of the semi-darkness in which we were. I could perceive that there was an alteration in his tone, as he said,—

"We must have lights—plenty of lights; darkness is terrible!"

Of course I made no opposition to his wishes, and in obedience to orders which he gave, a candelabra, holding four lights, soon spread something like a lustre throughout the huge apartment.

He was silent for some minutes, and I felt that he was relapsing again into melancholy, and that the pleasant feelings which I had recalled into existence by remembrance of our early days were giving place to the dread realities, or the equally dread imaginings, of his present situation.

This, then, was the opportunity which I thought would be the best at which to ask him for the narrative which he had promised me; so, after the silence had continued some time, I said—

" Franklin, I will not interrupt you while you recount to me the circumstances which have produced such a state of feeling in your mind which I so much deplore."
—" Be it so," he said; and then, for a few moments, he covered his face with his hands, as if in deep and anxious thought.

I forbore to say anything, for I considered it best to let his feelings have their full scope, and so I found it, for after a time he began : —

" You recollect that I had often boasted how free my heart had been from female influence, and how often I had painted, in all the colours of romance, some imaginary being whom I might love, while I despaired of ever finding such a one really in existence.

When the cares and the anxieties of the great world separated us, and that intimacy which had brought us so often together years ago had ceased, I was still in that condition of mind which may be denominated heart-whole—that is to say, I had no decided preference.

But this was a state not long to last. I went to reside at the house of a widow of the name of Litchfield ; she had a daughter, and from the first moment that I looked upon her, I found my boasted philosophy shaken, and that it would be hard to maintain the invulnerability of heart which I had ever boasted of.

She was beautiful. I cannot, dare not, tell you how beautiful ; there is nothing in art, there is nothing in nature, that I can compare to her, because she transcended both, and yet, it was not so much the beauty of form or the beauty of feature that made her so loveable, but it was the lustre of the sparking soul which adorned the human form, and, in a thousand graces beyond the faculty of acquisition, made her what she was.

" And now I could not tell you that she had such and such eyes ; I could not describe to you her cheeks, her lips ; but I can tell you that she was a being fashioned by Heaven in such a guise that she should be the special admiration of its creatures, and, in full measure, work to their weal or woe as they chose to make a good or a bad use of the great faculty of loving excellence with which God has gifted all."

" And you loved her?" I said.

He stretched forth his hands, and looked me in the face."

" There was a war," he said, " between love and pride ; one of those contests in the human breast that produce devastation upon the object of their rage. Look at me ; you have known me well, and tell me if I wear the aspect of a fiend or of a man. I did love her. I loved her with one of those passions which all the concentrated feelings of a man who, in his pride of independence, had held himself far aloof from all petty preferences, might be supposed to feel for the one object that awakened all the latent and hidden sympathies of his heart, that satisfied all its aspirations, and made him feel that the most glorious attribute of humanity was that which enabled him to comprehend and to feel such an affection. Yes, God knows how I loved her !"

" And what followed?"

" What was the sin which hurled an angel from its abiding place in Heaven, and peopled a pandemonium with those who had been ministering angels round the throne of God?"—" Pride," I said.

" Yes, pride. That shallow, empty mockery of a passion; that feeling which, as a grain of sand in the balance of human anticipations and human happiness, has often succeeded, by a marvellous necromancy, in outweighing a mountain of holiness and goodness. It was that by which I fell."

"And with a consciousness," I said, " which enables you now so vividly to depict to me the evils of such thoughts, could you greatly err?"—"Yes; it is no unusual phenomenon of mind for man to do that which his better nature wages an unequal warfare with."

"That is true," I said.—"It is far from unusual for some unworthy motive, which cannot lay claim to be even the faintest exhalation of a high resolve, to usurp the place of the best and the noblest feelings, and give an impulse to human actions achieved in a moment, and regretted for an eternity."

"A melancholy truth."—"Like most truths. But let me proceed. Her name was Margaret. Oh, if there ever lived a pure, holy, and a sinless being, it was she; and although to worldly ears it may sound a strange and inexplicable doctrine, I can tell you truthfully that it was her innocence that was her greatest foe, and stripped her of that armour of virtue which clings with calculation to the more worldly minded. And it is a holy truth, which those who look more deeply than the surface of humanity will surely find, like a rich jewel far beneath earth's verdant surface, that those who fall, and are branded with the stigma of criminality, are often those who have known least of wrong, and who, suspecting not the seeds of evil that are in human nature, because none of the rank weeds that spring from such germs of wickedness have found a place in the garden of their hearts, are the least guilty of all the fallen."

I must own that I heard Franklin with pleasure; and although these remarks that he was making probably kept me from the actual particulars of his story, yet I could not help thinking to myself that they were most apposite, for if they had not been so, he could not have uttered them with the fervour with which they came from his lips.

He paused now for a few moments, as, no doubt, painful and bitter thoughts rose up in his mind; and I forbore to make any remark of an interrupting character, for I rather liked to hear those genuine emanations of feeling than to hurry him to a recapitulation of facts which I believed myself certain to arrive at in due time. He continued thus:—

"I know not what possesses me to dilate thus upon the excellencies of her towards whom I became an evil genius; but I have said enough, doubtless, to let you know what she was, and, therefore, to enable you to appreciate to its full extent the conduct of which I was guilty.

"I had got a reputation among a certain set for being a man who held himself aloof from that species of female fascination which would induce him to barter his liberty for any amount of loveliness or excellence whatever."

"I am aware of that," said I; "you took pains to acquire that reputation." —"I did."

"And often have I argued with you against it, telling you upon what a shallow foundation I thought you rested your hopes of happiness, both here and hereafter."—"You did—you did; but I was strong in the pride of my own purpose, and heeded no warning, cared for no advice."

"Proceed, proceed; I do not speak to reproach."

"It matters not, it matters not; I'm obnoxious to more reproach than ever you could feel inclined to level at me."—"I have told you that I loved her, and I have told you what a concentration of excellencies it was that won my affection; and then I began to think, not how I could make happy this object of my fondest adoration, not how I could secure for myself the haven of rest against all the vicissitudes of evil fortune, in a heart which could repay me all the tenderness I could bestow upon it a thousand fold, but how I could, in accordance with the evil principles which had found a place in my bosom, effect the desecration of the shrine at which I proposed to be a worshipper."

"Could you be so blinded?"—"Yes, I was so blinded; call it blindness, infatuation, what you will. I sought not the happiness of Margaret, nor my own contentment and felicity; but, because she loved me, I sought her destruction.

and the empty applause of the few heartless companions who deemed it a great triumph to achieve the ruin of a trusting, fond, and affectionate girl, whose only error was one of judgment—that she believed a liar, and trusted to a villain."

" You do not mean," I said, "that you deceived her thus?"—"Hear me out. With such practised arts as I professed—I do not scruple now to say, that I covered myself with odium and disgrace, these only are the proper terms to apply to such hideous conduct—I triumphed, and she fell. Oh, sorry victory! which has left behind it more stings and wounds than ever the vanquished felt. Far, far better is it to suffer than to inflict. Oh, that I had been born to be oppressed, and not to be the oppressor !"

" And did she love you ?—did you teach her to rely upon an affection based in faithlessness?"—" I did. Imagine all that the worst villany and hypocrisy could accomplish. Picture to yourself a being all sensibility, all innocence, all virtue, and call her Margaret. Then, as the very principle of antagonism, imagine one full of artifice ; one who strained every nerve, and who plotted deeply to deceive ; call that one Franklin. Oh, it was as if some fiend had for a time had power to assume a shape of goodness, and had deceived an angel, who, in its aerial dwelling-place, knowing nought but goodness, suspected no evil, from a want of knowledge that it could not exist."

" Go on, go on."

" It was on a summer's eve, when the soft balmy air bore on its breast the fragrance of many a flower, when heaven and earth seemed to mingle with each other in a dream of beauty, when, by some sympathetic influence with a better nature, which surely has yet to come for those who have borne themselves well in this earthly pilgrimage, the perceptions of the gentle and the good seemed robbed of all the world's bitterness, that we sat, hand in hand, beside an open casement.

" A garden, rich in floral sweets, was spread out beneath our feet. She was mute, and drinking in the honeyed words that fell sweetly upon her ears from the lips of—of—there was a time when I could not have pronounced the word, but I am confessing all to you—of the seducer. Yes, that is the epithet to which I am justly entitled ; and she who imagined no wrong, she who fancied that, because my words sounded like the true reality of a heart devoted to her service, believed them all, hearkened to me with that feeling of beautiful devotedness which is the truest characteristic of a heart such as hers which truly loves.

" I told her that she was dearer to me than an universe with all its riches. I told her that I did not divide with her my thoughts of Heaven, but that all my dearest aspirations belonged to her, and that rather would I have renounced a hope of bliss in a world which was to come, than forego that which might be mine with her in this.

" And she gently chid me for so much fervour, bidding me love her not less truly, but less enthusiastically.

" ' You must remember,' she said, ' that I'm human, and have many faults—faults which, when your partial fancy has awakened from its dream of fancied excellence, your reason will not fail to show you. I tremble to have awakened the feelings which you profess.'

" ' And wherefore, dearest ?' I asked her.—' Because,' she said, ' my heart tells me that they cannot be of a permanent character. Nay, do not misunderstand me. I will not say, because I do not think that you would cease to love me, but be careful of loving overmuch.'

" You can imagine, my friend, what I replied to this ; how I threw into my manner, and the tones of my voice, all the eloquence that I was master of, and she listened to me, as she would have listened to the outpourings of an inspired intellect, believing all I said, and basking in the delicious sunshine of such a dream of hopefulness and joy, that she paused not to think if really all could be truth, lest she should too rudely awaken herself from the dream of felicity that was hers.

" Look at me, Mortimer. Can you see aught of the devil in my countenance ? Can you conceive it possible that, loving this gentle and affectionate creature as I did love her, I could sit down in the solitude of my own chamber, calmly and deliberately to plan her total and irretrievable destruction.

" Yes, for fear a few empty-headed coxcombs, for whose intellects and real opinions I had the most profound contempt, should utter a jeering comment, or, perchance, smile at my being what they would call booked into matrimony, I chose to be a villain.

" It is needless that I should pursue so painful a retrospection, as to relate to you, step by step, how I won her confidence to such an extent, that at last she would have trusted her very soul into my keeping, and wagered all her hopes of bliss hereafter, upon my truth and constancy. The tempter triumphed, and she, the loved, the trusting, and the beautiful, became my victim.

" Oh, bad is it to betray those who trust us little, and who, in the conceit of their own worldly knowledge, fancy that they may defy the tempter; but a thousand times worse is it to deceive one who trusts wholly and implicitly, without a shadow of reservation, even as she whom I betrayed trusted me.

" But let me hasten onward. The busy scenes of the past creep over me again with a frightful reality. Let me hurry on to a dreadful day, upon which she first awakened to a sense of the treachery with which she had been treated.

" She hung about my neck with all the confiding fondness of a bride, and without urging half so much as she was entitled to urge such a suit, she asked me to name the day which should make her mine at the altar.

" I felt that an explanation must come sooner or later; the truth of my villany trembled upon my tongue, but I dared not utter it. My heart sank, and my courage failed me, when I would speak the words that were to condemn that innocent being to despair. I changed the subject of conversation, and did what I could to get rid of the necessity then of answering such a request.

" She saw that I was distressed, and did not press me, and yet strange to say, she suspected nothing, so absolutely perfect was her faith. But I felt that the crisis had come, and that I could not go through another interview of such dissimulation as the last.

" When I was alone, I wrote to her. It was a brief note, not over full of reflection or of sentiment, and in it was a question as hideous and as dreadful as it was possible for a man situated as I was, with regard to her, to ask. It is the only portion of the note which clings to my memory, and it will cling there for ever. Some accusing angel has those words ready to confront me with on that awful day, when all that is human shall appear before the God of heaven and of earth, for judgment.

" They were these :—' How can you expect me, Margaret, to make you my wife, after what has occurred? Men do not wed those who fall before their solicitations, but they adopt that step only towards some one whom they have loved, but whose virtue they have found as an impregnable fortress, which they could not otherwise conquer than by the assistance of the church.'

" Can you conceive it possible, Mortimer, that such a letter as this was my production, and yet I tell you it was so, and that at the time, I actually thought it, or deluded myself into the belief that it was a clever, spirited, and philosophical production."—" That was, indeed," I said, " Franklin, a miserable piece of fatuity on your part."

" It was ; and yet, from your knowledge of human nature, you can doubtless understand the feeling which swayed me."—" I can, I can."

" I had a number of associates whose principles consisted in having no principle, who made a sport of the best and the holiest feelings of human nature, who thought it fine and great to outrage every virtue, which from age to age had been sanctified as the best portions of humanity, and this they called philosophy."

" Alas !" I said, " Franklin, that is a word which has been more misused than any other that was ever invented. It is a spurious plea to cover any hideous doctrine which the passions of man may give existence to—anything may be called philosophy. The apathy which teaches inanity, and a disregard for every social virtue, as well as the most active villany which proclaims war against all which the mass of mankind held dear, became each, in the popular cant of the age, philosophy."

"You are right, and I was a victim to such fancies, therefore I destroyed myself and another, in support of so vile a theory. But I was not at ease here—no, no. A shadow of some impending evil was resting on my very soul."

He struck his breast as he spoke, and groaned deeply.

"What happened next?" I said; "did she send you an answer?"—"No; I expected one, I waited for one. I called upon a friend and told him the tale, and what I had done."

"And did not he awaken you to a sense of—of ——"—"Nay, do not spare me—of my villany, you would say. He did not; he thought it a capital joke, and that I had acted with commendable spirit. Yes, spirit—that was his opinion. Oh! miserable substitute for virtue, for honour, and for happiness. I had acted with spirit—that, while it destroyed my victim, was likewise paving the way to my own destruction."

"And what then happened?"—"I knew nothing for weeks. I received no answer to my note, and I began to affect to plume myself upon the manner in which I had got out of an intrigue, the consequences of which might have been most serious. And those persons whom I called my friends, congratulated me upon my cleverness, declared me a fellow of infinite spirit, and applauded me to the very echo, for that which should have consigned me to odium and disgrace. But I was ill at ease—there was still a something which whispered to me, in a voice that would be heard even in the moments of my greatest pleasure, it is not over yet. When the brimming wine-cup was at my lips, when I was affecting to be the gayest of the gay, and apparently as careless of the past as though it had never taken place, I still in my mind's eye could see Margaret, and fancy the aspect that she wore.

"I have talked to you of the shadow of some coming evil I said was resting upon my soul. That shadow increased in intensity day by day—ay, hour by hour, until at last it poisoned my enjoyment, and three months having elapsed, I thought I would certainly inquire how it would fare with my victim.

"With such discrimination as I could, I made inquiry, but I could learn nothing, although I went to a friend of her family, and was received with a haughty diffidence, and a kind of shuddering repulsiveness, that let me know full well my guilt was suspected, if not actually and accurately known.

"I shrank from before the eyes of those people as they looked upon me scrutinizingly, and I returned home humbled, cowed, yet angry, anxious. I could not rest; an unknown sort of terror sat upon me, and then at last there came a note. I have it here; read it for yourself, and let me have a pause of thoughtfulness, even if it be one of agony, while you peruse that document which will speak to you, trumpet-tongued, of my shame."

With trembling hands Franklin handed me a torn and crumpled letter. With some difficulty I spread it out, and read as follows, while he rested his head upon his hands, and seemed possessed with grief. It was this:—

"Sir,—She who has become the victim of a deception such as none but the mind of a fiend could have compassed, is dying. I need not tell you who she is. Your own conscience will sufficiently point out to you the name of her of whom I write. After long struggling with herself, and much pleading by her friends against so dreadful a wish—for it would be dreadful to them to have their home polluted for a moment by your presence—she has prevailed upon them, and they have yielded to a request, uttered nearly in the pangs of dissolution. She wishes once more to see you; to tell you that she forgives you, and to implore you to pray to Heaven for the mercy which to her you showed not, but which to you she hopes may yet be granted."

This letter, which had no name in it, and no signature, I read with some surprise.

"Why, Franklin," I said, "how could you tell from whom this came?"—"Too well—too well!" he said; "conscience told me. I needed no other monitor."

"And you turned out to be right?"—"I will tell you. Long I considered and trembled—when I say long, I mean I counted the time by hours, before I could make up my mind to accede to the request contained in that horrible but brief epistle. At length I made up my mind I would go and bear all consequences ; for I was not without a suspicion that, when I got there, some indignant kinsman would spring upon me, and make me expiate with my life the evil I had done.

"I shall never—never forget that evening, as, with reluctant, dragging steps, I reached the abode of that beautiful being, who, in all her innocence and all her virtue, I had destroyed. I paused on the threshold of the house, and yet an invisible agency seemed to drag me on, and when I turned to go away, dreading the reception I might meet, I felt as if chained to the spot, and that it was impossible my lagging feet could take me from it.

"At last I made known my presence, and was admitted. Oh ! how they shrank from me, as if there were contagion in my touch. I was shown into an apartment where there was a young child of tender years ; the little creature gathered its garments closely around it, and shuddered as it passed me.

"There were no reproaches ; I could have borne them, and perhaps have replied haughtily : but it was the absolute silence and the solemnity which overcame me.

"A man, whom I knew not, conducted me to a chamber above ; he opened the door, and motioned me to enter. I thought that I was alone, but, by the dim light that came through the partially closed shutters, my eyes rested upon a bed, where lay all that remained of the once beautiful and excellent Margaret. She seemed to be sleeping. I tremblingly approached the couch.

"'Mercy !' I said—'mercy !'

"She answered not, and then I knew that such vengeance as such a being might feel was busy at her heart. I knelt down by her side, and, in imploring accents, I again spoke to her.

"'Margaret—Margaret,' I said, ' you sent for me, and I am here. Oh ! I have suffered much, and the vain pride of such a conquest as that which I have obtained over you, dearest and best, has passed away. Let me, in the face of Heaven, now call you mine, and if a future life can atone for the evil which is already done, I shall yet live to see you smile upon me, and hear you say that I am forgiven.'

"I thought I heard her sigh ; but she would not speak to me, and again I implored her to do so, if it were but a word, to let me know that she believed I was contrite, and that the expressions of repentance, which, indeed, came from my heart, were real.

"'Reproach me,' I said, ' but do not treat me with this dreadful scorn. Why, oh, why have you sent for me, if it be but to drive me mad with your disdain ? I know that I deserve all the contempt which you can heap upon me ; I know that I have rendered myself obnoxious to a world of reprobation, but you, Margaret, are not the one to exact so stern a justice. I have come repenting, and, so near allied to Heaven are you, that you must share in its noblest and highest attribute—mercy.'

"She spoke not, and, with a kind of desperation, I seized upon her hand, which lay upon the coverlet. She was dead !"

"Dead !" I exclaimed.

"Yes ; in all probability, the shock of seeing me, as I entered the apartment, had made her breathe her last. She was dead, and I was alone with the poor and sad remains of my victim. Oh ! if I were to speak volumes, I could not tell you truly the rush of agonizing thoughts that came across my mind at such a crisis. I could not move, I could not speak ; I tried to scream, but my tongue clave to the roof of my mouth. I panted for very breath, and the life-blood seemed to coagulate around my heart ; and then I tottered from the room, I know not how, and reached the stairhead, and there was waiting the same man who had led me up to the chamber of death.

"'You have seen her ?' he said.—'I have—I have.'

"'And she said to you all that she ought to say?'—'Yes,' I gasped—'yes !' for I dreaded to tell that man that she was dead.

"He walked to the door and opened it wide, and pointed to the street.

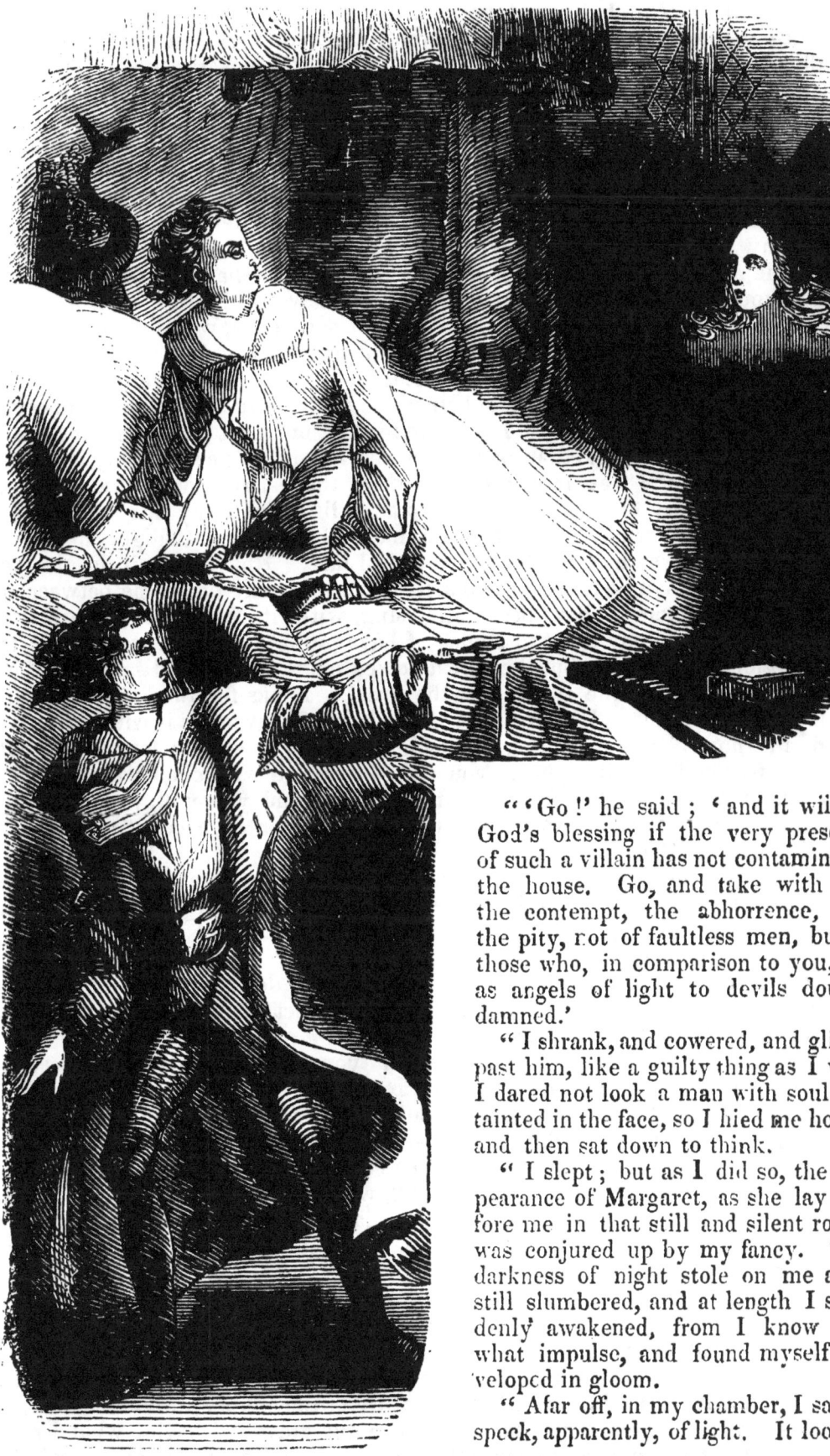

"'Go!' he said; 'and it will be God's blessing if the very presence of such a villain has not contaminated the house. Go, and take with you the contempt, the abhorrence, and the pity, not of faultless men, but of those who, in comparison to you, are as angels of light to devils doubly damned.'

" I shrank, and cowered, and glided past him, like a guilty thing as I was. I dared not look a man with soul untainted in the face, so I hied me home, and then sat down to think.

" I slept; but as I did so, the appearance of Margaret, as she lay before me in that still and silent room, was conjured up by my fancy. The darkness of night stole on me as I still slumbered, and at length I suddenly awakened, from I know not what impulse, and found myself enveloped in gloom.

" Afar off, in my chamber, I saw a speck, apparently, of light. It looked like a small flame from which there came no rays of brilliancy, and, as I looked, it came nearer and nearer, spreading out and becoming pale as it came. I gazed, with my whole soul concentrated in my eyes, and then it gathered form and substance. It came nearer—nearer still—I shook, I wept, I raved, I screamed. It was a face—nothing but a face—the face of the dead. Nearer still—nearer still! There was blood upon the lips, the cheeks were pallid, and the moisture of death hung, bead-like, upon the brow. It was her face—Margaret's—come to drive me mad. There—there, Mortimer; look again. Yonder by the wall—it moves across a picture—there where the arras falls in a wide fold—look—look! God, how the dead eyes are fixed upon me! Mercy—mercy, Margaret! have mercy even in death!"

He had risen from his seat, and now with a shriek, he fell back upon it, while, with many misgivings as to the reality of what he said he saw, glanced around the room, feeling myself anything but happy in that mansion of despair.

"Did you see it?" he said, after a pause.—"I saw nothing."

"Nay, from a friendly feeling, you will not say you saw the dreadful sight; but it was too true. From that dreadful night on which it first turned upon my gaze, it has been my constant and my dreadful visitant. If I were alone even for a moment, it would come and look upon me with those sad and accusing eyes, driving me almost to madness. If I looked into a mirror it was there, instead of my own image. If I walked abroad it followed me, flitting even by my side, and making me feel that I was never even alone. At the festive board it haunted me; it rested on the very brim of the wine-cup as I lifted it to my lips; it lay upon the same pillow on which I tried to sleep, morning, mid-day, twilight, night— all were the same, I was haunted by that dreadful face. I have seen it in the soft moonbeams. I have seen it in the dancing sunlight. It has come between me and those with whom I have been conversing, with its awful, cold, despairing look. It has turned my heart to stone. I have plunged amid the throngs of the gay and giddy metropolis, but there it followed me. In crowded saloons it has glided after me, amid the titled and the great. It has followed me out, and it has followed me home. It is with me now. God of heaven! it is with me now!"

I don't know if any of you, gentlemen, have been so circumstanced as I was with my friend Franklin; but if you have been, you will comprehend the uncomfortable nervous sort of feeling that beset me; and you will, probably, conceive how heartily I wished that I had not, as a matter of necessity almost, to pass the night at Bellenden Lodge.

As much for my own sake as for his, I used every argument in my power to dissuade him from a belief in the existence of the supernatural appearance which so tortured him; but all was in vain. He would not, and he could not, mistrust the evidence of his own senses.

"It is so—it is so," he said, "and it will be the death of me."—"But still you have not explained to me," I said, "how you became possessed of this beautiful place, with all its appurtenances."

"No—no," he said, "I ought to have told you, that not only had I deceived her, but I had deceived myself. Too late I discovered that she was entitled to considerable property, and a communication was ultimately made to me by a solicitor, that she had actually left me—she whom I had betrayed—she whom I had brought even to death, a handsome competence in the shape of rentals, from houses in the metropolis, and this hall, with its beauties, which you admire so much, beauties I am in no mood to appreciate, but which every one of them seems to me like a reproach, and are almost sufficient to drive me to distraction to contemplate."

"That was singularly generous conduct," said I, "of one who had abundant reason, if she chose, to feel resentment, rather than any tender passion."

"And yet had she sought for the most subtle means of being revenged upon me, she could not have found a means more adapted to the end. Imagine what I must have felt at feeling myself the creature of the bounty of one whom I, by the most frightful treachery, had hurried to the grave. Imagine what I must have thought at knowing and feeling that she had done so much for me, while I had been the very bane of her brief existence, opening to her pure spirit the gates of eternity, which should have been long closed upon one so gentle and so good; if for no other reason than that she should have been an example of holiness and goodness to all humanity."

"And then," said I, "you shook off that gloomy impression which had so long clung to you."—"Shook it off!" he said; "would I could. No, far, far from it. If, before it clung to me, with an intenseness which could not be gainsaid, I found that when I came to contemplate all that I owed to this pattern of excellence, the dim shadow of what she was in life, as represented by that awful dead face that haunted me, came across my imagination with two-fold force, and more than once I contemplated suicide, as a means which might possibly rid me of a torment of existence, which had become nearly insupportable."

"And how long ago was that?" I said.—"Only two miserable years. Look at me. Would you believe it possible, that, in that time, I could change, as indeed I have, from an appearance of strength and manhood, to one of premature decay?"

"I must confess," said I, "that you are changed; but it is no new phenomenon to find the imagination working wonders upon the physical structure. Why do you not seek society? Why do you not endeavour, amid the amusements which must be open to you now from your extended means, to forget these painful thoughts and feelings?"—"You speak in vain," he said, "and contrary to your own conviction; you know the utter futility of attempting to do so. Let us have more light; the room is in a state of semi-darkness."

"Well," I said, "Franklin, whether we have more light or not, I think that the subject which we have been discussing, is one that had better be deferred until day dawns again. It is not a fit one to talk of among imaginative persons after sunset; and I am convinced it had far better be delayed. Come, we will think of some more cheerful theme. Let us recal to our minds some of the scenes of our early boyhood, and possibly you may be able to shake off some of the influences of superstitious feeling that now oppress you."

"Oh! if I could but hope to do so," he said, "I should begin then to think it possible that time might alleviate my anguish; but it cannot be—oh! no, it cannot be! And, although I can fully appreciate the kindness which dictates the delusion, I still believe it a delusion, thanking you none the less."

Notwithstanding, he thus repudiated any attempt to withdraw him from those feelings which had taken such possession of him, I found, that in the course of time, he was withdrawn somewhat from his gloomy thoughts, and entered with something like an appearance of pleasure into the reminiscences of the past.

An hour or two went on pleasantly, and save that he occasionally glanced around the room with an uneasy gesture, no one could have taken upon himself to say that he was suffering to such an extent, as I knew he was, and from such a cause, too. At length, eleven o'clock sounded from an old turret of the building, and I ran, saying,—

"Well, now, you must excuse me, Franklin, for you know, early to bed and early to rise, has been one of my mottoes for many a year."—"I'm aware," he said, "I'm aware. You wish to retire to rest—be it so—do not stop for me; I dare not go yet."

"Dare not! what do you mean?"—"I mean, that I am forced to remain up until the dawn of morning. If I were to go to bed before then, I should awaken up full of horrors; but you, who have a free conscience, may repair to rest when you please. Do not let me stay you."

"Nay," said I, "if you sit up, I sit up with you. But let me reason with you on this subject, and prevail upon you to break this supposed spell which holds you in this bondage. Come, now, Franklin, for once—now that you have an old friend in the house with you, who will be ready at your call at any moment, retire to rest at once, and fear nothing."

"If I thought I could—if I thought I dared ——"—"You know you can, and, as for daring, what is there hindering you from summoning up some of your ancient courage, which made you foremost in every description of juvenile peril, which, at different times, we have encountered."

"You inspire me with a fresh courage. I have allotted you a chamber next my own. Will you promise me meantime that should you hear any cry for help, you will come to me."—"Oh! most assuredly."

"A thousand thanks. Be it so. And for the sake of the exhortations you have bestowed upon me, and to assure you that it is not fear, but reality, from which I shrink, I will now retire to rest."

"Do so. Do you sleep with a light?"—"Think you that I could endure darkness with the knowledge of what it might produce?"

"Well, Franklin," I said, "you will please yourself, but it seems to me that you surround yourself with aids and appliances to superstition."—"No, no, do not reason with me on that head—it is not so. Heaven knows what efforts I have made to shake off those dreadful feelings that oppress me, but in vain. It is not likely that I should give any aids or appliances to a feeling that has already nearly driven me to my grave, and, as you see, has made me the very shadow of what once I was."

There was something about this too true for me to deny it, and I therefore got out of making such an admission in the best manner that I could, merely saying,—

"Well, well, Franklin, I consider it a point gained in prevailing upon you to retire to rest at a proper and a Christian-like hour; and you may do so, I think, with a full assurance that you will meet with no disturbance."

"There is always something," he said, "in human nature showing that great confidence in one person begets it in another; and I must say that I do not feel so much beleagured in my fancy as I have been; and yet, do not imagine that I have any thought which would bear you out in your supposition as to all that I say I have seen being the effect of imagination. Mortimer, I know it to be real."

"And," I said, "I feel it to be otherwise; and I do hope that you may date from my visit a flesh and blood one, as it is something like an impunity from the visits you complain of as being those of a disembodied spirit."

"You cannot hope so," he said, "more sincerely than I; and now, since it is a wish of yours that I should do so, I will retire to rest, attempting for once to taste of repose as I used to do in those happy days ere my conscience was tainted with that deep sense of injury to another that now clings to it."

He ordered candles to be brought us, and conducted me himself to a long corridor, from whence issued a number of chambers. The lights we carried cast uncertain and flickering shadows upon every object, and I could not help remarking to him that it seemed to me he was feeding that very imaginative power that peopled his brain with such teeming fancies by living in such a place as he had chosen.

"I have my reasons," he replied; "and one of them is, that it seems to me, that by forcing myself to reside here, I was undergoing a self-imposed penance for the evil that I have done, instead of making an effort to escape from it, which, of course I might do."—"Well, if you can please yourself with such a doctrine as that, be it so. But which is my bedroom, and which is yours?"

He led me into one of those stately old-fashioned chambers which laugh the dimensions of modern sleeping-rooms to scorn. So spacious was it that we seemed lost within it, and the lights we carried were all insufficient to shed any rays beyond its limited extent.

"This is where I sleep," he said, "when I can sleep; but that, alas! is seldom now; and in the adjoining chamber to this, which is of equal dimensions, I wish you, if you will, to repose to-night."—"With pleasure."

I was quite fascinated with this extensive, and really beautiful apartment. It was furnished very similarly in style to the room below, which had so much struck my fancy; and in one corner, or rather in the centre of one of the side walls, stood one of those ancient carved oaken bedsteads, the like of which we seldom see now, except as curiosities shown to lovers of the rarities of past ages in some old mansion or gallery of art.

Its massive pillars, even from the very floor upwards, were elaborately adorned with saints and cherubims, while the canopy over head was one of the richest pieces of that species of art that I had ever seen. At each of the four corners was a massive plume of what, no doubt, had once been extremely handsome, drooping feathers. And now, indeed, they drooped, but not from the natural grace which this structure gave to them, but from the weight of dust, and the progress of decay.

The hangings to this most exquisite piece of chamber furniture were of quilted damask, so thick and massive, that I could well imagine that when they were drawn, the most profound darkness to reign within the space they enclosed.

The floor was partially carpeted, and here and there some of those high-backed chairs, with their low seats, that, notwithstanding their ungainly appearance, are, after all, luxurious to sit upon, met my eyes.

But soon the exquisite adornments of the chimney-piece caught my attention, and I could have lingered for hours gazing with delight upon the mass of exquisite carving which surmounted it.

"You see," said Franklin, as he noticed my enthusiastic glances around me, "that I am surrounded by much that should make life delightful, and yet am I certain that in the wide world there cannot be a more unhappy wretch than I am."

"You are, indeed, surrounded with what to me would be never-ending subjects of pleasure. Oh! I should dote upon such an antique chamber as this. Visions of ancient days, when our ancestors were merry in the hall, would be continually coming across me ; and I should fancy I heard the loud and gladsome shout of Christmas sports below, as I lay upon yon antique bed, and carried myself in imagination back to the time of the Edwards and the Henries."

"There is a bell," said Franklin, in an abstracted manner, "which has been made to communicate between this chamber and the next. Mortimer, should you hear it in the night, will you come to me ?"—"Assuredly."

"Upon your word you promise me you will."—"Most certainly. I have said as much, and I will keep my word. Why, Franklin, curiosity to see if I could not obtain a glimpse myself of your strange phantom, would induce me, if friendship had not sufficient power."

"I care not what motive you do it on, so that you do it," he said. "Come to me if you hear the bell, or I may go mad in some sudden extasy of terror ; for a something seems to whisper me, even now, that this night will be one of horror."
—"Ay, because you are going to bed earlier than your wont ; but when you awake in the morning, I make no doubt but that you will be able to tell me quite satisfactorily you have seen nothing more than yourself, and that only in your mirrors as you dress for breakfast."

He seemed better pleased and cheerful at the manner in which I spoke. There is something irresistible in cheerfulness, and, like grief, it is contagious.

"Come," he said, "I will show you to your own chamber, which, I believe, in ancient times, was the practice of the host in such mansions as these to do."—
"Yes," I said; "in those times the like of which we shall never see again, when the poor were far happier with no rights at all, than they are now with nominal ones, which they lack the moral influence to enforce."

"Come, come," he said, "we will have nothing of political economy. I know you have some odd crotchets upon that subject, so let it rest. This way, Mortimer, this way."

We went into the next chamber, the door of which opened but a few paces to the right in the corridor from the one we left.

I found that in regard with what he said to it, he had by no means deceived me, for it was quite equal to the one devoted to his own use, as large, as handsomely furnished, and as replete with what I considered beauties, although the colours of its embellishments were a little different, affording a most pleasing variety to the eye from going from one to the other.

In his room the hangings were of deep crimson, almost approaching to the colour called morene, a tint probably which they had acquired by age ; while, in the chamber to which I was shown, as that wherein I was to spend the night, they were a rich and costly-looking purple, which struck me as being extremely magnificent, and in excellent relief against the oaken carvings with which the place abounded.   And in my room, which was not the case in his, a wood fire fluttered and blazed upon the ample hearth.

"Franklin," I said, "does not your taste go in the way of this indulgence ?"—"I dare not," he said ; "I must be in total darkness, or in abundance of light ; it matters little which.   If I were to have such a fire as this in my apartment it would cast all sorts of strange shadows upon the walls, and then the giant, imagination, at such a period, would subdue the dwarf, reason, and I should picture to myself a world of horrors."

"I understand you," I said ; "be it so.   And now good night, go to sleep as quickly as you can, and take heed you wake not until the early lark gives salutation to the morn."—"Oh, would I could," he said ; "would I could ; good night—good night ; I will not keep you from your rest, although I fear that gentle sleep, nature's sweet restorer, will not rest upon these sorrowing lids."

"You will find it otherwise—good night."

With a slow step he left me, and I was alone in that large chamber. I forgot to say that he had pointed out to me the bell, which he was to ring if he felt so great an accession of alarm as to make it absolutely necessary he should have some one with him ; but it hung near the head of the bedstead in which I was to sleep, and was large enough, from the glance that I gave it, I thought, to awaken the "seven sleepers" themselves from their long repose, if it were hung as close to their beds' head as it hung to mine.

I felt fidgetty and uneasy, and yet I scarcely knew why ; I collected all the embers of the half-burned wood that were upon the hearth, and piled them upon the fragments that were still blazing, so that I felt convinced that I had provided, even should my candle go out, light for the greatest part of the night, as well as warmth.

"Shall I be disturbed or not ?" was the anxious question I repeatedly asked myself ; and never before, with such excessive deliberation, had I divested myself of my apparel.

I seemed somehow to dread going to bed, and yet I felt ashamed of myself, for giving so far the reins to fancy, for it could be nothing else ; and at length, with a kind of desperation, I undressed, and sprang into the ancient bed which had been prepared for my reception.

There I lay, deeply sunk in down, and I looked at the candle as it gathered a long and ominous wick—I looked at the fire until my eyes began to feel heavy and sleepy.   I watched the wreaths of smoke as they took their way up the ample chimney, and I speculated, as if they had been living things, upon the jets of flame that now and then shot out from the burning mass of wood.   I placed my watch upon the pillow by my side ; a delicious dreamy sensation came over me.   I left the light to expire of itself, the fire to shed its flickering radiance as it listed. A strange confusion of ideas came across my mind ; my eyes closed, and, thoroughly happy, I fell into a deep and dreamless slumber.

    *   *   *   *   *   *

What's that ?—how my heart beats—my head is in a whirl.   What is it ? help ! fire ! no, no—the bell, the bell—that dreadful bell, will it never cease ?

I sprang upon the floor—the alarm was ringing in my ears ; the candle was gone, and but a few red embers of the fire remained.   There, again, will that bell never cease ? Tinkle, tinkle, tinkle ! what a sound of alarm in the dead of the night !   Curse on the bell !   I've no light ; my own notion of the topography of the mansion is confused ; I know not my way to the door.   I come, Franklin, I come !   Now, all is still ; I grope my way carefully and slowly ; I believe I run against every article in the room that I could run against.

"I must have a light," I said ; "I must have a light."

The bell, again! it confused my very faculties—my heart beat in unison with it.

"Good God!" I said, "something is driving him distracted, and I cannot find the very door; I wanted a light, but how was I to get one? 'It was foolish of me to allow my candle to burn out; I might easily have extinguished it, and then relighted it; but now there was no resource; I must go in the dark. Surely I shall find the door; it is this way—yes, yes, I must find it. God of heaven! the bell again! My hand touched something cold—it was the lock; in another instant I was in the corridor.

"Franklin, I come—I come!" I said.

The bell ceased. I knew which way to turn, for I had taken especial notice; there was a dim sort of light from the night sky in the corridor which was not in the chamber; I saw the door of his apartment, for I was now more thoroughly awake than I had been when first roused by the sound of that terrific bell. I think I've had a dread of bells ever since.

To open the door and enter his room was the work of a moment. I closed it behind me, and stood about two paces within the chamber. He was speaking as if addressing some one palpable to his eyes, although not to mine.

"Mercy! mercy!" he cried—"have mercy upon me. I am lonely and sad, and have bitterly repented. Take, oh, take away that accusing face: let me sleep the long sleep of death. I only wish to sink to repose, and never again to awaken. No, no—no nearer; I am mad already. Do not bend that earnest gaze upon me. Accuse me before God, and hurl my soul to perdition, but leave me here to the undying worm of conscience. My days are full of melancholy; do not make my nights hideous. Help, help, oh, help! it comes! it comes! the dead face! the dead face!"

He uttered this with such frightful rapidity, that it was done and over before I could interrupt him; when, however, he paused, which he did once for a moment or two, I spoke aloud, saying,—

"Franklin, Franklin, I am here, I have answered your summons."—"My friend Mortimer," he said; "is it Mortimer?"

"Yes, yes, do you not know my voice? have you no light?"—"None—none. Oh, stay with me a little while; the servants will hear the ringing, and will bring a light. Let me implore you, until they come, not to leave the chamber. I have heard that the dead do not appear to two living persons at one and the same time, so do not leave me, Mortimer—oh, do not leave me."

"Hush! hush!" I said, as I groped my way towards the bed; "you're in a state of great excitement—you're in a dream."—"A waking dream—a waking dream; I have not yet slept. I heard the old turret clock strike twelve, and then it came to me like a pale beam of moonlight; it crept into the chamber, and yet I knew it was not that, for there is no moon to night. Where are you, Mortimer—where are you?"

"Here," I said, "here," as at that moment I stumbled against one of the bedposts. "I will stay with you. I have no light myself."—"They will come soon—they will come soon; the sound of that bell is well known here."

"Well, well," I said; "compose yourself, compose yourself; I will wait. Come, come, this is mere imagination; all is darkness, I see nothing. Have you a candle here? for I can light it from the fire in my room, which has yet sufficient vitality about it to enable me to do so. Where is it?"—"Here," he said; "here, by my side; but you will have to leave me—a moment will be an age of agony—you will have to leave me."

"For so brief a space," I said, "commensurate with the advantage of having a light, you will think nothing of it; besides, I will leave both doors open, and be within sound of the lowest tone of your voice."

He said nothing, and after some groping about, I found the candlestick, and as my eyes were now getting accustomed to the dim light that reigned around, I made my way to my own apartment, with more ease than I had come from it; and after some little trouble succeeded in illuminating the candle at the wood fire which still smouldered on the hearth.

Cautiously shading it from draughts by my hand, I went back to Franklin's chamber, into which I entered, and closed the door behind me.

I must own that I cast a suspicious look all around it, as I entered, but seeing nothing, I gathered courage, and approaching the bed, I held the light close to him, saying,—

"You are convinced now, Franklin, that it's only a dream?"

His face was the very picture of terror—pale and ghastly—and the perspiration stood in such heavy drops upon his brow, that it was quite a painful sight to look upon him. His very lips were white and his eyes dilated.

"I saw it—I saw it," he said; "it came to me more vividly than it has ever come before. There, from the window where hang those massive folds of drapery; it was from there it came. I could not sleep, for my eyes, with straining earnestness, sought that spot, impelled by a power more than human. The clock struck twelve, and then, as if a number of wandering pencils of light had suddenly assembled together to give the semblance of some human form—some frightful portrait of the dead—her face appeared—nearer then and nearer it came as of old—my shrieks could not appal it. I rang that alarm bell; but you did not come. I prayed to Heaven. I called even on Hell to aid me; but nearer—nearer, with a slow and horrible steadiness it came. It touched me. I felt as if a blast from the grave had come across me; and then I heard your voice, and it melted away. Why am I not mad—why am I not mad?"

"Why, Franklin," I said, endeavouring to assume a false gaiety which was foreign to my feelings—"if I were to say that you had arrived at that state, I should, perhaps, not be far from the truth; but now, as you have been so alarmed, you had better rise; you will not make me believe but what you have been to sleep and dreamt this much."

"You are hard of belief," he said. "I hope that it will come to you."—"Thank you," I said. "I am very much obliged; but I don't want any such thing to be demonstrated to me."

"Yes, you shrink," he said.—"Naturally I do. But now, Franklin, I tell you what I will do; lend me the coverlet of your bed. It is large, I perceive, and thick. I will wrap it round me and sit down in this chair and keep watch and ward by you while you sleep. I give you my word that I will not leave you, and I think I may likewise venture to give you my word that you will be undisturbed. Mind you, my object is to convince you that it is but a dream which has laid hold of you so strongly—a dream with which your imagination is so affected, that you continually repeat it over and over again. Now I shall watch you, and I make no doubt that you will call out again and ring that confounded bell, actually in your sleep."

"Oh, how I hope so," he said; "if you can but convince me of that, much as I now esteem you, I shall consider you as a dearer friend than it is possible any one else can be to me in this world; but you are not deceiving me—you will remain?" —"I declare to you," I said, "upon my honour and conscience, that I will remain."

"I am satisfied," he said. "I am satisfied. I know you will now pardon me for doubting you for a moment, and I will try to sleep, too. After all, Mortimer, this visit of yours may bring me some consolation, and this may be the last night I shall be so afflicted."—"I think it will, Franklin."

"God send it may! that is my prayer. Will you say amen to that?"— "Amen, most devoutly!"

"I feel moral peace and happiness. I will try to sleep. Good night."—"A wise resolution, and do so. Good night."

I had drawn off the coverlet from the bed. Massive and thick was it, and a capital protection against the cold, and so ample likewise was it in its dimension, that I found I could wrap it round and round my feet, and over my head, so as to have nothing but my face visible; and there I sat, looking more like an Egyptian mummy than anything else, while Franklin gathered the clothes about his ears, and prepared to go to sleep.

And now a strange and intense stillness reigned in the chamber. I thought

that he was sleeping, and I did not put out the light, because I saw that it would soon save me that trouble by going out of its own accord, as it was nearly exhausted; and most fervently did I hope that Franklin would go on sleeping till daylight, without any more superstitious terrors, that I might have the triumph of proving to him in the morning, that the imagination had everything to do with this supposed vision.

Notwithstanding I was so well wrapped up, I felt cold and uncomfortable; and, really, but for the great friendship I felt for Franklin, I should have given up the job; but I had given him my sacred word that I would remain, and so I did.

The candle began to wane, and a feeling of uncomfortable anxiety somehow or another crept over me as it did so. I did not feel at all the thing, and although I cannot say I was in a state of fright, yet I will confess, that, like the man in the play, I did feel some of my courage oozing out of my fingers' ends.

The candle burnt dimmer and dimmer. I looked at it, and saw that in a few moments the last remnant of the wick must fall into an ocean of fat, and be extinguished for ever. There was no saving it—and if I had propped it up for a time by any means, I should e but protracted the affair a little, which was not worth while; so I gathered the ck counterpane more closely around me, and resolved to abide whatever might ensue.

This very resolution augured a fear that something uncommon might ensue, and I put it to any of you, gentlemen, if you were placed in a similar situation, whether you would not have felt something like superstitious fears creeping over you.

I do not mind confessing that such was the case with me, and when at last the candle wick made a desperate plunge into a sea of fat beneath it, and I thought it had gone completely out, I felt a little scared; but candle wicks don't do that sort of thing all at once—it still burnt with a sickly star-like flame, now and then rising a little higher, and then sinking until it became of a faint, blue colour, and cast no rays whatever around it.

The turret clock struck one—the little flame that had lingered upon the point of the candlestick shot upwards; I was in darkness, and in silence, as if the very grave reigned around me.

*   *   *   *   *   *   *

I opened my eyes wider than I had ever opened them in my life before; it was with a vain effort to pierce the darkness that was around me, but I could not do so. I saw nothing, if that could be called seeing, but that wavy confused mass of nothingness which at such times comes over the senses, as if darkness was a kind of atmosphere of itself, and something almost to be felt.

I listened, and heard that Franklin was breathing slowly and regularly. I could have sworn he slept, and that serenely, too; but whether he did, or not, is a matter that to this day I know not, and you will soon perceive, by the sequel of my narrative, how and why it was that I had no means of ascertaining.

The time wore on, and I thought that if I could get myself a quiet, comfortable slumber in that ancient chair, it would be about the best thing I could do; but that I tried in vain. If I closed my eyes for a moment, some strange instinctive kind of dread induced me to open them again. In real truth, I was far from comfortable, although I combatted, as far as possible, with the feeling of dread that was creeping over me.

"Oh!" I said, " the night will soon pass away, and such ideas as those which now beset me are natural, under such circumstances." How very dark it was! Being accustomed to reside in London, where there is something like a constant hum of life even in the darkest nights, I have no doubt that my imagination was acted upon by the intense stillness, as much as by anything else; but certainly I was most truly uncomfortable; everything that I had heard and read of the terrific, paraded before me in solemn procession. All that had been related of vampyres, of ghosts, of hideous spirits, and apparitions, came vividly before my mind's eye. My imagination became perfectly bound, and as I tried in vain to pierce the intense darkness which was around me, I could, if I had chosen to give way to such fancies, have believed myself surrounded, as it were, by a compact moving mass of the unreal.

Horrible shapes seemed to roll round me, and career around my head. Thousands of strange demoniac looking faces, in horrible contortion, gibed and flouted at me; the very element of darkness, so to call it, for it seemed like something tangible, and not a mere negative condition, I could have sworn was teeming with life.

A strange dreamy kind of sensation crept over me. I was awake, I am certain I was awake, but I had not energy enough to move, and so shake off the spell that bound my physical powers as slaves to the overwrought mind.

There I sat, motionless as a statue, gazing upon vacancy, but peopling it with all the wild phantasma of the brain that an excited imagination could call into existence. And yet I could reason, and told myself repeatedly that I knew it was a delusion.

But this state passed away, and the clock struck two. The many strange shapes which appeared to have filled the air, dissipated, and yet it continued as dark as before. I knew not why they fled, for I was just in the same state of excitement, but I remember at the time thinking it was the sound of the old clock which cleared them off, and that they would come again, when its echoes had died away upon the night air.

But I was mistaken—I waited for them, but they came not, and a feeling of great relief crept over me, as I began to hope and to think that the phantasma of that night had at length passed away, and the happy and beautiful morn would come, bringing with it joy, serenity, and gladness.

But I reckoned not wisely. I might wish, and hope, and expect such a result, but you will soon perceive how frightfully I was disappointed, and what terror I was yet doomed to know.

I listened again to the breathing of Franklin, and I envied him the quiet repose he was enjoying; and then, I know not what on earth induced me to look in the direction of the ancient fire-place, close to which was a screen similar to the one in the room below. It seemed to me, as I looked, as if some faint tint of early morn had crept into the apartment, for I could suddenly see the outline of the screen, and a chair which was placed against it. The blood rushed back to my heart with a frightful gush—the chair was occupied. Yes, the shadowy outline of some form was most certainly there; it was but for a moment I saw it, and I became convinced that the pale reflected light, which I had mistaken for early dawn, came from that figure, which had a strange phosphorescent luminosity, that made it so faintly and fearfully visible.

All was dark again. I saw nothing more just then, but I had the horror of knowing that amid that darkness something not human was near me, and gazing at me with eyes not of this world.

I could get no further back, for the chair touched the wall. I could not shrink away, for the massive bedstead flanked me on one side, and to have moved in the direction that was open to me, would have brought me nearer still to the dreaded object from which it was my whole desire to escape.

There I sat with my eyes rivetted to the spot, which had presented to me so terrifying a spectacle, and yet seeing nothing—and yet for all I knew, that apparition might have glided up close to me, and been within an inch of my face.

I drew back instinctively at the thought. It was a dreadful one, and not long to be endured; so to satisfy myself I just stretched out my hand a little in the darkness. Oh! what a moment of agony was that! Somthing cold and clammy met my touch! I thought I should have died! It had a damp and slimy kind of feel! I was paralysed, and yet by some dreadful fascination I could not take my hand away! I knew it was a face I felt, for my fingers trembled upon the lineaments! A frightful sensation of thirst came over me, and it was by one of the greatest efforts in the world that I at length contrived to say, in a husky voice,—

"Help! help! Franklin, help!"—"God, have mercy!" said the voice of Franklin, "the hand of the dead is upon me! Mortimer, Mortimer, save me!"

The sound of his voice a little recovered me, and I withdrew my hand.

"Where are you?" I said. "Where are you?"—"Leaning out of the bed," he said. "Something touched my face."

"D—n your face!" I said. "You don't know the fright you have given me. I shouldn't wonder but my hair's turned grey. Did you see anything?"—"Hush! hush!" he said; "it is coming! I know that it is coming! The scent of the charnel-house is in the air! Look, Mortimer, look—the dead face! Look on yon light! Do you not see it—like a faint star! It is the concentration of that despairing look, which will yet drive me mad! Mortimer! Mortimer! save me! save me!"

"Don't clutch me in that way, Franklin!" I cried. "Your grasp is one of iron! Leave me free to act. Lie down; for God's sake, lie down!"

"Do you see it?" he shrieked, in a voice that sounded to me like the blast of a trumpet.—"Yes—yes—yes; by the God above us yes!"

His hand relaxed its grasp upon my arm and neck, and I heard him fall back upon the bed with a deep groan. And now for what I really did see.

Somewhere about the spot where the chair was situated, I saw hovering in mid air a speck of light. It had a strange, dancing movement, and it differed from any other light I had ever seen, in so far as it cast no rays whatever around it, seeming not to be possessed of the power of reflection.

I continued looking at it as I had never looked on anything before, for I was terrified to think that, after all, that question which had so often agitated my mind with regard to supernatural appearances, was about to be so suddenly and strangely settled.

Gradually it increased in size, or it became nearer—perhaps both; and in a few moments I began to perceive something like the outline of a human face.

It would be quite impossible for me to attempt to describe my feelings at that moment. The chaos of thought that took possession of me, defies all classification; but soon absolute terror overwhelmed every other feeling, and I felt as if my very eyes were staring from their sockets, as I continued to gaze on that strange and fearful apparition. It grew more and more distinct each moment, until there could be no mistake about its identity with the dead face described to me by Franklin as that which haunted him.

There was the singular opaque look about the eyes which he had talked of. The pallid cheek, the compressed lips, bloodless, and bespeaking a world of woe. It came nearer, moving on through the murky air; nearer, nearer still. It might be coming to Franklin, but it must pass wonderfully close to me—too close for my nerves to stand; and yet how was I to escape? Already it was within half-a-dozen paces off me. I was blocked in—the face before me—the wall behind, and the bedstead by my side.

With a sudden and a desperate resolution I flung that massive counterpane, in which I was enveloped, from me, and with difficulty turning my eyes away from those cold, glassy orbs, which gleamed from the spectral visage, I took but one spring, and very nearly cleared the whole width of the bed.

I fell on to the floor on the other side, but, heedless of consequences, I gained my feet in a moment, and dashed out of the apartment like one possessed.

By great good luck I reached the head of the grand staircase, down which I plunged with frantic speed. A light flashed in my eyes—there was the growl of a dog, and in another moment I almost fell into the arms of Franklin's serving man, who was holding up a lantern, apparently in the attitude of listening.

"Why, what's the row?" he said. "Where's the governor?"—"God knows!" I said. "Go up and get my clothes, and let me be off."

"What, have you seen it?"—"Yes. Have you?"

"Lor, yes. I didn't believe it till I did see it. It gave me a sort of turn. But I tell you what's the best thing to do."—"What? Keep that d—d brute of a dog quiet!"

"Down, Cauliflower, down."—"A most euphonious name for a dog," I said. "But for God's sake, run up to your master at once!"

"Wait a bit," he said; "I knows what's what on these ere occasions. Hold the lantern."

I took the lantern from him, and then he went round the corner of the deep well-shaped staircase, and produced a large jug, with a foaming top upon it, betraying the presence of some infusion of malt.

"Stingo," he said; "that's the caper."

He gave me a sort of nod, which, I've no doubt, implied "good health to you;" and while I stared at him with a lantern in my hand, and the dog sat upon his haunches, with his head upon one side, looking him knowingly in the face, he took a long and deep draught from the jug.

He had not removed it from his lips ere such a shriek came from above, that involuntarily I ran half way up the staircase, calling aloud to the fellow,

"Follow me—follow me! You must, at least, feel bound to render him some assistance, who puts bread int your mouth. Come on—come on."

I held up the lantern as high as I could, and it shed a bright light up the remainder of the staircase; but scarcely had these words passed my lips, than I heard a rush of feet upon the corridor above, and in an instant, shrieking and wringing his hands, Franklin made his appearance.

"The dead face!" he cried, "the dead face! Oh, God! the dead face! Horror—horror—horror!—save me from the dead—oh, save me! It pursues me, and it will pause not but upon the grave's brink; the world deserts me; I am abandoned by Heaven, abandoned by earth; off—off, keep off. Don't bend those sightless orbs on me—take—oh, take away those glassy eyes! No—no—I am not guilty! Avaunt, spirit—avaunt!—Help!—help!—oh, help!"

I stood like one petrified; the voice in which he spoke, awakened shrieking echoes; he bent back against the top of the balustrade; his hands were stretched out before him; he ceased to speak; but scream followed scream, and then—my heart sickens at the recollection—he fell over.

There was an iron bar which connected the staircase with the wall, supporting both; even now I shudder as I speak, and the blood creeps with a strange motion through my veins; his back fell across it; I heard the snap—a crushing, grinding sound. There was one shriek, the lower half of him was paralysed; his back was broken, and, like a lifeless mass, he fell upon the stones beneath.

I dropped the lantern; my trembling hands could not hold it; that frightfu crash of Franklin across the iron bar, had sickened me. I was completely enervated, and had I not sat down upon the staircase, I must have fallen to the hall.

I can scarcely tell what happened for the next half hour; but when I recovered, I found that the dawn was indeed breaking in upon every object, and the sound of a bell was tolling in my ears.

It was an alarm-bell, situated in one of the towers of the mansion. Franklin's servant was ringing it to some of the neighbours far and near, to come and be witnesses to the dreadful catastrophe that had occurred.

To this day—I have but a dim remembrance of how I succeeded in doing so—but I certainly did go up stairs to the room in which I had for so short a time slept. I dressed myself with speed. I spoke to no one, but came shuddering down again. I cast but one look upon the dreadful spectacle that lay upon the diamond-shaped, marble stones that paved the hall. It looked like a heap of coagulated blood, pregnant with corruption, and in the midst a strange, glassy-looking eye was glaring on me.

I rushed out like a hunted hare; I flew through the pleasure-grounds; I surmounted a wall, that, at any other time, I should have shrunk from attempting to scale. The high road was before me; I breathed more freely, and sped along it at my utmost speed.

I knew that I was unknown by name, and I thought that I might avoid being even a witness upon any investigation that should ensue. Franklin was dead, and what good could it do to recapitulate the dreadful tale of how he sinned, and of how he suffered? I walked the whole distance to the market town; the sound of a horn met my ears, and the tramp of horses' feet. It was the mail—the mail for London.

"Thank God!" I said, as I mounted on its roof, and I bade adieu for ever to Bellendon-lodge and the dead face that haunted its gloomy precincts.

END OF "THE DEAD FACE."

CHAPTER II.

THE CONSULTATION AND THE ALARM.—THE SEPARATION.

THE president finished his tale, and a dead silence reigned throughout the vault in which that singular association met.

Some looked at each other, and shuddered; others, again, glanced uneasily around them, as if each moment they expected to see that dreadful face, such as he had described it, glaring upon them.

There was no remark made for many minutes; each person there present seemed anxious that some one else but himself should address the meeting upon the subject. At length one rose, and all eyes were immediately bent upon him.

He was evidently about to say something of importance, as appeared by the gravity of his deportment, and the look of deep interest that sat upon his brow.

An uneasy sort of movement pervaded the assemblage, and then several cried, "Hush!" for they were extremely anxious one and all to catch whatever should fall from the speaker's lips. The chairman courteously inclined his head, and looked attentive, and then he who had risen spoke, saying, amid that wrapt and solemn attention,—

"Mr. President, is that all?"

Disappointment sat upon every countenance. The president looked astonished, and he who had spoken, placing his hand behind his ear, seemed extremely anxious to catch what should be said to him in reply.

"All!" said the president; "yes, sir, it is all; and, if you don't think it's enough, I must say, that, to my belief, you are the only gentleman present who is of that opinion."

"Ah!" said the captious person who had spoken, "that may be; my own opinion is, that the minority are generally in the right on all subjects whatever; and I again ask you, Mr. President, emphatically, is that all?"—"Yes, sir, it is," said the president.

"Very good," said the speaker, and down he sat.

Now, the rest of the society could not make much of this; there was no such thing as finding fault with the man for asking if that was all; he was perfectly justified in so doing; but the most provoking part of the business was, that he had, as it were, thrown down the gauntlet to the president, and given everybody a vivid expectation of a row, after which he had quietly picked it up again, in a manner of speaking, and sat down as composed as if he had done nothing, or said nothing at all.

"Gentlemen," said the president, and it was perceived by those most accustomed to him, that a ruby sort of tint, indicative of growing anger, was gathering about the apex of his nose. "Gentlemen, I put it to you, one and all, individually and collectively, whether it is right and proper, after I had with immense difficulty and great perseverance unfolded my tale, for any gentleman to get up and ask me if that's all? What more would he have, gentlemen? I ask you emphatically, what more would he have? Is his imagination not sufficiently acted upon by these dreadful images of the dead? Are his sympathies, gentlemen, not sufficiently awakened in the cause of virtue, to make him feel something for the deluded Margaret, who fell a victim to treachery, in the disguise of affection? Is his morbid love of the horrible not sufficiently gratified by my poor friend breaking his back across an iron bar, and then glaring at me with an eye which, I believe, was forced from its socket, as he lay horribly smashed and mangled, along the marble floor of the hall?

"Gentlemen, I say I do not envy the feelings of the individual who, after that, could stand up in this enlightened assembly, and ask if that is all. I do not envy that gentleman his heart, nor do I envy him his head, nor anything that is his. I look upon him as one of those persons—but no, I will not say what I look upon him as. I will leave the iron to enter into his soul, and there corrode—yes, gentlemen, corrode—corrode—d—e! corrode."

The chairman sat down, and—as they say in the reports of the Chamber of Deputies in Paris—there was a great sensation—to the right, and to the left, and in the centre, and up the middle, and down again, and everywhere else.

It was evident that now there must be something serious, and all eyes were turned upon the audacious man who had provoked so cutting a reproof from the president.

He must have been a most obdurate individual that, for he did not seem one penny the worse; and, after a few moments' awful silence, he rose again.

"Attention, gentlemen—pray give attention. Let me be impartial. I will hear what that gentleman has got to say, although it may be of the most dreadful nature to my feelings. Now, sir, what are you going to remark? In my presidential capacity I will hear you."

Again was the full tide of attention awakened, and again did everybody lean forward, with a look of anxiety, to catch what would fall from this man's lips. Something now it must be desperately dreadful, in the way of a retort, for the stinging sarcasm with which he had been visited.

" Sir," he said, " I rise again, after having my feelings lacerated, to ask you one question."—" Ask it, sir," said the president, fiercely.

" Do you allow smoking?"—" Sir!"

" I say, sir, do you allow smoking? The air here is damp—my feelings have been harrowed—I've been held up to opprobrium, and I now ask if you allow smoking? because, if you do, I'll light a cigar, and if you don't, I think I'll take a pipe."

Now it became evident to those serious assembled persons, that this audacious man was actually making game of them; that he had actually come there for the purpose of turning them into ridicule, and, consequently, that it was highly desirable he should be immediately expunged from the society.

Was this the way in which a harrowing recital—consisting of a seduction, a dead face, and a man with an awful injury to the vertebræ, was to be received? No; forbid it Heaven, earth, and the other place! This man must be obliterated—dissolved. The expression of the chairman's face said it as plainly as if he had shouted it through a speaking trumpet.

And now a gentleman among the assemblage nodded to the chairman, and the chairman nodded to the gentleman, and the result of this telegraphic communication was, that the gentleman rose to his feet, and, in a voice that betrayed he was a little afraid, but not much, he said,—

" I move that the gentleman who asked the president if that was all, be politely requested to go away."—" I second that," cried a voice.

The chairman looked bland and pleasant, as much as to say, " Well, gentlemen, if you will turn him out, I can't help it. It's moved and seconded, gentlemen, that —— "

" Stop a bit," said the individual against whom this motion was directed—" stop a bit. I wish to say, gentlemen, that I have joined this society, and here I am, and here I intend to remain. I rather like, myself, to be in opposition, so I shall vote for the motion. I've lots of leisure, and am a dead shot. Major O'Blazes, my friend, resides a short distance out of town, and I shall challenge everybody who holds out his hand in favour of my exclusion, excepting myself, and we'll make it up over a bottle. And now, gentlemen, blaze away."

" I—I—upon consideration," said the gentleman who had moved the motion, " I think I'll withdraw it."

At this instant, and before anybody else could utter one word, the sound of a footstep over head came upon their ears, and a deep, sonorous voice said,—" Past four!"

There was a dead silence among the assembled association, and then one said,—

" You needn't be alarmed; I know what that is. It's a private watchman that's kept in the cathedral at night. He takes the round of the vaults, with a loaded blunderbuss, between four and five. The mouth of it is about the size of a wash-hand basin, and they do say he loads it with handsfull of buttons, old nails, screws, and such like matters."

" The devil he does!" said the president, and he made a rush to the door.

This was the signal for a general alarm. The coffins were upset, the candles extinguished, and in a few minutes the vault was left to itself, for the members of what might be called the Ghostly Association, had made their escape, and repaired to their several homes, to ponder over the dead face, Bellenden Lodge, and the fearful, decomposing mass that might even now be still resting upon the marble pavement of its hall.

It will be recollected that these meetings were arranged to happen once a week; but owing to the extremely precipitate manner in which the members had separated, the next night of meeting had not been precisely arranged.

But, then, they were mostly acquaintances, and in the course of the next few days they had all seen each other, and come to a general opinion that, on the whole, it was rather a false alarm, than otherwise, that that had been said about the private watchman ; because, in the precipitation of their leaving, they had left quite sufficient evidence of their presence behind them, and if he had been in the habit of visiting the vault, as was asserted, something surely would have been heard of it before now.

Acting upon the supposition, then, that all was safe, they mutually agreed, the one with the other, to be present at the next regular night of meeting, and again to draw lots to see which of their number should be called upon to contribute his quota of the supernatural for their amusement.

By common consent, however, they took care to exclude from this arrangement the obnoxious individual who had asked the president if that was all ; so that they were quite in glee at the idea that they would get the better of him entirely, and, notwithstanding his bellicose propensities, they would hold a meeting without him, while his cause of complaint would be too general to enable him to fix it upon any one individual.

The president was particularly gratified ; for really he had exerted himself in his tale of "The Dead Face ;" and after that, as he truly and emphatically observed, —" Who likes to be asked if that was all, just as if something had been left out, or the episode from human nature had had a bad and imperfect conclusion."

" All, indeed !" he said, to every one of the members he met during the week— " I should say it was all, and a very tolerable all, too. Confound the fellow, what did he want ? I suppose he would have liked me to have broken my back across the rail, and then the old Tudor hall to have been burnt down ; ay, and half-a-dozen catastrophes at the back of that. That man will come to no good, you may depend upon it, my good friend."

This was a sentiment responded to, for the gentleman had certainly made himself very obnoxious, so that everybody congratulated themselves upon holding their next meeting without him.

And now the eventful night drew nigh, and all those who had intended visiting the vault there to hold their weekly meeting, wore on their countenances throughout the day a mysterious look, as if their thoughts were far away upon some subjects very different from any connected with worldly things.

After sunset they avoided ordinary society, wandering about alone until the hour arrived when they might make their way to that dreary place of meeting.

Each one, too, had a pleasing kind of doubt upon his mind about the possibility of its being his turn to enlighten his companions with his experience of the supernatural, so that, we really believe we might, without any exaggeration, take upon ourselves to say that each member of the society prepared himself with some narration of the horrible connected with his personal experience, the truth of which he could vouch for, and which he fully expected would make the warm blood curdle in the veins of his auditors.

The solemn hour of midnight came ; the vault was reached ; those who arrived first waited at the entrance for their later brethren, so that four or five went into the dreary abode of the dead at once ; and, being provided with the means of doing so, they illuminated that sombre-looking lamp that hung from the ceiling, and its rays shed a feeble, mysterious sort of light, throughout that charnel-house.

What was their horror and surprise to find seated upon one of the coffins, smoking a great German pipe, the very man whom they had taken such pains to avoid, and who, but for his suspicious acquaintance with Major O'Blazes, would have been expelled from the society.

" The devil !" said one of the company.

"What's that you say ?" said the gentleman who had thus unexpectedly made his appearance ; " do you mean me, sir ?"—" You, sir—you, sir ; oh, dear, no, I meant myself, sir."

" It's a good thing you did. I should have felt it my duty to society to exterminate you ; but, you see, here I am. I thought I'd lay the war hatchet between us, and so, you perceive, in a manner of speaking, I'm smoking the camulet o peace all to myself."—" Yes, sir ; oh, dear, yes, sir, you're quite right. D—n the fellow, what will the president say when he sees him ?"

"If it should happen to come to my turn," said the gentleman with the pipe, "I shall stun you all—positively stun you. I know something that's never yet passed mortal lips. Ha, how do you do, old boy? you're rather late, ain't you? Take a whiff?"

These last irreverend observations were made to the president, who at that moment made his appearance, and who was so struck at the unexpected pleasure of

meeting this malignant man, that he staggered back until he came to a coffin, on which he sat with a crash that broke the lid, landing him in the interior, on the top of a very unhandsome corpse.

"So you've come," he said, "have you?"—"Yes," said that desperate man "and so have you."

"I have; but, permit me to say ——"—"What?"

No. 6.

"Nothing. I'm a peaceable man, sir; I don't want to quarrel with anybody. Are we all assembled?"—"Yes," said one, "except Mr. Angelo Dawson; he who, if you recollect, Mr. President, made that horrible proposition at our last night of meeting, that we should visit each other after death, in order to settle questions which, in my opinion, it's much better to go on talking about, than to have settled in such a way."

"Oh," said the man with a pipe, withdrawing it from his mouth, and puffing a cloud of smoke up into the air. "By-the-bye, I can tell you a pleasant little incident about him."

"Can you, sir?"—"Yes, he's dead; flung out of his gig this morning; broke his neck."

Again there was a terrific sensation among the members, and the president was remarked to look uncommonly grave.

"Gentlemen," he said, "this is a dreadful event. It is one which fills us all with grief, I'm sure; and it is one which reduces our number from twelve to eleven."

"I beg your pardon, sir," said one; "I've been counting—there are twelve already."—"But I had only twelve names originally, and one is dead."

"Then that gentleman in the black cloathes, sitting on the end of the coffin there by the wall, is a stranger."

All eyes were now bent upon the individual thus pointed out. He was tall, thin, and of a deathlike paleness. There was a wild, strange lustre about his eyes, and a fixedness about the pupils, that gave him an odd look. His arms were crossed upon his breast, and he sat perfectly motionless for some few moments, the observed of all observers.

But he did not seem in the least disconcerted, which many men would unquestionably have been, at exciting such particular and marked attention. It was impossible that he could grow paler than he was; and as for any accessories of colour, to look at him, one would not suppose he had enough blood in him to produce any such effect; or if all that sanguine fluid that he possessed had flown to his face—and it would have taken all to produce then any effect—it must have left the rest of his corporeal frame so destitute, that death would have ensued.

And now, after a few minutes thus spent, he, with a coruteous salutation, somewhat after the manner of an age long gone past, bowed to the assembled members of that singular society, as if he would have said: "Gentlemen, I'm your most humble servant, and wait your leisure; what is it that you require of me?"

All eyes were then turned upon the president, who was, sitting in his official capacity, expected to say something upon this occasion; and, after a moment's pause, he addressed the stranger.

"Sir," he said, "I beg to inform you that this society is, in a manner of speaking, strictly private; and although, of course, we have no reason on earth to know that you would be other than a most unexceptionable associate, still, as you are not such, I beg, in the name of myself, and the other gentlemen present, without intending or meaning the least possible offence, to direct your attention to the fact that we—we—that we'd rather you'd go, in fact."

"Nothing," said the stranger, breaking the dead silence which he had hitherto preserved; "nothing, I am certain, could be more full of politeness than this unobtrusive and gentlemanly mode of showing me the door; but, as I have been introduced by one of the members of this most learned and honourable association, I do hope that I shall be permitted to remain a spectator of your proceedings, and that it may not be considered too bold of me, if, perhaps, eventually I should venture, from my own experience—which is not slight—to add something to the fund of information which you gentlemen are getting upon subjects from which the vulgar mind shrinks aghast, but towards which you, with a more exalted philosophy, advance with giant strides."

The association looked at itself, if we may use such a term, and then the president spoke, saying,—

"Sir, you will excuse me; but we are all here, and it's rather singular that no gentleman stands forth as your sponsor on this occasion. If any gentleman here present knows you, it seems to me rather an extraordinary thing that he should remain silent."

"Oh, that is easily accounted for," said the stranger; "my friend is not come yet. Mr. Angelo Dawson introduces me."—"Why he's dead," cried the whole eleven in a breath.

"Dead!" said the stranger. "Dear me! Well, gentlemen, if that be a fact, I can only assure you that I came here under his auspices, and as his melancholy end causes a vacancy in your association, I shall feel but too proud and happy to fill it up."

It was quite a remarkable thing to see how the guests looked at each other—these guests at a banquet of superstition. No one seemed inclined to say to the stranger "we won't have you," and yet it was evident there was a great disinclination on the parts of all present to have anything to say to a man of whom they knew positively nothing, except that he came with a dead man's recommendation attached to him, and that they had only his word for, for not one of the members remembered ever having seen him, or of having heard Mr. Dawson talk of any one whom he intended to introduce into the society.

On the contrary, the principal thing that was remembered of Mr. Dawson was, his uncomfortable proposal that the members, as they should die off, were to visit each other, making the night hideous by so doing, and filling, with a vague and undefined terror, every one belonging to the association.

It was no recommendation, therefore, for him to say that it was from Mr. Dawson he came, and there was a look of confusion upon the face of the chairman, and upon every one else, to know what was to be done in the emergency.

And when they came to consider, likewise, that Mr. Dawson was not in the flesh, the affair became an emergency indeed; for a question arose as to how far it was safe to put any slight upon Mr. Dawson's friend, even supposing he were dead, lest he should come in the witching hour of night and execute a terrible revenge; so that when we call the affair an emergency, an emergency it really was, and one the responsibility of acting in which each man then present would gladly have shifted on to his neighbour.

The chairman made a gasping attempt to get out of the difficulty in which he was placed, for he said,—

"Well, sir, you come well recommended to us from our esteemed friend Mr. Dawson, and I can assure you that between this time and our next night of meeting, we will duly consider upon the propriety, or otherwise, of admitting a new member."

"Thank you, sir," said the stranger. "I cannot be too much indebted to you, gentlemen, or express to you sufficiently my thanks for treating me with such a world of courtesy, and, in the meantime, to show how highly I appreciate such conduct, and to show how certain I feel of a favourable judgment from gentlemen of such great liberality, I will remain where I am."

This was a most unexpected declaration, and the whole association looked as fidgetty as possible. But what was to be done? The man was too quiet and too gentlemanly to be turned out, and, besides, if they could have got over these feelings, it came to something like the question of belling the cat—who was to do it? Collectively, they had no objection to vote him out of the vault, but that was quite another thing to taking him by the shoulders and putting him out; so that the stranger stood a good chance of remaining, whether his presence was wanted or not; and, doubtless, conceiving this to be the case, he clenched the matter by saying,—

"Gentlemen, allow me to return my sincere thanks for the very handsome manner in which you have permitted me to intrude upon you, and in which you have unanimously—for I perceive that such is the case—granted a request that I would hardly have dared to put into language. But my lamented friend, who is now no more, you inform me, once told me that I should find this a most gentlemanly assemblage, and my only regret is, that he is not here to speak for me himself, although that regret is tinctured by one circumstance of congratulation in which I know you will all join me."

It was with something like a groan that the president said,—

" And pray, sir, what may that subject of congratulation be ?"

" Why, it is, that our late respected friend will now be able to discover the grand secret we have been all so longing for ; and, no doubt, that to-night he will endeavour to make a round of visits, so as to satisfy most of the gentlemen present of the fact, that apparitions really do exist, and that they not only exist, but that they can make themselves tangible to other men, to all appearance, without their ghostly origin being suspected."

All eyes were now bent more curiously than before upon the stranger.

" Do you mean to say," said one, " that you have no objection to a gentleman's ghost coming into your chamber at night, just for the purpose of convincing you of such an abstract proposition ?"—" Objection, sir !   I should glory in it."

" Then every one to his taste ; and I here say, publicly, that I glory in no such thing, and I do trust and hope that Mr. Dawson will have the goodness to leave me alone, for I am quite convinced without."—" And I—and I," said several voices.

" Then it seems generally to be understood," said the chairman, in a quiet, placid sort of voice, " that we decline Mr. Dawson's promised kind visit, and should very much regret, indeed, giving him the trouble of making it ; which it is to be hoped (and here the chairman raised his voice, as if there were a remote possibility of Mr. Dawson's ghost hearing what he said, and profiting thereby), he will see the propriety of keeping himself quiet in his awful grave, and not come visiting people who don't want him."

" Hear—hear—hear !" cried half-a-dozen of the members ; and as nothing occurred to disturb the full harmony of such a proposition, the point was considered settled, and, as one remarked, *sotto voce*, to his neighbour, " the ghost who, after that, could come troubling anybody, must have a pretty good face indeed."

And now, because, rather that it seemed too difficult to get rid of Mr. Dawson's friend, than that there was any wish to detain him, his presence was tacitly put up with, and, as an hour had been unprofitably expended in these affairs, it was considered high time to proceed to the more legitimate business of the meeting.

The skull which, in the scramble on the preceding occasion, had been mislaid, was, after some difficulty, found ; and there were the papers containing the names one of which was to be drawn forth, for the purpose of discovering who was to be the individual next in order to favour his associates with some tale of the terrible.

After a great deal of preliminary shaking of this *caput mortuum*, the chairman, with due solemnity, drew forth one of the small written papers, and announced the name of a Mr. Amble Wade as he upon whom the lot had fallen.

This was a gentleman who had not said much during the various proceedings that had taken place. He seemed to be one of those quiet kind of men, more accustomed to think than to talk, and he had played the part of a listener, almost entirely throughout the singular proceedings that had taken place.

He seemed a little disconcerted that he should be the party next called upon to contribute to the general quota of information ; and he made an attempt to get out of it by asking if any gentleman would be his substitute upon the occasion.

This was a notion, however, universally repudiated, and consequently Mr. Amble Wade soon found that he had no resource, but with as good a grace as possible, to submit to what was inevitable, and forthwith do his best in the terrific.

" Gentlemen," he said ; and an air of deep candour and sincerity came across his countenance as he spoke—" Gentlemen, I do certainly regret, that your choice of some one, or rather the choice of fortune in this matter, has not fallen into better hands.   I fear that I shall want the graphic power to paint to you the circumstance which I shall make the subject matter of my narrative, and the only recommendation I can give you to it must consist in the fact that it is strictly true, and that in telling it to you I shall not embellish it in the least, but shall leave you to draw your own conclusions from an affair which, as it happened to myself, I can vouch for in every particular."

This was an exordium rather calculated to excite curiosity than otherwise. There was a murmur of approbation, and after a few moments, Mr. Amble Wade continued,—

" Gentlemen, I shall name my narrative

THE SPECTRE HANDS;

OR, THE DROP OF BLOOD.

WHEN first I came to the metropolis, as a single man studying the law, economy and quiet were two great objects with me. My family was not a wealthy one, but my father had a fancy that, if I went to the bar, there was nothing on earth to prevent me being Lord Chancellor, and so far he was perfectly correct—there was nothing to prevent me; but, at the same time, I am afraid there was nothing to assist me in obtaining that enviable office.

With limited resources, therefore, I came from Magdalen College to London, and entered as a student in one of the inns of court.

My father, who was considered a skilful financier, had made out for me a kind of balance sheet of expenditure and income, by which it was proved to me with most unimpeachable clearness that, after payment of such necessary expenses as my choice of a profession induced, I had to subsist upon the amazing sum of 95l. 6s. 4d. per annum.

Out of this I was to provide myself with the four essentials, bed, board, washing, and lodging, and I was dismissed with an injunction not to be extravagant.

I often asked myself how I could possibly accomplish such a desideratum as that. But, however, one of my first considerations when I reached London was to ascertain what was the most desirable and cheapest mode of lodging.

With this view I called upon an acquaintance of the name of Eccleston, who was pursuing his medical studies likewise in London.

He occupied an obscure and dingy looking lodging in a street in the Borough; and, with two glasses of cold brandy and water before us, we entered upon the important subject matter of the where and how to live upon 95l. 6s. 4d. per annum, so as to be remarkably genteel and keep out of debt.

Eccleston looked at me, and winked his eyes knowingly.

" I tell you what it is old fellow," he said; " there are more ways than one of hanging a cat."—" Oh," said I, " are there? I thought there was but one."

" There you are mistaken," he said; " you can hang her by her heels, you know, if you like; but, to the point—you'll find that what are called furnished lodgings for gentlemen will not suit you on any account."

" Good God! then," said I; " you don't want me to take a house, do you?"—" No, but I tell you, as regards lodgings, you'll be eaten up, done for, swallowed before you know where you are. You're a great deal too green for furnished lodgings, and you havn't got money enough to spend in acquiring the experience that fellows get in London; that is to say, you might get it in a low way, but that won't suit you, for you must be decent."—" Yes—I suppose so."

" Or whimsical, and that's what I advise you to be."

" What do you mean by that?"—" I will explain to you. You have a small sum to subsist upon, and there's no avoiding people seeing that you do subsist upon a small sum. Now, as regards that, they must come to one of two conclusions."

" And what are they?"—" Why, that it's choice or necessity."

" A difficult thing, I should say, to convince them of the former."—" Yes; I grant you that; but you may raise such an amount of doubt in their minds, that they will not be able exactly to decide which it is; and, as you are studying the law, you know that it is one of the principles of English jurisprudence to give people the benefit of a doubt.

"Yes," said I, "in criminal cases, if you please."—"Well, you will be virtually put upon your trial, and so you may get clean through an affair which, otherwise, might act very detrimentally to your interests."

"I have a glimmering," I said, "of what you mean. You wish me to affect to choose to be economical."—"That's about a second Daniel."

"Good; and now for the how such a state of things is to be brought about." —"I am not one who gives advice, and then leave people to find out the way to follow it themselves. Can you cook a chop?"

"A chop! they put it in a frying-pan, don't they?"

"My God! where were you brought up? Did you never see a gridiron? Why, that's one of the punishments of hell—they give you fried chops—fried in dripping, too—from some fat sinner—but, however, you will learn all about that in time."

"What about the fried chops in a certain place?"

"No, no; but the broiled chops in another; the idea, now, of frying chops— gracious! But, to put the question to you in a more enlarged shape; have you any objection to carrying home a sheep's-head at night in an old newspaper?"

"A sheep's head!"

"Yes, a sanguinary James—a gay mountain-pecker. If you have a fire, you know, you can burn the bones; and, if not, you can drop them down some one else's area."

"Well," I said, "I'm in the dark, and don't know what you mean."

"Then," said he, "it becomes my duty to illuminate a mental candle, and hold it to your brains. I perceive that you are uncommonly green about life in London, and what I want to let you know is, that you may unquestionably live, and live well upon the sum you have named—ay, live luxuriously, provided you are not above spending it yourself; but, if you let others spend it for you, you will find a lamentable difference as regards the proceeds."

"I can understand that," I said; "it's a reasonable proposition; and, if you will condescend to illuminate me as to how I'm to spend it, you will not find me above taking your advice."

"Then, in the first place, you must not go into furnished lodgings and be done for, for, if you do, you will be done up in the literal sense of the word, as well as in its figurative. Now, I'll tell you; you are studying the law; what can, therefore, be more proper and appropriate for you to do, than to reside in chambers? —there you can do just as you like. Take a desperate dingy set of chambers, in one of the cheap inns of court—you'll get them for a mere bagatelle, as regards rent; and there you can do just as you please. You may live upon a thousand pounds a-year, or a thousand shillings; you have as respectable an address in the one case as you have in the other. You are a Mister Somebody, of such an inn, and that's all that can be said of you; you will do just as you please; you have your own keys—go out and in to suit your own convenience—nobody to trouble you—you might shut yourself in, and die and be d—d, and nobody would come near you till quarter-day."

"Well," said I; "there's something independent and pleasant about that mode of life."

"It's the best for a fellow like you, that can possibly be desired. You can sit and study Coke upon Littleton, and coals upon anybody else, as long as ever you please; make yourself thoroughly acquainted with jurisprudence; although, in my opinion, to perpetrate a horrible pun, for which I ought to be prosecuted, juries have no prudence. You can cook your own chops, broil your kidneys, and solace yourself with a slice of your own hams whenever you please—there's nobody to say nay to you; you may make the grate as greasy as you like, and there's no officious landlady to make a fuss about it. You can boil, bake, stew, fret, fume, frizzle, and do yourself continually from morning to night. The best way in winter will be, to have your bed made next to the fire, and get in before you cook your supper. Take my advice, my boy; that's the life for you; I'll come and see you; I'll put you up to all the moves and dodges, which will enable you to get the good and economical, while you eschew the cheap and nasty."

"I'll do it," said I; "you've determined me."

"Oh! it will be delightful! you'll find it a capital thing, my good fellow. Why, d—n it, you'll be able to pickle your own legs."

"Yes," I said; "I shall depend upon you to find me out some locality in which I shall be able to carry out this really pleasant scheme. What do you suppose it will cost me for rent?"

"You can suit yourself from twelve pounds to twenty, and I recommend you Lyon's-inn—dark, dingy, and terrific—a regular kill-joy sort of place; enough to give a man of the world the horrors, but just the thing for a studious fellow like you."

"I'm not afraid of solitude," I said.

"And if you are ever, and feel in the mopes, you can run out into the Strand, you know, for you know it's close at hand; and there you are, in the midst of life, bustle, and activity, in a moment. You can't do better than locate yourself at once. Come with me, and we'll take a prowl, and see what there is to be had in that quarter."

There was a kind of charm to me about the sort of life my friend had painted. I fancied myself occupying the chambers of some deceased worthy of the law, breathing a very atmosphere of legal erudition, and nobody to interrupt me; while, as for the cooking part of the business, I recollected reading a treatise, by a learned philosopher, on man, at the commencement of which, he defines him from the rest of the animal creation, as being a cooking animal; and, surely, therefore, I was sufficiently like my species to be enabled to play the part of cook to myself, should occasion require; so that, as regarded that part of the business, I did not hesitate a moment, but accompanied my friend towards the locality which he had pointed out, as that most suited, in all respects, for me to reside in.

We soon reached that extremely dismal quadrangle called Lyon's-inn, which dates from the time of the first Charles, and certainly it strikingly displays how much our ancestors had to learn in the way of domestic architecture.

There are the most ingenious modes that any one could think of for excluding light, and making every apartment as uncomfortable as possible. The staircases, of course, are always put in the wrong place, the doors abominably fixed, and the fire-places always in some obscure corner, which prevents them from throwing any genial heat into the apartment.

Then, if there are three rooms to any one set of chambers, by some horrible contrivance or another, two of them are sure to be dark ones, and you are looked upon as frightfully fastidious, if you make an objection upon that account.

An application at the porter's lodge procured us the company of a female, who carried with her several keys for opening the different chambers that were to let.

I must own I revolted from them all, and shook my head at the dingy staircases, sunk corridors, and wretched rooms into which she conducted me.

"Well, sir," said the woman, when she found that nothing she had shown me would suit, "I'm sorry that you don't seem to like what you've seen, and it's a thousand pities that Mr. Ingram's are the best set in the inn."

"Why, what's the use of Mr. Ingram's being a good set," said I, "if I cannot have them."

"Ah! sir, you know what I mean well enough, only gentlemen will have their jokes; you know you might have Mr. Ingram's set in welcome, for an old song."

"And wherefore," said I, "does it happen that a set of chambers which you describe to me as the best in the inn, are to be procured upon such remarkably easy terms?"

"Ah!" said my friend, "I should like to know?"

"Is it possible, gentlemen," said the woman, looking at us both, "that you don't know afore you come here, that you might have the haunted set almost for nothing? Poor dear Mr. Bullwhistle, he was took out a matter of five months ago in a hackney-coach, with two keepers and a strait waistcoat—that set of chambers druv him mad ; and Mr. Chinnery, as had 'em afore him, a bold man he was, and well I recollect his waking up the whole inn in the night, and going away, and never showing his face again."

" You interest me," I said ; " I'd no idea you'd a set of haunted chambers here."

" Yes, sir, I believe you ; and they do say—I wouldn't try it for worlds ; but they do say, that if you was to go up the staircase, atween twelve and one, any night, and put your ear to the key-hole, you'd hear something as would make you come down again quicker than you went up."

" Can you show us those chambers ?"

" Oh, dear, yes, sir ; now as it's broad daylight, and seeing as I ain't going by myself, I can't have no objection. If you'll come this way, gentlemen, I'll take you ; and as nice a set of chambers you'll find them, as you wish to see ; only, as I say, with such a drawback to them, who'll have 'em ?"

We followed her across the quadrangle, and into one of the best houses, and upon proceeding up stairs, we found that these chambers were upon the first-floor, and consequently in the best part of the house.

She then left us, for a moment or two, while she went to the lodge to fetch the key, during which time I told my friend, that if they suited in other respects, and were so remarkable cheap as they were represented, I should not hesitate to take possession of them, for that I held perfect defiance to all kinds and classes of superstition.

" As you please," said my friend ; " I must confess that, for my part, I don't like these kind of things, especially when you come to be shut up in a place all alone. You don't know what strange tricks fancy may play you, and although there may be nothing in reality at all in what is asserted, yet it comes to much the same thing to you, whether you conjure up for yourself the apparition that terrifies you, or have it conjured up for you by somebody else. But you will see how you will like the place, and we can make further inquiry."

By this time the woman returned with the key, and after several abortive efforts she succeeded in turning the lock of the door, for it was much rusted, in consequence, as she told us, of the chambers never having been opened since the last tenant was taken away in the hackney-coach, with a strait waistcoat. And she adhered to that part of the story, too, so pertinaciously, that I had no doubt of the fact, though I had a great doubt of the inference—namely, that it was anything he had seen in the chambers that had driven him distracted.

A rather dark vestibule led into a room, spacious and light, the chimney-piece was curiously and elaborately carved, the roof covered with ornaments, and the walls richly panelled. It was certainly a very desirable and likeable sort of apartment.

Passing through this, we came into another, not quite so handsome, but nearly so, and then to a third, and finally, there was a little dark, square room, into which I just looked, and saw that it contained some lumber.

In fact, putting their bad character out of the question, these chambers were such as would at any time have fetched a large price, and been quite the fancy of any one having a taste for such an abode.

" Upon my word," I said, " this is as pleasant looking a place as I have had the good fortune to see for some time."

" Yes, sir," said the woman ; " ain't it a pity, a thousand pities, that it's haunted?"

" In a word," I said, " I'll take them."

" You, sir !" she exclaimed. "Oh ! sir, don't ; you'll be another Bedlam for a certainty—I think I sees you in a cell."

" Yes," said my friend, who never let a pun go by, " that would be a sell, indeed, and a lonely sell, too."

" I am serious," I said ; " these chambers shall be mine. Here will I locate, and defy the ——"

" Hush ! good gracious," said the woman, " don't mention him. But, if so be as you will take the chambers, Mr. Ingram as owns 'em, which is why we calls 'em Ingram's chambers, told me to say to any lawyer as took 'em to send 'em to him, but if a gentleman took 'em he left it to his conscience."

"Well, I ain't a lawyer yet," I said; "so I may be presumed to possess that article. You can tell Mr. Ingram, when you see him, that it is a gentleman who has taken them. Can you give me possession at once?"

"Oh! yes, sir, I can give you possession at once; here's the key, you must give me two references about your character."

"Very good," I said, "that will do. There is my word, and I trust that I shall redeem those really handsome apartments, from the ban which is upon them."

I took the key, and felt quite proud of my possession, scarcely believing the fact that in so short a time I had picked up so desirable a home, the rent of which, too, was left to my conscience.

"What do you think of all that?" I said to my friend, when we got out into the Strand.

"Candidly," he replied, "I don't like it at all; there's some confounded thing

No. 7.

connected with these chambers that you don't know of yet. " Now, take my advice, I'm an older man than you; go back again, give up the key; say, that upon consideration, you'll have nothing to do with it—that you have quite enough mortal acquaintances without wishing to drag a few more from another world. Get clear of your bad bargain? for I tell you, candidly, I have a presentiment on my mind that if you don't you will live to repent it."

" Now really," I cried; " this from a man of sense like you, a man of the world too—a man who has seen human nature in all its varieties, and who has been telling me how to live—I am surprised and shocked."

" Go on," he cried, " go on; a wilful man will have his way. If you have made up your mind to take these chambers, you will; I only tell you I wouldn't, and that I believe no good will come of it."

" But how and why?"

" My dear fellow, we live in a commercial country, everything fetches its price. Always be suspicious of what's given away; once for all, will you give them up?"

" For you to take them," I said, with a laugh.

" Holy Heaven!" he said; " but that's quite sufficient; I say no more."

" Excuse me there," I said, " I only jest; but I don't intend to give them up, and we shall pass many a happy hour in them yet."

" Amen!" he cried; " and now, since that's settled, you must think about furnishing. Come along."

In the course of the next two hours I laid out, under his judicious auspices, about five and twenty pounds; and I was amazed at the quantity of the useful and the ornamental which we procured for that comparatively insignificant sum. These things were all moved to my chambers—I need not go through details; but, in the course of three or four hours, the place was tolerably comfortable, and a bright fire fumed and flustered in the grate, sending its revivifying influence throughout the principal apartments of the chambers.

My friend now left me, promising, however, to look in in the evening, and christen the place by taking a social glass in it.

It must have been in consequence of what I had heard that, somehow or another, the moment that he had left me, and I knew that I was alone in those chambers, a strange sensation crept over me, and I shuddered from top to toe. I got suspicious and fidgetty, caught myself continually looking over my shoulder, listening to little noises, peering into corners, and darting round suddenly, as if I expected to catch somebody unawares.

You will easily imagine that this was a state of things of a most uncomfortable tendency. In vain I told myself that it was silly, and poked the fire; as often as I did so I turned round with the poker, very sharp; and once, I actually said, " Eh!" for I thought I heard something.

It was only twilight, too, and not dark enough actually to afford me a reasonable excuse for lighting up; and I could not help saying to myself,—

" If I feel like this now, what shall I feel late at night, when I have closed the outer door, when I know that I must be many hours alone, when all is still around me as the very grave? What shall I think then? Eh! what's that? Oh! that's nothing, only a coal dropped out of the fire into the fender; courage—courage— what a laugh my friend will have at me if I give in this way. I'll read."

I took up a book, but, some how or other, I was always glaring over the top of it, and I felt uncomfortable unless I placed the back of my chair against the wall; and every ten minutes or so I half closed my eyes, so as to concentrat my powers of vision, and look all round carefully, to satisfy myself there was nothing unusual.

An hour or two thus passed, and I had succeeded in reasoning myself a great deal out of my fears. The room was immensely ample, as far as appearances went. I had lit a couple of candles, and tapped a bottle of port, and was in momentary expectation of my friend's arrival, when such an unearthly and horrible noise sounded immediately outside the door leading to the staircase, that, in my agitation, I very nearly sat upon the fire.

"Yes yes," I cried, and down went one of the candles.

"Hilloa!" said my friend, as he popped his head in; "did I startle you?"

"Curse you," said I, "what did you do that for?"

"Oh, indeed," he said—"you can't stand that—very good—and you're the fellow who has taken possession of the haunted chambers, out of which one fellow ran away in the middle of the night, and another was walked off in a hackney-coach, with two keepers and a strait-waistcoat."

"Ha, ha!" said I, "a good joke—all moonshine."

"Well, it may be a joke, but I must confess that that laughing of yours is just what I should expect from a hyena who had lost his mother; and, for a man in a pleasant state of mind, you look as uncomfortable as any Christian gentleman would wish to be. Why you are positively pale, and what a look you have got about the eyes. Have you seen anything?"

"Ha, ha!" I began, but he stopped me abruptly, saying, with all the seriousness in the world—

"I'll trouble you not to laugh in that way again; you may like it, but I tell you I don't. It's one of the most deadly living things I've come across for a long while, so pray drop it."

"Oh, you're jesting," I said—"you're jesting, and want to make me nervous."

"Do I—that's superfluous; but, however, I don't want to say anything about it. I see you've drawn a cork, so let's talk of other subjects, and dive into the reasons of that bottle."

I was not a little pleased that my friend was willing to divert my mind from the subject, too painfully, uppermost in it; and we were soon engaged in an animated discussion respecting field sports until I was quite restored to equanimity, and forgot all terrors incidental to the haunted chambers. And yet, now and then, it would occur to me that I had to pass the night there alone, for all that, and but for the outrageous manner, I was perfectly convinced he would laugh at me, I don't know but what I should have actually asked my friend to stay, and share with me any dangers that might arise from the spirits black, white, or grey, that were supposed to hold their fearful orgies in Mr. Ingram's chambers.

I managed, however, to repress this feeling, and we got through, not only that bottle, but another at the back of it, so that by the time I was about being left alone again, I might be considered to have acquired a certain amount of courage from my potations, and I could have almost defied the devil and all his imps.

"Well, my boy," said my friend, rising, "you're at home, you know, and I'm not so, I must go."

Those words sounded most uncomfortable upon my ear. "Go—nonsense!" I said, "not yet; it's early."

"Don't delude me with such an idea as that—you know it's late; but I tell you what I'll do now—I'll look in to-morrow, just to——"

"To what?"

"Why to ask you if you've seen anything."

"Oh, confound you, I suppose I never shall hear the last of that, but I'm not so nervous as you take me to be; and I've every reason to believe, after all, that I shall see nothing worse than you or myself, as long as I remain a tenant in these chambers."

"Well, well," said my friend, "I approve of that—there's nothing like putting a good face on it—once give way to your fears, and it's all up with you. I don't wish to make you in the slightest degree uncomfortable—it would be too bad for me to think of such a thing. I may be wrong, but the real fact is, that from the first moment I set my foot in these chambers, a kind of strange, charnel house, uncomfortable chill, shot through me—I felt as if I were in the presence of something which I could not dissolve; and, upon the whole, not that I wish to make you uncomfortable, far from it—the man who would come to enjoy another's hospitality, and then say anything at all calculated to have an effect upon his nerves, is unworthy the name of a man—only this much I will add, that I'd rather you slept here to-night than I. Good night to you."

"Go on, go on," I said ; "as you please—I understand."

"Now really you think I'm trying to annoy you, but you're very much mistaken. Don't imagine such a thing for a moment—only I think it would be just as well, if you were to make up your mind what you mean to do, in case you see anything ?"

"I'll tell you," said I, what I mean to do, "If I see my ghost I'll give him your address."

"Aye, very well, good night, I'm afraid your booked, I'll be hanged if I ain't sorry for you, good night, good night."

He was gone, I looked at my watch, it wanted a quarter to twelve, I closed the outer door and shot a massive bolt into its socket. How profoundly still and calm everything was, if I had been in a city of the dead a feeling of greater repose could not have stolen over me, and yet I knew that I was in the midst of bustle and every day existence ; still was I shut off as it were from human society, cribbed, cabined, and confined in those chambers, to be made, for all I knew, the sport of some malignant beings, who might even now be glaring at me with their supernatural eyes. But no, no, I must not think of such things. I tried to hum the air of a popular song, what a dreadful failure that was.

I battled against my feelings as much as I could, but before five minutes had elapsed I caught myself at all the old manœuvres that I had practised early in the evening, dodging about to see that no one was behind me, listening attentively to nothing, and working myself to a pitch of nervousness beyond all expression.

I got extremely uncomfortable, and more than once I thought of sallying forth and going to some public house, a measure which I believe the dread of ridicule alone stopped me from carrying out. I could not bear the idea that my friend, and others, should have such a laugh against me.

All at once it struck me that I had never thoroughly examined the rooms, and although it was a ticklish task just then to do so, I thought it possible that it might allay some of my nervousness, and lifting one of the candles from the table, I walked slowly towards the door of the adjoining apartment, I think my very hand was upon the lock of it, and I felt rather better than I had for some few minutes previous, when suddenly from the interior of that room, there came upon my ears one of the most awful and diabolical yells, that ever I had heard in all my life, and then it was followed by such a shouting shrieking kind of laughter, that one would have thought that the very devil himself was in a fit of hysterics.

I dropped the candle in a moment, and gained the other end of the room having a distant recollection of shouting out as I did so, some incoherent words, consisting principally of—

"Stop ! stop ! that'll do, that'll do."

Then all was quiet—a quiet which seemed the more profound in consequence of the volley of sound which had immediately preceded it ; and then I sat, I think for full half an hour, with the perspiration rolling down my face, and making vain efforts to account for the dreadful shout, and equally dreadful laugh, that had disturbed the solitude of my chamber.

I should certainly have flown from the place but for one supposition, and that was the remote possibility that it might be a trick. How did I know but that some chambers immediately contagious to mine, might afford facilities for somebody waggishly inclined to play off so cruel a farce at my expense.

This circumstance, and this only, gave me a little nerve. I did not like being beaten ; and although I shook in every limb, and was as dreadfully frightened as anybody need wish to be, I screwed my courage to the sticking place, and said aloud,—

" I will sleep here to-night. I am armed ; and woe be to him who is foolhardy enough to bring down upon his head the consequences of trifling with a man who is familiar with the use of the fire-arms he has about him."

⟩ I thought it possible that this valorous speech might produce some sort of rejoinder, but it did'nt. Nobody of this world, or of any other, took any notice of it ; and yet it was no idle threat, for in my carpet-bag which I had brought with me, I had a brace of loaded pistols, and it was quite wonderful the amount of self-possession that I felt when I grasped those weapons which were familiar to me, in my hand.

"Now," I said, "I will not be trifled with. I have done nothing that should make me afraid of the supernatural world, if there be one, and I can take my own part against anything human."

It was with a feeling of something like desperation that I now snatched up my only remaining candle, and without waiting to think—for if I had attempted to go through that process I should have shrunk back—I made my way suddenly into the adjoining room.

I walked into the very centre of the floor, and then I turned round, and moved several times, looking curiously around me, with a half sort of expectation of beholding something horrible glaring upon me from some corner.

I was agreeably disappointed, though nothing met my gaze but what I expected there to find. It was the room in which I was to sleep, and in it I had placed a French bedstead, and the usual appurtenances of an ordinary bed-chamber; and yet I could have sworn in any court of Christendom, that from there I had heard that diabolical noise, and that it was not fancy, but a dread reality of some sort or another. After satisfying myself by this cursory examination, that nothing of the terrific was present, I took a more enlarged and comprehensive view of the apartment ; and, finally, I peered into every corner of it, looking under the bedstead and into a cupboard that was very large, to convince myself that nothing lurked within the precincts of the room.

But there was a room beyond this, which I hadn't looked at, and into which might have retreated the being who made that terrific uproar. The sudden flash of courage that had carried me into the first apartment, did not suffice, on the moment, to take me into the second. But yet, how could I think of going to bed without thoroughly examining the whole of my domain ? I could not dream of such a thing ; so carrying one of the pistols in my hand, ready for immediate service, and the candle in the other, I with, I dare say, as anxious looking a countenance as ever mortal man wore, took my way into the end apartment.

An examination of that was a very simple affair, for I had placed no furniture whatever in it. The two rooms were enough for one, and I had much rather that there had not been the third, and the little closet that made the fourth.

A glance sufficed for the third room, and then I opened the closet door. In it were some old, musty looking boxes, an old chair—with a fractured leg, and behind the door, which made me start a little at first, hung a musty looking, ancient garment, in the shape of a grey morning gown.

My sudden opening of the door gave it a movement, so that, at the moment, I could have fancied myself almost face to face with some one, but this feeling was transitory.

It had evidently hung there for a long time, and as I had no disposition to disturb it, I closed the door again, saying to myself,—

"Well, I shall go to bed, and perhaps, after all, what I have heard is everything that will occur; and if so, and it should occur even every night, I think I can accustom myself to it. Let me see, my best plan will be to say nothing of it to any one, and if it be a trick, then I shall disappoint the perpetrators of it ; for now, that I have thoroughly examined the apartments, I am certainly inclined to suspect —. Good God, there it is again !" I staggered back till I reached the wall, against which I supported myself, holding the candle in one hand, and the pistol in the other, while from the room which I had devoted for the purposes of a bed-chamber, came again that fearful and awful shout. I know not how to describe it ; and never but once did I hear a sound at all equal to it, and that was in France, where a man was being guillotined, and by some mismanagement of the apparatus, the descending axe stopped, after inflicting a gash of about an inch in depth in his neck ; he uttered some such a yell as that which came upon my ears in those lonely chambers. God knows, it thrilled through my heart, and made each nerve of my body vibrate again. It stopped the healthy current of my blood ; and, by some frightful sympathetic effect, confused for a moment, my very eye-sight.   I almost lost perception of where I was, and of who I was ; and then came the horrible ringing laugh—a laugh so totally destitute of mirth, such a hideous mockery of every thing that was pleasant in cachination, that in itself it was enough to make, popularly speaking, one's flesh creep upon one's bones ; and produced that strange feeling about the roots of the hair which induces a full belief in the fact, that if the ghost of Hamlet's father had said what he might have said, the waving locks of the former would have stood on end,

" Like quills upon the fretful porcupine."

I drew a long breath, all was still again ; twice in a night—I said, I can't stand this—there's no sleep to be had here—I shall have to go out—I never felt so unnerved in all my life—I haven't the strength of an infant ; any one might brain me with a lady's fan.   Truly, there are more things in heaven and earth than were dreamt of in my philosophy, and this is one of them.   What shall I do? my evil stars had pitched my bed in the apartment which seemed so pregnant with horrors.   I wonder if any one else sleeps above or below ; if so, they must be plunged, indeed, deeply in slumber not to hear that frightful cry. Why, its enough to awaken the whole house—it rings in my ears even now ; the echo of it fills the still air.   Now—now, I shall see something.   Confound Ingram, and his chambers, too ; well may the rent of such a place as this be left to his conscience.

With faltering steps I reached the door that led into the bed room ; I opened it and put in the hand that held the candle, and then my face ; and there, for a few minutes, I looked, I dare say, more like an inhabitant of another world than of this, fully expecting to have my eye-sight blasted by some frightful sight that would turn my very heart to stone, and kill me at once, by its supernatural aspect.

But I was mistaken again ; nothing—nothing ; all was as usual, or just as I had seen it before, and I do think that I suffered more terror from this state of uncertainty than if I had actually seen something, the aspect of which would have been dreadful to me ; but still something definable to my fears, which I might have battled with.

I sat myself down upon the side of the bed, after placing the candle upon the dressing table, and I asked myself the question—

" Shall I, or shall I not retire to bed in such a place as this ?"

Then arose a host of arguments upon each side of the question ; at one moment I told myself that it would be ridiculous to attempt to sleep ; and then again, I asked myself what I should say in answer to the questions that would be put to me, regarding my reasons for so suddenly leaving the chambers.

Pride, for it was nothing else, prevailed over prudence, and I determined upon remaining.   It was with many a mental throe and struggle, though, that I came to such a resolution, and now, when I had arrived at it, and half repented me, and looked wistfully at my hat, which seemed to invite me to go forth and leave that place, and all its terrors, to itself.

I looked into the next apartment, and found that the fire was nearly out, so that there was no temptation to again leave the bed-room, but although I had made up my mind to pass the night there if possible, I did not at all see that there was any necessity of denuding myself of my apparel.   I took off my coat, my waistcoat, and my cravat, and then, I thought I had done quite enough.   I kept on my boots, I suppose on the principle of having a last kick for my life. I set up a whole candle, which I calculated would last well till day-break, and then I slipped into bed accoutred as I was.

It was cold, but I had no sooner laid down than a feeling of drowsiness crept on me, which I didn't half like.   It was unusual, almost unnatural, and I had a dim idea that if I went to sleep I should be awakened again, with a vengeance, by something.

Oh, how I fought against that propensity to slumber. There I lay, winking and blinking at the candle, and trying to persuade myself that it was all right, until now and then, I caught myself with my eyes closed, and just dropping off, at a rail-road pace, into the land of nod.

Then, I would rouse myself by a violent effort, and actually wrenching open my eyes, I would look about me in those haunted chambers, to see if aught new had occurred.

No, all was still; all as before; and now, more than the interval between the first and second occasion of frightful sounds had passed away, and nothing came to disturb the stillness; so that I felt a little comforted, and almost thought that I might venture to yield to the drowsy influence that was stealing over me.

The effort to keep awake when a somniferous influence has once crept over the senses is to the full as painful, if not more so than the restless unavailing effort to get to sleep, I shook myself, I opened my eyes and glared at the candle till I winked again, I moved my leg up and down in the bed till I tired it out; I tried to speak and uttered only indistinct murmurs, objects became confused before me; my eyes closed, and with a delicious sensation of doing something wrong and fell fast asleep.

"Fast as a church," is a common saying, but I was faster than that; aye, faster than a cathedral; the last thing I saw was the candle, it had a long and ominous looking wick, I couldn't have got out of bed and snuffed that candle if anybody had laid me down a hundred pounds upon the spot.

I don't know how long I slept. It is said, that the mind in its marvellous activity will depict, in the space of a few brief moments, a world of thought; certainly a number of images floated across my slumbering imagination, and then suddenly I was awakened by fancying I heard my own name pronounced in a loud shrill cry.

I started up, and on the impulse of the moment I cried—

"Yes, what?—who calls?"

All was still; I saw by the look of the candle that I could not have slept long, and then I sunk back gently upon the pillow again, but I was wide awake. The somnolency of a few moments seemed to have but an end to all desire of repose, I was evidently wide awake now. It was a French bedstead in which I slept, and I knew I looked very carefully beneath it, before I stepped into bed; it was so placed too, that from where I lay I could see the whole apartment.

I felt my heart beat with a sudden quick emotion, which assured me something was going to happen of no desirable character, except that it would partake of the terrific; yet I heard nothing, but oh, how I wished, and wished in vain, that I had left the chamber.

My breath nearly left me, there was a sound, it was of some one too, half sobbing, half laughing, the very madness of woe; and then there came a strange scratching, —scratching, and a singing sort of laugh, as if something, at once demoniac and malicious, was chuckling at the thought of coming mischief.

The hair bristled upon my head, I compressed my lips until I felt they were bloodless, I breathed short and thick, I felt the painful protusion of my eyes; and the scratch,—scratch, as if somebody with a multitude of nails was climbing up a wall, came a fearful sound upon my ears.

In a moment it localized itself—that dreadful sound—it came from beneath the bedstead in which I slept; I fixed my concentrated gaze upon the footboard, there was nothing yet—nothing—nothing; but it was coming, I knew it, I felt it through every fibre of my frame, and then slowly, but with a terrific perseverance, there slid over the edge of the wood-work two hands; I never saw such hands, the fingers long and corpse-like looking. I saw them to the wrists, and there they hung, and shook, and wrung themselves, as if in mental agony, before my very face; and even as this, with a horrible-pictured intensity they depicted the agony of a something or a somebody, wild and shrieking sobs and laughter came upon my ears.

I tried to move—I think I cried help, help! I felt a sudden sensation, as if the bedstead, the room, and every thing in it were whirling round and round ; my senses left me and I knew no more.

    *   *   *   *   *   *   *

How long I lay in this seeming trance of death I, of course, could have no perception ; but I think it could not have been many minutes, for the first sensation I had, was of the light glancing painfully in my eyes, and I lay in that confusion of thought. which for a few moments holds possession of the whole mental system, after some dream of more than usual vividness and intensity.

Then gradually there came back to my mind the remembrance of what had happened, and I knew I was in the haunted chamber still, exposed to all the horrors incidental to them. I felt that I was fastened into those rooms of terror, and that voluntarily I had shut myself up from society, as if for the very purpose of being almost driven mad with terror.

I dreaded to move hand or foot, lest by giving any indication of having again recovered my perceptive faculties, I should again draw down upon my head the vengeance of those malignant beings, who had made a sport of my fancy, and unnerved my whole system.

I thought that I would lie there till day-light, till some early farm cock had crowed his salutation to the morn, and dispersed into thin air those hideous fumes of the night which could only hold their reign while darkness, like a black pall hung upon the face of nature, which with other unwholesome and noxious vapours, must fly before the light of day, leaving the sweet earth green and beautiful, as God had made it ; and the mind of man free from the cobwebs of superstitions, which the absence of the glorious sunlight had permitted hideous things to weave within the chamber of his brain.

There I lay, hoping, wishing, for the morn, as never prisoner in a weary dungeon wished to see the first faint pencil of light that might come struggling in to visit him, a blessed messenger of hope from heaven, through the grated parture of his prison-house.

Never did expectant lover sigh more fervently for the coming morn, that was to unite him for aye and for ever in the holiest of bonds, to her who was his first, last, and only idol, as I did for that daylight which was to bring repose to my mind, and enable me to shake off the fetters of abject fear, the massive links of which were clinging round my very soul.

No shipwrecked mariner clinging to the last faint fragment of a wreck, tossed at the wild mercy of the wind and waves, with nought above but a sky of darkness— nought below but a sea of howling gloom, could stretch his hands to heaven with more fulness of supplication, than I whispered to myself a prayer for sunshine.

I think an hour must have passed thus, and strangely and fitfully my mind flew back to the days of childhood, of youth, and of that period still partaking of something of the latter state, but upon the threshold of what might be called a mature existence, on which I stood. There was not an incident in my whole life but what seemed to pass before my mental vision—beings numbered with the dead came stalking by me again, instinct with life.

It is said that in the last agony of drowning, the gasping wretch, who has sunk beneath the billowy surface to rise no more, sees depicted in a moment the whole of his former existence, as if the character, the events, the dialogue, plot, everything of his existence were concentrated into one flash of thought, to be presented to him, in what may be called a blaze of memory, ere death claimed him for its own ; and so it was with me, only that the operation was not so rapid—more slowly, and with a heavier kind of solemnity, the events of my past life marshalled themselves before me, until I began really to think that my last hour had come, and that this mortal review was but the mind's preparation for that other world to which I was so swiftly hurrying.

I made a great effort to move, for I felt as if to continue in that pacific state of thought must result in madness. I was convinced that if I would preserve my sanity I must, let the consequences be what they may, shake off the state of mind in which I was.

I held up my head; I thought by such a movement I might at once provoke some evil act on the part of the supernatural beings that were around me in those chambers, but if such were not the case, if I could make so decided a movement as that, and no consequences arose, surely I might consider it safe wholly to rise, and make a brave effort wholly to shake off the oppression that sat so heavily upon me.

All was still; such a stillness as, popularly speaking, would have enabled me to hear a pin drop; and then I felt a little more assured, saying to myself,—

"Surely the great danger is past, the evil spirit that haunts these chambers has had its will; it had filled poor humanity with sufficient terror, and now, until the morning, I shall be suffered to be at peace, but I cannot sleep—I will wait—I will not leave the place, but I dare not venture again to close an eye within its precincts."

Although I uttered these words in a low tone of voice, yet I was by no means
No. 8.

assured of the truth of the proposition which they conveyed. I still had my doubts and fears ; and it was with a feeling of absolute dread that I tremblingly sat up in bed and looked around me.

I saw nothing but what I expected fully to see, namely, the various articles appertaining to the apartment, which I had myself placed there.

Everything seemed just as usual, there was no confusion ; and, by the appearance of the candles, I judged that about half the night had expired.

I cautiously put one foot out of the bed, and then, somehow or another, a disagreeable idea shot across me that something was about to lay hold of it, and I took it in again with a precipitation that, I dare say, to any one who had seen it, would have partaken of the ludicrous.

But it was no joke to me, and I was a considerable time before I could again muster courage firmly to get out of bed. When I did, it was only with a spring that I accomplished my purpose ; and then, with a desperate sort of feeling, I at once seized the candle, and dropping on my knees looked under the bed.

There was nothing there but before seen ; as I was of the idea that the two dreadful hands that I had seen over the foot-board must belong to some equally dreadfully body, it would not, in my then state of mind, have surprised me had my eyes been greeted by some frightful spectacle beneath my couch.

It was a great relief, however, and a world of mercies to find that such was not the case. I breathed more freely, and I sat down on a chair with a deep sigh of relief as I wiped the perspiration from my brow.

" Perhaps," I said, " it was only imagination after all."

As if the very thought had enabled my mind to summon up all the evidence that could possibly occur to it in favour of the truth of the reality of the appearance, I remembered that I had seen, as if hanging by the fingers of those dreadful hands, what Macbeth calls, in speaking of the air-drawn dagger that invites him to a deed of murder, " gouts of blood."

With a feeling in my mind that I cannot explain or define, I approached the bed to examine the coverlet ; for I felt convinced that if the vision had been a real one I should there find some evidences of its actuality,

It was a strange feeling that prompted me to this examination, and at the moment I seemed to have no difficulty in reconciling to my mind, the substantial with the unreal.

I examined the counterpane, which being completely new was free from every spot or soil which might have produced a mistake, and there, exactly beneath where those long and haggard fingers had vibrated, there was a large, deep, red stain—a spot of blood, and yet something more than a spot ; for it must have been a huge drop indeed if the ensanguined liquid could have produced such an effect.

I was much affected, for this seemed a damning piece of evidence as regarded the actual presence of the apparition that had appeared to me. I might have argued myself out of every thing but that. What sophistry, however, of the reason, could get rid of such a frightful evidence ? there it was—blood ; there could be no doubt upon the subject, it had the colour—it looked fresh and new ; and it might have been fancy, but I thought it had the odour of the life-sustaining fluid.

I staggered back and resumed my seat upon the chair which I had left.

" It is true," I said, " I am convinced—there is no longer room for doubt ; scepticism itself must quail before such evidence as this, and, while I live, the circumstances of this night will rouse up in my memory as most abundant proof, that the connection between this world and that which is to come is of a closer and more intricate character than most people imagine, although there are times and circumstances when all admit as much, of the fears that creep over their distracted senses.

I had a thought now of leaving, for I felt that I had a means of disarming ridicule and of proving that I was right ; for who could gainsay the existence of that drop of blood upon the bed. Was it not sufficient to convince any one ?

Did it not give a 'vraisemblance' to the story, which otherwise it might have wanted, and which no asseverations of mine could have made up.

"Yes," said I, "I have a right to leave now;" but yet I lingered, partly, probably from a dislike to be the hero of such a tale, and partly from a feeling that, having gone through so much, it would be a thousand pities if I didn't stay the night out, and so ascertain all the terrors that could be crowded into one twenty-four hours spent in those chambers.

I am free to confess that I had a suspicion to the effect, that those terrors were over, or, probably, I should not have been so valiant; but, as it was, I took the candle with me and went into the front room, making up my mind to light a fire to sit by for the rest of the night, and to indulge myself with another bottle of that port wine which I had laid in for my own especial use and that of my intimates.

But you will bear in mind, gentlemen, that this indulgence in this extra bottle was after the vision and not before it, so that don't suspect that what I saw was elaborated out of that vinous fluid.

I felt a little assured as the fire crackled and blazed up about me; it was pleasant to feel its influence, and as the wood crackled and shattered living embers, I felt as if I was not wholly alone; and I wonderfully revived under the cheering influence.

But still I had no thought whatever of passing another night in those chambers.

"No," I said, I shall have a good tale to tell, and I do not see why I should take any pains to repeat it. I have had a complete dose of Ingram's chambers, and may congratulate myself that I am not so far gone as the last unfortunate tenant, who put the strait-waistcoat in a state of requisition, and the two keepers.

As I took glass after glass of the grateful beverage, I revived more and more; and at last, spreading myself out cozily before the fire, I fell into a deep and profound slumber.

From this I did not awake until I thought or rather dreamt that a great illumination was taking place, which produced an amount of heat from innumerable candles, sufficient to scorch my very face. I sprung to my feet, rubbing my eyes, and wondering for a moment where I was, and then, all of a sudden, I found that a sun-beam had had the bad taste to come into Lyon's Inn, and the philanthropy to disturb my slumbers, and fall full upon my countenance.

So the morning had come, the bright and beautiful morning, the harbinger of the heart's delight; the morning, in which men feel courage proportioned to the extent of their fears at night—the morning, when young blood dances more pleasantly and joyfully through the veins; and when, one would have as well think of being a Mahomodan as of being superstitious.

And now all the events of the night crowded upon my recollection, but I did not shudder now,—on the contrary, I felt quite at ease and pleasant, and if a whole legion of ghosts had suddenly made their appearance, I think I could have faced them all, and said :—

"Pray gentlemen, what may be your pleasure? I look upon you as natural curiosities, but you are quite mistaken if you fancy you alarm me in the least."

I rose, and looked out of the window, into the sombre square of the Inn; the most romantic object that met my eyes was an old woman carrying a dust-pan in one hand, and a tin pail in the other, from some of the chambers.

"Elderly female," I apostrophised her to myself, "how welcome you would have been last night, if you had but made your gracious appearance, as I lay shaking in bed, with those frightful hands exhibited before me." But pshaw! it must have been a dream. Stuff! Nonsense! Spectre hands, indeed! the idea of such a thing coming into my brain. Nobody will believe it, and I can't compel them to do so ; seeing I have no evidence myself, I have no evidence to offer. Evidence—no evidence !—the drop of blood !

A cold chill crept over me, but I soon recovered from that as I looked out upon the bright sun-shine.

"Oh!" I said, that was imagination, too ; after fancying the vision, it was easy to fancy a confirmation of it ; nothing but fancy—a spot in my eye perhaps ; in fact, at such a time, it would have been wonderful if I had not seen something of the sort, most wonderful ; but however, I'll just go and satisfy myself upon that head ; I'll be quite assured that it was imagination, and nothing but imagination ; and then—why then, I'll go me and have as jolly a breakfast as ever mortal man tasted ; and I'll keep possession of Ingram's chambers, in spite of the very devil. I won't be beat. I'm convinced its only imagination."

While I spoke, I made my way into my bed-room ; and, by the time 1 had got thus far, I reached my over-night's couch, off which I suddenly pulled the counterpane, and held it up to the light.

It was a very uncomfortable thing, but there was the spot of blood, sure enough ; there was no mistake in that ; there it was, just as I had seen it over-night, with its unmistakeable colour, and even its very odour. I could have sworn to its being blood ; and here had I been congratulating myself upon the absence of proof of something which was proved to me in a moment, whether I liked it or not.

I did not feel half so jolly as I had before ; on the contrary, a state of decided uncomfortableness came over me again, and my resolution of holding possession of Ingram's chambers fell at least fifty per cent. "I don't think I will," I said, "its really not worth while ; I shall never be very comfortable here, because I shall always be thinking of what has happened ; besides, when night comes— night, that's conclusive. I wouldn't stay another night for a thousand pounds.

I dropped the counterpane, put on my hat, and was hurrying to the door, when there came a sudden and startling knock at it.

I recoiled for a moment, for the question occurred to me, should I tell my friend, for I felt assured it was he who knocked up my night's adventures, or would.

It was a serious question. I dreaded ridicule, and disbelief ; and yet, I did not see how I could keep it to myself.

While I was cogitating, the knock came again, louder than before, and I was forced to make up my mind with tolerable precipitation ; like other great men, I decided upon being controlled by circumstances ; so I opened the door at once, without any fixed determination in my mind.

My friend made his appearance, and he looked at me with a comical kind of expression, which quite prefaced the question I knew he was about to put to me of—" did you see any thing ?"

" Good morning," said I.

" Good morning," he said, " well, well.'

" I'm very glad to hear it," I said.

" Glad to hear what ?"

" Why, you said you were well, didn't you ?"

" Oh, pshaw ! pshaw ! nonsense, you know what I mean ; come, and be candid, have you seen anything ?"

" Yes."

" Ah ! indeed, what ?"

" The bottom of another bottle."

" The devil !"

" No, not exactly, but come in, I want your opinion upon something, just come this way."

I led him into the bed-chamber, and lifted the counterpane from the ground ; holding it close to his face, I said :—

" To the best of your belief, now, what should you say that spot was ?"

" That spot ; that great red spot ; why, if it ain't—damn it ! its blood !"

" I know it ; and now, sit down, I'll tell you a tale whose slightest word will harrow up your soul, and make your young hair stand on end."

" Then you have seen something."

" Rather."

" And you will tell me all the particulars, without stint or reservation."

" In good sooth, then, I will: you shall hear everything. But not in this place, for I've an old habit of taking some breakfast as soon as possible after I get up ; and, as you have no doubt already luxuriated in that morning meal, you can look at me while I partake of it at some neighbouring tavern, and I will relate to you the adventures of a night in Ingram's chambers."

I could perceive that he was greatly interested, and we walked out together.

As we crossed the inn-yard I met the woman who had shown me the chambers ; and, coming up to me, with a curious expression of countenance, she said—

" Did you see 'em, sir ?   How do you feel ? "

" See what, I said. I'm very well, thank ye."

" Why, sir, the last gentleman as went away raved horrible. Mind you, I don't know but what it might have been what they calls imagination, as they say people as is book-larned sometimes has.   But he raved horrible ; and, he says, says he—' Ive seed 'em,' says he ! ' The hands of the dead !' he says ; and then he bursts out a laughing quite oysterical ; and then he says, ' Oh, those gray fingers ! The drop of blood,' he says ; ' the drop of blood !' "

" The deuce he did," I replied.

" Yes, sir, that 's what he said: and then they gived the strait-waistcoat a extra buckle as nearly doubled him up ; and I've heerd since that he's in the what-may-call-it in the Old-street Road."

" That 'll do," said I, as I urged my friend forward, " that 'll do. I don't want to hear any more. Come on—come on."

" Well, but you don't mean to say——"

" I've said nothing : so ask no questions ; but imagine, if you please, that I have said everything. Come along, and I'll unfold to you a tale such as you never saw unfolded before."

I saw that he looked curious ; and no doubt my countenance amply testified to the fact that I had something to tell him that was worthy of his attention in the readiest manner in which he could bestow it.

We went to one of the coffee-houses with which the Strand so abounds ; and, after breakfasting, for I did not commence my narrative beforehand, I informed him, with all due particularity, how I had passed the night in my new chambers, ending by saying—

" Now, if you can start any hypothesis whatever, which shall have the effect of giving me a loophole by which I may successfully creep out of a belief in the full reality of all I saw, I will not only retain these chambers, but I shall feel myself most particularly your debtor for enabling me to do so."

" My dear fellow," he said, " the thing just, to my mind, comes thus far—I know you, and am well aware that you have each made up this story, to fill the ear of credulity. Had any one with whom I was less acquainted than yourself told me such a tale, and then asked my opinion I should in all probability, have given one that the narrator would not have considered, favourable to him."

" I understand you : you would not have believed one word of it."

" I certainly should not."

" Well, as regards myself, all I can say is, that I have abstracted nothing from the narration, and added nothing to it. You have it just as it happened ; and the only evidence I have, is that drop of blood which is on the counterpane in my bedroom."

" You want my opinion," he said, after a pause, " as to whether or not you should continue the occupant of those chambers."

" I do."

" Then, in strict accordance with what I said to you from the first I say now, leave them as quickly as you can. Do not attempt to sleep in them another night, on any account. Haunted or not haunted—imagination or reality—it is all the same. You never will, and never can, have a comfortable home in them."

"But people will laugh."

"Pshaw! They will laugh, or ought to laugh much more, if you were so foolish as to remain in a place which was uncomfortable to you, in consequence of a dread of ridicule from fools who would have lost altogether the small share of intellect they possessed had they but seen one half of what crossed your observation last night. Let them laugh. You can laugh, too, if you like; and your laugh will have the right side."

I must aver I was well enough pleased to find that any one would take the trouble to persuade me to do what in my heart I was very anxious to do, namely, leave Ingram's chambers; for, as to sleeping there another night, and being transfixed by those dreadful hands, it was what I shrunk from doing; and if I shrunk at that time in the morning, what was I likely to do as the evening set in, and all the accummulated horrors and superstitions of darkness were about me.

No, no! Had my friend been as urgent for me to remain in the haunted chambers as he was for me to leave them, I could not have followed his advice; but as it happened, I quite congratulated myself that he gave me so good an opportunity of doing just what I liked.

I now thought that it would be a very friendly thing of him if he would go and say as much to the woman who was to take back the key of the chambers, and likewise arrange to bring away all my goods and chattels which I had left there; but notwithstanding I was so intimate with him that I could say a great many things with a good face, I certainly did not get so far as as to ask him to take so much trouble for me; and, as he made me no offer to be so complaisant, I was compelled to go through that somewhat uncomfortable ordeal myself.

If anything disagreeable has to be done—from the making an ungracious remark to the having a tooth extracted—the sooner it is over the better : so, I set about the affair manfully, and at once. By noon I had cleared out from the haunted chamber all my effects; and as I left the inn, and gave the woman a gratuity for the trouble she had had, she said, with a shake of the head—

"Ah, sir! you needn't mention it. Don't make any apologies. I know well how it would turn out. Janie saw the spectre hands, as they call them, and I only hope."

"Hope what?" said I.

"That they won't follow you about wherever you go, for they did one gentleman till he threw himself into the river."

CHAPTER III.

THE NEW NUMBER VOLUNTEERS A TALE OF A COFFIN.

Mr. Amble Wade ceased speaking, and the assembled society suspended the fixed attention which it had been bestowing upon him. There occurred, now, that murmuring buz of amusement which occurs after some speaker who has been charming a multitude, either by the force of his eloquence, or charming their attention by the important matter of his subject, has ceased; and it is no longer necessary to preserve so fixed a silence.

There can be no doubt, that the tale which had just been recited, in many respects interested those who had listened to it. There was an air of truthfulness, too, about it which although no one present could think of impugning for a moment the accuracy of M. Amble Wade's statements, still for all that, it lent a considerable charm to the narrative.

"And so you left the chambers," said one, "and never returned to them'

"Never! I was but too glad to get away, and escape at the same time the' of that place, and the ridicule of being compelled, after a vain effort to remain, to leave it. In these cases there is nothing like taking the invitation at once; so I gave up all thoughts of Lyon's Inn, and it is a locality that I cannot pass, even now, without a shudder; for I have not forgotten or ever can forget those ghastly hands which hung over the foot of my bed, and which really were enough to drive any one mad to look upon."

"But the most remarkable feature of the whole business," said the president, "to my mind was the diabolical speech of the old woman, when you returned her the key, to the effect, that she hoped the spectre hands would not follow you wherever you went."

"Yes," said Mrs. Amble Wade, "it was a diabolical idea of the old beldame, but the spectre hands did not follow me; for that night I slept at an hotel—that is the night of the day on which I left, and I never, in all my life, enjoyed a sweeter or a calmer repose."

"That broke the charm," said one; "to pass the night without a visitation took your mind off it, and prevented the imagination from playing tricks, such as it otherwise might have served you."

"Well gentlemen," said the president, "we have yet some time upon our hands—it is my duty to ask if any one has a remark to offer upon the narrative we have just heard. It is an open matter of discussion, and I need hardly say, that the remarks of any gentleman, be they for or against supernatural appearances, will be listened to with attention."

One rose and said, in rather a captious, hesitating tone of voice,

"Mr. Chairman, with all due deference to our honorable friend, who has so graphically and eloquently described the adventures in the haunted chambers, it appears to me, that the whole affair may be accounted for upon the most natural and conclusive principles."

This was such a sweeping assertion, that the society looked amazed, and an accession of colour came over Mr. Amble Wade's face as he looked, fiercely, at the individual who thus strove to undermine the structure of his capital ghost story; and blew, to something thinner than air, the phantoms that had perplexed him.

"Mr. President and gentlemen," continued the speaker, "we met here in the pursuit of truth, and I trust there will be an amount of forbearance extended towards any gentleman who may utter an unpalatable sentence which will have a tendency to bring forward that talent that may exist in members of this most honorable society, who, like myself, are timid and bashful."

Loud cries of "oh! oh! and hear, hear!" resounded through the vault.

"Gentlemen," continued the speaker, "I assert, that I am timid and bashful, therefore do I throw myself upon your indulgence, hoping in time to acquire that brazen sort of countenance which will make me say, what I think, and what I don't think upon any subject, whether I know anything about it or not, without feeling my hair standing an end, and the perspiration bursting out of every part of my body."

"Question, question!" cried several.

"Well gentlemen, I will keep to the question, I have asserted, that it is easy o account for the phenomena which our friend Mr. Biggleswade ——"

"I beg your pardon, sir," said the narrator of the spectre hands, rising, "I beg your pardon, sir, with all humility, sir. Damn me, curse me, but the man, sir, who calls another out of his name, is a man who—— who——"

"My honorable friend is right," said the speaker, "interrupting him, and most accurate in his description of the man. I find that I have mistaken the honorable member's name which he must attribute to my bashfulness, and my being so completely unaccustomed to public speaking. I know that this expression of my unfeigned regret will ameliorate his feelings towards me. I believe I called the honorable gentleman Biggleswade, instead of Bumblepuppy, which is his accurate designation."

The consternation of the society was intense—the members rose tumultuously from their seats—the chairman in vain tried to preserve order, by rattling a thigh-bone against the lid of the coffin, which was nearest to him. Mr. Amble Wade was furious; while the orators, who had created all this consternation, in a loud and stentorian voice, tried to excuse himself, on the ground of extreme bashfulness and maiden modesty, which no one seemed inclined to give him credit for.

At length the president, by dint of waving his hands, and making use of the gestures of a maniac, succeeded in procuring a hearing, and said—

" I have to inform the honourable member who spoke last——"

" Who do you mean ?" said somebody ; " for we all spoke together."

" Really," said the chairman, " this is indecorous—of course I mean the gentleman who got up for the purpose of giving us some natural explanation of the incidents in the episode of the spectre hands. I have to inform that gentleman that the narrator's name is Amble Wade, and to sincerely hope that he will not call him Bumblepuppy, or Bigglewade, or anything else for the future."

" Sir, I stand corrected," said the speaker; " and for fear of mistake, I had better call the honourable member nothing at all, but to proceed with what I have to say concerning his narration, which I admit to be deeply interesting, artistically put together, and well told; but, at the same time, there occurs to me the natural explanation of the whole affair."

Everybody looked intensely curious to know what these explanations could possibly be, of a subject which seemed certainly to forbid anything of the kind. The story was so precise, so unambiguous, and, altogether so clearly and finely narrated, that it was indeed puzzling to think how the most ingenious sophist, or the profoundest natural philosopher could find a loop-hole at which to creep out of a belief in the supernatural character of the whole affair.

Even Mr. Amble Wade himself looked curious and anxious to hear what the speaker should say next.

" Mr. President and gentlemen," he continued, " the first way in which I account for all which has occurred is this—I think the honourable gentleman, whose name I will not now venture to pronounce, must have been asleep when he thought he was awake, and awake when he thought he was asleep, and so he passed the night dreaming and dosing, and jumping and starting, and not knowing whether he was on his head or his heels—sitting up or lying down, or whether the candle was out or the candle was in, until morning came, and he gave up the ghost, in the shape of the nightmare. Gentlemen, that is the first explanation I shall offer to you, with regard to the narrative we have just heard."

Mr. Amble Wade sprang to his feet—he flung his arms about for a few seconds, like the sails of a windmill; and his mouth opened and shut, without saying anything, like some gigantic cod-fish, nearly caught and struggling for life on the brink of the stream which was his native element.

" Mr. Gentlemen and president," he at last cried, " the honourable damned wretch who has last spoken, with a mouth in horrible—and, hang me if I know what I'm saying. Gentlemen, I'm in a state of excitement, and I glory in it. I did know, gentlemen, when I was on my head or my heels; and as a proof, I assert that I was on neither, but on the flat of my back, gentlemen, except when I sat up to look at those ghastly spectral hands, gentlemen, and then I was on something else—I did know whether I was awake and whether I was asleep, and as a proof, gentlemen, I am now sufficiently wide awake to know and to feel that I have been frightfully insulted, and that the man, or rather the fiend, who has risen up among us to produce discord, has done so, gentlemen, with malice aforethought."

Down sat Mr. Amble Wade, with a complete consideration that he had crushed his adversary.

As to the members of the society, they looked from one to the other, as if they did not know very well what to do. Of course they liked the row; for that, at any rate, was amusing, and probably the mental insinuations of some of them consisted of how they should prolong this state of things, which tended to create so pleasant a disturbance.

He who had thrown the apple of discord thus into the society, had remained on is feet during the whole of this time, and now again he spoke, saying—

"Really, Mr. President and Gentlemen, I am shocked and amazed that the few remarks I thought it my duty to make upon this subject should have produced so much bad feeling on the part of my honourable friend. Let me beg of him to recollect that I did not assert any want of knowledge, upon his part, whether he was upon his head or his heels—I merely stated the thing as a supposition, that it might be so."

"But it was not," cried Mr. Amble Wade.

"Very good—since the gentleman is so positive, I give in entirely, freely surrendering my hypothesis upon his dictum, and admitting to you all that the opinion which I hazarded was nothing but a supposition, which I am now willing to abandon, since it is not at all favoured by the gentleman whom it mostly concerns. That gentleman ought to know, and therefore I beg his pardon."

"Hear, hear," cried everybody; "hear, hear," and there were loud cheers,

No. 9.

"I hope, Mr. Amble Wade," said the president, with an amiable smile upon his countenance, "that now you will feel yourself quite satisfied. The gentleman has retracted what was offensive to you, and behaved in the handsomest manner."

"I am satisfied," said Mr. Amble Wade; "of course the gentleman having apologised, and I am satisfied."

"Here Mr. Amble Wade rose, and it was quite a delightful thing to see how he and his late opponent shook hands amid the plaudits of those assembled, and that they appeared to be on the very best of terms.

"There is nothing," said Mr. Amble Wade, "that I admire so much as free discussion; and you shall find, sir, from the patience with which I will listen to the second argument which you will bring forward against a belief in the supernatural character of what I saw, that I am satisfied you have no intention of being offensive."

"None in the least, sir, none in the least; and now, gentlemen, I hope you will dismiss from your mind all considerations connected with this first idea of mine which implied a want of knowledge of Mr. Amble Wade; but I congratulate myself upon having the gentleman's name right at last, with regard to whether he was asleep or not, and I shall proceed at once to state to you my second argument, or rather hypothesis upon the subject of what he considers his supernatural visitation.

"We shall hear you with pleasure," said the chairman, "and I trust that the harmony of this meeting will not be again in the least danger of being disturbed.

"Not by me, sir, I can assure you; what I am about to say can be summed up in a very few words indeed. If the gentleman who has narrated this interesting tale to us did not dream it, my firm opinion is that it is what may be vulgarly called a thundering lie, from beginning to end. You will excuse me, gentlemen, for using rather strong language, but, as I don't wish to say anything offensive, I thought it best to sum up in as few words as possible what I really had to say, and what is my firm opinion upon this subject—an opinion which I believe it will be very difficult, indeed, to alter or in any way to compromise."

No language can convey an adequate idea of the sensation which was produced by these words: they were so utterly unexpected by every one present, that each sat looking at his neighbour as if paralysed for the time being, and hardly believing the evidence of his own senses that anything so audacious and outrageously libellous had been uttered.

What the stranger said at first was mild, and quiet and gentlemanly, in comparison to this, and, if that offended Mr. Amble Wade, what can we expect were his feelings now at this dreadful additional insult that had been heaped upon him.

But it very often happens, that on great occasions people are much cooler than they are upon small ones; and so it appeared with Mr. Amble Wade in this instance. He turned very pale, but he did not burst into any fury. He merely walked up to the individual, and inclining his mouth to his ear, said in a hissing whisper—

"Sir, you're a humbug."

"I know it," said the other.

"You shall hear from me to-morrow, sir; I shall send a friend to call upon you, do you understand that, sir?"

"Yes, I do, and am much obliged to you for the warning. I shall put away all the silver spoons, and take care that there is nothing portable about of a tempting character."

"Sir, will you give me your card?"

"No sir, you'll get into some street row and leave it instead of your own, and so get off upon a false plea of respectability.

"Damn it, sir, do you want to drive me mad?"

"Not at all; I consider you mad enough already."

The eyes and ears of the society were wide open to this short colloquy, from which nothing but something extremely hostile in the matter could be inferred. Ah! perhaps one or both those members of the club might, ere midday, be reduced to a state which would enable them to solve at once the interesting question that agitated them in life regarding supernatural appearances.

The chairman, with almost tears in his eyes, begged that the affair might be allowed to drop, and proceed no further. He much blamed the gentleman who had stated the possibility of Mr. Amble Wade telling a falsehood; and he said, if he were Mr. Amble Wade, he should consider the affair as a long way beneath his notice, nor really at all worth consideration or putting himself out of the way about.

"I am sure, sir," said Mr. Amble Wade, "I am sure. I rather believe I can vindicate my own honour. Let the proceedings of the society go on sir, I beg."

This was a proposition received with acclamation, for it was evident that the dispute had reached its climax, and came down again, so that no more amusement was to be expected from that quarter.

"Gentlemen," said the president, "it wants yet a considerable time to the first dawn of morning, and I do not see why we should not at once call upon some gentleman to contribute to our edification and our amusement for the time we have to stay here."

Even as the president spoke, the mysterious-looking man, who had been, according to his own account, invited to the meeting by Mr. ————, who had been thrown from his gig and killed that day, rose to his feet.

"Sir," he said, in a solemn tone, "various circumstances, the principal of which is, that I am obliged to leave early—I feel that to a certain extent I am an intruder here, and that he who would have been my sponsor, had he been alive, has left me to speak for myself. It behoves me therefore, gentlemen, under these circumstances, to say something, or to do something, that shall place me on goods terms with you; and, as I must leave early, I will, with your permission, relate to you an incident which will illustrate the subject for which you hold these meetings.

There was something so handsome and so gratuitous in this offer, that the stranger, notwithstanding his mysterious appearance and his ghastly and horrible looks, was looked upon with benign eyes by every one present.

Cries of " Hear, hear !" resounded from all parts of the vault ; and after bowing repeatedly in acknowledgment of these continuing plaudits, the stranger assumed a fixed attitude, and, gazing intently in the chairman's countenance until that individual did not know which way to look, he said, I shall call the incident to which I am about to call your attention

A TALE OF A COFFIN.

The members of the society looked at each other, and several of them nodded, as much as to say, there's something coming now.

Everybody settled himself in his seat in as comfortable a position as possible, so that there should be no occasion, while the narrative was proceeding, of disturbing the even thread of it ; and then all eyes were bent upon the unknown, as, after a slight pause, he commenced as follows :—

Gentlemen,—It so happened, that in early life I fell in love with one of the most beautiful and one of the most accomplished of human beings ; but she was as proud as—but no matter—she was very proud indeed. She had met with no man whose adoration she considered a sufficient tribute to her charms, and yet, whenever she found that she had enslaved any fresh heart, it was a great trial to her to lead the poor deluded victim so far that he believed himself beloved, then to crush all his hopes for ever.

I was young and enthusiastic—a worshipper of the beautiful in nature and in art, and, from the moment that I looked upon this fair, but, alas ! not faultless creature, I adored her.

Soon she saw that she had entangled me in the meshes of her fascination, and I spoke to a friend concerning her, who knew more of her history than I did.

I was informed that she had been the cause of deaths innumerable ; that duels had frequently happened, in consequence of rivalry about real or supposed favours which she had granted to different suitors.

"But," said my friend, " what is the most extraordinary thing of all is that I

have been informed to a certainty that for the last forty or fifty years in differen
cities of Europe she has been carrying on this game."

"Oh, most monstrous," I said; "forty or fifty years? Why, all her angeli
beauty has not yet graced the earth twenty-six summers! There is all th
grace and delightful bearing of childhood about her.

"That may be," said my friend; "but I have spoken with persor s who hav
assured me they have seen her at Paris, Rome, Madrid, Venice, and Milan, as we
as other cities, many years ago — that she had the same train of courtl
worshippers—that she spread destruction wherever she went by enthralling i
her charms the young, the gay, and the thoughtless.'

' You must be mistaken," I cried; " it is not possible !"

"So you think; but, hark you, a word in your ear—I've heard an opinio
expressed of this mysterious female which I believe to be a correct one."

" And what may that be ?"

" She's not mortal."

" She's not mortal! she not mortal?"

" No, hark you—there was a young count, of the Roman empire, who, it is saic
she really did love; her domestics overheard one day a passionate intervie
between them; they declared that they never before had heard their mistress spea
with so much tenderness of any one; and yet, at the termination of the interview
the count rushed out with all the frantic bearing of a madman."

" Oh ! she—she—she—had rejected him ?"

" I think not."

" What can account for his behaviour ?"

" You shall hear: he made his way to the banks of the nearest river, and ther
he was heard, by some fishermen who could not get sufficiently close to him, fc
they were on the opposite bank to stop his purpose; declare, that life had bee
loathsome to him, and that he could not exist, under the load of care that nov
oppressed him."

"Gracious Heaven!" they heard him cry; "to be received—to be accepted—and yι
to be so wretched: but no, I cannot—I dare not—I can die and trust to Heaven
mercy; but I dare not yoke myself to one who is without the pale of its holie:
influences." With this he plunged into the river and was drowned.

" Well but, I argued, for I did not half like what was said about her upon whor
I had fixed my best affections; " well, but, after all, there was no particular reaso
to call her anything more than a human being, because this mad-headed count chos
to commit suicide for love of her."

" Well, well," he said " draw your own conclusions and be as wilful as you like
I only tell you what is the general opinion of those who have given the subjec
attention, cousin. It is their belief that she is not mortal, but that she is endea
vouring to entangle some human soul in some way to its undoing."

" Then she may entangle mine," he said, " for I want not Heaven if I canno
share it with her."

My friend was shocked at this speech, as well he might be, for he was no
a man of those stern and powerful passions which oppressed me, and so I lei
him.

But although I had combated while in his presence the opinion he hai
uttered respecting her whom I loved, it had made a far greater impression upoι
me than I chose to admit, and really caused me a world of disquietude.

But oh! how quickly all this vanished, like mists before the morning sun, wher
once again I looked upon the face of that beautiful being who held his heart ir
such delicious thraldom; she received me on that day with a sweeter smile thaι
she had ever worn before, and I felt as if I were at once lifted to a very haven ol
delight. She was alone, too, so that I could say to her what I pleased: feeling aι
the same time a consciousness that no other ears but his drank in the words ol
affection that fell from her lips, a feeling of intoxication of the mind came ovei
me, and in all the eloquent language which characterises man's expressions of the
first, best, and holiest affection, I told her that I loved her.

She smiled upon me a smile so full of the very witchery of loveliness, that, had there wanted anything to complete my fascination, that would have done it; and in a voice that was the very soul of music she replied :—

"And can you love me with the intensity of which you speak? Is it possible that you can feel for me one tittle of such a passion as seems to animate you?"

"Love you!" said I; "oh, find some other name, not so cold and passionless as that, by the use of which ordinary mortals express their heart's devotion, and I will use it to tell you how dear you are to me. I do not love you, I adore and worship."

"Oh," she said, "if I could believe the existence of such a passion; but these are all words of course, uttered by men to delude women, until, thinking herself too happy, she falls a victim to a deceit which came to her in the garb of the greatest purity, and with a mask of such sincerity upon it that the doubt would have seemed like only heaven itself."

"Oh, what can I do?" I said; "what can I say to prove to you the sincerity of my heart's devotion?"

"What would you do?" she said.

"What would I do? anything, everything; the catalogue of what I would do would swell into an enormous amount, but that which I would not might be recorded upon the narrowest scrap of paper that ever held a few isolated words."

"I'm tempted," she said, "I'm tempted almost to believe that there is such faith in a living being. Oh, if I dare trust you!"

I cast myself at her feet, I wept, I raved, I prayed to her, I covered her hands with kisses; and at last she was moved, and she spoke to me tremulously.

"Arise," she said, "arise, you have conquered; and now tell me—oh, tell me truly—has the busy tongue of rumour not been prating of me; have you heard nothing against the being whom you would wish to call your own; has no one insinuated to you aught prejudicial of me? Upon your answer to this depends all that I shall continue saying to you. I pray you, therefore, to be candid and to conceal nothing from me."

"When beauty," I said, "escapes hypercriticism, and virtue detraction, then may you and such as you hope to walk scatheless through society without one word being utterred to your prejudice even from the mere envious and the most bitter."

"Then you have heard something?"

"Yes," said I, "I have."

"Ah! as you love me—you'll tell me all."

I could not refuse, but related to her distinctly what my friend had said regarding her. She heard me to the end without interruption, and then, clasping one of my hands in both of hers, she said—

"I am better pleased that it should be so, because it prepares you a little."

"I started, and, she continued—

"Yes, it prepares you a little: it enables you to hear without, probably, so much shrinking, that which it is necessary I should relate to you. But mark me—it is only from an overweening confidence in your genuine affection that I thus far break through the great rule of my existence to intrust to you what I never but once before revealed to any living breaths soul."

The count, I thought to myself—the count!

"You must know, then, that those charms which you affect to admire so much, and which I believe you really do hold dear, are not such as bloom only to decay; my existence and my youth are alike eternal, but I hold both by a frightful tenure."

"Go on—go on, I beseech you."

"At midnight I am compelled to leave the busy and the bustling world, to return to it again after some few hours of a sojourn in my coffin."

"In what?" I exclaimed.

"In my coffin! I have died once, and was consigned to that narrow resting-place; the gloom of the tomb surrounded me, but I was snatched from the cold embrace of death, by one who offered me life, youth, wealth, and all the capacities of worldly enjoyment upon that one condition. But at midnight, and for the few succeeding hours, during which time he was powerless, I should repair again to my coffin, and there lie until I saw the faint lines of daylight, which he assured me I should see, for that the trance of death would then dissipate, and I should know that it was time again to rise ; but he told me that if I could find one living mortal man, who, for me, would take the penalty from off my hands and himself each night for that period of time, take my place in the dismal coffin, with the grave shutting about him, I should be free, and that for the remainder of the time he might enjoy my society, share my wealth, and make himself as happy as the day was long."

You may guess with what singular feelings I heard this speech, and how strangely it was likely to affect me. I sat down paralysed, and it was many minutes before I could frame an answer to what she had related.

I looked in her beautiful beaming countenance as she spoke, and could not believe that my ears had properly conveyed to my brains the words that she had uttered. They were so ludicrously out of all the order of nature, that for a few moments I could almost have fancied myself dreaming.

She observed the expression of my countenance and she said to me in a vein of deep affliction,—

"It is enough : I can too well perceive that you shrink from such a test of affection. I ought not to have expected but that you would so shrink. It is enough; and all now I have to ask of you is, that you will keep to yourself the secret with which I have made you now acquainted."

"Do not mistake me," I said, "oh! be not too hasty in judging of one who loves as I love."

Animation again sparkled in her eyes, she clung to me ; in another instant her head was pillowed upon my heart, and in soft, dulcet accents, such as went to my very heart, she breathed gently.

"Oh! righteous Heaven, and have I indeed found such a heart, as I have in vain sought amid the crowd of flatterers that have so long surrounded? Is there really a human being who for me is willing to make a sacrifice? Can I hope to be happy?'

I was maddened with an intoxicating joy. The idea of holding, as I then did, half-encircled in my arms, so much loveliness, overcame my reason. I pressed my lips to hers ; I vowed that she was dearer to me than life itself ; that without her the whole world would be to me but as a charnel-house ; that, deprived of the joy of looking upon her, and feeling the warm soft pressure of her lips I should feel that death had indeed crept over me—the death of the soul. Could I then hesitate to accede to any conditions that should promise me, if it were but for one hour out of the whole twenty-four, the blissful consciousness of loving her, and of being beloved again? The tears fell like rain from her eyes, and for many minutes she did not speak to me. I begged, I implored her to utter to me some words of consolation, to give me some assurance that she really loved me. I entreated her not to think me exacting in demanding of her that she should tell me in actual words that she loved me, and I succeeded. She whispered in my ear those three soft words, which from the lips we love are so full of a world of exquisite melody.

"I love you, I love you, yes."

This paragon of charms, this very divinity of perfection, this being of such refulgent beauty, that she had been sought, and sought in vain by the high, the gifted and the noble—had singled me out from among all her worshippers, to tell me that she loved me. Oh, what an hour of joy was that ; I would not have bartered it for a kingdom. It seemed but like a fleeting minute. I pressed soft kisses on her brow, her cheek, her lips. I felt the warm fragrance of her breath upon my face, and I saw the minute image of myself reflected in the depths of those beautiful eyes, which to me were glimpses of heaven such as some saint, in the fervour of his enthusiasm, might suppose that he saw in his dreams.

And now she spoke to me so unreservedly, treating me with all that delicious confidence which mutual love inspires; she spoke to me of the brilliant fortune which was hers, but which had failed to impart to her any pleasure, because she had until now—yes, she said, until now—not found any heart to share it with. How happy was I! At once would I have sworn those vows which would for ever have bound me to her, but she insisted upon the delay of two weeks.

"No," she said; "you shall have time for thought—time to see and to know more of me, and, perchance, to find out some faults that I have, but which now, to your too partial eyes, do not show themselves. You shall not hurriedly, and in the excitement of a feeling which may be compounded as much of gratitude as of love, bring yourself into engagements which there may be even a possibility of your regretting."

In vain I tried to combat her resolution, in vain I told her that it was as impossible for me not to love her as for the sun not to shine upon the following morn in a cloudless sky.

"No, no; it would kill me afterwards to see or even to fancy I saw the least appearance of neglect upon your face, or of regret that you had pledged yourself to me."

"That you will never see, dearest."

"I do not," she said, with a trembling smile, "expect that I shall; if I did harbour such a thought I could not look upon you as now I do, or speak to you as now I speak. But I will have nothing to reproach myself. You are dear to me, but you must wait the time I have mentioned; let me see you each day. Observe me well; be critical as to all I say and all I do."

"No, no, no; such perfections disarm all criticism."

"Nay, but you must; and, above all, do not forget the condition upon which I have consented to love you. You will take my place in the coffin at the time I have mentioned, and there remain, in the cold and sullen apathy of death, for a time."

"It is a condition only rendered hard from one circumstance."

"And that?"

"That is, that I am for some time separated from thee."

"And can you still think of that dreadful condition with no other feeling?"

"Yes, yes; there is another feeling connected with it that I shall never forget—a feeling which almost suffices to make it a pleasure; and that is, the conviction that by taking upon myself voluntarily this strange and, no doubt, what would be to many persons most terrifying condition, I am sparing you. I am rescuing you from that house of death which such beauty, such gentleness, such intelligence should never be doomed to."

She listened to me with a look of pleasure; she held my hand between her own, and called me by endearing epithets: I could not doubt that she loved me well and truly. I felt very happy—most happy indeed; and now, for three or four days, the thought of the new existence which my love had opened to my enraptured eyes, and all the thousand fascinations of her who was the idol of my existence, more than sufficed to chase from my mind every melancholy thought; and, even now, I look back to that time as the happiest of my existence—a time which I can never know again. I know not now whether to chide the hours for passing too quickly or too slowly. I could not but be happy, because I passed the most of my time in the company of my beloved one; and yet I was waiting until that day should dawn on which she had consented to become all my own. A week passed—I know not how it was, for my love had not moved, but yet, now and then, a shudder came across my frame unawares, and then I would think of that gloomy condition to which I was to consign myself, for some portion of my existence, each night.

I had no thought of making the slightest effort of freeing myself from my engagement. Ah! no, that would have been too great a struggle with my feelings; but still it was not in human nature but that I should feel something occasionally of the dread that such an ordeal as that I had to go through was likely to awaken in my mind. To be immured alive in a coffin! there to remain for a time in a reverie—health exposed to Heaven only knows what malign and dreadful influences, how could I tell what dreadful images might take possession of my brain?—what fearful company the liberated spirit, when, even for a brief space, it had seemed to leave its earthly tenement, might get among. Truly I did tremble, and well might I. As the time drew near, I awakened, more and more fully to a dread of that to which I had pledged myself; but I allowed her, the chosen of my heart, to see none of those feelings. To her I was all smiles, and the sunshine of my heart must to her perceptions have been undimmed by a single cloud. She could have detected nothing, unless her eyes were preternaturally acute to the feelings that had for days been creeping over me. And now, one-half of the time had elapsed which had been named by herself as the period of her probation. We were together, and alone too. She had gradually, as she had told me she would, withdrawn herself from the crowd of worshippers around her, after we had made our mutual engagement. To be sure, she saw nearly in amount as much company as before; but, from her cold and altered manner to the mere butterfly gallants who thronged around her, like moths around a candle-flame, they could not but perceive that their addresses and compliments were no longer required, and that there must be some favoured mortal in the case, who had succeeded in monopolizing to himself the attentions of the beautiful being whom each had fondly hoped to call his own.

This thinned her saloons of those whom of course I liked least to see there, and afforded more room for the thoughtful and the to my mind, better-mannered portion of her acquaintance. But on this particular evening she had, at my persuasion and instigation, consented to receive no visitors, but to pass it wholly with me. The fact was, that I had in my own mind made up a little plot, which I fully hoped and expected to be able to carry out as regarded her I intended to engage her in conversation, and protract my stay, if possible, to the hour, when she had told me she was compelled to submit herself to the frightful change of place, from her brilliant and beautiful house to a coffin. I presumed much, as indeed what lover does not? upon the affection she had for me, to think that she might be induced to allow me to see something of the strange scene —bu I will not anticipate.

I put on an appearance of perfect ease and cheerfulness, which I was really far from feeling, and we passed some hours in the most delightful tete-à-tete. Scarcely any allowance had been made to the conditions upon which our union was based, but we talked of the future, and of the happiness it would bring us, as if there was no secret alloy connected with it. It was she, at length, who made an observation that brought that subject upon the tapis.

" Do not imagine," she said, as she fixed her beautiful and lustrous eyes upon me, " do not imagine that the gift of immortality that I possess will ever make me anothers. Do not suppose that I can ever love one as I love you. When the cold hand of death shall approach you, the destroyer shall likewise reach my heart. I do not intend to live beyond the time which Heaven has allotted you. When you are gone from me, the only true light that ever shone upon my existence will be gone likewise, and I shall no longer desire to live."

"Nay," I said, "do not talk thus; far distant, let us hope, may be the day which beholds our separation."

" Far distant, indeed!" she said, as she glanced at a time-piece that was in the apartment in a manner which I considered was a hint that I ought to go. But I was proof against it, and heeded it not.

A light and elegant repast was served, and thus another half-hour passed away, and the time-piece, with its silvery tones, gave notice of the hour of eleven.

A shade of uneasiness crossed her brow, but she shook it off quickly, as she said, with animation—

" Shall we meet to-morrow?"

" Most assuredly," I said " Think you I could pass a day without looking upon you, and hearing the tones of your voice? Ah, me! was it not a superfluous question for you to ask of me if we should meet to-morrow?"

With a smile that had more of sadness about it than I had ever seen a smile of hers wear, she assented, and the conversation proceeded rather painfully for another quarter of an hour. Then, as the colour went and came upon her fair cheek, she rose, and taking from her bosom a small bouquet, that there had had a happy home, she handed it to me, saying—

" This shall be our parting gift to-night, and we shall meet again to-morrow, shall we not?"

I could not affect to misunderstand her; I should have been rude to do so. In a moment I caught her gently in my arms, and as I knelt at her feet, still clinging to her, I said—

"Dearest and best, do you really believe that I love you? Have you real faith in the existence of my heartfelt attachment?"

"As I have faith in Heaven," she said.

"Then, then, you will trust me to remain here to-night?"

With a half scream of alarm she shrunk from my touch. I never shall forget the look of exquisite misery that she cast upon me as she replied; and, when she did so, the deep pathos of her voice went in reproachful accents to my heart.

"And is it so, indeed?" she said; "have you come with a determination to test

NO. 1o.

your power over the weakness of one who has confessed to you a passion ; oh, i
this generous—is it just ?."

"No—no—" I cried; " hear me, and then judge not so harshly of me. Yo
mistake—"

" Have I been then mistaken ?"

" Nay, hear me ; if you were less noble and less virtuous than what you are
you would not be the idol of my heart, as now you are ; but that fatal hou
approaches at which, you have told me, you have to render yourself up to death
not many minutes must now elapse ere that midnight hour arrives, and, till then,
would fain stay."

" Oh ! no—no—"

" I would fain watch by you for the time that you remain in that cold and drea
embrace of death; and, oh, may it not be possible that the embrace of one wh
loves you as I love you might rescue you from—"

" This is madness," she cried, interrupting me, " and it is what I feared too
Oh ! leave me—leave me."

" Do not force me from you, I implore you, do not ; I shall, if you turn me fron
your home, this night do some desperate act, against, perchance, my ow
existence. Do not tempt me, in my present state of mind, to war against mysel
and Heaven's holiest behests."

" What mean you ?"

" I mean that I cannot live in this state of afflicting uncertainty ; my sympathies
which have been all awakened by the dreadful tale you have poured into my ear
have really maddened me. All I ask—is to remain with you—to watch by you ; t
pray for you, and, in my arms to receive you, when you shake off the trance c
death to which you are subjected."

" No! no! no!" she cried, sobbingly, " that must not be ; go, and go at once
I implore you, I entreat you, by all you hold dear and sacred, to leave me. Ol
can you love me, and yet hear me thus appeal to you in vain ? You do not—yo
cannot love me, and I have awakened from what was but a dream of constancy an
excellence."

This was an appeal which shook my resolution. I rose, and was silent for
few moments. I glanced at the clock—it indicated half-past twelve.

"Farewell!" I said.

" Farewell! leave me now. Oh, a thousand thanks ! You have though
better of this wild idea. I know it was born of your love for me; I know tha
Do not mistake me, now that you are going for ever. I do not doubt you. Ol
no! in your honour I am safe. Farewell! the blessings of love fall upon yot
We shall meet to-morrow."

I shook my head, and she looked alarmed. There were some desperate passion
tugging at my heart. I said, "Farewell ! I go in obedience to your express com
mand—but I go—for ever !"

" For ever !"

" Yes—God's blessing be upon you and around you. May you find anothei
who, not loving so fervently as I, is better able to control his passion."

She stood like a statue for some moments. My words had so deeply affecte
her, that she could not speak ; and already had I reached the door of the apart
ment, when she flew towards me, and hung around my neck.

" Cruel—cruel !" she exclaimed ; " oh, cruel! how could you utter such word
to me ? Do you wish to kill me ?"

" You force me to love you. You will not confide in my honour."

" Yes—yes—I—I—will."

" I may remain?"

" Yes," she said, faintly, " yes—you have conquered."

Her head sunk upon my breast, and for a few moments no sound was heard i
the apartment, but her low sobs ; suddenly, then, she glanced towards the time
piece, and the sight of it roused her.

" It is now the hour," she said, " you must seem to go. Descend the stair case, and then turn into a small room on the right of the hall. At its further extremity is a door, which you can open with this key. You will find that that door conceals a staircase—pursue it, and then wait in the room to which it leads until I shall come to you."

"Yes, yes, I understand. Shall I encounter no servants in the hall just now?"

"Go at once, and you will find no one."

I hastened down the staircase, and saw none of the domestics. I crossed the hall, and, opening the door a short space, I slammed it close-shut again, so as to convey the impression that I had gone out of the house, and then I darted into the little parlour to the right. It was a small room, and but dimly lighted by a lamp held at arm's length by the hand of a statue, but I at once perceived the door that had been mentioned to me. The key fitted glibly into the lock, and then I found, when I had opened it, a very narrow, winding staircase, which was in complete and pitchy darkness when I had closed the door behind me, and taken the precaution to lock it in the inside. I carefully ascended a number of stairs, feeling all the way I went carefully on the walls for a door which should admit me into the apartment that had been mentioned, until as I was wondering to where the staircase could possibly lead, I saw a streak of light apparently coming from some crevice in the wall, and doubted not but that now I should soon come upon the room I was in search of. My suspicions were correct. By attentively feeling the wall, my hand encountered the handle of a lock: I turned it, the door instantly yielded, and I found myself in a moment in a splendidly appointed bed-chamber. A small elegant chandelier of ground glass, which hung from the ceiling, was lighted, and shed a pleasant softened radiance around the room. Some Indian perfumes impregnated the air with a most delicious fragrance, and I could not but admire the wealth and luxury that were the concomitants of that chamber. It was carpeted with some fabric I had never before beheld, but it looked like a parterre of living flowers, in the bloom of their summer beauty. Works of art of the highest order of excellence graced the walls, and there was not one direction in which the eye could turn but it was met by something rich, and rare, and beautiful, belonging to that most costly apartment.

Even full as my mind was, it may well be supposed to have been of far other thoughts. I could not help making some exclamations indicative of my admiration for that place, in which was concentrated so much that was calculated to elevate the senses.

I thank my stars that I had persevered in my intention, and taken no denial from the charming being whom I adored; and yet do not, gentlemen, misunderstand me for a moment—I harboured no evil thought. What I had said was really what I thought and what I intended. I did, with an ungovernable feeling of curiosity, wish to be a witness to the change from life to death which she had told me of, and which I had pledged myself to undergo so shortly in her stead.

Whether she were wise or not in submitting to my entreaties is quite another matter.

And now I took a more deliberate survey of the place, and the more I saw the more was I charmed with that most delightful chamber. It was a room calculated to exercise upon the mind the most pleasant influences—a room which, to be doomed to repose in, was almost sure to bespeak by its very remembrances dreams of beauty, taste, and harmony.

"And is this the chamber," I asked myself, "in which the dreadful change from life to death takes place?"

I looked around in vain for any indication of the coffin which she had told me she had to inhabit. There was nothing in the shape of aught so ghastly and distasteful in that apartment which might have been devoted to the chamber of the Graces themselves.

She came not so soon as I anticipated, and yet I could have sworn that it must be twelve o'clock; but, just as I was fatiguing my imagination, by endeavouring to invent reasons for her absence, she entered the room.

I flew towards her, and she met me half way, and flung her arms around me, exclaiming, as she did so—

" Oh ! what an injustice I have done you !"

" Injustice, dearest !" I exclaimed ; " in what way is that possible ? Have you not shown the noblest confidence in my affection ? Does not my presence in this sacred place speak eloquently of the faith you have in my honour ? How, then, can you have treated me with injustice ?"

" You will not even seem to blame me," she said ; " you are too kind and too good to me ; you know well that I did not detect the artifice of love ; nay, until a few moments since, it did not occur to me."

" That I love you with all my heart," I exclaimed, " is true.   It would need more artifice than I am master of, to conceal the passion."

" It would, it would !   But now I know what has prompted you to remain here to-night ; oh, how blind was I not before to guess it ! "

I looked a little puzzled, but she soon explained herself by adding :

" You have resolved to take upon yourself the trance of death in the coffin thus sooner than I anticipated ; you have determined upon that, before the church has made us one, to convince me that you do love me with a passion, and with a sentiment only equal by my own for thee,"

What could I do? what could I say?   Had the penalty that I had thus brought upon myself been the taking of my very life, I must have endured it.   I did love her likewise, although of late the love had been not unmingled with dread.

" You are right, dear one," I said ; " you are right."

" I knew it," she exclaimed, as she clasped her hands ; " and even as you talked of watching by me, will I watch by thee ; oh, how can I sufficiently reward the affection that is willing to go through so much for another ?"

" It is already," I said, " rewarded by the delight of knowing that the feeling is reciprocal ; but I see no preparations here for such a scene as that you have taught me to expect has to be gone through."

" No ; but hear !   There is a room adjoining : were I to keep the coffin here it would be impossible to hide it from the observation of the servants.   Come this way ; the time has arrived—and to delay brings pain ! Come, come, dear one, follow me—follow me !"

She led the way to the further end of the magnificent bed-chamber, and touching a spring—which was so well concealed amid the rich ornaments of a moulding that it could have been only some accident that might ever have discovered it—a small door opened gently upon its hinges.

All was darkness beyond, but she lighted a wax candle, and, motioning me to follow her, she led the way into the adjoining chamber.

Oh, what a contrast it presented to the one which we had left! There—from whence we had come—all was beauty and splendour ; here—all was gloom and blackness.

The apartment was small, being not above a fourth of the dimensions of the one which we had left, and the walls were hung with black cloth.   Windows in it there seemed to be none—no other entrance than that through which we had come ; but soon an object attracted wholly my attention.

In the centre of the room was a coffin.   The lid was slid a little on one side, disclosing the interior, in which there lay some vestments of the grave ; and as the lovely being—for whose sake I had expressed a willingness to do so much; and encounter so much unknown terror—held the light so that I could look upon that last earthly receptacle of humanity, I felt my blood run coldly in my veins, and a sensation as if the hand of Death were already upon me.

                *   *   *   *   *   *   *

The narrator of this strange story here paused for a moment, and looked around the vault upon the eager listening faces by which he was surrounded.   Then he said, in an earnest tone :—

" Gentlemen, I shall be better able to explain to you what followed, if you will lend me some assistance."

Everybody looked intensely puzzled to know what sort of assistance he required, and he soon explained.

" If I can be accommodated with one of the empty coffins that we have, I shall be able to proceed well."

"Several of the coffins," said the president, "which we use here for seats have been by us emptied of the dust—for it was little more that remained in them—so that you can be easily accommodated."

There was some little bustle consequent upon this requisition on the part of the stranger for a coffin, but after a time one was placed at his disposal, which contained nothing whatever.

"Ah," he said, "this will do; I should not wonder, now, if some of the church-yard authorities know more about the emptying this coffin of its contents many years ago than any modern disturber of the remains of mortality."

There would seem to be indeed some grounds for this supposition, for the coffin was wonderfully well cleared out, but the members of the society were much too eager to hear the denouement of the stranger's tale to enter into any inquiry upon a less interesting subject, so, with one accord, they begged of him to continue.

"Well, gentlemen," he said, "even as this coffin now lies before you all, did the coffin in that small dismal chamber, to which I was introduced, lie before me: I looked upon it, as I told you, with a shudder, which she observed, and said in a faint voice, expressive of great anguish,—

"You or I must be its occupant!"

All manly feeling now revolted against shrinking from the task I had undertaken, and I at once said to her, "No, dearest love, no; I will, for your dear sake, essay this adventure, and one kiss from those soft lips, when the time shall come for me to rise again, will repay me for all."

The tears streamed from her eyes, and she was much agitated; her hand clasped mine, and she trembled, so that I forgot what probably I had to endure, and became her comforter and consoler.

"Be calm, dear one," I said, "and you shall see how love can conquer all things; even the most rife and current feelings of apprehension with which from earliest infancy the mind is filled, may be overcome by the influence of that master-passion, pure and holy affection."

"Oh, God!" she exclaimed, "when can I be worthy of such a heart as this? never, never—oh, never."

"More than worthy," I exclaimed; "'tis I who have been distracted by doubts and fears, and live but in the joy of calling you my own."

"It is here," she said, pointing to the coffin, "it is here; you or I must be there; the time has come!"

"Now, gentlemen, in order that you may have as graphic an idea as possible of the scene, I will now lie down in the coffin, and you will do me the favour to place the lid on me."

The secretary looked amazed, and upon several of their faces there was an expression which plainly expressed, "rather you than I;" but the stranger was not to be diverted from adding such a zest to his story, and in another moment he laid himself fairly down on his back in the coffin.

"Thus, gentlemen," he said, "I laid myself down, while she for whom I was consenting to go through such an ordeal looked on me with a torpid expression, that was very far from increasing my courage to go through the scene."

"Would you like the lid placed on now, sir?" said one.

"Not yet!" I felt the moment I laid down that a dreamy, sleepy, half-choking sort of sensation crept over me; objects grew dim and confused before me, I could not—have—risen—if—I—"

"Sir—"

"You—may—put on—lid."

The lid of the coffin was placed on according to his desire, and then all was still.

The members of the society looked at each other in astonishment, not unmingled with a little dismay. In vain they waited for some signification of his pleasure—but no sound whatever reached their ears: and now any one would have thought that a kind of dread crept over them of personal mischief for those who were closest to the coffin. Some established themselves at a great distance; and it was only a strong feeling of curiosity that prevented many from at once leaving the place.

"He says nothing," remarked one.

"Well," said another, "perhaps it is a part of his story. He intimated his desire to present it to us in as graphic a shape as possible, and this may be his means of getting up a necessary effect."

"But what shall we do?" said the president.

"Oh, let him alone until he comes to speak of himself: there can be no doubt that in a short time he will do so."

This advice was followed; and, probably, not so much with a conviction of its reasonableness, as from a disinclination, on the part of any one there present, to meddle with the mysterious stranger, or his singular proceedings. It is not every man who would like to get into a coffin, and have the lid closed upon him; nor is it every man who could muster courage, on the spur of the moment, to open that coffin-lid again, to ascertain what he was about: therefore was it that the stranger was left alone, in the singular situation which he had chosen of his own accord to occupy. A short time only elapsed—but, under such circumstances of excitement, minutes swell into hours—and the impatience of the members of the society became ungovernable. Murmuring inquiries arose among themselves as to what was to be done; and at last one, more bold than the rest, advanced, and, tapping with the knuckle of his forefinger upon the coffin-lid, he said—

"Sir, sir, if you please, we quite understand it now; if you will be so good as to go on with your narration and come out, we shall feel so much obliged. Eh? does he say anything?"

"Nothing," said several, who had been attentively listening together if any reply was made to this moving appeal. All was as still as the very grave itself, and it became quite clear that, unless some means were taken to put a stop to so cruel a jest, that mysterious man, whom no one knew, and who had introduced himself there with the name of a dead man in his mouth, would go in, no doubt, with what was a practical jest, for the purpose of trying, to the utmost extent, the nerves of his auditors.

"Gentlemen," said the president, rising, "this will not do; I propose, and I shall consider it carried by acclamation, if no opposition is given to me, that the lid of the coffin be removed, and our friend, if we may call him such on so slight an acquaintance, be requested to oblige us with the denouement of his story in a more rational manner than he can possibly do in his present situation."

"Hear, hear," cried every body; but somehow or other, as they said it, they got further off from the coffin, and although they carried by acclamation the president's suggestion, it seemed more than probable that, if he wanted it carried a little further, namely, carried out, he would have to do so himself.

"Really, gentlemen—really, gentlemen," he said, "I may say I'm surprised, as well as a little shocked at this apathetic feeling. Let me earnestly request you, Mr. Brown, to have the kindness to remove the coffin-lid."

"I thank you, sir," said Mr. Brown, "and highly esteem the honour; but, when you want any hot chestnuts off a fire, put your own hand to them and don't expect to make a catspaw of me."

"Perhaps, sir," said the president, "you think that's facetious, but I can tell you you're most profoundly mistaken. You are no wit, Mr. Brown."

"You're no judge, sir."

"Sir!"

"And sir!"

"Really, really, gentlemen," said a quiet-looking man who, as yet, had made no remarks, but who had paid great attention to what was going forward, "really, gentlemen, it strikes me that this contention is about the merest trifle in the world. I have no particular objection, if any other gentleman will lay hold of one end of the coffin-lid, in assisting him to raise it; humanity calls upon us to do so, for how can we tell but that our own friend, who has so much amused us by his tale of the Mysterious Lady, may have been taken ill or fainted, perchance?—a confirmation we none of us would wish, and therefore humanity, gentlemen, should prompt us to look to his condition."

Thus appealed to, several stepped forward, and it became evident that the stranger, who probably had fainted in consequence of having his feelings worked upon by the narration he had himself given utterance to, would soon be rleased from his voluntary at first, but now involuntary place of confinement. There had been some jagged sort of nails sticking up from the sides of the coffin—or screws, perchance, rusted sufficiently to deprve them of their character—and these when the lid was fitted on above the singular being who had chosen to get into such a receptacle for the purpose of illustrating his tale, had fitted into their old places in the lid so that there was some little trouble in lifting it off, especially when it is considered; that a coffin-lid is an article which admits of no good hold until it is partially removed.

He, however, who had urged the matter upon the score of humanity, was not to be deterred, but, after two or three unsuccessful attempts, he did at last succeed in wrenching up his end of the coffin-lid. At the moment, the whole of the society might be said to be assembled around that sad and solemn resting-place of poor humanity. Some were stooping, to allow others to look over their heads, and, in fact, by one means or another, almost every individual present had some glimpse of that coffin upon which the dim rays of the ceiling lamp shone with spectral-looking beam.

It was a moment of intense excitement: of course every one expected some exclamation from the denizen of that narrow chamber of the dead. For a brief moment conjecture indulged in some of its wildest dreams, and then the lid w s removed, and a cry of surprise and terror burst from the lips of all present.

Within there lay nothing but a mouldering skeleton, with the yellow damp of age upon its loathsome festering limbs, and an exhalation arose from the putrid mass, filling the air of the vault with a noisome stench. It was a frightful sight— the ghastly orifices, where once the eyes had been, were filled with a slimy glittering matter, reflecting the dull rays of thelamp, as if the decomposed organ of vision yet shone amid that mass of putridity. Portions of integument yet clung to the yellow bones. It was a frightful sight indeed—a lesson to pride—a something to shudder at, even at the best of times; but now, vested as it was with all the accumulated terrors of surprise, and unexpected horror, the half-stifled cry that burst from those who looked upon it was not more, and certainly not less, than could have been expected from human nature under such circumstances.

Then the cry was hushed, and not a sound disturbed the solemn stillness of the place. Each man seemed fixed in the very attitude he had assumed at the moment when that humiliating sight had dawned upon his faculties—a sight which no one could have looked for in the wildest stretch of imagination—a sight to chill the very heart's blood, and make each there present feel as if the blight of cold and terrible corruption was slowly and insidiously taking possession of his own faculties, giving to each a feeling as if they, too, were hastening to such a consummation as they saw achieved within the narrow precincts of the last home of that suffering humanity.

And none there were who thought that the ghastly countenance of the dead form that lay before them—deprived as it was of all its pathological identity—yet bore a frightful and terrific resemblance to him who but a few short moments before had spoken to them, even as one of themselves—as a breathing, living man —an inhabitant of the earth—one who might look forward to length of days, and for whom—although the grave must ultimately be his resting-place—grim-visaged Death might long have waited.

But now to see him thus blasted in a moment—the body parted from that soul which had given utterance, throughout the mortal faculty of speech, to soft and sweet poetic fancies—to flights of that imagination which we call genius, and which assimilates those who are yet of the earth earthly to that heaven which must have been their bright and glorious origin, as it is and will be—aye, and must be—their haven of rest in that time which is eternal.

Oh, it was horrible to think that even an inch of humanity should be thus snatched from among the living things, and made to look so like one who has passed away with his generation and belonged not to that great struggle for life and for happiness which had succeeded the era that belonged to him. The silence was broken, and it was broken by that man who had first suggested the idea that sickness might have overtaken the graphic delineator, who had stopped not short at such a personal exemplification of the narrative, the vivid particulars of which he wished to bring before his hearers.

"Great God!" he said, "what is the meaning of this? tell me, I implore all of you—do you see this sight as I see it?—what do you behold int his coffin? is it a living man, or is it a hideous mass of corruption, dragged forth in all its frightful horror to that light which should have shone upon such a spectre?"

The looks of those around were a sufficient answer; and, now that the spell was broken which had held them all in silence for a time, exclamations of terror and of wonder burst from every lip.

There was an uneasy movement, as if each was inclined to move away from the presence of that dreadful sight, and yet as if they could not, but were detained by some fascinating power that compelled them to look until they had drank in with their external senses all the horrors of the scene.

And there it lay, that ghastly form, so mute and yet so eloquent; so absolutely harmless, and yet such a thing of dread!

How long they might have gazed upon those sad remains we may not know, for he who had spoken most upon the subject with a shudder took up the coffin-lid, and, replacing it upon the terrific spectacle, he clasped his hands, and lifting up his eyes to heaven, said—

"May the great God, who watcheth over all, receive this soul, which by some judgment should surely have been surrendered up to its Creator long ago, else could not the mortal tabernacle have suffered such decay; but, as in the case of those who have merely left us living behind them, the cold and pallid semblance of what once they were, we should yet have traced the familiar lineaments of him whom we know not well, but sufficient for recognition, in those sad remains. Friends, there is a mystery here which mortal eye can never fathom. God send that it is over!"

The spectacle of terror was shut out from mortal sight. With pallid visages and shuddering limbs those who had looked upon it turned aside, and slowly and silently they resumed their seats, as if it were requisite to do something of a serious and important character after what had occurred. Scarcely had they done so, when one rose again, and in a voice which seemed strange and unnatural, because he spoke as it were through the shrill clarion of his fears, he said, "Gentlemen, you can do as you please; I can well perceive that the faint tints of morning are beginning to show themselves in the glorious east; after what has passed I cannot, I dare not; and I must not remain in such a place as this. Heaven have mercy upon us all!".

As he spoke he rushed from the vault. It needed but such an impulse as that to give the impetus to every one present; three minutes, not more elapsed, and the place was left alone with its dead; the lamp burnt dimly for another hour, and then expired with a stench.

* * * * * * *

It seemed a most doubtful question indeed if ever this society, established for such strange purposes, would ever again show itself within the gloomy precincts of that vault wherein such horrors had been enacted.

They were men who were in the habit of meeting each other in the busy world, sometimes on business, and sometimes on pleasure, so that it was probable enough that between the intervals of that last night of meeting and the next which was to follow, most of them would have an opportunity of comparing their feelings and sensibilities with regard to the singular circumstances that had occurred respecting the mysterious stranger and the coffin.

The current question among them was, " shall we meet again ?" and some put it in a more fearful shape, saying, " dare we meet again after what has occurred ?"

And yet none gave a clear or positive answer to these questions, but each seemed to wait for each to express some determination upon the subject.   It was evident that if some went all would go, although it was not equally clear that if some stayed away the whole would follow their example.

Curiosity, however, and the earnest desire which is ever existent in the human mind to be improved concerning the occult and the terrific, no doubt had their full share in producing a distinct line of conduct, and what that was we shall shortly perceive.

It will be borne in mind that the unhappy member of the society, who had lost his life in consequence of being thrown from his gig, was the same individual who had made the extremely unwelcome proposal that the members of the society should, after death, visit each other, at some certain time, in order to put at rest that question which agitated them all with regard to the supernatural.   And, although this proposition had been repudiated most expressly by those who were

No. 11.

then assembled, it was not to be expected but that there should remain, in the minds of them all a lingering doubt and a great suspicion that he now, who was numbered among the human beings who had been, might, if he had the power so to do, carry into effect the idea which he had given utterance to in life and activity—

"Revisit the glimpses of the pale moon;"

and make night hideous by showing himself at one time sacred, under other circumstances, to repose before the bewildered visions of the individuals whom he had known in life.

This was a thing much talked of among them, that is to say, those whom chance brought together during the week which elapsed when the next night of meeting came round.

But at last the auspicious day—auspicious to us, because it has furnished us with a theme by which we hope to interest our readers—arrived, and, no doubt, the most vexatious question that could possibly arise in the minds of the members of the society consisted in an inquiry whether it would be desirable to go, or not, to the dismal vault wherein already such agitating scenes had taken place.

The morning matured itself to dawn—the dawn passed away and the decline of day crept on—that saddened into twilight, and that again deepened into night. It wanted but an hour of midnight, and the vault, as yet, in which that strange inquisition was wont to hold its meetings, remained untenanted.

A quarter of an hour elapsed and the two entered, arm-in-arm—one would not have ventured. These two lit the lamp which depended from the ceiling, supplying it with fresh oil, kept in a secret nook for that especial purpose, and, ere they had concluded this necessary part of the duty of the first arrivals, a third, who had been watching uneasily around the entrance until he saw some of his fellows enter, and then a fourth, and then two more, so that there were seven.

And now the vault began to fill—each new-comer was hailed with looks of silent satisfaction by his fellows—and at last, strange to say, despite of all their fears, which had crept across them at their last interview—despite of everything which had assumed a character of terror—the whole of the society, with the exception of that one who had come to death by violent means, was assembled in that dreary place of meeting.

But there was a subdued tone about them—they looked suspiciously around from one countenance to another—they seemed as if they dreaded something was about to occur of an alarming character—and yet, like men whose destiny hurried them on, despite their will, they felt as if they were compelled to make their appearance where they did, and being members of the fraternity to which they belonged, it seemed as if a kind of moral obligation beset them all to carry through their purpose to the end, despite any terrifying circumstances that might occur as they proceeded.

The president, in silence, took his seat, and the members arranged themselves around him, but, although they looked at him furtively, it was briefly, for their principal attention was most unquestionably fixed upon that coffin into which the mysterious stranger had gotten, and from whence he had never come, but had left such a frightful evidence within its gloomy precincts of the progress of decay as was not likely for many a year to fade from the memories of those who had been a witness to it.

The president spoke :—

"Gentlemen," he said, "we meet to-night under the most peculiar circumstances. I cannot but feel that circumstances have occurred which render this night's meeting a painful and a serious one; but still it is with a feeling of intense gratulation that I look around me and perceive, without exception, the whole of our members present, for he who has come by his death of course can no longer be considered as one of us; therefore the whole of our living members constitute the whole of our members."

This sentiment was applauded by several present, because it was a tolerable hint to anything connected with the supernatural world that they were not wanted, and if the ghost of the individual who had suffered so sudden a death, by a fall from his gig, was present, and heard how such a declaration was received, it ought to be quite sufficient to convince him that he was not wanted, under any circumstances whatever.

"Gentlemen," continued the president, "I feel convinced that it would be quite a work of supererogation to call your attention to what occurred on our last night of meeting; the strange, and, I may add, inexplicable events of that evening, must be fresh in the memory of every gentleman here present. Now we have made a rule, gentlemen, to discuss after its recital any incident that may be brought before us, illustrative of the object for which we hold our meetings."

This was assented to by the silence of those present, and then the president continued :—

"Gentlemen, it is not for me, acting in my presidential capacity, to trouble you with any opinion of my own; I sit here, of course, to hear what others may have to say, and not to intrude my own feelings; but most happy shall I be to listen to anything which may be suggested by those respected friends whom I see around me."

There was a silence for some time, and then one of the members rose.

"Mr. Chairman and Gentlemen," he said, "it strikes me that the ancient proverb, which remarks that 'the least said is the soonest mended,' becomes most peculiarly applicable to our present circumstances. It seems to me, gentlemen, without encouraging any useless fears, or attempting to put a worse construction upon matters than they will reasonably or creditably wear, that it will be prudent to drop the subject altogether, as a matter of public discussion, which I have no doubt has engaged the imagination of the whole of us during the past week."

There were some murmurs of dissent to this, and, when the speaker perceived it, he added—

"Of course I only express this as a private opinion, which can have nothing to do with the feelings or prejudices of other parties. For my own sake, I decline entering into any discussion upon a subject which I think is far better left alone."

As he spoke he sat down, and it was some minutes before any one else rose to address the president. The last speaker was supported in his remarks by the individual who, on a former occasion, proposed the expulsion of the person who proposed the plan of that ghostly visitation which was to set at rest the question of supernatural appearances.

There was such an appearance of fear about this gentleman, and he trembled so excessively before he could utter a word, that it was with the greatest difficulty, even when he did speak, that he could be understood. His friend, too, all the while encouraged him, telling him to mind nothing, but to tell plainly and intelligibly what he had to relate, so that at length he gasped out—"I will!" and, amid a profound stillness around him, he spoke as follows :—

"Mr. President and Gentlemen,—I—have got something dreadful to relate, and I do hope that it will not take too strong a hold of your imaginations, but I have seen him; yes, he has been to me—it was an ungracious thing; but, thank God, it's over; yes, thank God, it's over! He'd no business to come—he oughtn't to have thought of such a thing, alive or dead, gentlemen; but he did, and he has, and so there's an end of that."

"Pray, sir," said the president, "will you be a little more explicit? I am sure I am extremely anxious, and I can read the same expression upon the faces of the gentlemen present, to hear what you have to relate; but let me beg of you to do it in a systematic manner, so that we may have no questions to ask you, but may understand calmly and easily that which you have to tell us."

"Well, well, gentlemen, you shall have it. I have come here purposely to put you on your guard. It's a duty I owe to you all, I own at once; so, without further reservation, I will relate to you some circumstances which have horrified me, and which, I doubt not, you will find, even upon recital, to be of the most interesting character."

This explanation, of course, was calculated to excite a great deal of expectation, and there was not a soul then present who did not wait curiously to hear what next should be said by the individual who had uttered it. He shuddered yet before he spoke, and seemed once or twice upon the point of giving up the attempt. But then, at last, as if with a desperate resolution, he proceeded—

"Gentlemen, you all remember the marked disapprobation with which I received the proposal of our late friend to visit us after he had shuffled off his mortal coil, and how I actually went so far as to move that he be expelled this society, which I have no doubt excited his ire. Well, gentlemen, who would have thought he was going to be thrown from his gig, just at such a juncture, too? Not I, gentlemen, nor I am sure any of you; but so it was, and the moment I heard of it I felt a sort of conviction that something uncomfortable would happen. But as a week passed on, and nothing of an alarming character occurred, I took to congratulating myself that such would not be the fact, thinking, upon the whole, that he must really have taken a better thought, and declined visiting a gentleman who did not desire his company. But last night, gentlemen, last night!"

Here the speaker paused, as if quite oppressed with his feelings, and unable to proceed further. All he could say for several moments consisted in the words—"Last night, last night!"

It seemed as if he could get no further than the utterance of these two words, "last night, last night!" and it was clear to all that something of a most desperate and alarming character must have taken place to mark that last night with such a remembrance of horror. The members of the association looked at him with the most lively sensations of surprise and curiosity; anxiously they listened for the next words that should fall from his lips, trusting that from them they should acquire sufficient information concerning his subject of alarm to enable them to understand how it was that he was evidently in such a state of mental perturbation and alarm. But still it was some minutes before he could command his feelings sufficiently to allow himself to speak again, and the president, as well as several of the members, had to speak to him in encouraging phrases, before he could trust himself to the sound of his own voice. Then still trembling, but certainly not so much affected as he had been, he spoke :—

"Mr. President and Gentlemen, I feel that I owe much to your kind indulgence, in pardoning this excess of emotion, which almost forbids utterance ; but when I inform you, which I shall now at once proceed to do, of the ample cause for agitation, I am certain that you will withhold any censure from me, and consider me an object of commise ation."

This speech was received with demonstrations of applause of an encouraging nature, and then in a somewhat firmer voice—for he was human, and to what human heart is not applause grateful?—he continued :—

"Gentlemen, it no doubt is fresh in your memory that I, along with others, expressed my most decided disapprobation of the course which our deceased friend proposed, namely, the re-visiting each of us at night, in order to set at rest the question of supernatural appearances. I decidedly, gentlemen, demurred to any such experiment being tried upon my nervous system, and, in so demurring, I believed that I expressed likewise the opinion of many gentlemen present."

"Hear, hear! yes, yes!" cried several.

"Well, gentlemen, you all know how short has been the interval of time since that gentleman, who is now no more, was among us, and we were all, from a consideration of his melancholy fate, the more and more impressed with a conviction of how slight is the step from this world to the eternity that lies beyond it.

"I must own, that when first I heard of the sudden and awful death of our friend, the thought of what he had proposed came across my mind with a shuddering intensity, and I told myself that I would not be in the position of having agreed to such a proposition for the best 1,000l. that was ever placed before a mortal man.

"For the remainder of that day, the idea haunted me that his disembodied spirit might make some attempt to carry out the suggestion he had given utterance to while living; but, surely, I told myself that I was free from the chance of such a visitation.—I who had objected so strenuously to anything of the sort, and who had stood up here and repudiated the very idea of any such bargain! Yes, gentlemen, one would have thought that I of all men would have had nothing to apprehend upon that score."

Here the narrator wiped the perspiration from his brow, and heaved a deep sigh, after which he added :—

"I went that night to bed, gentlemen, certainly with not the most agreeable feelings in the world. It was in vain that I strove to chase away from my mind all thought of even the possibility of my being horrified by the appearance of a spectre—the thought would haunt me, despite all my exertions to shake it off, and I passed a sleepless night."

"But did you see nothing, sir?"

"Absolutely nothing."

"Then pray what have you been exciting our expectations in this way, for if you saw nothing?"

"Wait a bit, wait a bit, the villany is yet to come; I awakened at mid-day, for although I could not sleep the whole of the night, on account of my extreme nervousness, I did, when the light of morning dawned into my chamber, succeed in catching some repose, and when I awakened it was, as I say, mid-day.

"You all know, gentlemen, how different a man's feelings manifest themselves, upon some subjects at twelve o'clock in the day, to what they do at twelve o'clock at night;—therefore it is needless for me to say that I almost blushed at my own fears. Well, the next night came, and I was not quite so feverish and anxious. I saw nothing of an unusual character—heard nothing that could excite in me the least alarm—and now I put it to you all, gentlemen, whether after that, you would not have considered yourself quite safe from any visitation, and dismissed all fears upon such a subject?"

This was understood to be one of those pulpit questions which nobody is at all expected to answer; so no one took any notice, and the orator continued—

"Well, gentlemen, the third night I slept pretty well—the fourth night quite well—and then I gave up all fears whatever; and the affair was rapidly fading from my mind, or assuming the shape which events take in which we have no great interest, although at the time they may have made a sufficient impression not to allow us readily to forget them. And now I come to what I do consider is a grievous complaint. If the ghost of our departed friend intended to come, he had no business, with a malicious ingenuity, to make his coming a worse infliction by throwing one off one's guard completely, and making one believe that he did not intend putting in an appearance at all, and then afterwards doing so with a vengeance."

"Then he did come?" said several.

"He did."

Eager questions were now propounded as to the how, the where, and the when this ghostly visitation had taken place. The narrator waved his hand for silence, saying—

"Gentlemen, be patient, and you shall hear all from your unhappy but most obedient servant. You shall hear every particular; I will keep nothing whatever from you that I consider is calculated to interest you."

This liberal promise of course satisfied every one, and all eyes were bent upon him who made it with a gaze of the deepest interest.

"You are all aware, gentlemen," he added, "that our friend who was thrown from his gig executed that feat this day se'nnight, and that yesterday he was duly consigned to the tomb. As I knew something of him, but not much, I was asked if I would be present at the funeral; and being willing to do everything of the most conciliating character, I consented, and made one among the mourners, who saw him to his last home.

"Little did I think I was to see any more of him. The funeral made but little impression upon me. We live too much in this world in the midst of death to think anything of it, unless it approaches us nearly; and so, in an hour or two after the ceremony, I dismissed it from my mind wholly, and thought no more of our deceased friend than I did of Adam. It was in such a calm, serene, and comfortable state of mind, as a man of clear conscience, who is well enough to do in the world may be supposed to have, that I retired to rest last night. I had no terrors—no nervous misgivings—no presentiment of anything out of the way going to happen. I got into bed, gentlemen. It was eleven o'clock, and I put out the light. In a quarter of an hour I fell into a deep slumber. You know that the back of my house is very near to the cathedral wall; and, when first I occupied it, I used to be awakened, almost every hour of the night, as a regular thing, by the striking of the old clock. But habit accustoms us to anything; and I soon slept on, as if I had no means of hearing such a sound; and it might strike away, possibly awakening any stranger who was near at hand, but never for a moment disturbing my repose. On this night, however, the case was different; for I was awakened by hearing the old cathedral clock striking. Now, of course, although a man in his sleep has no means of measuring time, yet I always fancy that when you awake you can have a sort of consciousness as to whether you have slept a long or a short time : at least I have; and I at once, when I was thus awakened, felt assured that I had not long enjoyed the sweets of slumber. If any thing had been wanting to convince me I was right, the old cathedral clock would soon have accomplished that for me. I counted the strokes : they were nine; and as I knew it was past eleven before I went to bed, and could not be nine in the morning, I came at once to the natural enough and perfectly correct conclusion that it was twelve o'clock, and that three of the sonorous announcements of the hour had gone by, while I was awaking and before I began to count them.

"Then the pleasant and easy state of feeling in which I had gone to rest completely changed, and all at once a state of dread crept over me, which I could not account for in any way, for I had heard nothing, nor seen anything, which ought to produce or account for such a feeling. I trembled in every limb, and yet, somehow, I dreaded to get up, which, undoubtedly, would have been my best plan of operations, but there I lay with such a mass of strange images and thoughts flashing through my brain, that I thought more than once I must be going mad. And strange to say, in the midst of all this, I did not give the least thought of our deceased friend, or in any way connect my painful state of feelings with him ; no, I had, from the whole week's quietude, been so lulled, as regarded any idea of a visitation from him, that his name came not to my lips, nor did any image of him associate itself with the numerous others with which my teeming fancy was filled.

"I am thus particular in informing you that my mind was not dwelling upon him, or upon the idea of his ghost visiting me, in order that you may feel convinced, as I am, that what did occur is not a mere thing of imagination. Well, gentlemen, this state of things became worse and worse, and the chimes of the old clock announced that a quarter of an hour had passed away. By degrees my eyes had got accustomed to the darkness of the room : it was not a very dismal night, and there was light enough, I presume, from the young moon, to enable me to distinguish objects faintly and confusedly, the one from the other, in my chamber. There was a chair by my bed-side, and somehow, after I had bent an anxious gaze all around the room, my eyes became fixed upon that chair, and, in the space of a moment, I felt certain that it was occupied. Yes, gentlemen, that chair was occupied—a dim-looking, shadowy form was there seated, and from that instant I felt as if the eyes of the dead were looking into my very soul. I was astounded, fascinated, terrified. I could not have taken off my glance, had my life depended upon my so doing ; and as I looked the spectral form grew more and more defined, until I knew who it was, and saw as plainly as I now see any of you that it was the man whose funeral I had that day attended. A cold perspiration broke out upon me, and for a few moments I think I became perfectly insensible, but it could have been only for a few moments, and when I recovered, there, in the chair by the bed-side, sat the spectral form, and the old cathedral clock chimed the half-hour past twelve.

" It did not speak, but it only looked upon me with a strange and terrifying glare, with those horrible opaque-looking eyes that belong to a corpse. He seemed attired as he ordinarily was in life ; but there was upon the countenance an expression of great anguish, probably the same expression with which he had died, after the accident that had befallen him. More than once I made an effort to rise, but my limbs refused to obey the mental impulse—speak I dared not, and yet I wished after a time that the spectre would itself break the awful stillness that reigned within the chamber. The cathedral clock announced the three-quarters past twelve, and still the spectre sat looking at me, a mute but horrible evidence of the reality of those existences it has been our wish to investigate by the researches of this society. Another quarter of an hour of dread I passed. The cathedral clock struck one, and then a strange fluttering noise sounded in the room, and as I looked upon the ghostly form that had been seated so close to me at my bed's head, it gradually became more and more confused in its outlines, until I could not at all distinguish in it the appearance of a human form, and then it slowly melted away before my vision. The chair was vacant."

" And did it say nothing?" asked the president.

" Not one word."

"'Tis very strange!"

" Strange indeed! To-night I dread not its presence, because if, between the hours of twelve and one, be the only time that it is permitted to show itself to mortal eyes, I shall not be in a situation, of course, to be alarmed."

" It is not far from one o'clock, now," said the president ; " I cannot help thinking, and perhaps you will excuse if I say, I hope that this, after all, was nothing more than an extremely vivid dream."

" Mr. President, far from being in any way offended by the expression of such an opinion, I only wish you could convince me of it. If I could but really think it a vision of disturbed slumbers, I should be a happier man than I am now."

" Will you allow me to offer a suggestion?" said one, rising from the further end of the vault, which was very much enveloped in gloom.

The moment the voice struck upon their ears, all rose in alarm ; and various exclamatory observations testified to the sudden shock which they had received : it was no other than the mysterious stranger, who on the last night of meeting had illustrated his own story by getting into the coffin, where, to all appearance, he had undergone so horrible a transformation.

" Good God!" said the president, heedless of his speech at the moment, " that's him! that's him!"

And then the stranger stood alone, with all eyes turned upon him, while he affected a look of surprise, as if he wondered what there could be of an extraordinary nature in him that should attract such general attention.

" Gentlemen," he said, " I am much obliged for this marked attention, but I assure you I merely rose to offer a suggestion to our friend, who has narrated how he was alarmed last night."

One more bold than the rest looked to the coffin into which the stranger had got on that night week, and pushed the lid on one side—it was empty! Not the least vestige of the hideous mass of bone and flesh that they had seen in it, was visible.

" This is terrific," cried he who opened the coffin. " Speak! who are you? and what are you? speak, in the name of Heaven!"

" Speak," said the stranger, " I have only just done speaking. What is terrific? pray enlighten me."

There was so much coolness and easy assurance about the manner in which these words were uttered, that they staggered everybody ; and no doubt there were some present who were almost inclined to doubt the evidence of their own senses on the last occasion, and to ask themselves if it were possible that they could have been mistaken in what they supposed they saw upon the opening of the coffin.

It was the president, at length, who spoke. Probably he thought he was in duty bound, to a certain extent, to be the mouthpiece of the society, so he addressed himself to the mysterious stranger, saying—

"Sir, if your first appearance among us was rather strange and inexplicable, I need hardly say that your second partakes of the horrible."

"The horrible! Well, sir, you are certainly very complimentary; I don't think that I have any larger claims to be called horrible than any member of this society, yourself included."

"You mistake, sir, or wilfully misapprehend me. Did you not tell us a story on the last night of our meeting concerning a beautiful young female whom you fell in love with?"

"I!"

"Yes, sir, you."

"God bless me! I told you no story."

"You deny it, sir?"

"Most unhesitatingly."

"This is the very height of assurance. Did you not tell us that she hung back from reciprocating your attachment, until at last you caught her in a neighbouring wood, and she informed you how dreadfully she was circumstanced?"

"How? I should really like to hear."

"This is insufferable. Do you deny that you got into that coffin?"

"What coffin?"

"That coffin. There, sir, that coffin by your feet."

"Oh! by my feet. Oh yes, I deny that. It strikes me you are not quite right in your head. I don't know what you are talking about; I never was here before in my life; I am introduced by a friend—the very gentleman who met with a melancholy accident a week ago. It was the day before he came to so sad an end that he invited me to meet him here, where he said I should find some choice pirits; but, as I had not time on that night of your meeting, I have ventured to intrude upon you now, gentlemen, and have only to hope for your kind leave and indulgence to remain."

Well might the members of the association look at each other with such bewildered expressions of countenance, that some of them partook quite of the ludicrous. The stranger spoke so fairly to the ear, and so quietly, and withal there was a gentlemanly manner about him which forbade any rude speech, that they mutually waited for each other to say something, rather than venture upon what individually their feelings dictated.

"Sir," added the president, "I have, during the course of my life, met with various instances of effrontery, but never one like this."

"Sir," said the stranger, "had I not been invited I should not have come here at all. My friend it was who combated with my scruples, for scruples I had, and in abundance, too, about introducing myself among a body of gentlemen, none of whom but himself were known to me. He, however, said, that even if he were not there the use of his name would be sufficient, and that I should receive a gentlemanly reception. I much regret that in that respect he exaggerated."

"But, sir!"

"Oh, you need say no more; I can very well myself understand how all this has taken place: my friend has played off upon me a practical joke, which, had he been a living man, I should not so easily forgive and dismiss from my mind, as, of course, common feeling prompts me to do, now that he is no more among the living."

"A practical joke, sir! And pray in what do you consider the practical joke consists? It seems to me that you have played us a practical trick, which we are not likely soon to forget."

"Sir, the practical joke consists in this: my friend led me to believe that this honourable association was got together for various purposes, and not consisting, as I see it does, of a number of gentlemen fond of jesting at the expense of a stranger."

"You are mistaken, or you know better; I appeal to any gentleman present, if you were not here on our last night of meeting, and if you did not tell us a story which you left unfinished, because you got into a coffin by way of illustrating it, and did not come out again. That is the truth, so help me Heaven! and you cannot convince us that you are not fully aware of it. It is you who are the practical jester, although, how you have contrived so to impose upon our senses, I know not. A fearful suggestion, of course, under such circumstances, crosses my mind."

"And what may that be?"

"That you are not of this world."

The stranger was silent for a few moments, and then he took up his hat, and walked slowly towards the entrance of the vault. Several of the members thought that, without another word, he was going to leave, but when he had nearly gained the threshold he paused, and turning, he addressed the president in a fine, deep, calm, and respectful voice :—

"Sir," he said, " you have used an asseveration, which I cannot entertain so bad

No. 12.

an opinion of human nature, as to suppose for one instant would have come from your lips, had you not really believed in the truth of what you have uttered. You have called upon Heaven to witness to your belief in the fact of my presence on your last meeting night, and certain occurrences which you have vaguely hinted to me as having then taken place."

"I have, sir."

". Well, sir, then all I can say is, and I say it with some amount of dread, that you must all of you have been made the dupes of some dreadful delusion. I can prove to you that I was elsewhere on the night you allude to, and the only explanation which I can for a moment hope to offer of what has occurred, is almost too horrible to think of."

"Go on, sir."

" It is that some supernatural being assumed my form, and so introduced himself to you; gentlemen, I have the honour of wishing you all good night. Heaven forbid that I should intrude myself upon this respectable and talented body, if my presence is unwelcome."

The mysterious stranger would have left the vault, but several of the association were so much struck by his gentlemanly bearing, and the polite manner in which he had last spoken, that they called upon him to stop, and the president in particular said :—

" Sir, if we have done you an injustice, believe me that no one can regret that more than I, and I am likewise certain that I could not regret it more than the other gentlemen composing this association."

The stranger bowed.

" May I then beg, sir, that you will take a seat, and we will talk this matter over; for it is one of the most mysterious and most deeply interesting that ever I have yet encountered."

The stranger hesitated, and seemed to be in doubt as to weh er or not he should accede to the request that was made to him. At length, he said :—

" Mr. President, so chary am I of hurting any gentleman's feelings in the least, that, although I shall have some trouble to convince myself that my presence here is not an intrusion, I will do myself the honour of remaining."

Some applause followed these words, which were as judiciously spoken as they well could be, and the stranger took his place upon the end of the very same coffin from which he had been supposed to emerge.

There was a silence now of many minutes' duration, for the real and the unreal were so mixed up together in the minds of all present, that no one knew what to say. The stranger must have thought that the pause was an awkward one, and that he was, to a great extent, the cause of it, so he broke it, by saying, in a voice of anxiety :—

" And was the spectral form of which you speak very like me ?"

" It was exact, sir."

" Indeed ! the thought gives me uneasiness ; it is said that such things presage death sometimes."

" I have heard so, but in this case there may have been other motives altogether for the spectral appearance."

". There may, indeed ; but when I first rose here to-night, little dreaming of creating the alarm that I did, it was for the purpose of making a suggestion to our friend, if he will permit me to call him such, who saw the apparition of our deceased other friend seated in a chair by his bed-side."

" We shall hear your suggestion with pleasure, sir."

" Oh! it is a very simple one. It is generally believed—and possibly the belief is founded upon fact -that the supernatural beings who are permitted for a brief space to revisit the earth cannot speak, unless they hear the sound previously of human voices."

" Yes," said one, " not until they are spoken to."

" Why, not exactly that, I think," said the stranger ; " but they cannot break a silence at the sound of a human voice, although the words they utter may not be addressed to them, they can speak, since they do not, of themselves, break the stillness of the air around them. The suggestion, therefore, that I would make to the gentleman is, that, should he ever see this spectre again, he should by all means speak to it, as it may have a something of importance to reveal."

" I only hope I shall never have an opportunity," said he who had seen the spectre of the deceased member.

" I hope you will not, then, sir, as you do not wish it."

The stranger was so verbose, and spoke in such a mild conciliatory tone of voice, that those who heard him were quite charmed, and one rose, and said :—

" Sir, I move that this gentleman, if he be pleased to be so, become a member of this honourable association.'"

The proposition was not a moment without a seconder, and the chairman declared it carried by acclamation. Then the stranger rose, and bowing gracefully, he placed his hand upon his heart, saying :—

" You will, gentlemen, I am certain, do me one favour, and that is, to imagine for me what I should say upon this occasion. I can assure you that no man can, more than I do, fully appreciate such a mark of kindness. Gentlemen, I am overwhelmed and know not what to say."

" Hear, hear, hear !"

" Gentlemen, I emphatically thank you."

" May we trouble you for your name, sir ?"

" Oh, certainly, my name is Annesley."

" Thank you, sir, thank you !"

" Annesley ? I have heard that name before," said one, " but I cannot just now call to mind where, really."

" And now, gentlemen," said the newly-elected member, " permit me to say that nothing shall hinder me from being always present at these delightful little meetings ; and, if it be not obtrusive, I have a little anecdote, which I can relate to you, that bears upon the subject of your labours in the way of the supernatural."

This intimation was received with much applause and satisfaction by every one ; so that whatever doubts Mr. Annesley might have had of his welcome among those persons who had assembled together for so singular a purpose, they must now have completely vanished, and he looked, as indeed no doubt he felt, quite at home.

" We shall listen to you, sir," said the president, " with the greatest possible pleasure, I assure you."

" Gentlemen, then, after the very flattering manner in which you have been pleased to signify your kind intention to listen to what I have to relate to you, I shall, as the time is fast slipping by, and I must home early, at once commence by telling you what I shall call my tale—

THE GHOSTLY SENTINEL ; OR, THE HAUNTED KNOLL.

This was a title which awakened expectation, and all sat devouring every word that came from Mr. Annesley's lips.

" I was once in the army," he said, " holding a commission in a regiment of light cavalry, who had the chance of being ordered more frequently upon actual service than any other regiment of its class. Well, that was a matter that to the officers was rather pleasing than otherwise, for, strange as it may seem, some men who take up the trade of war get their feelings so blunted, and all the better part of their valour so degraded, that they sit down to dinner together one day, and the next have a hope that some of their number may be shot off in order to make way for promotion.

" However, not to fatigue you with any of my own reflections upon a profession which I consider the worst under the sun, and which I left from that conviction, I will at once proceed to the incidents of my tale.

" It so happened that one under the government had intelligence of an expected outbreak, which would take almost the character of a serious rebellion, in a particular district of Ireland, and my regiment, along with others, was ordered to the spot *instanter.*

"This, as you may well imagine, was anything but an a agreeable duty for a soldier, and yet it was one which, under orders, we were of course compelled to perform. Fighting the enemies of one's country—people who are aliens to us in blood, in manners and in religion—is quite another thing to suppressing a civil outbreak.

"But it so happened that the rapid movements of well-organised light cavalry regiments were considered as best adapted for the proposed service, but it turned out that a greater mistake could not have been committed, for the country we had to act in was hilly, and we were comparatively with infantry useless.

"It was the first time I had ever been in Ireland, and the novelty of the scenery and the difference in the habits and manners of the people, were some recompense for the service I was on.

"We were landed, and had then a distance of about one hundred and sixty miles to go before we came to a place called by some horrible Irish name that I never could pronounce properly, and where we were to go into quarters.

"Horses and men were both in prime condition. The weather was delightful, and, as we passed through the romantic scenery, we were much pleased with our route.

"Certainly, when night came, our accommodations were seldom of the most agreeable order ; sometimes, to be sure, we came upon a large town, where we did get tolerable accommodations, and sometimes we officers were well entertained at the seat of some landed proprietor, who was sufficiently patriotic to risk his life, by remaining on his own property and endeavouring to do all the good he could for his tenantry.

"And these are two offences that in Ireland have often been sufficient to send a bullet through a man's brains.

"At length, on the evening of the fourth day—for we did not make fatigue marches—we arrived at the place of our destination.

"It was a district rather than a town, and most of the houses were in the most miserable condition. There was a barrack, which was held by a company of infantry, and that was to be our head-quarters. With some trouble we found stabling and fodder for the horses, and then the colonel and two or three officers, one of whom was myself, sat up to talk over what we had to do more particularly.

"'It's a troublesome and an uncomfortable service,' he said, 'but must be done. In my instructions, I am told of a house in the immediate neighbourhood of this place, which goes by the name of Knollwood House—an old mansion now inhabited by a family who have always made themselves conspicuous in Irish politics, and where, it is believed, meetings are held, and matters arranged concomitant upon the projected outbreak.'

"We had all seen a handsome old-fashioned house, as we came along, which we, upon comparing with the written description the colonel had of Knollwood House, found to be that edifice.

"'Now,' he said, 'my instructions are rather curious as regards that house. I am directed to place a sentinel in such a position, so that he shall only seem one of our regular outposts, but yet be able to keep an eye on the entrance-lodge of that house, and take a note of every person who enters it. This system is to be pursued for a week, and then, if I receive no counter orders, I am on the first occasion, when the greatest average number of male visitors have entered the house, to beleaguer it, and take every one prisoner without any further ceremony.'

"We all agreed this was rather a strange proceeding, but still, as it was in the orders, it had but to be done. There were four officers of us now, and after we had partaken of refreshments and rest, we sallied out to reconnoitre and see which was the best point at which to place our sentinel. The night was a dark one, which was all the better for us, so long as there was just light enough for us to see where we were going to, and there was just that much and no more. We walked in the direction of the house, and soon found ourselves close to some of its enclosures.

There were lights from some of the windows, and it looked, as indeed it was, an immense building of most imposing architecture; whilst the lands, comprising gardens, a magnificent park, and waving plantations, and fir-trees about it of great extent and beauty, as far as we could judge by the luxuriant growth of the timber, which was the finest I think I had ever seen, not excepting some that had come under my notice in the most favoured counties of England.

"'Now,' said the colonel, 'where shall we place our sentinel?'

"'Do you,' said I, 'intend to make a secret affair of it, or an open one?'

"'Oh! quite open. If any attempt were made at secrecy, it would be sure to be discovered. He shall have a horse from the barracks, and be regularly posted, as if a thing of course.'

"'We passed a very eligible spot,' said the major, who was with us. 'There is a piece of rising ground, which we skirted, and which, I think, not only commands a view of the lodge of that house, but can be seen from the barracks.'

"'Then that,' said the colonel, 'is the very place. The sentinel can be so placed as not to face the house, and then there will be nothing to excite suspicion; at the same time, he will have no difficulty in taking notice of whoever goes in.'

"We walked back to this little knoll, and we found that it was so situated, that the corner of a plantation hid the lodge of Knollwood House from all but one spot of it, while the whole of it was visible from the barracks.

"'This will just do,' said the colonel. 'One of our fellows dismounted can pace here, taking a view of the lodge each time he walks forward, and yet not being constantly within sight of the house itself.'

"We all agreed in the excellence of this position for the sentinel, and then we slowly marched back to the barracks. A corporal's guard of our men dismounted, and, armed with their sabres, was marched to the spot by myself. They carried with them a light sentry-box from the barracks, and put it up where I directed them. I gave the order to the man we left, who was to be relieved in a couple of hours. Thus far all was well, and as the evening was not so far gone as to make it necessary that we should retire to rest, we sat up together, played a hand at whist, and had some supper. Just as the captain of the infantry company that was there was in the middle of a capital story, a tap sounded on the door of the apartment. The intruder being requested to show himself, an orderly of our regiment made his appearance with a very grave face indeed.

"'What is it?' said the colonel. 'You look as if the enemy had surprised you, Johnstone.'

"'Your honour,' said the orderly, 'is about right. Fawcett has disappeared.'

"'And who may Fawcett be?'

"'The sentinel that was posted at the knoll, to watch the lodge of Knoll House.'

"The colonel immediately rose as he lost all the bantering tone in which he had spoken, and cried with real energy,—

"'You—you do not mean that, Johnstone. Did you say he had disappeared?'

"'I did so. We went with the relief about ten minutes ago, and found him gone. Not a vestige of him is left, sir. The box is there, but that is all. There is no sentinel, or rather—there was none. Of course I have left another man now there; but he is half frightened out of his wits.'

"'Frightened! One of my men frightened?'

"'Not, sir, at any mortal foe, you may be quite sure,' added the orderly, 'but among themselves, I am certain the men think there's something out of the ordinary way of nature in the affair.'

"'Pshaw! This must be seen to, gentlemen. Will you be so good as to give me your company to the knoll where the sentinel is posted?'

"Of course on the moment we were all astir. Swords were buckled on, and off we started to the spot which had been selected as so judicious a one on which to post our sentinel. We soon reached close to it, and, as we did so, we could see the new man that had been put upon duty walking to and fro, and looking about him with a wary eye.

"'Who goes there?' he cried, when he heard our footsteps.

"'Friends,' said the colonel; and the man knew his commander's voice.

"'Have you had any alarm?' he was asked.

"'No, sir. I ought I heard something—I don't know what it was, but when I listened again was gone.'

"'Wh .. resemble?'

"'A kind of suppressed groaning; and it seemed to come from somewhere very close at hand, as if some one was in pain, and trying to suppress an exhibition of it.'

"The colonel considered for a few moments, and then he said:

"'Gentlemen, as we are here, let us make a thorough examination of this place. We may possibly make some discovery which may account for the mysterious disappearance of the former man. Have you your pistols with you, sentinel?'

"'I have, sir.'

"'Then do not hesitate to give an immediate alarm, by the discharge of one of them, should anything suspicious occur. You will be excused, even should it turn out to be nothing. And now, gentlemen, let us look about us a little.'

"We made as thorough a search of the immediate vicinity of the part on which the sentinel was posted as we could, but found nothing at all suspicious. There were bushes growing in great luxuriance close to the place, and some few fir-trees, but there seemed no possibility of any one being concealed close at hand.

"The sentinel looked uneasy as we walked away, but of course he said nothing, and we all went back to the barracks, determined on the morrow that no little stir should be made for the rescuing of the man Fawcett, whose fate seemed to be involved in such profound and fathomless mystery.

"We spent some time in talking it over, I think about an hour, when the sharp report of a pistol came upon our ears. I sprung to my feet in a moment, and exclaimed—

"'That's an alarm from the sentinel on the knoll.'

"'Turn out the guard!' shouted the colonel.

"There was one blast of the trumpet, and the guard was in full movement towards the knoll.

"We—that is, the colonel, myself, and the other officers, who were present—walked quickly after the guard, so that we reached the spot almost as soon as they; at all events, the serjeant had only to walk about half a dozen paces to meet his commanding officer, and say, as he did respectfully—

"'Sir, the sentinel is gone.'

"'Gone?'

"'Yes, sir; he is not there. There seems no trace of him. All is quite quiet, but there is no sentinel, sir.'

"I saw the colonel almost stagger, as he said—

"'Good God! What can be the meaning of this? No sentinel? Gone? Why, this is the second man we have lost in this way to-night.'

"'It is, sir.'

"He turned to us, and said—

"'Gentlemen, what is to be done, now? There is some mystery here which we must unveil before we think of retiring to rest. Search the ground well, and see if you can find anything indicative of a struggle. Send to the guard-house, serjeant, for torches.'

"This was done, and a thorough examination of the ground took place, but with no satisfactory result; nothing whatever was discovered to give the least clue to the means by which the two sentinels had so mysteriously disappeared from their posts. Men, arms, and all had gone, leaving no trace behind, nor could we perceive the least mark upon the grass of anything like a struggle having taken place.

"We certainly all of us felt anything but comfortable. However, nothing more could then be done, and we refrained from giving utterance to any wild conjectures on the subject for fear of alarming the men.

"With an assumption, therefore, of indifference, which I was quite sure he was far from really feeling, the colonel ordered another man to be posted on the spot. When that was done, he spoke to him, saying—

" ' Now, my man, you know what has happened; you will, therefore, look sharp; keep as much out from the trees and bushes as you can, and don't relax in ur vigilance for a moment : I shall order a relief to come to you in an hour, and, during that time, I will myself visit your post.'

" Again, then, we left the place, and walked slowly towards the guard-house, fully expecting each moment to be called back by some alarm from the new sentinel, but such was not so immediately the case, and down we sat again, with full resolution, at all events, to remain up the whole of the night, in case anything unusual should happen.

" We might have sat a quarter of an hour or so when we heard some sounds of bustle outside the barrack. There were voices, some in remonstrance, and some in threats, and while we were wondering what on earth it could all be about, the serjeant of the guard came into the apartment, with a troubled-looking countenance. After saluting the colonel, he said—

" ' Sorry to have to report, sir, that the Sentinel of the Knoll has come back. The man seems half dead, sir.'

" ' Come back!' said the colonel, in a rage; ' put him under arrest this moment. Damn him, I'll make an example of him! Leave his post—the cowardly villain!'

" ' Yes, sir; he came rushing into the guard-room as if he were pursued by all he devils from below, sir. He was as white as a sheet, and we all thought for ome time that he was dying.'

" ' Bring him,' said the colonel, suddenly: ' he used to be a brave man, and as good a disciplined soldier as any in the regiment. Bring him here; I will question him myself upon this most unparalleled act of desertion of duty.'

" The serjeant left the room, and when he was gone we all coincided in opinion that it must have been no trifle that could have induced a tried and faithful soldier, such as we all knew that sentinel to be, to leave his post. However, the mere act itself was such a flagrant breach of all military discipline, that it was quite impossible it could be looked over; so, although the colonel had no doubt that he should hear some amply-sufficing cause for the circumstance, yet he prepared himself to act with all necessary severity.

" When the unlucky sentinel was brought into the room he was under the escort of a file of men; he presented an appearance of absolute fright, such as I never before saw upon any human countenance. His very lips were pallid, and the muscles of his countenance seemed all distorted. He shook from top to toe, and his eyes glared with a wild expression.

" ' You deserted your post?' said the colonel. ' Have you been so long in the service as not to know that such an act is the most serious breach of military discipline you could commit?'

" ' I—I know,' he said.

" ' Then what can you say in your justification? I am willing, patiently and calmly, to hear you, because I cannot but remember past acts of courage and discipline which led me to entertain a high opinion of you as a soldier.'

" ' Sir,' said the man, ' do with me what you please. I know that I ought to be shot, but I could not stand it."

" ' Stand what?'

" ' What came to me as I held my post on the knoll.'

" These words, as may be supposed, excited our curiosity in the highest degree, and we waited impatiently for an explanation of them.

" ' Go on,' said the colonel; ' tell, without reserve, your story, and if I can find any cause for your conduct, it will give me far more pleasure to do so than utterly to condemn it.'

" Thus encouraged the man, after a brief pause, continued—

" ' Sir, I thought I feared nothing; but I was resolved to keep a sharp ook-uot after you had left me on my post. I listened with all my might, but all was still for some time after. I walked round the sentry-box to satisfy myself that no one was hiding there, and then I stood in the centre of the knoll, ready for anything that night, and determined that nothing but a bullet should take me by surprise. Nothing occurred for another five minutes or so, and then I saw a faint light among the bushes, a little to the left of the sentry-box. My first impulse was, of course, to rush towards it, but before I had got three steps I found myself face to face with Fawcett and Clifton, the two sentinels who had preceded me at my post, and so strangely disappeared.'

" ' Who? The two sentinels ?'

" ' Yes, sir. I came almost upon their heels. The moment I looked into their faces, the blood curdled at my heart, and I could not move a step. They were dead men, and blood was smeared upon their accoutrements, while a ghastly wound in the forehead of one, and some dreadful-looking lacerations about the other's face, showed by what violence they had come to their ends. They were dreadful to look upon. They bent their sorrowful eyes upon me, and stood between me and the light that shone among the bushes, but yet I could see it through them. Twice I tried to pass them, but they would not let me. I rushed upon them with my sword; it passed through them as through air merely, and then I scarcely know what I did; for, until I found myself in the barrack-room, surrounded by my comrades, I was unconscious of my actions.'

" He ceased. And certainly there was enough of the marvellous about the story he told fully to account for his conduct in a natural point of view, however little it might be estimated in a military one.

" The colonel saw, as indeed so did we all, that the guard in whose custody he was, had listened with greedy ears to the tale he had told, and being willing, as no doubt it was good policy to do, to reduce the effect of such asseverations as much as possible among the men, he said—

" ' Oh, you were dreaming, that's all about it. Remove the prisoner. We will investigate this matter to-morrow.'

" ' Shall I place another sentinel on the knoll, sir,' said the serjeant.

" ' Not till further orders.'

" When the room was clear, and we officers were alone together, the colonel looked at us for some moments in silence, and we looked at him.

" ' Well,' he said, at length, as he drew a long breath, ' what do you all think of this ?'

" We confessed the truth, namely, that we did not know what to think. The tale was too strange a one to believe, and yet by far too circumstantial to doubt. Besides, there was no such thing as getting over the fact, that the two sentinels had by some means or another very mysteriously disappeared, and that gave a sort of colour of truth to the whole affair.

" ' It would be cruelty, as well as I fear useless,' remarked the colonel, ' to place another sentinel on the knoll.'

" In this we all agreed; and then, as a slight pause ensued, I looked at my watch, and seeing that it wanted yet some time of daylight, I said—

" ' Colonel, the knoll ought not be left thus, in the hands of what we may call the enemy. It is, however, a service that you do not like to issue your commands to any of the men to engage in; will you permit me to go and hold the post ?'

" The colonel shook his head, dubiously, as he replied—

" ' I don't know that I ought really to consent to anything of the sort. My duty I think, clearly points out that I ought to send another of the men to act as sentinel in that place.'

" ' Yes, sir,' I replied, ' but you do not wish to do so; and recollect, whatever happens to me, I go as a volunteer.'

" ' True, true.'

" ' And these kind of acts on the part of officers always do good to the service by giving the men a sort of confidence in those whom they have to command them. I therefore make it a particular request to you that you will grant me permission to take the post.'

"I do not like to refuse you," he said, "and yet, at the same time, I must confess I do not feel myself justified in consenting."

However, after a little more pressing, he told me I might go; and accordingly, after seeing to the priming of my pistols, I, with my drawn sword in my hand, passed out of the colonel's room, and went through the guard room to the door of the barracks; but, as I passed out, I said—

"Let a guard be in readiness, if you hear the discharge of a pistol, to come to the Knoll immediately, and support me."

The soldiers said nothing, but I saw that they looked after me with regretful eyes, as I walked away upon a mission from which they never expected to see me return again with life.

"I beg your pardon, sir," said a sergeant, addressing me, "but I will go and take the post, if you please."

"No, no," I said, "I thank you. This is my own choice; I have volunteered, and will go through with the adventure."

No. 13.

I walked out and took my way to the Knoll. I must confess, although I had thoroughly made up my mind to go through with the adventure, that some misgivings as to what might be its result came over me as I did so, and I almost repented, not of going, but of not having a companion with me.

It was now, however, too late to think of mending the matter, so on I went, and in a very few minutes more I reached the spot which was said to have been fatal to two of our men, and which had driven another nearly out of his senses, and involved him in a serious breach of military duty.

There was a dim and uncertain sort of light in the air, which had about it something of a misty character, so that you could scarcely say whether you saw objects well around you or not. The sentry-box was there, just in the same place in which it had been left, and all was profoundly still.

I glanced towards Knollwood House, a necessity for watching which had given rise to all the disasters of the night, and I could see that lights still faintly gleamed from some of the windows, as if even at that hour—and it was one fast approaching the morning dawn—there were still persons up, and moving about within its chambers. I took good care, however, not to be for an instant off my guard, and I kept my pistols loosely in my belt and ready for action, while I held my sword, so that at any instant I could act upon the defensive. Now and then, too, I gave it a sweeping movement around me, which made it whistle through the night air, and may, for aught I know, have divided the incorporeal forms of a million of disembodied spirits.

But still I saw nothing, and heard nothing; and I began to think that, after all, I should hold the post quietly enough, for that either what the last sentinel had reported he had seen could not appear twice in one night, or was entirely the produce of his own excited imagination. The latter I thought the most reasonable proposition of the two, and I was getting quite boldly philosophical upon the subject, when suddenly, among the bushes to the left of the sentry-box, just as the soldier had described it, there came a faint, dancing, flickering sort of light.

"Gentlemen, I shall be better able to explain to you what followed, by a little aid from your own imagination, because much depends upon a knowledge of the relative position of one object with another. Let me see : we will suppose, then, if you please, that this vault in which we are assembled represents the Knoll, and that the door of it is the Knollwood House. Then, gentlemen, our president sits in the direction where you may suppose the barracks to be—"

"Yes, yes," said everybody.

"Very good :—my only desire, gentlemen, is to make my narrative perfectly plain to you all. Well, then, as I stand here, you will suppose, if you please, that the sentry-box is to my left hand."

"Yes, yes."

"Oh, but we can add much to the seeming reality of these points of my story, by pitching upon some object to represent it. Let me see—oh, this will do—will any gentleman assist me? Thank you, thank you—capital! You perceive, gentlemen, that, by putting the coffin up on end, we make a capital representation of the sentry-box."

The coffin on which he had been sitting was lifted up on one end, with its face next to the wall, in the direction he averred the veritable sentry-box stood, as regarded some trees that grew on the knoll, or, rather, on its borders.

When these arrangements were complete, he smiled and added :—

"Now, gentlemen, I shall be able to make you thoroughly understand, almost as if you were there when it occurred. The mysterious light continued dancing about, in the sort of hedge where it had first appeared, in a most inviting manner, and I thought I could perceive the dim outline of a hand holding it ; but of that I cannot speak with any degree of positive certainty.

"Unlike the soldier who had been so terrified, I would not advance towards the light, but had made up my mind to take no immediate step myself, but to wait and see what actually came to me, if anything; so that I could not be thrown off my guard.

"After some time, the light moved along a little in a horizontal direction, and I slowly turned, so as to keep my eyes fixed upon it; but as I did so, and it moved on still, it would in a short time be hidden from my sight by the intervention of the sentry-box.

"Before, however, that could occur, I popped into it, as I may now be supposed to do."

As he spoke, Mr. Annesley popped into the coffin, and was hidden from the view of the society, in consequence of its face being next to the wall. At the instant that he did so, they heard a strange, rattling sort of sound, as if something had fallen; and the coffin shook a little, and seemed nearly on the point of toppling over; but it did not do so, however, and they waited with breathless anxiety for him to go on with his narrative.

All was still. The narrator of the strange story was wonderfully quiet in the seclusion of the coffin. They waited with more patience than, under the circumstances, might fairly have been expected; and then, as no sound whatever reached their ears, something like a feeling of apprehension began to find a home in their hearts.

"What can be the meaning of this?" said one. "He does not speak, and he does not move."

"Something has happened to him," exclaimed another. "He is ill—perhaps dead."

"Then let us not," said the president, "allow fear to unman us. An instant examination of the coffin will put an end to all conjecture."

This was an evident enough proposition; and it was at once assented to by two or three of the boldest, who now advanced towards the coffin, and laid their hands upon it. From the first moment that they did so, a conviction came across all their minds that it contained nothing half so weighty as would have been a human being standing within it. It shook easily, and then it fell over on to the floor of the vault.

No Mr. Annesley was visible; but there was lying, in a huddled-up heap at the spot where he had last stood, some human bones, that fully, by their fall, might account for the strange noise that had been heard, immediately after he had disappeared from observation.

Now the full explanation of this phenomenon came at once to every mind; and with one accord they shrunk back from the ghastly remains of poor mortality, while the president exclaimed,

"This, then, is the same dreadful and mysterious being who, on the last occasion of our meeting, disappeared so strangely before our very eyes; and we have been again deceived by him!"

"It is too dreadful," said one, in a loud, excited voice. "This will lead us all the road to madness. I will not—I feel that I dare not—stay here another moment."

As he spoke, he rose and snatched up his hat, and then rushed from the vault.

It needed but something of this kind to give an impulse to the wavering feelings of the others; and, before all ordinary speed of enunciation one might have counted twenty, the vault was completely cleared of its late occupants, and left to the dead alone.

This second mysterious appearance and disappearance of the stranger, who had come among them with the very equivocal recommendation of a dead man on his lips, was such as might well excite an amount of terror and consternation far beyond the control of ordinary reasoning powers.

It seemed now quite clear to every one that the beings of another world were resolved, for good or for evil, to mix themselves up in the investigations of that fearful subject, to examine into which the club had been formed in the first instance.

In fact, the great question had thus become virtually settled, for who could any longer entertain the least doubt with regard to the capacity of the spirits of the dead to revisit the earth and mingle with its inhabitants in the likeness of what they were in life?

Here was an instance, not of a solitary individual whose imagination might have been acted upon by time, place, and circumstance, seeing what he believed to be a supernatural being, but twelve persons, or rather eleven, for we will not count the dead—eleven persons had actually looked upon the seeming form of a living man; had heard him discourse; had held conversation, and question and answer with him; and then, almost within the very sphere of their vision, they had beheld him change to a heap of loathsome bones.

Truly he who had rushed from the vault, giving utterance to the opinions that such scenes and occurrences were calculated to produce madness, was right.

Heaven only knows what effect the event was likely to have upon some of those who had witnessed it. Imaginative men they all were: the mere fact of joining such a club betrayed a half conviction of the truth of the opinion that spectral appearances may take place, but still there was something about the absolute demonstration they had now received upon the subject, which came home to every heart with a chilling, withering sensation.

There was no room for doubt—not a shadow of a loop-hole for scepticism to get in by; there was the skeleton that constituted the only tangible remains of the man whom they had been listening to, and thinking was a most eligible member of the society, both from the manner and the matter of his narrative.

It could be no trick—that was impossible, for there was no means of outlet, so that they were denied the consolation of thinking that possibly some day they might arrive at some rational solution of the mystery.

In this state of mind, then, they had all left the place, but there were two, whose roads being the same, kept together, and after a time, as they increased their distance from the vault, they began to talk more composedly upon the subject.

CHAPTER IV.

THE CONSULTATION, AND THE DEAD MAN'S SACK.

"I must confess," said one of these two persons to the other, "that what has to-night occurred has dissipated any lingering doubts I might still have entertained regarding supernatural appearances."

"Had you doubts?" asked the other.

"In truth, I had. There were some parts of the subject so difficult to reconcile to all our known experiences of the phenomena of nature, that I had many and serious doubts upon the subject."

"Which are now removed?"

"How can it be otherwise, when with my own eyes I have seen such things even as have taken place to-night?"

"True—most true—we cannot all be deceived. And in what way do you explain the strange proceedings?"

"It appears to me that our association has attracted the attention of the supernatural world, and that thus it is we are haunted. I have no doubt whatever but that our friend, who was killed by a fall from his gig, has been, although not visible to us, present at our meetings."

"Indeed!"

"Yes, we may know, we may even see—we may feel convinced of the fact of the appearance of supernatural beings, without being aware of the laws which operate upon them, so as to give them only certain powers at certain times, for that they, like all other creatures, are controlled within certain limits of action, I think we may fairly enough assume."

" Certainly."

" Well, then, for aught we know, our deceased friend may not have the power yet to make himself visible to our perceptions in the vault, although he may, for all we know to the contrary, have full power to show himself to an individual, as we are told he has done."

" Yes, yes. And now, with respect to this mysterious being, who has twice disappeared from among us ?"

" Then, as regards him, my opinion is, that he is the apparition of some one who has died so long ago, that his remains were in the state of decomposition and decay that we remarked in the skeleton form to which he undoubtedly changed when he lay down in the coffin."

" And you consider that heap of festering bones now lying on the floor of the vault to be that man ?"

" His earthly frame, certainly."

" Good God! it is horrible to think of."

" The probability is, that he only has the power of making his appearance within certain hours, and then is compelled to drop into the state of decay that has, by force of time, come over his mortal tenement."

" It must be so ; if you recollect he has, on both the nights of meeting, disappeared at as nearly as possible the same hour."

" He has; and that hour is the one at which the first dawn of daylight peeps up from the eastern sky. Now, do you think your nerves would permit you to catch a ghost ?"

" Catch a ghost ? What do you mean ?"

" I have a plan in my head, founded upon that mysterious individual, which I should not like to attempt alone, but which, if you will aid me in, I do not mind adventuring."

" What is it ?"

" This—it strikes me that his appearance consists in the reanimation of the remains of his mortal frame, by which means he is alone enabled to make himself visible, or otherwise the subtle spirit would not be of sufficient capacity to become discernible to our senses. Do you understand me, my friend ?"

" Perfectly ; go on, go on."

" Well, then, what I propose is this—that we take possession of his bones, and so prevent him from making use of them. In that case, if his spirit comes, and animates them with life, or the semblance of life, we shall have him in our power, and otherwise he will be rendered innoxious.

" What ? Take possession of his bones ?"

" Yes ; and why not ? It seems to me that we have but to go back to the vault and do so. Only consider, now, what strange revelations we may possibly get from him, if we once had him securely. The secrets of the immaterial world might be wholly at our disposal. There is a tempting prospect for you. Is it not worth a little trembling—aye, and even a little real risk?

" I do tremble indeed."

" Of course, it lies not within the compass of belief to expect that human nature would be able all at once to shake off completely the bonds of tyrant Custom, and look calmly on circumstances that it has been accustomed, from the earliest years, to regard with a shuddering horror. But, for all that, I cannot help believing that if you reflect upon this my proposal, you will soon be able to divest it of much of the terror with which, at the first glance, it seems to be associated, and to entertain it in its more interesting aspects."

The other (whose name was Bellamy) was silent for some time, and then, in a low, hesitating sort of voice, he addressed his companion—

" Mr. Harcourt," he said, " I cannot but own that you have done much to awaken my curiosity. But yet I cannot so quickly, as you appear to have done, get over the feeling of horror which your proposal has called into existence."

" You will soon."

" No, not soon, if ever. You are a man of stronger mental calibre than I, or such a strange, wild, and, I must add, positively fearful thought, would not have entered your mind."

"Oh, no! you do not, I am confident, give yourself credit for the real amount of resolution which, I dare say, you would in a little time find that you possessed, if you give the subject another thought."

"Well, well, while I am considering it, and endeavouring to reconcile my mind to it, let me know some of the details of your plan."

"Willingly. What I propose to do is to get a sack from somewhere, and go back to the vault with it at once. Then, into it we will place all the remains of our friend, who told the story of the sentinel, the conclusion of which I hope to hear from him yet."

"Yes, yes!"

"Then you and I can take the skeleton home to my house, where I will have it placed in perfect security, and at sunset to-morrow—or rather this day, I should say, for we are dipping into the morning—you can come to me, and we will watch for the result.'

"A strange plan!"

"And yet feasible enough. Do you see any objection to it?"

"None in execution—none but the world of terror which we may be doomed to endure eventually upon our success."

"Nay, why such a world of terror?"

"Can it be avoided? What would be our sensations to find that the skeleton was becoming actually before our eyes reanimated and instinct with life? Think you we could look upon such a sight and yet preserve our reason?"

"Aye, most assuredly! You view the matter much too seriously. Come, come; look upon it more with the calm and sober eye of reason; do not torment yourself with new fancies of fright that might arise, but rather ask yourself what real cause there is for terror."

"You cannot reason with the imagination."

"Yes, to a certain extent, you may. Now, to show you that the appearance of a supernatural being brings with it no real natural terror to the soul, if I may so express myself, I need but adduce the experience of to-night, when, for more than an hour, we sat all of us in the company of one whom we are convinced, as far as ocular demonstration can convince us, is a spectre, and heard it talk without any alarm or terror. It was not until the imagination was set to work upon the ascertained fact of his supernatural character, that we all became terrified."

"I grant all your reasoning—it is quite just and correct—I grant it all; but the effort will be a great one."

"You say will be."

"Yes—yes!"

"Then, you consent to be my companion in this enterprise?"

"I do."

"That is well. I rejoice to find that I have not mistaken my man. We will set about it instanter. I know a man in this immediate neighbourhood who keeps a public-house, which is open the whole night long, and from him it is highly probable I shall be able to procure a sack, with which we will go back to the vault."

This was assented to by Bellamy, and, as if fortune was determined upon giving them all the aid in its power, they found the publican both able and willing to lend them what they wanted, although he seemed not a little curious to know what it was wanted for.

Of course they evaded any explanation, leading him to believe that it was merely some practical jest they were about to play off at some one's expense, and that satisfied him.

"Now," whispered Mr. Harcourt, when they had gained the street again, "now, we are all prepared, and the sooner we get done that which we have to do, the better; for already I can perceive a difference in the aspect of all things, which proclaims that the dawn is coming rapidly."

This was indeed the case. The east was brightening each moment, and becoming more and more refulgent, while a soft, balmy sort of feeling in the air, proclaimed that the damp and cold mists of night were absorbing before the coming glory of the day.

They walked rapidly, and reached the old vault, in which the association held its meetings, in a much shorter space of time than they had succeeded in getting so far from it as the public-house.

They spake but few words, for the minds of both were full of the project upon which they were bound, and, no doubt, conjecture was most busy with them both, as to its probable and possible results.

They had facilities for getting into the vault, which we need not trouble the reader by detailing; suffice it to say, that every member of the association could, when he pleased, find his way to that place.

As they entered the gloomy abode of death they found that the ceiling-lamp was not quite extinguished, but appeared to be nearly at its last gasp, shedding but uncertain and feeble rays upon the melancholy-looking objects in that place, and the niches in the walls where reposed the dead.

By a little attention, however, to the lamp, they found that it would burn quite long enough for them to accomplish the business they came about, and burn well, too, for that period; so they proceeded towards the coffin so close to which lay— just as they had been left—that collection of bones, so yellow, humid-looking, and ghastly, which had surely constituted the corporeal fabric of him who had so abruptly terminated his anecdote of the ghostly sentinel.

"All is just as we left," said Mr. Harcourt, "and we have nothing to do but to place the bones in the sack."

"A loathsome task!" said Mr. Bellamy, with a shudder; "but still one which we will not now shrink from. Does it not strike you, however, that this supernatural being has a strong *penchant* for this particular coffin? On both the occasions on which he has appeared among us, and then disappeared, he has managed to do so in this one particular narrow house of the dead."

"You may depend it was the coffin in which he was buried."

"May we not possibly find a name upon it, and so set that question at rest?"

"A good thought!" cried Harcourt; "we will examine it carefully. Stay a moment; we want a better and a closer light for that purpose."

As he spoke he screwed up a piece of paper and lit it at the lamp; then, both he and Bellamy, by its assistance, looked narrowly along the lid of the coffin until they made out that there was a plate upon it, although much obscured, as was the inscription, by damp and time.

With some difficulty they did, however, at length succeed in making out the whole of it, and read it as follows :—

Robert Annesley,

DIED DECEMBER 18, 1762,

ÆTAT. 40.

"This, then, is the very man," exclaimed Mr. Bellamy. "If you recollect, he said his name was Mr. Annesley."

"He did; and by the date, he must have been dead, you perceive, somewhere about half a century, which fully accounts for the state of decay in which the body is, if body that can be called, which now is nothing but a collection of putrid-looking bones."

"Most true. This, then, is another piece of conclusive evidence as regards the supernatural character of the appearance."

"It is, indeed."

"Come on, then, Harcourt; we will not shrink now that we have gone so far; but I cannot bear the idea of touching the bones, and, without doing so, how is the body to be placed in the sack?"

" We must manage that somenow. Do you hold open the mouth of it while I push the skeleton in, and he will surely find it difficult now to appear without this part of his system."

Bellamy held the mouth of the sack open, close to the ground, and Harcourt having defended his hands from actual contact with the humid-looking remains of Annesley, succeeded in getting the whole of the skeleton into the sack, which they then closed and tied up firmly.

They glanced in each other's countenances simultaneously, as if each wished to read the thoughts that were busy in the other's breast; but they had not much time for such an examination, for the lamp that had only burnt well for a short time, in consequence of Mr. Harcourt having propped up the wick, showed sudden symptoms of going out, and then, before they could reach the door of the vault, all was darkness.

" Come on," said Bellamy, as he dragged the sack after him, " come on— come on. Harcourt, where are you ?"

No one spoke, and Bellamy again called to him :—

" Mr. Harcourt, why do you pause? Come on. This way to the door—this way. Are you not coming ?"

There was a death-like silence for a moment or two, and then Mr. Harcourt said in a choking whisper of the most fearful character—

"Something has got hold of me—I cannot come."

" Good God !" exclaimed Bellamy.

"Help, help!" gasped Harcourt. " Some bony fingers are round my neck! Help! Oh, help !"

A strange shrieking voice came then upon both their ears, which said—

" Away, away ! The dead with the dead ! The living with the living !"

" Leave it ! oh leave !" said Bellamy. " That is enough. Leave the sack and its frightful contents. The air is thick—I feel choking."

He made a desperate rush out of the vault, but such was the state of wild excitement and terror he was in, that although such a thing was most contrary to his intentions after what had occurred, he did actually drag the sack with him without knowing it.

" Fly, fly!" cried Mr. Harcourt. " By a miracle I have loosened my throat from the dreadful grasp that was fixed upon it ; I thought my death-hour had surely come, and that I should never look upon the light of day again."

They both stood in the open air. The first faint rays of the sun were now showing themselves on the tops of the church steeples and on the towers of the old cathedral, from one of the vaults of which they had just with so much terror and so much difficulty emerged.

" Thank God, we've abandoned the skeleton," said Bellamy.

" Abandoned it !" cried Harcourt. " Why, then, what is that you have in your grasp ?"

" That!—this!—what!—Bless me, I have brought it with me, unawares !"

" You do not know what you are about, you are in such a state of confusion but I am very glad you have brought it, for I should have felt loth indeed to have had such a fright, and all for nothing too."

" Are you glad ?"

" Aye, surely. But come on. Quick, quick! or we may be questioned as to what we have in the sack, and an examination of its contents would place us in an extremely awkward situation."

" Oh, Harcourt, had we not, even now, better take back this dreadful burthen to the resting-place of death, from whence we have taken it ? Who knows what may be the consequences of this violating the sanctity of the dead ? Let us take it back, and think no more of the desperate and ill-judged enterprise on which we came, and which we have had ample warning to desist from carrying out further."

" No," said Mr. Harcourt, " no: if you will not aid me any further, I will alone pursue this adventure. After all the trouble that has been taken, I will not now abandon it."

"Think again."

"I am decided—quite decided: but far be it from me, if it has become unpalatable, to wish to drag you into the affair. Now you may, if you please, wash your hands of it entirely."

"No, no; I will not do that: if I cannot persuade you to abandon it, you shall not find me abandon you."

"Well said: so now come on. Why, what did we expect, but some sort of strange results, from what we are about?"

"Well, well—be it so; but what was it, do you think, that detained you in the vault, Harcourt?"

"I scarce can tell you. All I know is, that the moment the light went out something laid hold of me by the throat. It felt so cold and hard that I can think it could be nothing but the fleshless hand of some of the skeleton inhabitants of that dreadful place. I felt my heart cease for a moment to beat, my breath going, and I could scarcely speak at all."

No. 14.

"And when you did, your voice was strangely altered."

"No doubt; but yet I think that, whatever it was that held me, it had not much physical power; for, when I made an effort to do so, I soon freed myself from the strange grasp. Then I heard a rattling sound, as of bones; and, waiting for no more, I rushed out after you as quickly as I could."

"This is a night of horrors, and Heaven knows what the next one may be."

"Think nothing of it, Bellamy. I am myself inclined to believe that these super-natural beings would have but little power indeed, if we did not give it them by our fears. Once confronted, and they are virtually beaten. Come down this street—it is a shorter cut to my house, as well as a less populous road."

About a quarter of an hour's walking brought them to Harcourt's house; and, as he was a bachelor, he could go in and out at any hour that suited him, and no one could ask him a question upon the subject. He let himself and Bellamy in with a latch-key, and then they carried the sack, with its strange contents, into a small room, which Mr. Harcourt used as a little library and study. He locked the door of that apartment, and put the key in his pocket, so that there could be no possi-bility of any one interfering with the sack and its contents; and then he, by the loud ringing of a bell, succeeded in arousing an old woman who waited upon him, and ordered some breakfast to be prepared.

As they both partook of this meal, Bellamy agreed that at sunset that evening he would come to Mr. Harcourt's house, and that together they would watch the skeleton form that was in the sack, to see if any process of revivification took place during the night.

No doubt the whole of the day that had to intervene before they met was passed by both in reflections upon what had so singularly occurred, and in antici-pation and conjecture as to what might yet result from the adventure, which, the more it was thought of, assumed a more fearful aspect.

Mr. Harcourt being of a somewhat wild and adventurous disposition, no doubt did not at all repent of what had been done; but Mr. Bellamy as certainly did—although a sort of chivalric feeling which he had, prevented him now from thinking of abandoning Harcourt to go through the adventure alone. However much he disliked the affair—and whatever misgivings he had upon the subject—he kept to himself, and at the appointed hour he reached Mr. Harcourt's house-door. He found that gentleman anxiously expecting him; and, together, they proceeded to the room in which the sack was placed.

They had candles lighted, and every preparation made to enable them to pass the night there with comfort, if the state of their feelings would permit them to do, so, which was a very doubtful proposition. And there was a sack in the corner of the room lying in an odd, huddled-up, collapsed state, on account of the bones falling to the bottom of it.

"Well, Bellamy," said Mr. Harcourt, as he poked the fire, and elicited from it a cheerful, crackling blaze, "what do you anticipate will be the issue of our night's adventure?"

"I have no hypothesis upon the subject," said Bellamy; "I never was so lost in a complete sea of conjecture in my life."

"And I must confess to being really much in the same condition," said Harcourt. "It does seem something positively incredible that yon bones should ever again become vital, or that the spirit which death has released from its prison-house of flesh, should ever again inhabit it."

"It does; and yet, with our experience of last night, we can deny nothing, on the ground of its unintelligibility to use. If what we have seen be contrary to all that we know, or fancy we know, of the established and inimitable laws of nature, there may be some other laws regarding the immaterial universe, of which we have no possible idea."

"That is true. These are not days to doubt the existence of phenomena in, merely because we cannot understand them."

"Certainly not. But what now is the most advisable course to pursue as regards our friend in the sack? Is he to be left there, or taken out and brought into sight?"

This was a question which they both found it difficult at once to answer, but at length Mr. Bellamy said—

"My own impression is, that we had better leave him where he is. We shall soon find out if anything comes of the affair."

"Well, be it so!"

It was yet an early hour, so they amused themselves, partly with coffee and cigars, and partly by conversation. They would not, by mutual consent, drink wine, because they were so determined that they would be cool-headed, and thoroughly capable of looking calmly and dispassionately upon whatever might take place, so they kept to the coffee, which was a pleasant occupation the drinking it even of itself, and served very well to wile away the time.

Nine, ten, and eleven o'clock were announced in due order by a time-piece that was on the mantel-shelf, but nothing had occurred to disturb the repose of the place; and the sack of bones, to which it may be well imagined very frequent glances were directed, remained just as they had placed it.

Long impiety in anything begets a certain sort of bold recklessless, and, as hour after hour thus flew by, and nothing of an alarming character occurred at all, Mr. Harcourt began almost to feel disappointed.

"I certainly, Bellamy," he said, " did not expect all these hours to have passed away so peaceably."

"Indeed?"

"No; I did expect, after the sort of opposition we had experienced in the vault in taking the bones away, that we should, in some way or another, have been made subjects of attack by the beings of the supernatural world."

"Wait a bit," said Bellamy; "I think I may with propriety call your attention to that proverb which inculcates upon people the propriety of not hallooing until they are out of the wood."

"Very good!"

"Wait till the morning has fairly dawned before we venture to talk of the adventures of to-night."

"Spoken like a very Mentor."

"The clock on the mantel-shelf made a strange noise, which it always did at five minutes before striking any hour. What for, Heaven and the clock-maker only knew; but it always sounded as if somebody had said 'Hush!'"

"It wants but five minutes now," said Mr. Harcourt, " to the witching hour of night, and as yet nothing has happened."

"Not as yet."

"Bellamy, you expect something?"

"I do."

"Have you any special reason?"

"No—yes."

"No and yes! What —— God bless me, it moves!'

They both fixed their eyes intently on the sack, and saw that there was a slight motion towards the upper part of it. Then a deep groan came upon their ears, and the clock struck twelve.

"Look, look! Harcourt!" said Bellamy,—"look!"

They both fixed their eyes intently on the sack, which now began to exhibit some strange manœuvres. No sooner had the clock struck twelve, than in the first instance there came a short, stifled sort of cry from the interior of the sack, and in lieu of hanging about loose and flaccid as it had done, it filled out amazingly. Then it was violently agitated, finally falling upon the floor, where it tossed and rolled about in a most extraordinary manner, the short, half-smothered screams coming from it as before.

"Fly, fly!" cried Bellamy, " I cannot stand this.'

Harcourt held up his hand and motioned him to be still, and then he said, in a deep, serious tone—

"Be you what you may, strange and inexplicable being, whom we have brought hither, be assured that it is with no evil intent.   Speak to us, speak, we beseech you, Robert Annesley—for that we believe to be your name—speak to us !"

All was still in an instant.   The sack lost its rotundity completely, and lay upon the floor without the appearance of containing anything more than the few bones which had been brought home in it.

"He is gone !" gasped Harcourt, "he is gone !"

Even at the moment that he uttered these words, there came a sharp rat-tat at the street-door, and in a few minutes, the old woman who attended him, put her wrinkled face inside the study-door, saying—

"It's a fine time of night to come visiting, and so I told him, but he won't take a denial, not he."

"What do you mean ?"

"A gentleman has called to see you.   He says he must see you on important business, but I don't like the looks of him."

"Who is he ?"

"I don't know.   He says his name is of no consequence at all.   He's not a bad-looking man either, but still, there is a something about him that makes one give a sort of shudder, and one's blood run cold, somehow.   I don't like him, and I only hope he won't be here often."

"Admit him," said Harcourt, in a faint tone of voice, and he fixed his eyes with an uneasy expression upon the door of the room.

"Who is it ?" said Bellamy.

"Heaven knowns," replied Harcourt ; "hark ! he comes.   The adventures of this night, as you have said, are not yet over."

The tramp of a footstep came upon their ears, and the old servant opened the door wide for the admission of a tall, gentlemanly-looking man, attired with remarkable neatness, although in something of the costume of an age gone by. However, there was nothing so extravagant in the antiquity of his dress to make it a very marked feature in his personal appearance.   He bowed with much polite-ness as he came into the apartment, and in a rich, soft, bland voice, he said—

"Pray, gentleman, do not let me disturb you.   I fear my presence here looks almost like an intrusion, but it is not intended as such, and I can assure you Mr. Harcourt, and you Mr. Bellamy, that nothing but urgent business would have induced me to come at such an hour."

"Urgent business," said Mr. Harcourt, falteringly, "is a sufficient——"

"Exactly," said the stranger, interrupting, "a sufficient excuse for any intru-sion, but then he who comes upon such business should state it quickly, lest he be considered one of those troublesome persons who are always themselves in a trouble—keep every one else so, and yet get nothing done."

"Very good; and is, I think——"

"'That the sooner I say what has brought me here the better,' you were going to add.   Certainly, sir, certainly.   Will you oblige me with that bag and its contents, Mr. Harcourt ?"

"That—that—that bag ?"

"Yes, sir.   That bag which now lies by Mr. Bellamy's feet.   By-the-by, how is your wife, Mr. Bellamy, after her loss ?"

"Loss, sir !"

"Yes, when you go home, you will find a corpse in your house."

"A corpse !"

"Yes, don't be alarmed, your mother-in-law dropped down dead, just now."

"My—mother—in—law !"

"Yes, but you need not put yourself in the least out of the way about it ; your wife is, at present, inconsolable, but that is a safe feeling ; if left to herself, she will recover before a new moon."

"And pray, sir, who may you be ?"

"Oh, I may be anybody, or anything ; but permit me, sir, to   say,   that   it   is not the politest question which one gentleman can ask of another. Did I ask you now, Mr. Bellamy, who you were?"

"No, but you know."

"Oh, that is an accident: you might know who I was, and it would not put me in the least out of the way; but, honestly speaking, I have no time to spare, so, Mr. Harcourt, I have to throw myself upon your courtesy to oblige me with that sack, if you please?"

"The—the sack with the bones?" stammered Mr. Harcourt.

"Yes, yes; how quickly and pleasantly some people take one's meaning. The sack with the bones I mean; but you are reluctant, my dear sir, and why? now why should you be reluctant? it is really foolish. By keeping such a thing you accomplish a number of bad points: now, in the first place, you much disturb your own mind; in the next, you much disturb the mind of your friend, Mr. Bellamy, here. By-the-by, Bellamy, your wife has just fainted away, and it's next thing to a miracle she has not fallen down stairs and broken her neck: you had better go home now."

"Who the devil are you?" said Bellamy.

"Hush—hush—I really thought that in genteel society that name was never heard. I am surprised at you, sir! Mr. Harcourt, will you give me that sack?"

"You are a stranger to me," said Harcourt, "and I don't know why I should give up to you that which has taken me some trouble to get here. If you will tell me who you are—now—"

"Pshaw! what can that matter to you? I am a friend, an old friend of Robert Annesley, and, therefore, have a right to demand him at your hands, if I choose to do so. Give him up to me at once, or I am afraid some of your windows will be broken before even I, if I feel inclined, could prevent such a catastrophe."

As he spoke, as if his voice had been a signal for such an outrage, there came upon the ears of the friends a frightful collection of howls and yells, as if from the back part of the house, and then nearly the whole of the windows of the room in which they sat were dashed in.

"Hold!" cried the stranger, rising and lifting up his hand; "Mr. Harcourt, may I take the sack?"

"Yes, yes," gasped Mr. Harcourt, "take it in God's name, and take yourself off too, as quickly as you can."

In an instant the mysterious stranger seized upon the sack containing the skeleton form, and throwing it through the broken window, he shouted—

"House! house! house!"

Another strange yell, apparently of triumph, broke upon the stillness of the night-air, and then the two candles, which were burning upon the table, instantly went out, and all was still.

"Lights! lights!" cried Mr. Bellamy, "have lights, Harcourt; don't let us be in the dark. Here, lights! lights, I say!"

Mr. Harcourt rang the bell violently. and, in a moment or two, the old servant made her appearance with a candle, looking very much confused, as she said—

"Did you please to ring?"

"Did I please to ring? why, do you mean to say you have heard nothing of this uproar that has taken place?"

"Uproar, sir!"

"Uproar, sir! why woman, have you been to sleep? The window is smashed to pieces, as you will see if you uncover the blind, and the candles have gone out mysteriously of themselves."

"Have they really, sir?" said the old woman; "I don't see nothing mysterious in a candle going out when there's no fat; they have burnt out, of course, and you can't expect candles to last for ever, sir, I suppose; and as for the window being broke I don't see as it is at all. No! now I move away the blind, sir, I'm sure it aint, it's all whole as it was afore. You must have gone to sleep yourselves, and have dreamed a dream, I'm thinking; a good joke, indeed, to tell me I have been asleep when it's yourselves all the while. A good joke, i'faith. Marry, come up! a very good joke, ah! ah! very good!"

"Will you hold your horrible prating?" cried Harcourt, as he hastily rose, and walked to the window, which, to his intense surprise, had not the least appearance of a fracture about it.

"Why, Bellamy," he said, "how is this? The window is perfect; and you know we could have sworn the greatest portion of it was broken, and even the framework of it smashed in."

"I cannot make it out."

"Nor I. I am completely beaten by all this. Two men may go to sleep at one and the same time; but they don't dream the same dream exactly, at one and the same time."

"Certainly not. Besides, I deny the fact of having been to sleep at all. It is ludicrous to suppose such a thing. We were both wide awake and watchful when the sack first began to show symptoms of something vital being within it. I do not pretend to be able to explain what has occurred; but, upon the idea of our having been asleep, I place a decided negative."

"And I."

"As far as the candles are concerned, I think, of course, that we may have over-looked the fact that they were nearly burnt out; and so we need not count the sudden darkness in which we were enveloped as anything extraordinary; although it favoured the disappearance of our mysterious visitor, by some means which, in consequence of the want of light, we were not in a situation to see or understand."

"Precisely. But the most mysterious affair still is, the disappearance of the sack. Is it not?"

"What sack?" said the old woman. "There's a sack there now—up by the corner of the window there."

They both cast their eyes in the direction she indicated; and there, sure enough, they saw the identical sack, which they supposed had been taken away, in the same place it had always occupied since it had been brought into the room, not-withstanding they fancied, and up to that moment would have had no hesitation in at once declaring, that the mysterious stranger took it up the moment he had received permission so to do, and cast it through the broken window.

But there it was. There was no mistaking now the fact of its presence; and, as the old woman, with much grumbling about the lateness of the hour, and audible wonderings as to how long they intended to sit up, had now accommodated them with fresh candles, they sat looking at the mysterious sack in silence, and occasionally casting a sidelong glance on each other's countenance.

"What do you think of that?" said Mr. Harcourt, at length, "what do you think of that, Mr. Bellamy?"

"What do you?"

"I don't know what to think; but I'll endeavour to furnish myself with an idea, by looking into the sack."

As he spoke, he strode towards it, and laid his hand upon it. It sunk down in a moment into a state of collapse.

"Holloa!" he exclaimed, "it's empty. Look—look."

He lifted it from the floor and tossed it towards Bellamy, who found, by the manner in which it fell at his feet, that it was indeed perfectly emptied of its contents.

"Whoever," said Bellamy, "our visitor was—and that he belonged to another world I think we cannot doubt—he has accomplished his purpose by taking away with him those sad remnants of mortality which we had possession of, and which, as things have turned out, I think we are well rid of."

"You are right: he did not belong to this world, or he could not have accom-plished what he did. But I will ask my old servant if she saw anything of him, as he left."

This was done; but, to their surprise and astonishment, not unmingled with some degree of consternation of them both, she declared that not only was she ignorant of any one leaving, but that it was all a delusion of their own to suppose that she had admitted any one. She denied *in toto* that there had been any knock at the door, or that she had announced or introduced any visitor.

This made the matter ten times worse; and both Bellamy and Harcourt were perfectly staggered at the affair taking such an aspect. They found themselves in a perfect maze of difficulty, from which they could see no escape; and not the least glimmering of light came to illumine the mental darkness in which they were enshrouded.

Mr. Bellamy felt some anxiety on account of the information which the mysterious visitor had furnished him with respecting some occurrences that were taking place at his house, and he rose to go, saying—

"At all events, Mr. Harcourt, we have no other means of knowing that what has passed to-night is not all imaginary, besides the abstraction of the bones from the sack. You recollect that the strange being who was here told me that my mother-in-law was dead."

"He did. Was she ailing?"

"No; I left her in perfect health; and no one for a moment could have expected such an occurrence as her sudden death. I shall now go home, and soon be able to test the truth of what he said. Will you, for your own satisfaction in this most mysterious piece of business, accompany me?"

"I will, if I shall not, at such an hour as this, be intruding on you by so doing."

"Not at all, not at all. Come at once, for I own to you I am anxious."

They both at once left the house, and as they walked at a brisk pace to Mr. Bellamy's, which was not far off, they conversed deeply upon the proceedings of that night of mystery, and in some respects of terror.

They arrived at length at Mr. Bellamy's door, and he knocked and rang for admission—a summons which was answered by one of the female domestics, who, the moment she saw her master, exclaimed—

"Oh, sir, I am glad you have come home! We have lost missus's mother, sir."

Mr. Bellamy looked at Harcourt, as much as to say, "There, you see he was right!" and the other only lifted up his eyes.

"And missus was so affected, if you please, sir," said the servant, "that after she left her mother's bed-room, sir, she fainted away, and fell down within a inch of the stair-head; if she had have felled down that stairs she'd have been killed as sure as my name is Jane, sir, and no sort of mistake. It was a whole two thousand mercies, sir, done up in one."

"There again," said Bellamy to Harcourt, "there again! Come in, come in."

"No," said Harcourt, "not into this house of mourning; but, as Hamlet says, 'I'd take the ghost's word for a thousand pounds.'"

"And I—and I."

"Good night, or rather, good morning! It will be our duty, as members of the club, to report all that has passed to our brethren when next we meet. Adieu, for the present—adieu!"

CHAPTER V.

THE THIRD MEETING OF THE ASSOCIATION, AND THE TALE OF THE WEDDING GUEST.

It seemed to be rather a doubtful proposition now, after what had occurred, whether the club would meet again or not, for they had all received so great a shock in consequence of the second appearance and horrible disappearance of the man who called himself Robert Annesley, and who contrived with so much ingenuity always to make his way into a coffin, that some of the less resolute members might be said to have actually made up their minds not to go again.

But the very irresolution of purpose which prompted them to come to such a resolve went a long way to prompt them to break it again. Timidity is a feeling of the human mind of the lowest class, and it goes hand-in-hand with many other low-class feelings, curiosity being one among the number, so that there was a likelihood of the latter feeling successfully combating with the former in many minds.

And then it must be considered, that it was not as if something had to be done by an individual, from which he might well shrink. Many a man, without apparently much shrinking, will look upon dangers and frightful sights, if he have others with him who are looking upon them likewise, who would no more dare to do so alone, than he would dare to leap off the Monument. And so it was with the members of this association. Whatever fears came over them, they always recollected that they were not alone; and, whatever dangers the love of the strange inquiry in which they were involved might lead them to, they always had others with and around them, to take share and share. This feeling then it was, that towards the night of meeting enabled those who had even the most firmly resolved not to go to shake off the inclination, and to think that it would be just as well to put in an appearance at the vault, in order to see if anybody else came, and if they found that such was not the case, why then of course, nothing would or could be easier than to come away again at once, and no harm done.

But the effect of all the recoverers pursuing such a course as this was, that by the time the hour of meeting came, there was a full assemblage of the association, and not a soul was missing.

To be sure, we must admit they did not, as upon the first occasion, walk in with that bold look of scientific cleverness which they had thought themselves entitled to, even as men engaged in a deeply philosophical inquiry, but they lingered about the entrance, first of all, until five of them had collected, and then they went in in a body, and replenished the oil in the lamp, and lit it.

There appeared nothing at all unusual in the vault, and in the course of another five minutes the whole eleven members had assembled.

Many anxious and uneasy glances were directed to the coffin in which Mr. Annesley had disappeared, but as it lay in the same position which it had been left in, no one but Messrs. Bellamy and Harcourt were aware that anything new had occurred in connexion with it.

And these two gentlemen, after a little debate with themselves, thought that they would defer until some other time the relation of what had occurred; besides, they had a sort of expectation that something would happen that evening in which the apparition of Robert Annesley might again figure.

It wanted yet some time to twelve o'clock, for, owing to the feeling of anxiety which had come over everyone present, to ascertain if his companions were likely to come, all had reached the spot uncommonly early, and the association ccordingly commenced business a good twenty minutes before its usual time.

"Gentlemen," said the president, "be seated."

The members seated themselves upon the various coffins that had been dragged from the niches in the walls of the vault for their accommodation.

Mr. Bellamy whispered to Harcourt:—"Let us take possession of Robert Annesley's coffin."

"A good thought! a good thought!" replied Harcourt; "we will; and so we can prevent him from playing off a third trick upon us and the rest of the association."

"Exactly; we will be proof against all he may attempt!"

"We will—we will!"

They drew that coffin forward, and, turning it bottom upwards, they sat down upon it to the surprise of some of the members of the club, who, in consequence of the part which it had played in the mysterious transactions of the other evenings, would not on any account have had anything to do with it.

"You are aware, I presume," whispered one to Harcourt, "that you are sitting upon the same coffin that Annesley disappeared in ?"

"Yes, thank you, I know."

"Oh, very well!   I only mentioned it, in case you did not know, that's all."

"I like it."

"The devil you do !"

"Now, gentlemen," said the president, "I don't know exactly really what to say to you this evening, for so many strange things have occurred in connexion with this society and its meetings, that I am—as I have no doubt you all are—completely in a state of amazement at them."

"Hear, hear !" said one, faintly.

"Gentlemen, let us, in the first place, ascertain exactly who is here.   Let us see if any stranger is among us, and if not we will close the door and secure it."

This was done ; the eleven were counted, and it was completely ascertained, by a most careful inspection of the vault, that no one was there hidden.   The door was made fast by an iron bar that went across it, and then the president continued,—

"Now then, gentlemen, we are for the present convinced that we are alone,

No. 15.

and that nothing human can come in without our sanction. Let us commence business at once in our regular way."

This was acceded to, and the skull which contained the names of the members of the club who had not yet told any tales to their companions, was produced.

The president, with great solemnity, put in his hand, and for a moment or so found a difficulty in getting it out again; but he at length brought out a scrap of paper, on which he announced that the name appeared of Mr. Rottibonum.

Some of the younger of the members laughed at the announcement of this name; but as he was known to be a highly respectable man, the president stopped such levity, and gravely rebuked those who had been guilty of it.

"You should recollect," he said, "that Mr. Rottibonum did not invent his own name, and I beg you will keep order."

The individual upon whom the lot had fallen to relate a tale now rose and said, in a voice which betrayed a little nervous agitation,—

"Really, Mr. President and Gentlemen, I must confess to you that I do hesitate to take up your valuable time after the great talent that has been displayed by various gentlemen that have been called upon."

Here there were several cries of "Never mind!" "Go on, sir!" "We know your talent, Mr. Rottibonum!" and so on, to all of which compliments he bowed, and added,—

"Do not suppose, gentlemen, that it becomes any part of my intention to evade the duty which you have been pleased to place upon me."

Loud cries of "Hear, hear, hear!"

"Do not suppose that, gentlemen, for a single moment—I should be a most unworthy member of this club if I did so; and so far as my poor abilities will permit me, I will contribute my quota to the general fund of information."

The president tapped upon the coffin before him with the knee-cap of some skeleton in order to procure order, and the members took up the posture that each best liked in order to pay due attention to the narrative of Mr. Rottibonum, which they doubted not would be deeply interesting. For a few moments he seemed to be collecting his thoughts. He looked up at the lamp, and looked down to the floor, and then his eyes wandered all round the vault.

In these preliminaries the members all imitated him; for, for aught they knew to the contrary, he might have a motive in them, and be upon the point of directing their attention in some way to some object which was within the sphere of their vision. Such, however, was not the case; and with a rapidity of utterance that, until they got a little used to it, they found it difficult to follow, the gentleman commenced.

"The tale which I am about to tell to you, Mr. President and Gentlemen, I shall, with your permission, entitle—

"THE WEDDING GUEST; OR, THE SPECTRE OF THE OLD CHANCEL.

"It must now be more than fifteen years since I travelled. I have left that off now, but I used to be here, and there, and everywhere, as the saying is, but now I am more at home, and less abroad; but yet I have seen a few things in my time. A man with any brains cannot travel without learning something, and I learnt a little now and then, which I have not forgotten, nor am I likely to do so.

"I was making a tour through some of the Northern Counties upon business, when I had occasion to pass a few days at Appleby, where I staid, more in consequence of an accident that compelled me to remain, than from any other motive, and before I was ready to prosecute my journey, I had several days' leisure. This time I used by visiting the neighbouring places, that were worth walking over, to see, and all was seen and examined as far as I could tell, but I couldn't unaided explore every nook and cranny in that county. It is a very picturesque part of the country, full of old recollections, both legendary and historical, for all places in that quarter have at one time or another been the scene of many fierce encounters between the borderers, and it was chiefly respecting these matters that I inquired about. I lodged at an ancient-looking hostel, where I experienced both civility and good fare, and there was certainly no stint. I enjoyed the rides and drives about Appleby much, so much so, that I shall never forget that journey, and the occasion which took me there, if I have to live as many years as those that have passed over my head. I said I had seen all, at least I thought so, and one morning, as I sat over my breakfast, pondering over my own thoughts and recollections on and of what I had heard and seen, I began to wonder if there was anything more worth seeing. It was this day's discovery, and what I heard, that makes the whole of that visit so indelibly imprinted upon my mind, so much that I shall not forget it while Memory holds her place as one of the faculties of my mind. Well, I was saying, I wondered if there was anything more that I could make myself acquainted with, but recollected no road, nor any place where there was any chance of lighting upon an old ruin, or a stray adventure. At that moment the landlord entered the room; he came in for the purpose of inquiring how I had slept during the night. I told him I had slept very well indeed.

"Why, sir," he said, " I thought you might have heard the strangers, who came here in the night."

"I heard no one come," I replied, "and, moreover, I have seen none this morning. All is quiet."

"Why, they didn't come until this morning, between one and two o'clock, and they are not up yet; they made some noise, and I feared they would wake you."

"Oh, no, I heard nothing of them. By-the-way, landlord, I don't know how to spend the day here; I have been about, and have seen everything worth seeing, or of which anything can be said, and I don't know where to turn next."

The landlord looked with a knowing look at the tea-pot for a moment or two, and then said—

"Have you been to the ruins of the old chapel?"

"No," said I, "I haven't seen any such thing; where is it?"

"About three miles down the lane, that runs through the fields here behind the town; the road is almost unused, only occasionally as a cross-road, and that not very frequently."

"What sort of place is it?"

"Oh, I can't tell, sir, but it's something like a church, with all the roof knocked off, and the windows knocked out, and the doors knocked down, and the walls re, some of 'em that is, knocked down, and ivy here, and ivy there, and is, in short, a very queer-looking place altogether."

"I should like to see it," said I; "if you will put me in the way, I'll spend a few hours in looking over the old ruin, for I dare say it must be more than a chapel after all, but more properly, the remains of some ancient church."

"Oh, why, as for that matter," said the landlord, in an important tone, "it is one of the 'has beens;' it certainly looks like a large place, but the size don't appear so great, when a good part of it has been knocked away."

"Certainly not; we cannot expect half an apple to look as big as a whole one."

"That's very true," said the landlord, "very true indeed, and if you go out at the north side of the town, you are sure to come into the lane, if you turn sharp round to the left, and then, about two hundred yards more, you are safe in the road and can't miss your way."

"About three miles," I said; "that, I think, you call the distance between this and the ruins."

"Yes—thereabouts; a little bit more, I reckon, but scarce anything to speak of."

"I dare say I shall get there in an hour: the walk will do me good."

After a little more conversation with mine host, I determined to set out, and did so accordingly. I left the town by the north gate, and went about two hundred yards to the left, when I came to the road spoken of by the landlord of the inn where I was stopping, and I pursued it for some time. The road was very picturesque, very beautiful, and, I may say, quite romantic. I never saw a place that pleased me better. The road, I should imagine, must be impassable sometimes in winter, for there was no road-making about it; and, in very wet weather, or after long rains, it must have been axle-deep in mud and earth. This, no doubt, was the reason why the road was so little used, save in the summer or in hard weather ; and then it must have been one that would give pleasure to any journey : and I had wandered a full hour-and-a-half before I began to think that I ought to have come upon the ruins.

"I have scarcely been more than three miles,", I thought ; "but he said a little more, and that may be another mile, at the least : and yet, I have been a good four miles to this place. However, I will pursue the road, for it is well worth the walk to see it—much less the ruin, if I find it, and if it be what it has been represented to me."

I walked on, well pleased, at every turning of the lane, to find some new feature presented to my view ; some new group of trees fantastically arranged ; old stumps decayed, but that at one time served as supports to the stems of ivy which now encircled them, and held them up in the same position they had grown in, and effectually hid them from the eye of the looker-on. Then again, the hedge-rows were filled with tall weeds in full blossom ; they looked gay and very beautiful— their blossoms jutting out of the green masses as if they had been so arranged for a nosegay.

It is very strange, but there are many beautiful flowers that grow wild in the woods and hedges that are neglected, though many that cannot boast of their beauty are cultivated in gardens.

" Where are these ruins?" said I to myself. I could give myself no answer ; and there was no one else to whom I could apply for a solution to what appeared a great difficulty.

However, I was not doomed to be long in the doubtful position I felt myself placed with regard to the discovery of the object of my search ; for when I had reached an eminence not far off, I could perceive on my left many old trees, and ivy-grown beds. I determined that I would make for the spot ; and accordingly did so—it promising some pleasing combinations.

Off I went at a hasty walk, and found myself going down the hill ; for it lay in a hollow about half a mile below the hill ; and, as I descended, the hedge-rows, which here grew very luxuriantly, not having been trimmed for years, completely shut out all view of the spot I was making for.

When I came down to the spot I saw there was, instead of a clump of trees, a number of old walls standing, completely encrusted with ivy and moss that had been growing for many years—long before the time of the decay of the edifice itself.

There were the ruins, certainly ; but they were not so old, and not such sheer ruins as what I had anticipated from the landlord's description. There were entire walls standing, but there was also a profusion of ivy ; the soil, enriched with the unction of dead men, seemed adapted to the luxuriant growth of the plant, and yew trees were abundant.

"These walls," I thought, "were never built by modern hands ; they bear the marks of antiquity about them ; and they also appear to have been the work of ruder artists than those who are employed in these days : but the material was lasting, and the masonry was well cemented with a cement which seemed very little less in hardness than stone itself."

There were many decaying monuments around, that told of dead men of many ages gone by : them were some of them crowned with the same plant that seemed so luxuriant in this place.

The entrance had suffered less, in some respects, than the other parts. The doors were thick, and they had so far fallen and decayed, that they became immoveable without entire destruction ; and the crumbling mass threatened any one who should attempt to remove them. The entrance to the pile appeared to be anywhere rather than by the doors ; for there were breaches in all the walls, and the windows were entirely gone. There were some few iron stanchions—but so thn and rusted that they might easily be thrust from their places.

" Well," thought I, " this is well worth seeing ; but it only stands because there is nothing to knock it down. Decay has been at work : the very walls now are soft, and many parts would fall down, I dare say, if I were but to add my weight to the mass."

There was no doubt of the truth of my surmise; and when I got through a breach, I placed my hand upon the wall to help myself over, when I nearly fell, for some bushels of rubbish gave way, and came to a heap at my feet.

"A few years more," I muttered to myself, "and then this place will be no longer what it is. I may, perhaps, in vain look for the site of the old ruins."

I walked about, looking at the ruins, examining the effigies, and trying to decipher the old inscriptions, but found this rather too difficult a task, except in a few instances. They were unimportant, and only served to enumerate the individuals of a family whose remains occupied certain vaults, or certain portions of the long since disused burial ground.

The sun was high, and the walls of the church, ivy-crowned as they were, served as a good shelter from his burning rays, and the shadows were deep.

I paused in the aisle, and saw that the marble pavement was sound—at least, portions of it; for there was one part that seemed quite fresh, and made a pathway right up to the church-door, with some dark spots, or rather, a string of them, some closer, and some larger than others.

The marble pavement, elsewhere, seemed to have followed the fate of the other parts of the building, and had, as far as the material permitted, decayed; and between the stones, the interstices between them, were growing rank weeds, that spread over the surrounding stones, but none of them encroached upon the stones with the dark spots.

There was something strange about this—very singular—for the stones did not follow each other in a right line, but in a somewhat slanting direction, and stopped at the chancel-door, and then there was no further trace of them. I could not forbear saying aloud—

"There is something very odd or singular about these stones. What can there be that makes them remain fresh from all the others? Surely none of the Reformation enormities were committed here; and the monks, rather than leave their houses, chose to stain the very stones. Surely it cannot be human blood that stains the stones."

"It is human blood that stains the stones," said a deep-toned voice beside me, but in slow and measured sounds, "it is human gore that marks the way to you chancel-door—yes, it is human blood."

I started, for I had seen no one, and you may well judge of my amazement when I turned round and beheld a tall, gaunt old man sitting upon a heap of rubbish.

He was no less picturesque than the building itself. There had many years passed over his head, as I could well tell by the weather-beaten and whitened and wrinkled brow; his high forehead was, however, smooth, though his brow was filled with folds of skin when he lifted his bushy eyebrows to look up at me, for I stood up.

There was yet a tuft of dark hair growing round his beard, and hardly grizzled; his frame was a large one, but it had shrunk from extreme old age; he wore a loose blue coat, light waistcoat, cord breeches, leather gaiters, and boots; he sat on a heap of rubbish, as I have before said, at the same time he leaned back, holding his knees in both hands, and by his side lay his hat and stick.

"Yes!" he said, seeing my inability to speak from sheer amazement, "yes; that is blood!"

It took a few moments for me to recover the use of my speech, so close had I walked up to him that I could touch him with my hand, and his voice sounded close at my elbow, it was so entirely unexpected; but, when I saw him, the old man kept such an immoveable posture that he looked more like an effigy than any thing else, that I doubted my own senses, but they could not in the end be deceived.

"You appear an old man," I said, "but yet I should have thought these stones to have been older than you."

"And so they are," he replied, "the stones are as old as the hills from whence they came."

"And these dark marks," I said, scraping one or two with my heel, "they appear to be as old."

" No : they are scarce a hundred years old."

" A hundred !"

" Yes; I should say they are scarce ninety-six years old, and I say they are caused by human blood."

" Well," said I, " I cannot see how it could be done; these stones are hard, and that they should retain any impression of such matters I cannot very well understand, especially for that length of time you speak of."

" We know what can be done by the will of God," said the old man, solemnly, " and the blood spilt by the hand of the murderer we know cries aloud for the vengeance of Heaven, if it even escapes the justice of man."

" Ninety-six years ago !" repeated I ; " why I reckon there are but few, indeed, who know anything about what happened ninety-six years ago."

" I do," replied the old man.

" Are you ninety-six years old ?" said I, looking at the old man, for though he did look old, he was hale and hearty.

"Ninety-six and seventeen years to boot," said the old man, "or else I couldn't remember what happened at that time, though I can remember very well what happened when I was a boy between nine and ten years of age."

" Are you a hundred and thirteen years old ?" I inquired with some wonder, if not doubt, expressed on my countenance, for the old man said in the same slow and deep-toned voice—

" Yes, I am a hundred and thirteen years of age, and many a serious struggl I've seen in these parts, and may be have had my share of 'em; but that's nothing to the purpose. I can recollect the time when there were no spots of blood upon those stones, which seem alike to defy the efforts of time and of man, to destroy the evidences of a bloody deed."

" They certainly do look strangely preserved, and clear from weeds, to what the others are ; besides, the black spots which I see plain enough, 'tis very strange, they never could have been in the stone before it was put down."

" No, no, long after that took place ; and when once stained, it seemed beyond the power of man to efface them without entirely destroying the stone."

" How came they there ?"

" Why, that's no short matter to tell; but if you have an hour to spare, I will relate to you the whole tale; it is many years since I opened my lips upon that affair, but now I am sure I have but a short sojourn in this world, I may as well let those know who wish, and show how Heaven, in its own good time, will punish the shedder of blood at the very moment of his greatest happiness."

" And was that stream of spots caused by an act of retribution for evil committed ; and the blood of the criminal, was it thus spilt ?"

" No matter," said the old man.

" If you will inform me of the legend," said I, " you shall not go unrewarded for your pains."

" Sit down upon that log," said the old man, pointing to a piece of timber that lay on some dry rubbish beside him, " and I will tell you, not a legend, but what was well known in my early days, and the actors of which I had often seen' and the last scene of all I also witnessed."

I sat myself down, as the old man told me, upon the dry log, and disposed myself to listen with patience and no little interest to what I shall call

THE WEDDING GUEST ; OR, THE SPECTRE OF THE OLD CHANCEL.

" It is now ninety-six years since the event took place that I am going to relate ; or, rather, it was somewhat more than that, when the spots of blood were first observed upon the pavement.

" I can tell you pretty well the whole history of the parties, because I knew them well. I was intimate, and was often a guest at their table, and they at mine."

I looked at the old man, and thought he was speaking strangely for one in his condition ; and his language was by no means such as the common peasantry made use of. I had not noticed it at first, so much had surprise and a sense of excitement at the story I expected to hear, created in my mind.

" You knew them, then ; what were they ?"

"People of some fortune. I should not say fortune—because you would, and the world in general, attach different meanings to the same word; but they were people who had a decent independent means, who need never have an hour's uneasiness on the score of all the useful enjoyments of life; but those sort of people, who have enough, are not always the happiest, nor the most fruitful in good works."

"And what were you, at that time?" I inquired.

"I was curate of this place you now see in ruins," said the old man.

"And now," said I, "what now?"

"An old man, tottering on the verge of eternity, and whose subsistence is derived from the parish he once was the shepherd of. "Yes, sir," he said, "I have outlived friends and foes, and am now a solitary and sad old man, waiting, with some impatience, for that time to arrive when I shall 'shuffle off this mortal coil,' and meet my Maker in another shape and a better world. I feel as if I had lived too long. It is unthankful of me to say so; but my death will be to me a moment of joy, for I expect to meet those I love in heaven."

"And you were curate?" said I, expressing my thoughts aloud, not with any intention of doing so, though —"What a change for such a man!"

"But I am not discontented."

"Satisfied?"

"Yes, quite. I fill my allotted sphere, and have now no ambition to be otherwise than what I am, save that I would not willingly be a burthen to any one."

"It is your right," I exclaimed.

"Yes, in case of necessity; but no matter, I am thankful. I am not able to do anything, and even breaking stones on the road is too hard, and they have kindly remitted that labour for me."

"How comes it," said I, "that this church was abandoned and left to its fate? I thought that such a thing could not possibly happen, for means were taken to prevent it by rebuilding the edifice."

"I will tell you how that happened, stranger: the steeple, which was very high, was stricken by lightning, and was thrown upon the roof, which was forced in and lies about as you see it now: it has never been disturbed since that day."

"It was too extensive a mischief to be repaired then; but I should have thought that it would have cost less to have rebuilt it than to have constructed another."

"I cannot tell you how that happened, but I believe the neighbouring gentry immediately went to another church which lay more at hand for them, and the place fell off, after which they made no attempt to rebuild it; besides, the walls were considered too far gone in decay to allow of any one to think of rebuilding. I lost my church and my living—there was some litigation about the matter; but rather than be the cause of any ill-feeling in the parish, I refused to proceed, and supported myself by teaching for some years."

"And they allowed you to come to the workhouse at last, have they?" said I.

"There are none living now who know me—who then knew me, and I have not even the poor claim of sympathy, though I have often expressed it."

"It is a great change."

"Yes, but it has happened now these ten years, and I find myself well reconciled to my lot; but that's not telling you my tale of the 'Wedding Guest.'"

He paused, and then, after a moment's thought, went on in the same words I now relate it to you:—

It causes some old emotions, that have long lain dormant, to revive in one's mind, but there is no fuel to add to mere recollection in an old man like me; yet the days of youth and manhood are not without their fruits, and the joys of life can never be indifferent to the heart of men until they become too old to enjoy them, and then they feel an imaginary superiority, and fancy they see the failing of nature when in this long day of youth they indulge in all that seems to them happiness and joy.

They are wrong, and so are the youth who think they never can go to too great an excess, and those who think Nature ought not to be indulged—they are both wrong—the one to abuse Nature by the excess, and the other by thinking her instincts and desires ought to be suppressed.

Well, there were, at the time I mention, three families, all united by the bonds of friendship, neighbourhood, and great similarity of tastes; they were all inde. pendent, and not one of them had a thought of seeking a profession for a son—so united and happy each family appeared, and so, in fact, they were, else means would have been taken to have separated from each other.

The family of the Frasers were highly respectable, and none more so about here; they were beloved by both rich and poor: there was a large family of sons and daughters, but only two of an age approaching to manhood and womanhood. Hugh Fraser was a fine young man, and just in his twentieth year; his father had served his country as a captain of horse with some distinction, and the son seemed destined to follow the same career as his father, for he too entered the army, and obtained a cornetcy in a dragoon regiment.

The daughter, Ellen Fraser, was a beautiful girl, who was scarcely eighteen, but an acknowledged toast by all. She was as good as she was beautiful-—she used to come into this very church, so absorbed in the duties she was called upon to take a part in, that there seemed so little of earth about her that you could have called her an angel with less impropriety than one-half her sex. Many an eye was turned towards the beautiful Miss Ellen Fraser, and I fear the thoughts of many a young man were not upon heaven, but centred in the attractive object of their senses, who was not less beloved for her beauty than kindness of disposition and goodness of heart.

About a mile from the house of Mr. Fraser lived a Mr. Thornton, a gentleman of some estate; he had but one son, a young man about two-and-twenty at that time—he was a fine young man certainly. I do not mean that he was particularly a big or tall man, rather the reverse, but his qualities of head and heart were good.

Mr. Thornton had been on visiting terms with the Frasers before Joseph Thornton came from the University; but afterwards there was a closer intimacy among them, for the children were the cause of still greater friendship. At equal distance from Mr. Thornton and Mr. Fraser lived a Mr. Briant; for I may as well introduce to you at first the persons who figured in the tragedy I am about to relate, and whose deeds yet stain the marble at your feet; for there is much of it that will serve as a warning to others, and much that will serve to interest your best sympathies.

Every year, stranger, I come and visit this place; sometimes oftener than once a-year. I hover round it like the giddy moth that finds its death in the object that fascinates it. I should like well to sleep my long sleep beneath this mouldering pile —it would be a quiet graveyard, and the swell of the organ would not even disturb the dead silence of the night.

Yes: such a resting-place I should choose, if choice were left me. But to resume :—

It was near about one time when the young men were introduced to the notice of Miss Fraser, and they were certainly young men of spirit, and, I believe, worth.

Men may commit crimes, when urged to do so by the demon within their own bosom, that, at some time previously, they would have deemed themselves incapable of committing, any injury to, if any one had [ventured to assert anything to the contrary ; and so, indeed,I believe such men are untainted in character.

Crime is more frequently the offspring of some opposed passion which has become too strong to contend with ; and in the heyday of blood, there can be no doubt but the moral powers are often the weakest in the contention, even among the best of us; and so, as my story proceeds, you will say.

My intercourse with my parishioners at that time was very great—I was as a brother. There was no feast, no party of pleasure, to which I was not invited, and expected to appear. I was young then, stranger, and so innocent and cheerful did the families about here appear, that it seemed the sunshine of happiness and gaiety was permanent, with no cloud to cast a shadow upon our felicity.

Well, sir, (said the old man,) the families seemed like so many brothers and sisters, while the younger portion appeared on the footing of cousins. It was delightful to see such an intercourse among people—it was an evidence that the world had not infused its gall and wormwood into the breasts of those who formed the members of this little community.

The time was at hand, however, when the peace of this little society was to be invaded in no ordinary manner—a time when not only would harmony be broken in upon, but crime darken the atmosphere of our bright homes.

There was an evening party given by Mr. Fraser to his neighbours: it was a common thing among them to do so. They used to begin about two hours before

sanset, and continue for several hours. It was considered that the evening was the pleasantest time for dancing, when the heat of the day had become moderated by the evening breezes; then the dances upon the well-mown lawn would commence, beneath the shadows of the fruit-trees or spreading cedars.

These, stranger, were moments of fairy-like happiness, the most innocent and the best of our lives, because they are innocent, and leave no sting behind.

No. 16.

It was at a meeting or party such as this that I first saw the parties together. Ellen Fraser, in all her youth and beauty, stood there, the pride of the throng; and there were many beautiful young women present besides Miss Fraser, but there was no jealousy or envy among them.

Ellen opened the dance, and her partner was Joseph Thornton. The pair seemed well matched, both of them being well-made and handsome. All eyes were fixed upon them; and none more intently than those of Frank Briant, who stood leaning against the trunk of the large cedar-tree.

I thought at that time I saw the gleam of his eyes; that there was more of what the world terms spirit or fire in them than was usually found in the quiet hearts of those who lived in our little circle.

He leaned against the tree, and seemed intent upon the evolutions of the dancers, especially the two figures of those who had opened the same. I approached him and thought I would speak to him, and, touching him on the elbow, said—

" Mr Briant, do you not dance?"

" Not at this moment," he said, suddenly; but then added in a calmer voice—

" I may by-and-by; but I feel slightly indisposed, yet shall, perhaps, feel inclined to do so in another dance or two, and then I may be better."

" These are happy moments," said I, "moments that are worth enjoying, because they leave no sting behind—because too they engender no selfish thought."

" No," he said. " I like them too, and I like the dance also, but one does not always feel in the humour to dance."

" In the humour," I repeated, somewhat surprised, "you do not mean that you feel displeased."

" No, no," he hastily added, "by humour I mean I feel indisposed at this moment to join the dance, though I may an hour hence. I am not very well."

" I hope you will be better," I replied. " I must go to the dance myself."

" I thought you would have opened the dance."

" I should," I replied, "I dare say, but I gave up my place to Mr. Joseph Thornton at his request, as he wished to open it with Miss Ellen Fraser."

His brow contracted for a moment, and his eye seemed to flash fire as I spoke, but the emotion seemed but momentary, and it passed away; and he said—

" Then it was at Mr. Thornton's request that you vacated your place at the head of the dance?"

" I cannot consider myself as entitled to lead the dance. I am here by the kindness of my friends, and not by any right whatever; and as to Mr. Thornton, he does well to open the dance with our host's daughter. Surely there is none more worthy to fill the station than either of them."

" Oh! certainly not," said Briant; "both are fitted for the station they have assumed of themselves, and by the tacit consent of those who admire them."

He then moved away, and I saw him no more for some time; and, in the meanwhile, Ellen Fraser and Joseph Thornton danced together through three or four sets, and then Joseph led his partner to a seat beneath the cedar-tree, where there were tables arranged, on which were placed refreshments of various kinds, and handed them to her.

Soon after, having occasion to leave the place, and Ellen was for a few moments alone, Frank Briant, as if he had only been waiting for the opportunity, stepped up to her, and occupied the place of Joseph Thornton.

" Miss Ellen," he said, "will you favour me with permission to dance the next set with you, if you are not already engaged to dance them?"

" I am not engaged," said Ellen; " and you shall be my partner, if you think it a favour."

" I do, and a very great one too," said Frank.

" Then I cannot refuse to grant so small a favour when it is so highly prized. I will dance with you with pleasure, but you must find Mr. Thornton a partner."

" Find me a partner!" said Thornton, who at that moment came up and heard the last words; " find me a partner! Have I not got one? What should I desire another for?"

"Because," said Ellen, "you will be without one."

"Shall I? How is that to be then? Are you going to desert me when I am at the happiest?"

"Not desert you; but seriously I am going to dance the next set with Mr. Briant."

"And then, Ellen——"

"Why, if you desire it, I shall be again disengaged, and then——"

"I beg to be your partner afterwards."

"Well, I must not say no, I presume, for if I wait till I pick and choose among the young men, I shall, according to the old saying, 'pick up the crooked stick at last.'"

"Miss Fraser ought to be the last who should fear that," said Briant, "for he will be a happy man who is picked out by Miss Ellen, be he who he may."

"Come, Mr. Briant, if you are going to be elaborately complimentary, and make set speeches, you will tire me, for I am at home, and desire to see you so."

"You are very kind," he replied, "and I will endeavour to do the same as you desire I should; and to begin, let me tell you they are about to take their places."

"I am ready," said Ellen, rising and giving her hand to Frank Briant, who led her away in triumph.

I watched them away, and saw them take their places in the dance, and they were soon in the gayest of the throng, that trod so lightly over the green and soft turf, in all the mad gyrations of the dance.

There stood Joseph Thornton: it was his turn so feel disappointment, or rather vexation. He bit his lip, but no very deep or dark emotion passed his mind, though he had been for the moment entirely forgotten, nor had Briant found him the partner he was desired by Ellen, not that he cared about dancing, for he preferred to wait till she had finished the dance with Briant, who was a young man of fortune.

Of the two, Briant was the most affluent, though they were young men of independent means, even while their parents lived, and at their death they had good expectations.

I could not perceive any of the same determined jealousy of deportment in Thornton I saw in Briant, and the reflection that came across me was, that Briant was the most fiery temper of the two, while I thought Joseph Thornton had less fear of a rival than he who was now dancing with Ellen.

It was the first time I had seen the seeds of disunion, or of any feeling save that of kindness and charity, and it was to me a marked epoch, and yet it was one in which I could interfere not even with counsel and advice.

Thus it was that I was a spectator rather than an actor, through all the scenes that follow. Indeed, I was intermixed with them, and I took my part—a passive part, it was true, but I had it not in my power to act otherwise, for my position would not permit me to interfere unasked into the private affairs of my parishioners; it would have impaired my usefulness in other matters had I done so, and, therefore, should see that which was not intended for my sight; besides, I thought I had barely any right to scold, save upon such occasions as were clearly against the welfare of a Christian community, and so I said nothing of my own suppositions or fears.

This was the wisest course, though events did turn up, but not from that cause —quite the reverse—it arose from the violence of passion, and the chiding of the pastor could not stem such a torrent as that—it would have its way; and, unless the heart and head of the man who gives rein to such a course of things aids in the suppressing of its evil effects, it can never be ever turned aside from the point upon which it has set in to reach.

When the dance had ended, Briant led his partner to her seat, and gave her up with a bad grace, endeavouring to secure her for another dance, but she had pledged herself to Joseph Thornton, who claimed the promise of her, and she laughingly submitted to perform it, declaring at the same time, she thought it was very hard to perform the promise, as it kept her so much to one person, and that was enough to tire any two persons.

Ah, stranger, well do I remember those days—they were days of youth and happiness, such as were ninety-eight years ago ; but times are altered—well, so am I—there can be no good cause to feel dissatisfied. I am here—they are gone to their homes, long, long ago, more than three-quarters of a century.

That evening showed me there were two rivals in the affections of Ellen Fraser, and I prayed that he who might best deserve her should have her, and that no evil might befal any of them, and that the rejected one might feel lightly his disappointment, for disappointment there must be.

I could tell they were both in earnest, so deeply did their feelings of rivalry at that, the first time it was exhibited show itself off.

Yes, they were in earnest ; but Frank Briant had more of malignancy about his nature than Thornton, though it may be true the latter did not feel those emotions of jealousy and hate so deeply and so rancorously as his rival, only because he felt that he was not called upon to exhibit them; that, in fact, he had not the same cause.

Each time they met the young men were friends ; they affected the utmost friendship towards each other, and never once spoke of what was so evident to all others—of the love they sought to gain of Ellen Fraser.

It was strange, but they must have felt they were rivals, and hence the feeling engendered the thought it were unnecessary; it was no doubt prudent in them to do so, for had they once spoken of it to each other they would have been open enemies, and blood would no doubt have been shed.

The first evening passed off, and so did many more, but not without producing the results they were calculated to produce, an estrangement of the two friends.

This was not done immediately ; there were many more such scenes as the one I have described to you took place ; they all passed off, but served to show the same events off in different lights, while at the same time neither party seemed nearer the object of their wishes than before.

It was strange that neither lover made any distinct proposal to the young lady, or if they did, it was not done so as to enable her to show a decided and unalterable preference for the one over the other, though it was easy to see who was the favoured individual.

This might have been an error of judgment to be deplored rather than blamed ; it was a matter that they who were concerned, rather than I, were the best judges ; but there was no doubt, at least, a tacit understanding amongst them, as to who was the received lover.

Indeed, Joseph Thornton seemed to be the accepted lover, for he used to go to the house of Mr. Fraser, and was welcomed as their child, and it was not much less frequently that Frank Briant found his way beneath the same roof.

On one of these occasions there was an altercation, and a serious one too, which arose from a singular circumstance.

Frank Briant had called at the house of Fraser and found Ellen preparing to take a walk, and he at once proposed to accompany her, and this was at once acceded to, and they left the house and proceeded to the enjoyment of the day and walk, which was very beautiful.

One of the principal walks which Briant used most to frequent, was this very church—there are many beautiful points about, and there were many more then— the woods in the neighbourhood ; but here up and down this very aisle he used often to walk and read the inscriptions upon the old monuments, for there were many at that time.

On this occasion he brought Ellen here, and here they had some conversation upon that subject which was nearest to his heart, but he could get no encouragement to pursue, and yet he did not feel so far sure of an ultimate refusal, as to feel induced to give up the pursuit.

If she did not love him, he thought she had, at least, a very firm feeling of friendship towards him, and that was, at least, a great point gained, and he would not despair.

Well, it would appear that Briant from this gained heart, and thought within himself that he might, at least, run equal chances, and determined that he would endeavour to make his chance as sure as he could.

To do this, he conceived it would be necessary to pay her as much attention as he could, and to be with her as often as circumstances would permit, and in order that no impediment might exist, he determined at once to declare himself to her family.

This was an open and energetic measure certainly, and the best he could have adopted—one well calculated to aid him in his object ; and he determined that that very morning he would put his resolution into force.

Ellen declined his advances, but not peremptorily, declaring at the same time she was not engaged to any one, and her heart was her own.

"Then, Miss Fraser," said Briant, "if your heart is your own, be not angry when I say I will do my utmost to deserve it, and to win it."

"You must be very bold and resolute, and have a very great deal of patience too," said Ellen, laughing.

"I can exert any thing in such a cause, and if Heaven pleases, I will yet be the happiest man in all England."

"Why are you not so at this moment?" inquired Ellen.

"Because I am not sure of your love ; were I so, then, indeed, I should really be happy."

"I cannot give you a heart not yet formed," said Ellen, "besides, I do not intend yet awhile to give up the liberty I have of choosing my friends and my own engagements."

"Surely those who loved you would put no restraint upon such a thing as that."

"I fear they would," she replied.

This kind of conversation continued until they reached the house of Mr. Fraser, when who should meet them in the parlour but young Thornton, whose looks were not such as at all conveyed the idea that he was pleased.

It could not be denied but that there was much to displease him, to see her whom he so dearly loved walking and leaning on the arm of his rival ; but then he forgot he had not so far declared himself as to secure the affections of the young lady, but had, for some reason or other, hung back.

True it was he had spoken to her of love ; he had declared he should never be happy with another woman ; that she, and she only, would ever possess his heart.

Now, however, the change was different : he came to make her a declaration of love, and to swear his truth to her; but let events speak for themselves at this juncture.

But first I will remark, that Ellen had no dislike to Frank Briant, far from it, and there can be but little doubt that, but for the fact of Thornton's addresses, she would have accepted Briant's love.

Mr. Fraser was in his library. I was with him at the time. Young Briant entered the room, and after a few preliminary observations, he said,

"I wish to have a few words in private with you, Mr. Fraser, when you have leisure."

"You can speak at once before our friend here, unless you desire not to do so."

"No, I can avow my purposes as well before our good curate as not," said he, "and since you invite me to do so. I will, I come to propose myself, Mr. Fraser. You may think me presumptuous, but love overlooks distances, and I am here to propose myself as a son-in-law to you, sir, and a husband for your daughter."

"Ah!" said Mr. Fraser, "that is very frank."

"Yes," said Briant, "Frank is my name, and Frank my nature. I may say, without impropriety, I am more blunt than is usual, Mr. Fraser, on such occasions, but I am so, because I would prevent misapprehension upon a subject that I am very anxious about, and upon the result of which my future happiness and welfare entirely depends."

"Well, Mr. Briant, there is no one whom I respect more, or would more willingly receive as a son-in-law, than yourself."

" No previous promise, I hope, stands in the way of my happiness," interposed Briant, hastily.

" No, no, I was about to say that I would willingly receive you in the character you propose, if you can gain my daughter's consent to become your wife."

" I hope by time and attention to deserve, and ultimately to obtain such consent, if she and fortune favour me."

" Then all I have to say is, there is no impediment from me, but here our compact ends. I cannot pretend to influence my Ellen's choice, further than circumstances shall warrant me, to prevent her placing her affections upon who is unfit or unworthy of them."

" And I hope you do not consider I am such ?"

" Oh, no, I have said the contrary ; but where I see her choice may be exercised with freedom, why, I cannot support one against her own feelings."

" I should scarce live happy with one who would not be my bride willingly."

" I think you are right," said I ; " a willing bride may make a man happy, but one presented to you with tears of sorrow for a dowry, would only heap future misery upon your head, and in future years you would sorely repent it."

" You do not think I am sincere, sir, in what I say," he said with a sneer.

" No, I am not afraid of that," I replied.

" I thought," he said, " from the manner in which you spoke, that you held rather a strong opinion to the contrary, but I take Heaven to witness the offer I have made, I have done so honestly and honourably."

" I believe you do," said Mr. Fraser, " and here's my hand ; on my part, I will do what I have told you, and no more."

" You have said all I could wish, while the young lady has in point of fact to be won," he added with a smile ; " I hope you wish me success."

" I do, my boy," said Mr. Fraser, grasping the young man's hand, and giving it a hearty shake, " now be off with you, and make your peace with my daughter."

" I will try."

He then rose, and left the room.

" He is a fine young man, that Frank Briant, with something like fire in him. I wish him success ; though I don't like to second his cause, because you see, if it should turn out not so happy as I could wish and expect, it may be said I have been the ruining of my child's happiness."

" You act very rightly," I replied, " as long as you exercise only a protective power over your daughter's fate, to protect her from the impositions of the world, you do well and act wisely ; but I think there is another in the field."

" What do you mean ?" inquired Mr. Fraser.

" I mean," said I, " there is a rival to Frank Briant, and one that is somewhat more favoured by the lady herself."

" I am not aware of it," said Mr. Fraser, " it is quite news to me, I assure you."

" Have you not seen Joseph Thornton ?"

" I have."

" Well, have you not noticed that he is paying a great deal of marked attention to Ellen ?"

" I have certainly seen him pay her attention, but then I have observed other young men do the same thing, and took no notice of it, being an ordinary matter."

" But she appears to have some partiality towards him, and his advances are by no means disagreeable to her, and of the two young men, Joseph runs the better chance."

" Indeed ; well ; I do not mind much, whichever makes the better husband, is all that I hope will influence her choice, in default of knowing that beforehand, I think young Briant is preferable."

" On what score ?" I inqu red.

" He can make the best provision for her, but that is an object of secondary consideration at the least."

" It is so," I said ; " but from wealth alone comes not happiness, you know, certainly."

"Exactly; I spoke of them as occupying but a secondary place; but even then it is no unimportant matter, because it is the duty of young people when they marry to consider how they provide for the future welfare of their children, and without means they cannot do it."

"That is certainly, correct," I replied; and then the conversation dropped.

*　　*　　*　　*　　*　　*　　*

An interview took place that evening between Joseph Thornton and Ellen; it was one of some feeling on the part of Thornton, who really loved Ellen, but he was somewhat more backward in pressing his suit than most men, and Ellen, too, felt a far greater preference for him than she did for his rival, who was a bold and resolute wooer, such a one as would often induce a woman to sacrifice her own opinion and accept one who wooed with such an air of superiority.

"Ellen," he said to her, as they were walking together in the garden, "Ellen, you were walking out with Mr. Briant this morning?"

Here he hesitated.

"Yes, I was; he came just as I was about to walk out, and then proposed to accompany me, which he did, and we returned at the time you saw."

"And what," said Thornton, "what might have been the object of his visit?"

"Upon my word that is a very pretty question to put to a young lady—to ask her the object of a gentleman's visit—you couldn't expect an answer."

"Well, well, I come for another purpose—that of telling you I am about to leave these parts for a time, and of proceeding at once to engage in some profession which shall add to my fortune, and place me in a yet higher rank in society than that which I hold now."

"And so you will leave us?" said Ellen, a shade of sadness coming over her features.

"Yes, Miss Fraser, I am about to leave, but I hope I shall not be forgotten by my friends; for my thoughts will always revert with pleasure to the happy little community of this place, in which I have seen so many pleasant hours, that will remain in my recollection as long as I have power to recal the past."

"And so, then, you have not fortune enough; but you have greater ambition and desire to shine in the world, and become, in fact, a great man?"

"No, Ellen, no," he replied; "I have but one object."

"And what is that?"

"To seek your approbation in the course I am pursuing; for without that my course will be a weary and barren one indeed—its result will be failure."

"You would not attempt what you believed would prove a failure," said Ellen; "but I have not the power of making fruitful your plans and prospects."

"You are the light, the sun of my existence—that warms all my hopes into life, and renders my exertions fruitful and productive in those results I am desirous of producing."

"Then go," said Ellen, "go, and you have my good wishes for your prosperity and success."

"And should I succeed, will you share my riches and my honours?" he said, seizing her hand.

"I?"

"Yes, you, Ellen; for without you all that I hope or wish to obtain will be but a melancholy possession: it will be the ball-room without the spirit of the dance, and the summer without the sun—the day without light."

"You are too rapid; you outrun your discretion and your good sense together."

"Indeed, indeed, I do not; I have said what I mean, and only what I mean, but I have more to say, Ellen—I have often been on the point of saying more to you, but I have not been prepared to give you reasons as well as words for what I should tell you."

"Well!" said Ellen, endeavouring to say something, and yet scarce knowing what she was saying, yet afraid to let his words fall dead on her ears.

"I love you, Ellen, and that you can be no stranger to, for some months past; but at the same time I have foreborne to press you too hardly upon that subject, and should not do so but for the fact that I am about to quit the country and seek a town life, where there is a better opening for me to push my way forward in life; but before I go I am anxious to secure that love which I covet above all things. Say, that if I return to you within a limited time—not wait until I have realised a fortune, but that I have a decided prospect of doing so—say that when I can come to your friends and say I am not only independent but have a good profession in my hand, and may, before many years are passed, be able to realise a considerable, nay, princely fortune—say you will accept me then."

" It is too much, Mr. Thornton, to expect you should, while in London, preserve such a self-sacrificing faith towards your friends in the country—it is too much."

" It cannot be so."

" Aye, but it can, though : there you must be much out in company, you will see new faces, form new friendships, from inclination and necessity, and why should you not form new loves ?"

" Never   never! never!" repeated Joseph Thornton.   " I swear by Heaven—I swear it."

" Nay, swear not at all."

" I do so, and may Heaven punish me if I fail in my vow to be true to you, to have no other love but yours ; do not, dearest Ellen, refuse me this boon."

" Refuse you—what can I grant ?"

" Grant me this—that you will solemnly pledge yourself to be true to me, to have no other love but mine ; that you will refuse all addresses during my absence, and remain single until I come to claim you for my bride ?"

" I am loth to pledge myself to what may be less to your interest than to mine, and to what you may have more temptation to break through than I."

" Never! never !"

" You do not know what may happen."

" I do not pretend to know futurity; did I do so, I should never taste the blessings of hope.   Say you love me, and will love me ;—I see by your blush you do add to this dear obligation, and say you will remain true and faithful to me while I am away."

" I will," said Ellen—" I will."

" Thank you for this; thank you, dearest Ellen ; may Heaven shower its choicest blessings upon your head ; you have nerved my arms for almost any-thing.   I can encounter almost any difficulty that fate can bring upon me."

" I wish you every success you can yourself desire," said Ellen ; " but how long do you think it will be before you can predict success ?"

" I cannot well tell ; but two years cannot pass over my head without my being able to tell something satisfactory about my prospects."

' And it will be, perhaps, two years before I again see you !" said Ellen.

" No, no, I hope not ; something more unforeseen than I can at all anticipate m. s happen to cause that.   No, no, I hope to see you every few months, at the least, and we shall have abundant opportunities of hearing from each other."

' Aye, we can write, if you tell me where; but you will find it a hard matter to please me in writing.   I shall exact such a long description of what you see and meet in the great metropolis of all England."

" You may rely upon it.   I will write to you at least once a-week, and certainly the day after I get to London, for I expect it will be night when I do get there."

" I shall be waiting anxiously enough for the receipt of your first letter."

" You shall not wait in vain, my dearest Ellen ; I will write within eight-and-forty hours after I see you on the last occasion ; and you will have the letter in somewhat less time than that, more or less, after I have written it."

" Have you informed my father of all this ?" inquired Ellen ; suddenly recol-lecting she had been acting without her father's knowledge in this matter.

" I have not," he replied ; " and I was not yet in a condition to do so, because I could not make any specific promise, or show him my plans, in a manner that would attract his approbation ; besides, when I return with far brighter prospects than even those I possess now, I thought it would be much better than going to him, and running the danger of his disapproval, which would place me in the worst position I could find myself. No, my Ellen, with your pledged faith I know I am secure; I will not run any hazard for such a formal declaration to him."

"As you please; but I thought my father might deem himself slighted if he were not made acquainted with your attentions," said Ellen."

"He cannot, my dear Ellen; nevertheless, if you thought so, I would at once return back and inform him of all that has taken place, and hear what he says."

"Do not do so, if you think you had better not."

"Should your father be unfavourable to my scheme, will you, nevertheless, continue to hold faith with me against all parental interference whatever?"

"I own I should not like to do that which my father has once positively forbidden me."

"Then, my dear Ellen, see what an unhappy position I should place myself in: I must give up all hopes of you and of the future; for under such circumstances

I should not leave—the object I should otherwise wish to attain would be value-less, and I should no longer have any motive in doing what I now intend."

"You do not mean to say," said Ellen, "you would not prosecute this journey."

"I do."

* * * * *

The lovers passed several hours together, and then, when the hour of parting came, they did so with more regrets than they usually felt, for the separation that was to take place would happen on the next day.

* * * * *

That evening, Frank Briant did not meet with the same friendly reception he met with in the morning; but he took no notice of that, but still pursued Ellen with many attentions, and without the slightest remark upon what might have been the waywardness of her disposition, but continued himself in the same tone as before.

And yet there was something in his eye which, had she noted it, would have alarmed her : it was now and then turned upon her with such a fiery glance, so full of ire and meaning, that, had her eyes met any one of those sudden looks, she must have been alarmed.

"You do not seem very well, Miss Ellen," said Frank Briant, after he had in vain endeavoured to carry on a conversation in somewhat a similar strain to that which he had carried on in the morning, but with no success; Ellen appeared thoughtful and absent at times, and his words fell dead upon her ears, and she knew not he was speaking.

"You are not well, I fear, Miss Fraser," he repeated for the third time, "for you have not heard me."

"Indeed I beg your pardon for being so inattentive, but I was absent."

"Have you such serious thoughts, then, that absorb you so completely that you seem as though your very heart was elsewhere ? "

"Yes,' said Ellen, "but that is past—I have something of a headache, and will retire early to-night ; you must excuse my bidding you early adieu."

"Certainly, since you are indisposed ; I had hoped it had sprung from a lighter cause, but permit me to ask and inquire after you to-morrow."

* * * * *

The lovers' adieus that were to be uttered the next day were probably the cause of Ellen's absence of mind on the previous evening; she arose with the sun, and was walking through the cornfields, long ere even the labourer was seen in the fields.

The lark springs from his couch in the corn and salutes the rising sun with his all-thankful song. The day's begun and the whirl of rapid events has commenced, and the world is once more in the course of fruitfulness of things and deeds, aye, even at that early hour !

Ellen paused when she had reached a certain spot—here she paused and then gazed around her, and saw not afar off the object of her morning's walk—seated on the style was young Joseph Thornton.

"Ah! my Ellen," he exclaimed as he walked towards her, "this is more than kind—you are here earlier by an hour than what I expected you."

"And you, Joseph, have you not come earlier ? I did not expect to see you."

"No ; but I suppose we are both actuated by the same spirit of love, and have guessed each other's feelings and thoughts, and have acted in accordance."

"Then you go to-day ?" said Ellen, sorrowfully.

"Yes, within a very few hours."

"And when will you reach London ? " she inquired with some earnestness.

"By to-morrow night."

"And then you will write the next day to me."

"I will, Ellen, I will—you may rely upon my faith in that matter ; and I shall be very exacting from you, for I shall expect to hear of every little occurrence that has happened, or may happen, during absence, for I shall still take all the interest you can imagine in our friends and acquaintances."

"Then I will write to you, and you shall find I will neglect nothing."

Lovers' conversation is interesting enough among themselves, but interests third parties but very little; I will, therefore, say no more upon that matter.

They no longer spoke of others but of themselves, and after about an hour they quitted the spot and bent their steps towards this church.

Yes, stranger, this old church was then a very different place to what it is now. Lovers' vows have often been plighted at these altars, and many a happy couple have been united here, and left this aisle man and wife.

But no more of an old man's regrets: I will return to my sad tale.

They bent their steps towards this altar: the church was open—there was no necessity for locking the doors; and, had there been, there would have been but little advantage in doing so, seeing that even then in some of the older parts of the building there were places that would have admitted the robber to plunder the holy place.

No—there were several dilapidations—old walls will crumble as men will decay—all things must fall beneath the hand of time; even the hills themselves will in time crumble down and change their places with the bed of the ocean—they all change, save the Eternal. The lovers reached the church, and entered it, and then, before yon altar, they plighted their faith to each other, and swore to remain true to each other.

"When I neglect you, Ellen," he said, "when I forget to do that which I have promised, or shrink from doing it, then I release you from your promise."

"And you will write to me?"

"Aye, that I will."

"It is enough; upon the regularity of your correspondence I shall depend, and shall fully judge of you by the regularity and fulness of your letters."

"You may do so most safely," was the reply that Joseph Thornton made; "if I fail in so simple a matter as that, I shall fail in a more serious and important one."

They quitted the church as they entered it, but they saw not the dark figure that stole after them and was hidden among the monuments, and who left the church by yon chancel door—that door where the spots of blood end.

"I see them," I replied, as the old man pointed first to the dark spots and then to the doors.

"Yes, they remain, and will be seen to the day of judgment, unless some hand destroys the stones altogether."

Well, they quitted the church and left together, and walked some distance towards the house of Mr. Fraser, when Joseph Thornton bade farewell to the beautiful Ellen Fraser.

"Farewell, dearest Ellen," he said, "remember my promise, and you are free when I forget to keep any part of mine to you. Farewell, we now part."

They parted; and tender was the parting of the two lovers, but more especially on the part of Joseph Thornton, who seemed to leave her with an impression that some evil was hanging over their heads.

As for Ellen Fraser, she seemed as though she had gone too far without her father's consent, and feared lest her own feelings had hurried her on without any regard to his approval, and she feared the result would end in some misadventure.

There was, however, no resisting the impassioned manner of Thornton, aided as it was by her own predilections; and she gave herself up to the impressions of the moment, and bade him a kind and long adieu.

He stood and watched at the style: he saw her until she was lost among the trees that led in an avenue to her father's house, and then he turned away slowly, and entered the church yet once again.

* * * * * * *

For several days Ellen Fraser kept hr room, under the pretence that she was indisposed, and did not feel inclined to see any one.

Frank Briant, however, came daily, and often saw Mr. Fraser, though he did not see Mss Fraser.

"Why, Frank," said Mr. Fraser, about the second or third morning, "you seem growing pale and sad, man. Can't you and my Ellen hash up matte between you?"

"I have not had the pleasure of seeing her at all this last day or two, and am somewhat anxious about her, as I fear her health has suffered of late."

"I hope not," said her father; "but now I think of it, she has not been about much during the day, except at meals, and then only for a time; but a little time may cause some change to take place in her."

"I hope so," said Frank.

"You have heard we have lost one of our friends lately," said Mr. Fraser, "I suppose."

"No, no, I have not."

"What! Have you not heard that Joseph Thornton has left us for London?"

"Oh, yes, I have heard something about it; "but, at the same time, I don't consider that losing him, because he lives and may return again to us."

"He may," said Mr. Fraser, shaking his head gravely, "and he may not. The change from this to the great city of London is immense, and I look upon his return as more than problematical."

"Do you think so?"

"Aye, that I do," said Mr. Fraser. "Why, you see there are pleasures so enticing to young men in large cities that they completely fascinate them; indeed, had I, myself, been sent to a large city, and made up my mind to return here, I am sure I should not; but you see I married in London."

"Aye, many do who leave their country circle."

"Oh, yes, very many, there can be no doubt of it, and then return to their country circle, unless they have business avocations that compel them to remain."

"Well, I hope Miss Fraser will be better against I call again; but I shall not be here to-morrow," said Frank Briant, "I am going on an excursion with some relatives, and I was about to beg Miss Ellen would be of the party."

"She is up stairs. I suppose, as you have not been admitted to the sanctum of her apartment, I must do the part of a messenger myself for you, and see what she says to it."

"You are very kind," said Briant, "and I shall be much obliged to you."

Mr. Fraser arose, and instantly repaired to his daughter's room, where he found her seated at some ornamental work, and apparently in very good health. He questioned her as to the reason why she had kept herself so secluded for some days past, and then gave her the message of Frank, or rather, repeated the invitation.

It was with a very bad grace that Mr. Fraser accepted of her refusal, and said he thought it was ungracious, especially as Briant had been repeatedly to see her of late, and ended the matter by saying—

"Young Frank Briant is a fine young man, and loves you, I am confident; there is no mistake about him; he has at once come to the right quarter to settle all about that—his hand and heart are placed aright."

"What do you mean, father?" inquired Ellen.

"That Frank Briant loves you; he has told me so in the most candid and honourable manner; what more you can desire for a husband than a fine, handsome, and honourable young man, I cannot tell; but they would jump at such a fellow in a picked regiment of horse."

This was no doubt a *summum bonum* in the worthy ex-captain of horse, to cap which he thought quite impossible, and he at once quitted the room.

"She won't go, Frank," he said, as he entered the room; "she is amusing herself with embroidering something or other, and has got a pain in her head or her temple, she says the former; but no matter, she can't hold that way long."

This was gulped down with the best grace he could put on by Frank Briant, and after some conversation he left the house, not so much cast down as would seem he was at first disposed to be, at which Mr. Fraser was much rejoiced, for he considered that he had been the cause of it.

There was a lapse of a day more before Frank Briant returned to the house of

Mr. Fraser. The last day on which Frank called was the one on which Ellen expected a letter from Joseph Thornton, and she was too much excited with the anticipation of the letter to permit her to mingle much with company; hence it was she refused Briant's invitation.

However, the letter came not, and Ellen felt a damp upon her spirits; but she buoyed her spirits up with the hope that if it were not there to-day, it would be there to-morrow.

" He may not get it in post-time," said she to herself; " but it will certainly be here to-morrow. There may be some delay of the post-office—some mistake— such things do now and then occur, and usually in important affairs."

The morrow came, but, alas! no letter came, and Ellen began to feel vexed. She thought she had been slighted. She gave him a day after his time. Surely he could have written, for that was so very easy a matter, and there could be no excuse for not doing so.

" If he could not find time for so trifling a matter," she said, " as that, after such solemn assurances, he will hardly keep other promises, when he sees more cause to slight them. It is not a matter that would have taken long to have written to me now that he was safe, and would write more at length as soon as he is more at liberty."

There was some justice in these remarks, and the day passed off in fretfulness and ill-humour.

The next day Frank Briant called, but it was towards the afternoon, and Ellen saw there were no signs of a letter. This was the third day, and on each of these she expected to receive one by post, and yet she had seen none; and she had taken care to inquire herself, so there could be no mistake.

" Well, Miss Ellen, I am glad to see you again about," said Frank ; " you have been unwell, I hear, and certainly you look rather pale and graver than you used."

" Oh! dear, do you think so ?" said Ellen, vexed at being thought altered in appearance, because she had been so deceived by Joseph Thornton.

" I certainly think so; but I hope to see the roses again reigning in your cheeks."

" I have confined myself too much to the house," she said, " and that may have done it. I had some embroidered work to finish, and stopped to do it."

" Oh! I fear embroidery will scarcely suit you ; you should take to the green fields and the woods again, they will restore you to your former self."

Thus by little he drew her out into conversation, and begged to accompany her in a walk, which she at first refused, and then allowed.

Frank did his best to entertain her, and he certainly succeeded until they returned, and made the walk more amusing than ever it had been before.

She remembered what her father had told her respecting Frank Briant—that he had at once sought her father's consent to woo her, and she could but compare the conduct of the two young men, and the advantage at that time certainly appeared in the favour of him who stood by her side.

Besides, she had not heard from Joseph Thornton, and he had decidedly broken his promise and released her from her promise—she was free.

And yet Ellen did not seem anxious for her freedom; she hovered for many days between hope and fear, and would not commit herself to Frank. Even yet might Thornton have reinstated himself in her favour; if he had but written and justified, nay, excused himself, he would have had a merciful judge ; but he did not.

Many days and weeks now passed and nothing was heard of young Thornton. His father being uneasy, though aged and infirm, journeyed to London with the intention of ascertaining the cause of his silence, but he sickened, and died as soon as he got there.

Nothing, therefore, was heard of them, and like a seven days' wonder, they were ceased to be remembered, save as what had been and was no more.

Ellen sorrowfully acquiesced in the general opinion, that he had forgotten his friends and married well in London, whence he would not return at least for years.

Frank Briant now made his way very fast in the favour of the Frasers, and Ellen herself seemed to yield willingly to his suit. There were times when she thought of Thornton, but the vexation at the slight that had been put upon her drowned all love.

She had, in fact, admitted to herself the superior claims that Frank Briant had upon her affections. and now felt a sincere regard for him, which feeling was daily becoming more and more ripened into love.

And Frank, too, was well aware of the progress he was daily making, and pressed his suit with an ardour that showed his earnestness, and had even induced her to name a day when they should be married.

I will now tell you of a matter I could not very well break before, and which may seem unconnected with the story, and that was, for some time past some spots of blood had been seen along the pavement of the church—such as you see them, and such they were and have been.

They were discovered one morning when the attendants were about to clean the church out previously to divine service being performed, and they set about removing them by washing them out, but this was a matter not so easily done as had been imagined.

They washed and scrubbed by the hour, but they did not remove the spots; there they remained, despite all efforts to efface them from the stone.

This caused some sensation among the pew-openers and others, and when I came the next Sabbath morning to perform the service, the spots at once attracted my observation. I called to know the cause of them, and why they had not been removed, and was unable to learn the first, and was told, for the answer to the second, that many efforts had been made, but they had proved unsuccessful.

" They are blood," said I.

" Yes," said the sexton, " so I think it is; and if so, they'll never come out, you may depend upon it."

I had many good reasons why they would never disappear, but not to me satisfactory, and ordered them to be scrubbed now before me, but all to no purpose. I then had the stone chiselled down, but the bloody spots appeared to be deep 'rained right through the stones, and it was, I found, quite impossible to remove .iem, so I gave up the attempt, and wondered what was the cause of these appearances.

However, we wondered in vain, and never could we hear anything of the mysterious marks that seemed to elucidate the mystery that was hanging over them.

*   *   *   *   *   *   *

The joyous time of Frank Briant's wedding was coming on, and he and his future wife appeared a happy couple. She appeared to have forgotten all about her former lover; so, indeed, she was quite right in doing, seeing he had entirely neglected her, and fixed her love on Frank, who was true and honest.

There was not a little sensation excited among their friends, and when the banns were put up, which they were in this very place, there was a strong muster of friends to hear them, and to greet each other with their smiles of approval.

They both came—the bride and bridegroom elect—they were determined to sit and listen to the sounds as they rang through the vaulted roof of the old church; but it was noticed that he invariably led her round to the farther extremity of the church, so that she should not even see the spots of blood upon the stones.

He used to look very pale and very nervous when he entered the church, which his young male friends used to rally him upon, by saying he was growing nervous now the day approached, and that he would not be able to go through the ceremony without fainting.

With such badinage as this they would laugh at him, but he was always ready to take their jokes in good part, and laughed loudest as they ridiculed him.

The day approached, and the banns had been duly published, the hour appointed, all things prepared, and the guests were invited ; but as the hours shortened, Frank Briant became once more what he had been—cool, collected, and his presence of mind was as great as ever, while the fire of youth, and the joy at his approaching nuptials, were conspicuous to all who saw him.

Then Ellen was by no means deficient in the general expression of joy that all seemed to feel. On her account, and on that of her husband, she felt proud of her bridegroom, for, in truth, he was generous and loved her well, he was handsome and young, while his fortune was such, that it appeared as though nothing but a life of health, wealth, happiness, and peace awaited them.

The morning had now arrived, the guests were arriving, and the tramp of horses was heard up the avenue of linden trees that led up to the main entrance, and every thing about the harness and trappings was as gay as decorations and a joyous occasion could make them.

The white favours shone conspicuously, and the sun of an August morning scarce ever shone, for the numbers and station, upon a finer or more brilliant scene.

The whole of the house was open to the visitors, which comprehended all who were known to the family of either side—to Mr. Fraser and his immediate friends, and to Frank Briant and his friends.

The house was large and capable of holding many, but it was on this occasion filled with friends, many of them strangers to each other, and there was none more happy than Mr. Fraser himself, who gave a hearty welcome to all.

Among the guests, however, was one individual who gave some cause for apprehension and dread. Surprise and amazement were the first feelings that seemed to take possession of them, and keen awe.

"Who can he be?" said one.

"Do you know him?" inquired another.

These were questions that were asked of every one, but not one in that company could answer the question. He sat alone, and had not been seen to touch a morsel or drop since he entered the house, neither had he spoken to any one.

He was a mysterious-looking man—one who never could have been invited by either of the families.

This was the impression that was pretty general throughout the whole number of the guests.

The joyous hubbub that reigned throughout the breakfast-room, which had been crowded, and enlarged to meet the wants of the occasion, was in time stilled when the presence of the stranger became observed ; there was something so truly awe-inspiring about him that none could explain or resist its potency.

For the first time, too, he was observed to be very pale, and drops of blood were seen upon his vest, and his eyes were fixed with a glassy gaze upon the door ; and even when Mr. Fraser entered the room, it did not cause him to take his dreadful gaze off the door.

Mr. Fraser soon espied the stranger, and looked amazed for a few moments, and then moved towards him, and had just opened his lips to inquire who he was, and his business there, when the door opened behind him and Frank Briant led in his happy bride by the hand to present her to the guests for the last time as Miss Fraser.

The moment, however, Frank fixed his eyes upon the stranger, he gasped for breath, staggered, and fell into a seat.

"Water !—water !" he gasped.

Water was instantly given him, and amid the consternation that prevailed, to turn the stranger out had been the first emotion, but to learn the cause of the change in Frank's manner at such a moment—

"It was a sudden faintness," he said—"a palpitation of the heart—I shall be better presently. Where is—?"

Everybody turned round and sought the stranger, and when they found he had advanced among them towards the spot where Frank sat in the chair, they made way, and left a lane between themselves, and the stranger advanced to within three or four paces of Frank, and then gazed fixedly at him.

Frank seemed paralysed—he was of an ashy hue, and his lips bloodless—his eyes fearfully dilated, and when the stranger turned half round and beckoned him slowly with his forefinger, Frank arose too, and walked with a tottering gait after him.

The guests were astounded—bride and her father—all were too much absorbed to notice each other ; but as if by one consent, by one irresistible impulse, allowed him to pass out, and he became the centre of their gaze—they stood gazing upon this singular occurrence, and then, by the same kind of universal impulse among them, they at one and the same moment followed the bride and father, who hurried after the retreating forms of the bridegroom and his strange guest.

It was strange to see Frank Briant, who appeared as if he were unable to stand, but yet had strength enough left only to totter after the figure, that every now and then turned its head and beckoned him onwards, until they reached the porch of the church.

Then, instead of entering by the usual door, the figure turned on one side and entered by one of the breaches made by time in the walls. Here the guests came up at the moment, and had entered the church by the usual way, except some few, who followed bride and father through the aperture. Then, in the presence of all, the figure pointed to the drops of blood ; they all paused—all save Briant, who tottered on until he came to the chancel door, and passing through it the door closed after them.

The spell was broken, and in another minute the guests had passed through and found Frank Briant lying on the cold pavement of the chancel in the last agonies of death. He was lifted up and carried out of the church and placed on the grass, with his head on a mound of earth, that seemed to be the grave of some one ; he was fast dying, and but little could he say, save to me, and when others were out of ear-shot he confessed that he had murdered the unfortunate Joseph Thornton within a short time after he had parted from Ellen. He informed me where to find the body, which we did, and gave it a decent burial. This confession ended, he breathed his last.

Ellen Fraser was carried home senseless, and never married afterwards, dying at an early age, carried off by melancholy, which resulted in consumption.

The old chapel, a year after this affair, was stricken by lightning, and the roof fell in ; and thus ends my narrative. Stranger, judge if I have not said that which you may remember as long as you breathe!"

" I shall," said I, "and I am well pleased with the visit I have made to these old ruins ; for more reasons than one, I am gratified."

I gave the old man some money, which he declined at first ; but I induced him to accept it, and then returned to my inn.

Mr. Rattibonum sat down amid considerable applause ; for his tale had excited an interest which probably depended as much upon the fact that it had quite a different complexion from any that they had as yet heard, as from the intrinsic merit of the narrative itself, or the style in which he had given it.

CHAPTER VI.

THE ARRIVAL.—A BOLD FACE.—THE FIGHT FOR THE COFFIN.

It is just possible enough that some of the guests were a little disappointed—we may call them guests at a banquet of the imagination—that the three hours, for that was the time, Mr. Rattibonum had taken in the narration of the affair to which he had drawn their attention, had passed off so quietly.

It was now a quarter to three o'clock in the morning, and in another hour the dawn would begin to make its appearance.

Yet nothing had occurred—no interruption—all was as 'calm 'and peaceable as before; they had not heard of Mr. Annesley, who was the being from whom of course they fully expected to receive some sort of interruption to the otherwise even tenor of their proceedings.

And we may well suppose that there were no two persons who looked forward with more expectation or anxiety to something of the sort arising, than Mr. Bellamy and Mr. Harcourt, for no two persons had equal reason so to look forward.

That the whole evening, or rather night, should pass off, and he (the spectre) break the word he had pledged on his last night of being there, that he would always be present at their meetings, was inexplicable.

"You may depend," whispered Mr. Harcourt to Bellamy, "that our having possession of the coffin is what stops him."

No. 18.

"So I should imagine."

"I fancy that I can get up a very good and reasonable hypothesis upon the subject. He is compelled at a certain hour to relinquish his evanescent and spiritual existence, and then, from old habit and association, he likes to get into his own original coffin again."

"It would seem so."

"Oh! I have myself no doubt upon the subject. It is so, you may depend, and our taking possession in the manner we have of the coffin, you perceive, at once leads him to a belief that we mean to contest it with him, especially knowing what we know about him."

"Yes, yes; truly!"

"But what do you think of stating what we know of the proceedings of this Robert Annesley to the club?"

"I think that now we may as well take this opportunity—there seems a sort of pause which we may as well take advantage of."

"So be it! Will you, or shall I, be spokesman?"

"I would rather you, if you don't object."

"Object? Oh! certainly not. By no means; and as I know you speak your mind and your real wishes in perfect sincerity, I will commence, and conceal nothing of what we have done from the members of the association, who, I think, will find what we have to tell them the most remarkable thing they have yet heard."

"In truth will they."

Mr. Harcourt was about to rise and claim the attention of the chairman, when he, Mr. Bellamy, and everyone else, was completely petrified with astonishment by hearing from the further end of the vault nearest to the door, the now well-known voice of Mr. Annesley, the undoubted spectre, say,—

"Mr. President and Gentlemen,—I have listened with great pleasure to the narration of our friend Mr. Rattibonum, which, as I came in late, it was quite correct to go on with, in preference to waiting for me to conclude my tale of the Ghostly Sentinel, which you will remember I left off while I was in the coffin."

It would be quite impossible to describe the astounding effect which these few words had upon the association. Every one rose and made a movement in the direction which was furthest from the ghost, and when the first confused rush had subsided he was standing completely alone, while around the chairman was grouped the whole of the members of the club, with the exception of Mr. Harcourt and his friend Bellamy, who manfully kept firm possession of the coffin.

"Really, gentlemen, and brother-labourers in the garden of useful information," said Annesley, "is there anything about me so frightful that you should thus shrink aghast from me, and gaze upon me with such terrified eyes?"

"Yes, yes!" cried several.

"And pray what is it, gentlemen? If there be anything that I can alter, you may believe me that I will do so with pleasure."

"How, in the name of all that's wonder," said the president, "came you here? The door is closed. How came you here?"

"How came I here, sir?"

"Yes; we counted heads before, and there were but eleven of us; now, with you, there are twelve."

"Exactly."

"Well, sir, I say, exactly; but how came you here?"

"Why, am I not a member of this most honorable and praiseworthy association? Have I not, by virtue of my membership, a right to be here; and have I not likewise, by virtue of it, told a portion of a tale, which now, as in duty bound to those gentlemen who heard what I did relate so patiently, I have come to conclude? Gentlemen, I was in the coffin, if you recollect, watching the Knollwood House lodge gate."

"We know you were; but how did you come out again? Avaunt,—avaunt,— avaunt!"

The president rose as he spoke, and seemed to be in a state of great excitement, as likewise were some of the members, who took the word from his lips, and likewise shouted, "Avaunt—avaunt!"

"Well, avaunt!" said Annesley, looking around him; "really, gentlemen, I join, out of my extreme complacency, in your cry of 'avaunt!' but I don't see anything at all uglier than ourselves within the vault."

"It is you we mean," said the president; "we have seen quite enough of you to convince us that you are not of this world, and therefore we desire none of your company. We do not want the conclusion of your tale, nor will we endure to have you among us. We are mortal men, and while we preserve our mortal being we have no wish to come into close contact with the beings of another world."

"Nor I," said Annesley; "and now, gentlemen, if you please, at the same time that I highly approve of what the chairman has said, who is clever enough in his way, but now and then a little prosy, I will continue my story. Gentlemen, be so good as to oblige me with that coffin, and assist me in putting it up on end to make a representation of the sentry-box again."

These last words were addressed, of course, to Messrs. Bellamy and Harcourt, who still maintained their seats upon the coffin, and continued to gaze with an intensity of surprise upon the whole scene which almost deprived them of the power of utterance.

"Will you oblige me?" added Annesley.

"No," said Mr. Harcourt: "Gentlemen, I call upon you all to witness that this is the undoubted spectre of one Robert Annesley, who died half a century ago and was buried in this very coffin, as a plate upon its lid will prove."

"Yes," added Bellamy, in an excited tone of voice, "we know it well, and have good reason to know it. We had him in a sack, and my mother-in-law is dead, and my wife nearly broke her neck. Know him! we know all about him."

"That man is mad," said Annesley, pointing to Bellamy.

The incoherent and strange manner in which Bellamy had spoken really went a long way towards proving the assertion of Annesley; for, although in his own mind he of course understood very well what he was saying, and our readers understand it well enough likewise, yet all the strange jumble he made about his wife, the coffin, and his mother-in-law, sounded more like the disjointed ravings of a maniac than anything else.

"No," said Mr. Harcourt, "he is not mad. I can explain everything. This coffin, gentleman, belongs to Robert Annesley, and there he stands."

"Well, then," said the spectre, "if it really belongs to me, by what pretence do you keep me out of it?"

"Hear him, hear him!" cried Harcourt, as he still sat upon the coffin. "He wants to get into it. Hear him!"

"To finish the tale, I do," said Annesley, "certainly want to get into it, and I here request some of the gentlemen present to lend me their kind assistance in dislodging you from it."

This dispute, strange and terrific as it was, was listened to with abundant interest by the members of the association, and more than one wished really that Harcourt should give up the coffin, in order that the ghost should bring to a conclusion the narrative, which they had no doubt had some appalling and strange dénouement that would be well worth the hearing.

But it was a most provoking thing for Mr. Harcourt, who was sitting upon the coffin, to see that his motive in doing so was not appreciated, and that there was, as he could not fail to perceive, a difference of opinion upon the subject of the propriety of his doing so or not.

Perhaps that fact only increased his obstinacy, but he said,—

"Mr. President and Gentlemen,—You surely must all of you perceive what a very advantageous thing it will be for us to drive that spectre to such extremities that he will be forced to make terms with us, and so, perhaps, we shall get from him all the secrets of a world which is to come, as a compromise for letting him have his coffin."

"Can anything be more ridiculous?" said Annesley. "Really, I do hope and trust that no gentleman here present takes me for anything else than a mortal man like himself. I can assure you that when, on the last occasion of our meeting here, there arose some sort of panic, I know not what it was about, but left the vault along with the rest of you."

"You!" cried Bellamy. "Why, you changed to a skeleton."

"And do you pretend to forget the sack?" added Harcourt.

"Oh! I see it all now," said Annesley. "The two gentlemen have not minds strong enough to stand these investigations. They are not quite right about the head-piece. You hear their talk about a sack. Now, gentlemen, I shall request our worthy and most exemplary president to put it to the vote, whether I am to continue my story of 'The Ghostly Sentinel,' or not."

"Continue, continue!" cried several.

"Well, gentlemen, if I must continue, I must have the use of that coffin."

"Why not another coffin?" said Mr. Harcourt.

"Why not that coffin?" said Annesley.

"Well, gentlemen," said the president, "if it be your wish that we should hear the remainder of the story of 'The Ghostly Sentinel,' I shall not' oppose it. I do not see what harm can come of gratifying our curiosity so far, and I do hope that you, Mr. Harcourt, will give up the coffin."

"No, no," cried Harcourt, and he rose to speak. As he did so, the coffin moved away from under him, although no one touched it, and, when he sat down again, with a determined sort of plump, he to his surprise found that it was upon the cold, damp floor of the vault.

He sprung up again in a moment and tried to regain the coffin, but Annesley already had pounced upon it, and a struggle ensued, which was put an end to by Annesley suddenly blowing slightly in the face of Harcourt, who fell immediately, in a state of complete insensibility, on the floor of the vault.

"Hold," cried Annesley, as he saw that the members of the association were not disposed to see one of their number thus summarily disposed of, "hold—he is unhurt. Dash some water in his face, and he will rise quite well."

This was done, and Mr. Harcourt rose up looking a little bewildered, but none the worse otherwise from his encounter with the spectre.

He seemed, however, to have no disposition to resume the struggle for the coffin, but he sat down gloomily enough, muttering to himself—

"Be it so, then! Be it so!"

"Now, Mr. Chairman and Gentlemen," said Robert Annesley, with considerable animation in his tone, "I shall proceed to relate to you how I fared on the occasion of my being by force of circumstances compelled, as it were, to take up my abode in the sentry-box on the knoll."

He raised the coffin as he had done on a former occasion, only this time he allowed the front of it to be next to the spectators.

"You will see and hear me better," he said, "in this way than as I was before, I think; and you will please to recollect that I was at that part of my story when the mysterious flickering light that appeared in the bushes to the left of the sentry-box, was being moved to and fro by some unknown hand."

Some of the members remarked that they quite recollected, and then he continued—

Well, gentlemen, I felt strongly tempted to go forward and examine the light, for it seemed to me, by the manner in which it was moved to and fro, to be inviting me towards it, and I felt strongly impelled to go.

This temptation I resisted for some time, but it grew upon me astonishingly, and at length I felt that I must to some extent yield to it, and I left the box and crept forward a few steps.

Scarcely could I be said to have got from under cover of the sentry-box when I started back again, for I found my course impeded by two figures that stood before me, and who, by a certain sort of luminosity that belonged to themselves, were plainly visible to me.

It took but a glance to convince me that these were the same two apparitions that had been described by the terrified soldier.

They were in the uniform of my regiment, but that uniform was in a most horrible and draggled sort of state. It was torn, stained, and covered with mud in all directions, while their faces and hands seemed to be cut to pieces. I was both surprised and terrified at the sight, and stepped back in dismay.

The moment that I did so, showing a disposition to retreat instead of to advance, they both vanished, and I could see no more of them.

That this was a warning to me to remain where I was, and not attempt to follow that light, or even advance in the direction where it still glistened and glimmered, I could not for a moment doubt, and so I accepted it, and let it act upon me. I retreated again under cover of a sentry-box, and resolved to wait with patience what should next take place.

The light continued visible, and now it was more agitated than before, and seemed actually to be beckoning me towards it. The impulse again grew strong upon me to go, and partly with a wish to try again the experiment, if the two apparitions would appear to me, and partly impelled by strong curiosity, I advanced a step or two.

Yes, there they were again, linked arm-in-arm, and opposing my progress.

I again shrunk back, ashamed of having a second time advanced in the face of so obvious a warning not to do so.

I think, then, about a quarter of an hour might have elapsed, when the light all at once vanished, leaving the place in total darkness. I listened now for the least sound with the most painful intensity, for I conjectured that since I had been, in consequence of the supernatural warning which I had received, enabled to resist the temptation of the light—which would probably have led me into some danger—something else would be attempted.

My situation was anything but a pleasant one. I did not like exactly, although after what had occurred I should have been quite justified in doing so, to fire one of my pistols, and so give an alarm, which would at once have brought down the guard, but I held one of them in my hand, all ready to discharge at a moment's notice.

Over and over again I hurriedly asked myself if, after all, it did not amount to a positive duty, on my part, to give an alarm, because, not only was my own safety compromised in the matter, and as an officer in the regiment I was of course of some consequence, but if I fell it might pave the way for more mischief.

The next officer—for that one would volunteer to do so—who took that most dangerous post, might not be really so careful as I was; and so, by not giving an alarm, I thought I should really, perhaps, be sacrificing his life.

The latter consideration had great weight with me indeed, and almost resolved me, at least it induced me, to make with myself a kind of provisional bargain.

If, I said, I hear any other sound of alarm, or see anything whatever, which I do not understand, I will give an instant alarm.

This I thought—and I think that you will all, gentlemen, agree with me—this was a prudent resolution, and a very just way of putting the question indeed, so I waited.

Nearly a quarter of an hour elapsed in this way when suddenly, from some-where behind, I heard a sharp, crashing sound, and something most extremely like a bullet went whistling past my head.

This astonished me, because I had heard no report, and unless the shot came from some diabolical contrivance in the shape of an air-gun, I could not conceive how it was possible any mortal man could have propelled it so forcibly.

Upon feeling carefully with my hand the back of the sentry-box, as I feel now the back of this coffin, I felt where the bullet had come through, for there was a slight jagged orifice.

This was amply sufficient cause for action; not only had something happened, but something that threatened my very life, so there was no occasion for any more scruples upon the subject, and I at once pulled the trigger of one of my pistols.

Judge, however, of my mortification when it only flashed in the pan, and I had no more powder to renew the priming.

I dreaded to try the other, because if, before the guard came there, I should be assaulted, I had nothing but my sword wherewith to defend myself; and yet, " what could I do?"

While I was deliberating crash came another bullet through the back of the sentry-box, and this time it passed my head so close, that when I put up my hand to the side of my cheek I felt that it was wet with blood, for the bullet had actually made a slight furrow in the skin.

This was anything but an agreeable state of things. I had no idea of remaining to be made an animated target of, so I of course pulled the trigger of my other pistol.

Alas! the night air had the same effect upon both—neither of them would discharge; another evanescent flash was all it produced, and here I was, then, with nothing but my sword to depend upon, and not the least means of alarming the guard.

If I were attacked by numbers, say three or four persons, of course I must be overpowered; for, under such circumstances, a man can do no more than sell his life dearly. And there I waited crouching down, and on one side of the sentry-box, while two more shots passed through the back of it.

Probably, if I could have made up my mind to condescend to shout aloud, my voice might have reached the guard; but that was so undignified a mode of getting assistance, that I really did not like to adopt it.

An officer is placed in a very peculiar position—he must not only take care what he does, but he must take care how he does it ; so I remained where I was, only taking care to keep myself thoroughly upon my guard.

In the course of a few moments I distinctly heard stealthy footsteps approaching, and I have no doubt but that it was presumed the shots had taken effect upon me.

The footsteps came from the same direction whence the firing had proceeded, so that they belonged, without any question, to the same party; and I waited, not a little anxiously, you may be sure, for them to reach me. I held my sword in a position to strike, and kept a wary eye around me, which I was tolerably well enabled to do, because I had been now there so long that I had got accustomed to the darkness, and could see generally pretty distinctly.

Towards my left hand, as I stood within the cover of the sentry-box, I heard some one approaching, and in another minute a face cautiously peeped round the corner of the box.

"Of course," said I to myself, " where there is a face there is a head close at hand, and that is a vulnerable point of attack."

Down went my sabre with the rapidity of lightning; there was a deep groan, and the owner of the face fell across my feet. That I had completely disposed of one of my enemies I felt certain, and now I thought it high time to sally out, which I did at once, with my sword in my hand. A few paces from the sentry-box I was met by a man who was similarly armed; indeed, I felt convinced he had one of the sabres belonging to one of the sentinels who had so mysteriously disappeared from the post upon that knoll.

He was a man of the most herculean build I ever saw, and the first cut he made at me beat down my guard, and very nearly killed me. I soon found that it was not by strength but by science that anything could be done with him, and I took good care that he did not get such another clear cut at me as he had already had. I was gratified to find, after a few moments, that all he possessed was mere brutal strength, and that I was wonderfully his superior in my knowledge of the use of the sword. From the moment of making that discovery I felt my victory over him to be certain, and I inflicted upon him several wounds, which instead of having the effect of disabling him, only seemed to add to his fury. It became quite necessary at length to put an end to a conflict which, after all, might by some accident go against me ; so I summoned all my skill to my aid, and while the big, burley-looking ruffian fancied I was aiming a desperate blow at his face, and carefully guarding himself therefrom, I ran him through the body.

The howl of rage he gave was perfectly terrific. He at once became a furious madman : I knew it could not last many minutes, but well I knew, likewise, how desperately dangerous a man under the mad paroxysm of such a moment is.

The only resource was flight for a short distance until he should fall, which was a consummation sure to be attained very soon. Accordingly, I took to my heels and galloped back to my sentry-box again, from which I had, in the heat of the conflict, strayed a considerable distance. I thought that if I could reach it I might successfully dodge him until he fell from exhaustion. But he rushed after me with such frantic speed that he was near catching me before I got there. You may fancy the state of mind I was in during this fearful race, as one of the most uncomfortable character that can be imagined ; but at length I did manage to reach the sentry-box, with what I knew to be a dying man close to my heels. All I could do, for I ran so directly forwards that I nearly stumbled over it, was to pop round it and get inside, holding out my sword at arm's length. I have no sword here, gentlemen, but popped into the sentry-box as I do now into this coffin, the great use of which, in my narrative, you now perceive.

As he spoke, Mr. Annesley got into the coffin and stood upright within it.

"Well, gentlemen," he continued, "on he came like a mad bull ; I think the anguish of his wound must have blinded him, for he did not appear to see the sentry-box at at all, but came against the back of it so furiously that over it went, shutting me up completely from his vengeance, because it fell upon its face and I under it. I will show you exactly."

Mr. Annesley gave the coffin a jerk forward, gathered himself into as small a compass as he could, and down it went flat upon its face, with a ringing sort of sound upon the floor of the vault, completely hiding him from the observation of the members of the association.

At this instant Mr. Harcourt sprung to his feet.

"Mr. President and Gentlemen, I knew," he cried, "how this would be. I knew it, I guessed it, all along, and I whispered it to my friend Bellamy, who knew it, and who guessed it likewise."

"Knew what, Mr. Harcourt ?" said the president.

"Why, sir, how can you or any intelligent member of this association ask ? I am astonished that you have not seen from the very beginning, that all this story we have heard to-night from the spectre of Robert Annesley was but an artful mode of again introducing himself to that coffin."

All eyes were directed to the coffin, which was perfectly stationary ; and Mr. Harcourt then added, in a very excited manner—

"Gentlemen, you will find, if you raise that coffin, nothing but the same collection of festering, loathsome-looking bones, which we have now twice seen that spectre resolve himself into."

"That can easily be proved," said Mr. Bellamy ; and he stepped forward and raised the coffin, adding—

"Behold, gentlemen, the narrator of the tale of the Ghostly Sentinel !"

He and Mr. Harcourt were right. There, beneath the coffin, lay a skeleton form stretched out upon the floor of the vault, and presenting all the ghastly appearances that it had done upon a former occasion.

Surprise and consternation kept the members of the club silent for a while, and then one said—

"Mr. President, this is too horrible. I move that we break up this association."

"Hold," said Mr. Harcourt, "before you do that, hear what I and Mr. Bellamy here have to relate to you."

He then, as shortly as it was possible to do so, explained how he and Bellamy had possessed themselves of the skeleton which they now saw before them, and how, having carried it home in a sack, it had been taken away from them by the mysterious visitor, whose very presence was afterwards denied by the old servant, but who had proved the fact of his having been there by the news he had given to Mr. Bellamy of the death of his mother-in-law.

"This, then, Mr. President and Gentlemen of the Club," he said, "will account for the seemingly insane expression which fell from my friend Bellamy; and I can only say that both he and I fully looked forward to, and expected what has been the end of the story, that the spectre of Robert Annesley has so highly entertained you with, and, I admit, told so well to you."

Mr. Bellamy, in a few words, confirmed all that had been said, and called attention to the coffin-lid, on which the name of Robert Annesley appeared, along with the date of his decease.

These things were listened to with the greatest attention on the part of the members of the association ; and then he who had taken upon himself to move the dissolution of the club again announced this proposition ; but before it was further proceeded with, the president addressed the members, saying—

"Gentlemen, I must confess that I do not see any necessity, from what has happened, of dissolving this club."

"Hear! hear!" cried several.

"It seems to me, gentlemen, that it would be tantamount to a confession of very great fear, and that we should be obnoxious to the charge of giving up our weekly meetings at a time when, above all others, they were becoming deeply interesting."

There was considerable applause after this observation, and, emboldened by such a demonstration of sympathetic opinions, he added—

"Gentlemen, it does appear, to my humble judgment, that if there ever could be a time in the annals of this association when we should feel induced to proceed with more deep interest in the subjects which we have set apart for inquiry, that time is the present."

The proposer of the motion to dissolve the club, now finding that popular opinion was so strongly set against him upon the subject rose, and very politely at once withdrew his motion.

Rather an animated discussion then arose as to whether or not it would be at all prudent to do anything as regarded the skeleton lying before them or not, and there was one member present who took such a rational view of the subject, that he ought to be allowed to speak for himself.

The gentleman was the same who had told the first tale of "The Dead Face," and rising, he addressed the chair with great courtesy, saying :—

"Mr. President and Gentlemen, I cannot help rising in defence of one whom I think we are using rather ill, and towards whom I do think we are scarcely behaving with the most common and ordinary courtsy."

There was a general look of surprise, which was none the less intense when the speaker added—

"The individual to whom I allude, as experiencing at our hands this discourtesy is the ghost of Mr. Robert Annesley. Yes, gentlemen, I do not see what quarrel we can have with that existence, and why we should go out of our way to annoy and trouble one who has gone out of his way to amuse and instruct us. Gentlemen, what has this spectre form done? Has it come in some terrific shape to endeavour to light up unmanly fears in my breast, or in the breast of any gentleman connected with this society? Has it done anything which is calculated to produce one bad result? Not that I can see, gentlemen. On the contrary, it appears to me that this spectral form has come here for our amusement and our instruction. It has, in good language, and a graphic mode of delivery, told us a tale which has amused us all, I am sure. Why, then, gentlemen, I ask—why, then, is it that we should set about at all interfering with this existence, which has been itself so friendly disposed and so utterly and entirely harmless towards us?"

These reasonable words sunk deeply into the minds of all, and changed the current of feeling entirely. They began to look upon the skeleton form of him who had so recently been conversing with them with a kind of awe and pity rather than with a feeling of antagonism or disgust.

"I hope," continued the speaker, "that we shall, on the next occasion that this mysterious being comes among us, receive him with that amount of courtesy which he deserves, and in the meantime let us respect those sad memorials of the dead now before us."

It is astonishing how a few words of sober reason will sometimes calm down violent passion. Now all was peaceful serenity, and as the dawn of morning was close at hand the members of the club bade each other adieu, and departed from the place, leaving in the peace and the security of the tomb the skeleton form of him whom they looked forward to seeing again that day week with the semblance of life about him.

CHAPTER VII.

THE NEXT MEETING.—THE TALE OF THE ELFIN LOVER.

NEITHER Mr. Harcourt nor Mr. Bellamy were bigoted men, and after what had been said of the injustice of meddling with the skeleton, the mere thought of No. 19.

committing such a lapse of right would have deterred them from again making the attempt to possess themselves of the bones.

As they walked home they talked the matter over calmly and coolly.

" It did not, I must confess, strike me," said Harcourt, " that we were about to do anything unreasonable by taking that skeleton away as we did. Because, you see, one does not meet such creatures as Annesley with those feelings of human nature which we have ourselves."

" That was my idea," said Bellamy.

" But, however, since the affair has been placed in that light by every one, I am sure that both you and I would shrink from any semblance of doing anything in the shape of an injustice, or setting about anything that would seem like a persecution of the dead."

" Certainly, certainly ; we will let the matter rest where it is, and you know we have not really yet heard the conclusion of the tale of 'the Ghostly Sentinel.'"

" No, because the spectre began his narrative so late that he had not time in which to finish it, before the early morning air most probably warned him through his subtle senses that it was now time to go."

" True ; and that arose in consequence of our assembling before midnight, which was earlier than, you may depend, he was permitted to appear."

" Precisely. Did you notice his first appearance ?"

" No ; did you ?"

" I did not, and yet I thought that I kept the strictest watch ; for, as you know, I fully expected it, and thought that surely, in a place of such confined dimensions, I should be able to see whatever occurred. But the first I knew of his presence was hearing his voice."

" The same with me it was."

" You may depend those subtle forms can appear with such marvellous rapidity and disappear likewise in the same manner, that it becomes impossible to catch them with the eye until they actually choose that you should do so."

" No doubt, no doubt. But come home with me and we will pass a pleasanter evening than we did on the last occasion when you paid me a visit."

" Nay," said Mr. Bellamy, " when you say, ' Come home with me,' and talk about passing a pleasanter evening, you quite forget that I am a married man."

" Oh ! so I do."

" I cannot think of such a thing ; but if you will pass the evening with me on our next night of meeting—that is, till it is time to go to the vault, I shall be very glad ; only you know you must prepare yourself to be proof against any questioning on the part of my wife regarding the club."

" I will ; it is one of our rules that no member shall tell his wife where the club is held or its objects."

" Yes, but it is a rule which I am afraid is broken by some, although not by me ; although Mrs. Bellamy is getting dreadfully curious to know what it is that keeps me out once a week nearly the whole of the night. I have told her it was business, but she does not believe the excuse I can well perceive."

" Well, I am glad you have put me on my guard ; for I otherwise might not have had all my caution about me. I accept your invitation with great pleasure, and will be with you at eight o'clock ; so that we shall have nearly four hours of confabulation before we need start to keep our appointment with our friends at the vault."

With this understanding they separated.

*   *   *   *   *   *

" My dear," said Mr. Bellamy to his wife, on the evening of the next meeting of the club, " I expect a gentleman."

" What !" exclaimed Mrs. Bellamy, " a visitor. Now really, Mr. B., that is so like you. You know how inconvenient a visitor is here to-day, and that's why you asked him, of course."

" Indeed, you are very much mistaken, my dear ; for I do not know that it is inconvenient to you to-day to receive a visitor. How should I so? I could not ask him for that reason, even if I had ever so little regard for his comfort."

" Don't tell me, Mr. B., you did not know. Is not to-morrow my washing day?"
" Well!"
" Well, well! Yes, it's all very well for you who are a man—at least who pretends to be a man, to say, ' Well!' but it is not well, sir."

" I cannot see how you having to wash to-morrow prevents you from receiving a friend of mine conveniently to-day."

" Can you not, Mr. B.? Well, sir, if you cannot I am not obliged, I suppose, to find you in comprehension."

" No, certainly not."
" Oh! yes; try to shuffle out of it, do."
" My dear, I was not shuffling; and I don't know what it is all about. I have a friend coming to sit a few hours with me, that's all, this evening."

" And I have a larger wash to-morrow than we have had since we have been in this house."

" But if you have I don't see what that has to do with it. My friend does not come here to be washed, so that he adds nothing to the soap suds commotion."

" Oh!" exclaimed Mrs. Bellamy, with the concentrated look of a number of martyrs all rolled into one, " oh! is not this enough to make any woman hate herself and all the world? Mr. B., you are a trying man; you are. It's well you have got a woman who gives way to you, and who studies you and puts up with all your whims and fancies."

" Now, my dear, really you know I study you; and I have a favour to ask of you, which is that you will put on that China silk dress with the Valenciennes lace, that you look so lovely in."

" Mr. B."

" Yes, my dear, you do look lovely in it. Now do put it on just to please me, and let my friend see that I have the handsomest wife in the town, so that he may give me credit for my taste."

Oh! artful Mr. Bellamy! you know how to manage your better half. Designing man, how could you think of saying anything about that China silk dress with the Valenciennes lace? But, however, all's fair in love, and when Mr. Bellamy conquered, no more was said of the great wash, and the lady appeared duly attired in the garments that elicited such encomiums.

Husbands — a moral: always pitch upon some one article of your wife's wardrobe, in which you declare she is irresistible, and when the clouds are in the matrimonial horizon, persuade her to put it on.

You have all heard of oil on the troubled water—poh! that's nothing to it. Try it.

Mr. Harcourt was punctual to his appointment. At eight o'clock he knocked at Mr. Bellamy's door, and was duly introduced. " Mr Harcourt, Mrs. Bellamy;" " My dear Mr Harcourt, my friend—ahem!" and then Bellamy pretended that Mr. Harcourt had said something to him in a whisper, although Harcourt was quite innocent of it; and he replied to the pretended saying, in a stage whisper,—

" Yes, she is a handsome woman, although I say it."

This piece of Machiavelian policy settled the business, and Mrs. Bellamy was in the very sweetest of tempers—an artful, managing man was that Bellamy.

Of course, now, nothing was to be expected but smiles and tea-cake. Indeed, Mrs. Bellamy did the amiable in such grand style, that any one who did not know her, would have gone away with the impression that Bellamy must be one of the luckiest fellows under the sun, to draw such a prize in the matrimonial lottery.

But the tug of war was yet to come. Mr. Bellamy was like a man who uses a two edge sword : it is cutting at the back, as well when he only wishes it to cut at the front.

In making Harcourt so tremendously welcome, and in exciting such a world of kindness and amiability in Mrs. Bellamy, he had made the task of getting away a little before twelve o'clock rather a difficult one.

Of course, Mr. Harcourt's going would have been nothing. He could go when he liked, being presumed to have a home of some sort, but when Mr. Bellamy talked of going, it was quite a different thing.

Mr. Harcourt was not a young lady who, as a matter of politeness, required that Bellamy should see him home for fear of the " fellows"—oh, no ! Then why need Mr. Bellamy go out ?

" You are not going out, B.," said the lady, " at this time of night, I'm sure."

" Why, my dear," said B., " you know I always go out once a week, and this is the night."

" Well, I'm sure, a nice, polite man you are to invite your friend to see you, and the very night, of all others, when you have an engagement out ; of course, Mr. Harcourt may think of it as he pleases, and, perhaps, he is too much the gentleman to say what he thinks exactly, but if I were in his place, I should feel myself very much offended indeed."

" Why, my dear," said Bellamy, " Mr Harcourt might feel very much offended indeed, if it were not for the little circumstance that he goes with me, so that, you see, alters the case."

" I am very glad to hear it."

" Are you ? "

" Yes—because now I shall know the truth : Mr. Harcourt is too much the gentleman, in every sense of the word, to refuse a lady anything—a-hem !— Mr. Harcourt, where are you going with Mr. Bellamy to-night ? "

Here was a case. What now would any one have given for all the popularity of Mr Harcourt at the tea-table of Mrs. Bellamy ? Alas, how fleeting are human what do you call its, and all that sort of thing. With the Psalmist we would say something, but we don't recollect it.

" Why—a—a—a—madam," said Mr. Harcourt, " madam, that is—a—you see madam."

" No," said Mrs. Bellamy, " I don't see—oh no ! "

" No, no—oh no !—poh, yet"—

" Well, I want to know where you and Bellamy are going ?"

" Oh yes, you want to know where Bellamy and I are going—you want to know. You are in a manner of speaking, desirous of knowing where we are going."

" I have said so, Mr. Harcourt, or what comes to the same thing."

" Yes ; your are quite right, madam." (Bellamy, damn it, where's my hat.) " You are quite right—amazingly correct. I am not, madam, of that class of persons who say that—

> " Men have many faults ; women have but two—
> There's nothing right they say, and there's nothing right they do."

Oh no, oh no, I don't agree with that at all."

" Nobody asked you, sir. All I want to know is—"

" Yes, certainly, madam,"—(my hat)—" of course, and extremely natural." (Get out as quick as you can, and I'll meet you at the corner, Bellamy.) " I have the honour, madam, of bidding you most respectfully good evening."

" Which means that you will not answer my question, Mr. Harcourt. Well, sir, I did think—"

" I know it, madam. A mind like yours must be always thinking, and so with a hope—a distant hope, madam—that you will sometimes condescend to think of me, I humbly and respectfully take my leave."

When Harcourt got to this climax, he made a rush from the apartment, snatched his hat from a peg in the passage, and bounced into the street, where he drew a long breath of exquisite relief, as he exclaimed—

" Thank God, I've got out of that, and if ever Bellamy gets me across his threshold again, I will tell her, that's all."

He walked to the corner of the street, where, in the course of six or seven minutes, he was joined by Bellamy, to whom he said—

" Why, how did you get away so soon ?"

" Oh, Mrs. B. is in hysterics, which makes it all the pleasanter. She says that she never did much with such a brute as you are in all her life, and that she never will forgive herself for mistaking you for a gentleman, although, from the mere fact of your being an acquaintance of mine, she had her suspicions that you would turn out something bad in the end."

" Upon my word, Bellamy, you got me into a pretty scrape. I never was in such an absolute fix all my life."

" But you got out of it remarkably well."

" Did I! I don't see any remarkable wellness in the manner of getting out of it. The fact was that I bolted, and so got out of it. That is the only way in which I managed it."

" No ; but you fenced very nicely with Mrs. B. before you bolted."

" Did I. You may do the fencing business yourself another time. But come on, we shall be late at the vault, and affairs, to my apprehension, grow more and more interesting each time of meeting."

" And to me likewise."

They pushed on as quickly as possible, and soon forgot all about Mrs. Bellamy and her indignation, in a retrospection of what had occurred at the vault, and anticipations of what was likely still to occur, more particularly in connection with the mysterious Mr. Annesley, who, they doubted not, would come again.

" If," said Harcourt, " he made his appearance among us, notwithstanding all that was done of an aggravating character towards him, he will surely come now when a good feeling prevails, and he is left alone to go into what coffin he pleases, and no plot is found to put him to any inconvenience.

When they reached the vault they found that most of the members had arrived, and the lamp was lit. Upon inquiring of those who had first reached the place of rendezvous, it was found, as usual, that the skeleton of Robert Annesley had disappeared.

Business commenced by the President—viz., counting the members ; but, as only 10 were present, it was proposed to wait a little for the absent members, and they separated into small groups, talking something with each other, principally upon the subject of the coffin-ghost, as some of them called Annesley.

The member who was not present was he to whom had appeared the spirit of the deceased member of the club ; and, it wanted but one minute to 12 o clock, when he made his appearance, looking so pale and agitated, and in so much dishabille, that any one who saw him felt in a moment convinced that something of a dreadful character must have happened to him.

All eyes were of course turned upon him and many eager questions were asked at once but the president interposed, saying—

" Gentlemen, let us conduct our proceedings regularly, if you please, I have no doubt but that our friend will, through me, relate to you whatever of the strange and the marvellous has occurred to him."

" Yes, gentlemen, yes ;" said the agitated man.

" There, gentlemen," added the president, in a tone of evident satisfaction, " I knew he would—I was quite certain of it. Pray be seated, sir, and calm yourself. You know that you are now among friends."

" Yes—yes—thank God !"

" Amen, sir. Well, sir, we attend. You have seen—"

" Again the ghost of our dead member who was thrown from his gig. He came to me last night and I have been trembling ever since."

" Take your time, sir."

" Yes—Yes—I will. I was absurd enough to take the advice that was offered to me here and—and—to speak to it ; yes, I absolutely spoke to it. I hardly knew what I said but I did speak to it."

" Pray how did it appear ?"

"Why I feel a little better now so I may as well tell you, systematically, how it all happened, I told you now, a fortnight ago, how, when I had altogether ceased to expect anything of the kind, I suddenly found it seated on my bed-side. I told you then how cruel I thought it of any ghost to throw a gentleman first so completely off his guard, and then come nearly driving him mad when he least of all expected such a visitation."

"You did, sir."

"Well, of course I fully expected to see it again the next night but I did not see it. The next night after, that's the next, and then the next again passed away, and at last a whole fortnight, so that once again I was thrown off my guard in the same cruel way as before, and I said to myself, oh, it has made its visit and met with no encouragement, so I shall certainly now see no more of it whatever, and so I satisfied myself and went to bed last night as contented as any man could. I dropped off into a quiet pleasant-enough slumber, and thought no more—no, not so much of seeing any ghost as I do now."

"And when did you awaken?"

"About twelve, as near as I can guess, indeed I am certain it must have been thereabouts, for I had a feeling that I had not been asleep long, and it wanted only a little of eleven when I retired to rest."

"And then you saw him?"

"At once—at once—it was moonlight you know last night—rather a brilliant moonlight—and although I had the blinds in my room all drawn closely down, there was sufficient light for me to distinguish any object as plainly as if the sun was shining at noon-day."

"My eyes turned mechanically and at once towards the chair, which I always have by the head of my bed, and there sitting upon it was the spectre. I saw its face, for the moonlight fell full upon it, it looked pale but it did not speak, nor could I for many minutes, for whenever I would have said something my tongue clove to the very roof of my mouth and I could not."

"But you did at last?"

"You shall hear. I do think that nearly an hour passed away in this state of silence and the spectre never moved, nor did I. It kept the same shady, sad-looking gaze, and I was too much terrified and fascinated by its awful presence to take my eyes off it for a moment."

"At length I made a desperate resolution, remembered the advice that had been given to me and what had been said about spectres not being able to speak until some human being had first addressed them, so while I was quite in a state of horror I did contrive to say."

"Will you speak?"

"The sound of my voice broke the spell. The spectre instantly moved, and stooping his head down till the bloodless lips came close to my ear, and I shook from head to foot in consequence of such close contact with the dead, he uttered such a horrible yelling shriek that it went through my brains like a flash of forked lightning and I became immediately insensible."

"My family found me in the morning still completely gone, and it took some hours of unremitting exertions of a medical man to restore me to consciousness again."

"Then after all," said the president, in a tone of disappointment; "after all it really made you no answer?"

"No answer do you call that! I beg to differ from you there, it was a most stunning answer. The sound of it is not yet out of my ears, nor do I really think it ever will be."

Everybody thought this very unsatisfactory—and so it was—there was nothing in it. What they wanted was, some revelation from the ghost, but a mere shriek was nothing to satisfy curiosity, however it might have completely bewildered him to whom it was addressed,

"Gentlemen," said the president, "we may as well announce the business of the evening. We are very much obliged, of course, for what our friend has told us, and we can only hope, that on the next occasion, he and the ghost will really have some rational conversation, of which we can make something."

This was generally approved of, but the gentleman whose ear had been screamed into, evidently thought himself slighted, quite forgetting that a scream, however horrifying it might have been to him, was nothing at all at second hand, and was not very likely to produce much effect upon the hearers.

The skull was once more dipped into, and the president announced the name of a Mr. Barrows.

There were general looks of satisfaction as this name was announced, because it had been talked about among them, that Mr. Barrows had been a great traveller, and, as great travellers see strange things, there could be no doubt but that he had seen his share.

This gentleman made no comment nor excuse, but merely rose and bowed in acknowledgment of having been chosen on the occasion. He said, "he hoped that what he should tell them, would not disappoint their expectations, and that, in order that such should not be the case, he begged that they would expect as little as possible from him, when, if they were agreeably disappointed, it would be all the better."

All was attention, for much was expected from this gentleman, who looked one of those thoughtful and considerate men, who are capable of storing up an immense fund of knowledge.

His ample brow betokened imagination, and there was a something in his voice, which ever invested a common-place sentence from his lips, with some weight and importance.

The president demanded silence, more as a matter of form than anything else, for all were silent and attentive ; and then, the narrator began in a pleasant tone of voice, to tell the tale of

THE ELFIN LOVER;

OR, THE HAUNTED ELM.

It is now more than twenty years ago since I was in a pretty village, of the West Riding of Yorkshire, and there I have never been since the last member of the only family I knew well there died. The family were unfortunate, not in circumstances, because they were beyond all fear of want, or even inconvenience on that score, for they had long been known as landowners for many generations, and now they occupy the family vault, which has received the last of their race.

It was in 17— when I was there. It was spring, and I had gone down to spend a few months. I had suffered from illness, and I went there to recruit my shattered frame, and this I succeeded in doing, in the keen fine air of the Yorkshire hills.

The family in which I was domiciled, was composed of but three individuals, the mother, father, and daughter. The latter, one of the most beautiful girls I ever beheld ; they formed as united a family as ever I saw, and acted so much in unison, and almost as if they spoke and thought from but one impulse.

Charlotte Jeffries, was just eighteen when I arrived, and she was the object of more than one young man's ambition in that place. There was a party, a kind of fete, given among the friends and neighbours, and there were no less than about twenty couples, who sat down to the tables, beneath the awning or the spreading branches of a tree, trained on trellis work, to cover tables for twice that number of persons, if it had been required.

This had been the work of years, and now it formed one of the most striking arboreal pictures that I know of, or that I ever saw.

Beneath this singular canopy, I was conducted and placed in an arm chair. At the same time, I was wrapped up so that no danger of catching cold remained.

Then on the lawn was a dance, and those engaged in it appeared amongst the happiest beings that ever I saw or observed before. It was on this occasion that I was introduced to my host's daughter. I had seen her before, but she was a mere child, now she was a growing woman, and one of the most beautiful that ever I saw.

" I am glad you are come at this moment," said Mr. Jeffries, when he sat down beside me, after he had been conversing, and attending to some of his other guests, " not but what it has its inconveniences, especially as you are an invalid and would prefer quietness."

" I am well enough to repay this," I replied, " and find no inconvenience from this, whatever you may, and you must get fatigued."

" I do, when I've done," he replied, " but, then, one gets fatigued with pleasure. I cannot complain since I am well pleased, and wished you to see how we do these things in the country, somewhat different to what you find it in the gay saloons of London."

" Yours is unique and characteristic."

" Yes, yes, entirely so—entirely so ; but you see you have the advantage in lights, appointments, and delicacies—things, in fact, that charm the taste, the eye, and ear."

" And what more would you have, then, than you have here ? You have all that we desire, health, and youth. Your gay dance resembles more the effect of enchantment of the scene of a theatre, where these actors appear what they are not, young and innocent—more, you are all this—you are what they represent."

" That it is very true, and we, who are used to it, feel it, especially when we go to London, we feel it in our health. I must admit the pleasures of the town are too seducing not to be indulged in, in moderation."

" There is so much that is mere glitter, mere show, that I prefer the real enjoyment of such a scene as this, which leaves no sting behind."

" I admit I enjoy a dance, and love to see my neighbours around me, there is the beauty of a country life. Such a party as this does not cause the waste and disarrangement it would cause in town."

" I can easily conceive that."

" And, moreover, it has its advantage in this manner, it is an introduction to life for my daughter, and it is time to begin to think of her."

" I thought I saw her dancing with a young man, who seemed more than usually attentive, and she appeared by no means displeased."

" Yes, yes, that matter is well nigh settled, though the marriage won't take place yet I dare say."

" Then, you have but little to fear upon that score," said I. " Your daughter has a husband in her eye."

" That is all very well, and I admit that to be the fact ; yet, young people will be young people, and they must have some kind of amusement or other ; but, at the same time, I am desirous they shall not seek it from my own fire-side."

" You wish to be witness to what goes forward yourself, then ?" said I.

" I am, and I have reason to do so—or then, I think no harm can come of my Charlotte. She is a very susceptible child, and liable to be easily imposed upon. She suspects no evil from any one, and, therefore, armed in her own innocence, she thinks herself triply strong."

" Such is a noble trait," I observed.

" And, so it is, my friend, and, so it is ; but, then, the re are many things that militate against the success of those who endeavour to figh t their way through life with some cunning in view."

" Yes, unless some stern ruggedness of nature aids the i nnocence of such a one. She will sink before the arts of practised men of the world." "

" I have every hope and expectation to the contrary, for, my opinion in Charlotte's virtue and rectitude of conduct, is such that I have no fear, yet I would not be without precaution of some kind or other."

" It is right ; but who is the lover, and what is he, if such questions are at all fair ?"

" However, I will introduce you to him this evening, for he is a fine young man, and one that will please you. He is just come of age, and will be going to town in a few days, thence to undertake the prosecution of some business which the death of his father left incomplete."

" He has arrived at his majority, then ?" I inquired.

" He has, and now is the moment he must take upon himself the management of his own affairs, and release himself from his guardian's hands, a man who has not been the pleasantest to deal with ever since he has become acquainted with the fact that Charles Osborne has been an admirer of my daughter."

" Indeed ; had he any views of his own, that were thwarted by it."

" Indeed, you have just hit it. He has a daughter, a nice girl enough, who took a fancy I believe to Charles, or perhaps to his fortune, which is large enough."

" I see he is anxious enough to keep it all to himself, I dare say," I replied.

" He would ; of this there can be no little doubt, for it is very ample and unencumbered."

No. 20.

"I am very glad to hear that her prospects are so very good, and I am persuaded that she will well deserve the fortune that awaits her."

"She does, she does; look at her how she stands now side by side with Charles Osborne—see, they dance—they are made for each other."

"They are without compliment," I said, "the finest and best matched couple in the room!"

"The room!"

"I mean on the lawn. I cannot yet accommodate my tongue to the change of things that I see here; and I may make a few mistakes."

"It matters not; but to return to what I was telling you of—Charles will soon leave for London, because his father's affairs are somewhat involved. Some legacy that was left him is in Chancery, and there are some deeds that he has to execute, so that a few weeks will elapse at the very least, before he will be back to take possession of the estate of his father, for good."

"It would have been a very good opportunity to have had the wedding first over, and have carried his bride to town with him, and there have spent the honeymoon."

"So Charles thought, but Charlotte was averse to that; and I myself would sooner see him return from London at the conclusion of all business that calls him away, to his seat, there to pass the remainder of the days."

"There is some truth in that, and yet he would run less risk in taking a young wife to town with him, than to go by himself, subject to all the temptations that single young men really are."

"That may be very true; but if he cannot, when on the point of marriage, be careful of himself, and true to her he is about to wed—if he cannot pass through such an ordeal, he is worthless."

"I cannot but admit there is much truth in what you say, but young men have not old heads upon their shoulders; you must expect that young blood will hardly bear such strict rules as old men."

"Yes—yes—that is all very true, but where they have had the greatest possible inducement, the greatest of all motives that can actuate them at their time of life, they may be expected to have more control over them, than any other time."

I said no more at that time respecting the affair, for I saw my friend felt strongly upon this matter, and held my peace, as he was better able to mind his own affairs, better than I could advise him.

When after a short time, I saw another young man approach her, he was a tall dark young man, with a handsome countenance, and the air of a man who had been used to society of the best class; he addressed Charlotte with an air of respect and deference that showed he was, by no means, indifferent to her good opinion.

Who he was I could not divine, for my friend was not near me at the time, he having gone somewhere to attend upon some of the numerous guests he had around him; and certainly they seemed to me, the whole of them, to be well worthy of his attention; for, to judge of their personal appearance alone, they all looked as though they were the pleasantest people in the whole world, aye, and the happiest to boot; and I believe it too.

It was possibly because I had been used to the care-worn and pale visages of London that made me fancy this, and I had, moreover, been long confined by illness, and the change was great and pleasing to me.

After a while he returned to me saying,—

"Well, I am sorry to leave you, but I am lost here you see, and have to do the honours to more than one person; and so I must flit about from place to place, and if I can't be ubiquitous, I must at least endeavour to visit, and have something to say to all."

"Very true," I replied; "it is the master of the feast that makes the feast, and not the viands provided, for without him, it is a body without a head."

"Yes, but it is growing too late for you to be out here in the cold air."

"It is warm."

"It is not cold, but it will be chilly ; allow me to recommend you to withdraw into the house : you will not be alone."

"I am not afraid of that; but first tell me who that is now dancing with Charlotte—a tall gentlemanly man."

"Ah! that is a rival to Charles Osborne."

"A formidable one, I should imagine," said I; "for he has a very prepossessing appearance."

"So he has, and yet he can make no head with our Charlotte; she cares nothing for him."

"And yet she is dancing with him."

"Yes, surely ; because he wishes to win her heart is no good reason for refusing to dance with him—a thing that she would do with any guest that might be here."

"Is not Charles Osborne jealous ?"

"God bless me, no; I hope not, he isn't such a fool. A man wouldn't be jealous of an open act like that before the whole company; if, however, she accepted of his attentions as a regular thing, then I should say he might be jealous, and nothing more natural."

"But jealousy is easily fed."

"But without plenty of fuel it would soon burn itself out ; however, I don't want to see anything of the kind, nor do I think I shall."

"Is he a resident about here ?"

"Not close at hand, about five miles off; he has a pretty estate—a very pretty estate, indeed—he is a very nice fellow, has travelled, and picked up a good deal of information."

"A very companionable sort of man then ?"

"Yes he is, but we will go and see him ; his estate is well worth looking at, and he will be happy to show it to us I am sure."

"I will go when I am well enough," said I, "and I thank you for the promise of good things which you offer."

*   *   *   *   *   *

That evening passed off well; I was introduced to the two young men, Charles Osborne and Francis Tyrrell. They were both fine young men, but of a very different stamp ; the former manly, frank, and generous, but somewhat hasty and blunt, the latter more polished, perfectly self-possessed, and free from any awkwardness.

There was, however, a kind of haughtiness in his manner that seemed to say he was aware there was a kind of superiority in himself that they could not deny, and which was too perceptible not to be seen. This produced an unfavourable impression at first, but it soon wore away.

There was a great charm in his conversation, above that of many persons which I have seen to exist in some men over and above all others in the same community, and thus they exert a great influence.

The time was now coming round very rapidly when Charles Osborne was to depart for London, there to arrange his affairs ; the parting was not, I believe, a very tender one, because there was every confidence in Charles, and the belief that it would be but for a time, and that time very short during which he would be away. It was, therefore, with the feeling that he was going upon a necessary but pleasant and safe journey that Charlotte bade Charles farewell with smiles rather than tears.

"You will remember my little commissions," she said, "when you have time ?"

"Remember ! when could I forget anything you desired ?" he replied. "Farewell, and remember you have deprived me of my chief pleasure in this journey."

"How ?"

"You ought to have consented, and then took your place along-side of me and gone to London too ; had you done that how much happier would have been the journey."

"Be content, you dissatisfied being," she said, laughing, "that I am here and shall remain here till you look for me."

" Then I will hasten on the wings of love and despatch that odious affair, return, and claim your promise."

" Unless you see fit to alter your determination in favour of the ladies of London."

* * * * * * *

A few more good-natured sallies took place, and then Charles, catching her round the waist, bestowed a hearty salute upon her lips, for which he was rewarded with a box on the ears, but also the hearty commendation of my friend, who seemed to enjoy the fun.

* * * * * *

" Well," he said, as he turned to me after he had gone, " well, Charles is a fine fellow, and if true, and I believe him to be so, he will turn out a good husband."

" I hope and believe so," said I.

" There can be no doubt about it. I am very glad he is quite clear of his guardian's fangs."

" Why so?"

" Because he was a source of annoyance to us all, especially to poor Charlotte; she fretted about the disagreeables he must endure, especially as she was aware of the design that they had formed of marrying him, if possible, to his own daughter, which is now frustrated."

" She felt, then, ill at ease now that he was in the habit of seeing her?"

" Yes, she was; though I see no reason why she should have been so; to be sure, people did say all sorts of things, and you know people will be censorious."

" There can be no doubt that there is much untruth in the reports that come under the name of the people; I scarce ever believe one and certainly never repeat one."

" You are quite right, quite right; but he is away now, and we shall see how he conducts himself while in London, and if he can do that as he ought there will be no fear of him afterwards."

" Will he live in his father's house when he returns and is married?" I inquired.

" Yes; it is a large handsome house with beautiful scenery around it; we will go round and see it as soon as you are strong enough."

And so my host used to say, " If you are strong enough, or when you are strong enough;" but I was able to walk about well enough in the warm air and sunshine of mid-day.

Several days passed, but no letter came, and this caused some sensation in the family; no letter—that was an ominous circumstance and one they scarce could brook. About three days after the first was expected, there came one; it was loving enough and filled with many protestations of affection, and spoke of his business in town, which seemed more complicated than he had imagined, and would take a far greater period of time than he had been led to expect.

This was news, and I thought my friend looked a little vexed, though upon what his vexation arose in particular I could not well devise; but I thought it might be at the peculiar nature of his daughter's situation with regard to Charles Osborne, and the unexpected delay that was likely to take place before the wedding should be solemnized. There was another cause for vexation, and that was no other than the way in which the prolonged duration of his absence was announced and its consequences commented on, and a brief regret that my friend did not permit him to have his wedding over before he went to town, and this I think myself was unwise. However, there was no doubt but he himself thought he had acted too wilfully by far in the transaction, and this, I have no doubt, was the cause of much of his vexation and trouble.

Charlotte herself seemed somewhat vexed; she was quick in her feelings, and soon felt any slight or offence, however it might be given, and I could see well that she felt deeply the letter that had been sent; however, she made no remark upon it, but gave it at once into her father's hands as a thing that might be read by all, for all it contained or was written in it.

" When do you answer it," I inquired, " my friend."

" I do not see any answer is required. I shall wait until I have several, and hen I will endeavour to find materials for an answer but now there are none."

Thus passed off the first letter, and I believe I saw some signs of dissension, I own, between them ; and when Francis Tyrrell called in the evening there was evidently a disposition to flirt with him, in which he was nothing loth, but immediately began to converse with her upon the footing of an old friendship, renewed but recently.

Several days passed before any more letters came, and I could not help saying to my friend,—

" What do you imagine can be the cause of Osborn'se silence and singular conduct ?" I said.

" It is neglect," he replied.

" But from what cause," I asked. " It seems to me very strange he should have acted in this manner—very strange, indeed—his motives must be inadequate."

" Any motive is adequate for a fool," he replied hastily, and I began to think he can be no better, I cannot conceive any motive stronger than the fact that the pleasures of the town or some new and pretty face."

" That ought not to interfere in such a thing as this, because he must be aware of the mischief he is likely to commit, and that of no ordinary or temporary character."

" Well, I know of nothing else that can cause the change I never expected in him. Why there is young Tyrrell, now he has been abroad and through the thick of dissipation, and yet he was never the man to lose himself—no, he passed through the fire, and came out brighter than before, for he is greatly polished in manners."

" And is a very intelligent man, too," said I.

" In truth he is, but what cannot be cured must be endured, according to the old saying, and I am in just the frame of mind to give him a dismissal."

" Whom ?"

" Why Osborne, to be sure," replied my host.

" Oh !" said I, " you were talking of Tyrrell, and I thought you might mean him."

" Ah, here is an old gossip comes—see, see, she has began to talk to my wife already—she is a dear soul for a talk, and is very amusing for a time, but only for a time, and if she once catches hold of you, she will talk for a month, and never leave off."

" Surely, she must be an acquisition to a ministry, and would make an excellent leader in the House of Commons, for she would talk everybody down."

" Yes, here she comes, and you listen to her for a short time—it will amuse you."

At that moment the object of our conversation came forward. After shaking several of the family by the hand, saying in an odd kind of voice,

" Ah ! well, well, and so here you are all. I am really glad to see you all looking so well. Ah ! there's my dear Charlotte—I am so glad to see her well, and that she has not gone to London with us."

" Are you though ; well I won't scold you—for you can't think how glad I am that I have not gone."

" But, Charles, you know."

" Yes, yes, I know all about that," said Charlotte, " but I don't like to leave my native place to go to London, even with Charles."

" Indeed."

" It is a fact, I assure you—have I not all my friends here—my father and mother and all are here, and can find no pleasure in going there."

" Well, since that is your mind, I will tell you something I have heard ; but I could not have done so otherwise, for it might have been said that I was the cause of dissension, and there is nothing I abhor so much."

" No, I dare say not."

" Oh, dear, I never was so hurt as I was the other night, when old Mr. Singleton told me I made him unhappy, because I told him the truth about his favourite son George being such a reprobate. Oh ! it did grieve me though. To be sure he didn't blame me, only he blamed his son."

"I recollect all about it," said Charlotte ; "but what about this affair you were going to to talk of."

"Oh! why it's a certain mysterious affair that has occurred in the family of Mr. Osborne's guardian—its very strange, very singular indeed, and to my mind cannot be accounted for, unless by supposing some very great piece of impropriety has been committed somewhere by some one."

"Indeed you make me sick at the very idea of some dreadful piece of villany."

"Ah, well you may say so indeed ; though how you came to guess I can't tell, unless you had a presentiment of evil. Some people, it's very strange now, but there's old Mrs. Higginbottom last night dreamed she had the misfortune to lose her thumb. During this morning I have heard she has lost one of her toes, and Mrs. Kitchener always had a presentiment she should, one day or another, have a fortune, and her husband has left her some money, enough to get out of debt with and bury kim, that is not much, but then she's got rid of the man."

"Well, but about Osborne?"

"Oh! about his guardian that was, you know."

"Yes—yes—about him and the mysterious affair that you were speaking of, but of which we have heard nothing."

"I understand, yes—well—you know they have a daughter, a very beautiful young creature, I believe, at least so people say, and so I think myself."

"Yes, I have often heard Mr. Osborne speak of her, she was a mild and gentle girl?"

"Yes, so she was, poor girl, but there's something wrong there, I can't say what."

"What do you mean ?"

"Ah, there's the difficulty," said the gossip, "she's quite altered in shape—much stouter—health very bad, and nobody knows what's the matter."

"Poor thing."

"Aye, poor thing, indeed ; but what are those that made her so? But he has sent her away, that's one thing, he don't want any one to be acquainted with the misfortune of the family, he's wise there because it would keep his father's house empty."

"So it would, but who is it that is the cause of all this? Does no one say a word?"

"It is whispered—but I musn't tell you."

"Well, well," said Charlotte, "I wont ask you to tell in that case, because it is not right."

"I feared it might take an evil effect upon you, my dear, but since you desire to know it is said, mind I don't say so, only people do say, that Charles Osborne is the cause of all the mischief."

"Good heavens !"

"Ah, my dear girl, he's a bad young man, no doubt, but never mind."

"Ah! I needn't mind. But where have they sent the unfortunate young woman too?"

"Her father has sent her to London, I believe," said the gossip, with a knowing nod, "but there, I have gossiped all my time away, and must leave you now. I declare when I do come here I have so many questions to ask you that I have hardly time to draw breath."

The old gossip was soon dismissed, having done all the mischief she could, and then proceeded to another quarter to find out some little thing or other that she could magnify into a great deal and so convey it about.

I could see that the news she had spread had its effects upon the different members of the family and was the cause of annoyance to them all.

Upon Charlotte it had its effect, and the poison was not without its sting, that was plain enough by her blanched cheek, but no notice was taken of the information that had with the same liberality been spread among those who would least care to hear it.

It is very strange but there are many people who care for nothing so much as to be able to pick up crumbs of mischief that they may be able to sow them in the first prolific soil they meet with, and they never hesitate about the putting of a person to any torture so they can but attract their attention, and the most they can do is to cause some extra strength in the desire of the party to become acquainted with what they have to tell them.

This is usually managed by the parties declaring they must not—would rather not—or it might be true, and they can't tell—or they are afraid of scandalizing—and so forth, until they are begged to say what they know lest their listeners should think worse.

Thus it was on this occasion, and now that there was a deep impression upon the minds of the whole family and that they said but little, yet they felt deeply the slight put upon them.

I took no part in the whole affair. I could advise nothing, and they did not appear inclined to do anything, but I saw that Charlotte grew paler each day, though her spirit was too good to sink under such a slight.

For him she had refused the love of others, and for him she refused to become a bride to one who would, even at that moment, have gladly received her into his arms, and how was she treated now—slighted and insulted—not to say injured, for of that she could hardly say she had the truth.

*　　　*　　　*　　　*　　　*　　　*

It was some weeks before Charlotte again heard from Charles Osborne, and then, when she did, she read his complaint of her silence with coldness, and wondered how he could expect an answer after such neglect—how, in fact, he could imagine that his letters, written at long intervals with complaints of her not answering his former letters, and in neither of which did he do all or in any part that which he promised.

There was none of that faithful description of the scenes he witnessed, nor the sights of London described, nor the many little incidents which he must have known would have been highly entertaining to a lover.

"It is not worthy a second thought," said Charlotte, "not a second thought. He never would have acted the heartless part had he not been one of the most vile and contemptible of men. I could not have believed so much of him; I thought it was foreign to his nature. I could never have believed him capable of acting in this manner; and what motive, for none he could have had in this short time of sufficient power, unless he was tired of the connection before he went."

Thus she reasoned upon the otherwise inexplicable conduct of Charles Osborne, who, while he was present, appeared to be the sincerest, and, in fact, the very impersonation of candour and honour, so well did his appearance speak for him.

Time passed on, and yet another week or two passed, and the like neglect was continued. It was very singular and exceedingly distressing, and my friend at once expressed his anger at such a proceeding.

"I don't care," he said, "one groat for the thing itself, save for the sake of my poor girl, who I fear may feel more than will at all agree with her health. The disappointment to me is absolutely nothing, but to her everything."

"Surely," said I, "he has behaved very strangely and shamefully; but you never knew of such an occurrence before. Had he behaved very correctly at first and then fallen off, I should have understood his motive; but now it would seem that he must have had a motive that existed anterior to his departure. If not, his conduct is a perfect enigma, which it is useless to attempt a solution."

"That is my opinion," said my friend, "that is my opinion; and, from what that infernal cat of a gossip said when she was here, if she speak the truth, one may make a guess at the cause, or, at least, one may speculate upon the motives that has led to this conduct."

"Some portion of it one would think untrue."

"Very likely; but one cannot tell which portion, and, moreover, though it may seem so, yet it is the only probable motive that I can at all conceive that would have the effect of estranging his affections."

"There is much mystery about it certainly," said I; "but don't you think you ought to write to him yourself and demand an explanation."

"No," he replied; "he has the matter in his own hands, and if he do not willingly wed my daughter, Charlotte, according to his expressed intentions and agreement, I will never by one word endeavour to induce him to do so, because, if he were to so marry her and unhappiness was to be the result, I should have myself to blame."

"I can hardly think that; because if we were to look at the reverse of a picture always, we should be terrified into inaction, and, therefore, permit everything to go on in the state which we find it."

"And so it must in the present instance," said my friend, "for I do not desire to tamper with Charlotte's affections."

"Surely that would not be doing so."

"It would, and moreover be directly contrary to what I believe to be her wishes; and moreover, I am convinced that, were he now to return to keep his promise, she would scarce permit him to do so. She is a very high-spirited girl when she considers herself slighted and ill-used, as she most certainly has in this case."

Where father and daughter were possessed by these feelings it was useless to combat them; and yet I thought that, had the case have been my own, I should have endeavoured to have elicited an explanation from Charles Osborne, and to have obtained from him, at the least, a confirmation of my worst fears, and then I should have known how to act without any delay; and it would have prevented any distress of mind relative to the supposition that some accident or some other cause might have caused the change in his mind, and thus done away with all uncertainty and the sickening effect of hope deferred.

Time passed on and nothing was heard of Osborne, though Tyrrell used to visit the house, and often accompanied Charlotte in her evening walks; indeed, I saw there was fast forming an attachment between these two, or rather the attachment had long existed on Tyrrell's side, and was a new born passion in the breast of Charlotte.

It might be that anger and revenge, which are not altogether without their influence on the mind of a woman, or even on their affections, and that it might have been so in that case I cannot pretend to say, but merely suggest it as not a probable but a possible motive of action, or at least, one that had some weight, though not a predominant or ostensible one.

Be it what it might, Francis Tyrrell was often there, and his insinuating address and manners won upon the hearts of those with whom he came in contact.

Being seated alone with my friend under the canopy of Heaven before spoken of —of trained trees—our conversation turned upon the presence of Tyrrell.

"What do you think of him?" inquired my friend. "Do you think him honest and sincere?"

"Yes, I certainly do," I replied; "he seems most anxious to become one of the family, and his attentions are too broad to allow of a misrepresentation; but at the same time I would speak to him about it."

"He has spoken to me," replied my friend.

"Then he has saved you the trouble. Well, I am glad of it, for I suppose you have given over all further thought of Charles Osborne and the inexplicable conduct he has been guilty of."

"Indeed, I have."

"And what does Tyrrell say?"

"That he desires to become my son. He has long loved Charlotte, and hopes that his affections will meet with a suitable reward from her; I told him I had no objection to him, quite the reverse, but that I would endeavour to influence my daughter's feelings in that matter, and he must make his way himself."

"Did he allude to Osborne?"

"Not once; this I consider as very delicate on his part, and certainly he could not have done better."

"I think not," said he, "is shews tact and good breeding. Is he a man of any fortune?"

"Yes a very handsome independence—a good estate, and I believe an unblemished character ; but he is considered as being haughty, and having a mean opinion of most people. He is a clever man himself, and had he the inclination to throw himself into any of the parties of the day, he would, no doubt, make his way to distinction, but he will not risk money."

"He is quite right, too," I replied. "But what does Charlotte say to all this, or rather, does she know of it at all ? Have you informed her of Francis Tyrrell's offer ?"

"I did not intend to do so at first, but I afterwards changed my mind."

"And what said she ?"

"That she had entirely dismissed from her mind all thoughts and hopes of Charles Osborne, his conduct had convinced her that he was unworthy of her affections, and she would not waste a thought upon him more."

"I see her feelings of disappointment are not so great that she has no room for other feelings—anger and pride have drowned the softer emotions."

"Indeed, they have."

"But what said she of Francis Tyrrell ?"

"Oh, she said but little, save that she believed he had long sought to make himself agreeable to her, but she should be more careful for the future of believing in the truth of any man, though, considering her disappointment could not be unknown to him, it certainly did how much disinterestedness on his part, in coming forward at such a moment."

"That is uncommonly true, and shows him to be a man above vulgar prejudice."

"I have thought of that myself, and so has she, and I think it more than probable that Francis Tyrrell will take the place of Charles Osborne, in her affections, in a very short time."

"I am glad to hear it," I said, "for I do not like to see any unhappy circumstance afflicting a family by the unfortunate condition of one of its members."

"No, no," he said, "I should be distressed, indeed, if I had illness, or

No. 21.

anything of that sort, from such a cause, it would be the death of me, I be-lieve."

*   *   *   *   *   *

It was not long before Francis Tyrrell won the esteem and regard of Char-lotte, and she soon learned to look upon him as the future controller of her fate, and in whose power rested her happiness and misery; they used to spend their time in each other's company, and became almost inseparable.

There was a beautiful spot, lonely enough—in a dell formed by some high grounds—a hill, where they used to frequent; one extremity of it, which abutted on a declivity, commanded a good view of the country, and the whole place was studded with elms.

Here they used to frequent—this was the usual end of all their walks, and Charlotte was much pleased with this place; it might have been that she had requented the same place when she was out with Charles Osborne.

However, here they used to walk, and paused as they gazed on the setting sun. This was an enchanted spot; it was one, too, that was known as being the most romantic spot for many miles around.

One evening, there was an unusual flush on the cheek of Charlotte, when she returned from one of their evening walks; she had been out with Tyrrell, and re-turned with him to the house, and the latter sought out my friend, and, when he found him, he took him a little on one side.

"Forgive me," he said, "for troubling you, but I wish to speak upon a matter which nearly concerns us both, and myself in particular."

"Well, Mr. Tyrrell, say what you please, I am ready to hear you."

"It is respecting Charlotte, and, in a word, sir, I am now waiting your con-sent to become your son-in-law."

"For my consent, alone?"

"Yes! yes! yours alone; I have obtained that of Charlotte's, and it entirely depends upon yourself to make me become the happiest man in the whole empire!"

"Well! Mr. Tyrrell, I can have no objection to you for a son-in-law, quite the reverse, I should be proud to acknowledge you for one, but it must depend mainly upon Charlotte, you know, for you to secure her good opinion."

"That, I hope, I have done," said Tyrrell: "and I hope she never will have cause to repent doing so, at least, I will take care never to give her any cause willingly."

"I am sure of that,—but do I understand you rightly? you have obtained Charlotte's consent to your speaking to me for permission to visit her as an ac-cepted lover?"

"Yes! and more, for I consider I have done so all along—but I now parti-cularly request you will take into consideration my previous probation, and permit me to hope for an early day, on which I may put an end to all doubts, and even hopes upon the subject, by turning it into a certainty, and expectation into possession."

"Well! hence you have so far settled matters, it remains but for me to con-clude the affair. Charlotte can name her own day—and I will place matters in rain with my attorney, who will communicate with yours."

"Exactly! that is what I desire at once to do," replied Tyrrell, "and at this point, I may conclude it settled?"

"You may!"

"And I hope the man of law will not be permitted to push this matter off, by a voluminous correspondence, that will consume much time and paper."

"Certainly not, it can take but a very few weeks to settle all that is required, nd then you must settle the remainder between your two selves."

"Thank you; you do not know the happiness you have conferred upon me"

"We will say nothing about it, my dear boy, until the first five years are over, and then we may talk of it, and if you are of the same mind then,—"

" Five years—aye, fifty, if I live as long."

" I hope you may, but if you say the same thing then, why you will deserve al that I can give you, and if Charlotte don't behave well—"

" She cannot do otherwise."

" I have taught her well, I know; and I believe she will, but we cannot always foretel what may happen; but I wish you both health, wealth, and happiness."

" Thank you," I said, " there is every element of it now, and every human prospect, and more than that we cannot, under any circumstances, expect or obtain."

They shook hands and parted; Tyrrell saying, he should go **to** his attorney at once, and put him into communication with my friends, and then qute th e house.

" You see," said my friend, " he has got some sense in him, and that is the way to settle the affair at once, and further, we pushed on to a conclusion; he means what he says now, the other couldn't have done so."

" Yet he offered to marry her before he left."

" And a pretty state of things would have happened, had she have been married to him."

" I cannot see what evil would have happened," said I; " he would have had a young wife to have employed his attention, and he would not have been carried away to excesses."

" Indeed, I have quite another opinion; but that's of no consequence. I am very glad now, as the result is, that he did not marry her; quite the reverse of sorrow for the occasion, because you see he could have had no regard for her, or else he never would have done what he has done. No young man could neglect a female whom he truly loved, for the sake of any momentary passion. I am sure there would have been much unhappiness in store for my Charlotte."

" I hope there will be none," said I, " as it is; but that her present love arises from pure affection, and not inspired by revenge, or any less noble motive than that which ought to inspire it."

There was no more said at that moment; a few days passed on and then came a letter from Charles Osborne, in which he requested the cause of her not answering his letters, but this Charlotte coolly burned, observing, at the same time, that it was useless to hold any correspondence at that late date.

The days passed by in rapid succession, and the time for the wedding was fixed, and there was every preparation made, and each day that passed lessened the distance of time, until at length there was but one day intervening between the hour of the nuptials and the present moment. On that day, a post-chaise was driven up to the house with furious haste, and out stepped Charles Osborne, nd he immediately entered the house.

" Where is Charlotte? " he said.

" Charlotte," said her father, " you inquire for Charlotte?—allow me to say, sir, we are strangers; your conduct compels me to say so.'

" My conduct! but I have no time—no desire to quarrel. I wish to see Charlotte to know from her if all this is true that I hear. She is about t be married to Francis Tyrrell? "

" She is."

" And the cause of this change in her intentions, and why I hae been thus used and neglected? "

" Come, Mr. Osborne, I have no time nor patience; your neglect ha been the cause of all—you have sown and now you reap—begone, sir."

As he spoke, he turned away and left Charles, who, catching a glimpse of Charlotte, sprang after her, but she waived him back, saying—

" I have nothing to say to you; I have heard what you said to my father, and his answer is mine; farewell, I desire to see you no more."

Charles Osborne appeared thunder-stricken, and staggered back somehow or other and re-entered the carriage, and then drove rapidly towards his own home.

The next day was fine, a brilliant and glorious sun shone upon the earth, and when the hour approached for the celebration of their marriage, the place was alive with guests, from one end of the house to the other. There was not such a scene in that neighbourhood for years.

They were all in readiness to proceed to church, when again Charles Osborne appeared, and endeavoured to get near the bride, but both bridegroom and father prevented it ; the latter saying, as he pushed him back,—

"I am amazed that a man possessing any feelings of delicacy and honour, should make an attempt to disturb any assemblage like the present!"

"I do not desire to disturb it. I only hope it may not yet be too late to induce Charlotte to alter her determination, and believe I have done nothing for which I am deserving of blame!"

Charlotte stepped forward, and said, in a calm voice :—

"Charles Osborne !—forget what is past. I do not desire to remember it my-self, you may depend upon it no effort you can make will produce any but an un-favourable impression for yourself."

"You believe I have neglected you?"

"I do !"

"As Heaven may judge me, you wrong me!"

"It is useless to argue. If you will take no answer from me, I cannot help it,—but I will not listen to you."

So saying, she turned around, and gave her hand to Francis Tyrrell, and he led her away.

"Charlotte !—hear me !" he exclaimed, but she was gone, and he turned away and fled from the spot.

*   *   *   *   *   *   *

The wedding was solemnized, and Charlotte became Mrs. Francis Tyrrell, and then the carriage took them away, amidst the adieus of their friends, and bore them to the neighbourhood of the Lakes, there to pass a few weeks before they again returned to the home that was preparing for them at Francis Tyrrell's house, which was being altered for them.

From that morning, none could tell what had become of Charles Osborne—no one could tell what had become of him, or whither he had gone, and some thought he had hurried away, perhaps, or gone abroad ; and others again thought he might have committed suicide, from sheer desperation ; in fact, all kinds of rumours were afloat until the affair grew old, and then he was forgotten.

After a time, Tyrrell and his wife returned to the neighbourhood of their birth, and the house having been beautified and altered, the newly-married pair returned and lived in it.

They appeared to be very happy, and one evening Tyrrell proposed to go and see the place they had so often visited before they were married.

This was the spot where the elms grew ; and towards sunset they all walked gently there, and, from the hill above, witnessed his dying glory, until he had sunk beneath the horizon, and then, in the beautiful twilight that followed, they came to the elms, but started, at what appeared to be the figure of Charles Osborne. It was a dim, shadowy sight, and seemed to beckon them onwards, and, impelled by some secret power, they followed onwards until they came to the spot where Charlotte had often spent an hour with Charles Osborne.

This was beneath the huge branches of an ancient elm, and another laid across it, and served for a seat.

There, upon that seat, they beheld a sight that almost froze the blood in their veins. It was the body of Charles Osborne, who laid there—his head shattered, and a pistol still hanging in his hand. The whole of the upper part of the head was literally blown off.

A shriek from Charlotte recalled Tyrrell from the state of stupor into which he had been driven by this sight, and his wife was in a fit at his feet.

There was no assistance to be had, and when he had succeeded in bringing her round, she cried so piteously for water, that he ran to obtain some. He was gone some minutes, and before he could return, Charlotte got up, and staggered to the body, but the offensive smell that arose from it was suffocating, and she was compelled to get up, and stagger away : not before she had picked up a letter, which she found, had been directed to herself ; and then she again sunk to the earth.

However, Tyrrell was now at hand, and had no sooner come up than he assisted, and, after some distress and trouble, they reached home, and then information was given of the discovery of the body.

When alone, and able to do so, Charlotte broke the seal of the note, and read the contents.

"Unfortunate man !" she said, "you little thought that she to whom you had addressed this letter would herself find it; you could not have anticipated such a circumstance."

The first few lines made her start, and change colour, and as she proceeded, she became ghastly pale,—for the letter revealed the cause of Charles Osborne's apparent neglect, and her husband's treachery and criminality.

The inquest was soon holden, and Charlotte expressed her determination to be present, although Tyrrell endeavoured to prevent her doing so.

When called upon to give her evidence, she said what she had seen, and the letter that was addressed to herself, at the same time she produced it. It was read in court, and, judge of the amazement of every one, and of the guilty Tyrrell, when he found himself charged with having bribed the office keeper, to permit him to have the letters from Charles Osborne, which he did.

* * * * * * *

The inquest was over, and it was found that Mrs. Tyrrell was so ill, that she could not walk, or stand ; and she was carried home almost insensible.

For many weeks she lay nearly dead, and was considered more than half dead, but she rallied, but never recovered the use of her senses.

She was insane. She knew no one, not even her father—she knew places where she had been in the habit of frequenting before her illness, and there she would walk, and remained chiefly at her father's house, and could not be induced to return to her husband, who was loudly hooted for his conduct to the unfortunate Osborne and Charlotte—for he had deprived one of his life, the other of her reason.

Poor Charlotte used to frequent the elm wood, and used to be seen walking and talking to some one ; and few would venture to go near where she was in the wood. The spot had become more deserted than before, and there were some who declared they had seen the form of Charles Osborne beckoning Charlotte, as she entered the wood ; and then, after that, the sound of voices were often heard, but none of them ever ventured to follow them, though it was asserted by one who had unknowingly strayed away, and found himself near the elm tree where Osborne had destroyed himself,—that Charlotte was seated upon the fallen trunk, with another person beside her, but whose solemn and grave countenance somewhat amazed them, but the description was so accurate, that there was no mistaking it. It was the spirit of Charles Osborne.

Time flew by, and the circumstance became known to all, and the appearance in the wood became so well known, that none would go near, for fear the Elfin Lover of the Haunted Elm should do them evil.

Thus, day after day, year after year passed by, and no change took place. Charlotte's case was hopeless, and Francis Tyrrell, the cause of all, bought a commission in the army, and served abroad, and fell beneath the steel of the enemy.

Charlotte died ! but still round the old elm tree wander the spirits of the two lovers. As in life they would have been, so, in death they are.

———

CHAPTER XIII.

THE TERRIFIED MEMBER OF THE CLUB, AND THE WAY HE TOOK TO CALM HIMSELF.

WE have seen what really alarming effects were produced upon the minds of some of the members of the association by the single circumstance that from time to time took place during the progress of the meetings of this association, which was certainly one, in an eminent degree, calculated to produce a great amount of excitement, and really to superinduce some very serious evils.

But when we say this much, we do not intend to imply that we calculated upon the affair turning out as it really did.

It was facetiously said by an old sportsman of India, that "it was capital sport to hunt tigers, but that when the tiger turned round, as was sometimes the case, and begun to hunt you, it was far from being so pleasant."

And so it is with regard to our friends who became such anxious and inveterate ghost seekers. So long as they were seeking for ghosts the whole affair went off very pleasantly and delightfully, but when, after a time, the ghosts, as they unquestionably did, began to seek them, the case was very much altered, and assumed a totally different complexion.

But still, one would have thought that some who had, in the first instance, the most courage to associate themselves together for such a purpose, would not have shrunk from any of the consequences arising therefrom.

The mere fact that they had actually formed such an association, was sufficient of itself to imply a belief in those immaterial existences they made it their special business to inquire concerning. It is perfectly clear that men having no idea or notion of the truth of spectral appearances, would never have banded themselves together as our friends did, to inquire into the subject.

And, therefore, it is that in gathering together the records for which these pages are compiled, we are rather surprised to find what great effects ensued in the case of individual members of the association.

But such was the fact, and there is no disputing it; the most remarkable effects were produced, and while some probably acquired great interest in the affair as it grew into importance, there cannot be a doubt but that to others it became a matter of the most alarming character, and materially disturbed the even tenor of their existences.

It was rather lamentable that such effect should be produced, and, of course, it would have been far better if those individuals upon whom they were produced had never interfered with the subject of so extremely tender and ticklish a nature, but had left it to wiser heads and sterner intellects than their own.

We have already had occasion to record how seriously affected some of the members of the association were by what occurred, and how devoutly they wished that they had never interfered with a matter which they began to discover, too late, would be to them productive of nothing but uneasiness.

We do not particularly pity those who talked much upon the occasion, because we consider that, in all probability, they were among the most superficial thinkers upon the subject; but the mental effect produced upon some of the quiet members who had not yet opened their lips upon the occasion was great indeed.

To one of these now we will draw attention for a brief space.

There was a Mr. Reuben Gregory who belonged to the club, but who had as yet not ventured upon making the shadow of a remark. He had listened to all that had passed, however, with most intense and marked attention, and being a person of naturally timid habit, and of retiring disposition, there came across him such a dread of being called upon to relate something for the edification of the members of the association, that he never attended one of the meetings without much fear and trembling with regard to the result.

Fortunately for him his name had not been called upon, but he knew that sooner or later, it must come, and he got into a state of torture and anxiety not only as regarded the general subject of apparitions, but on account of what he should say or do when it came to be his turn to dilate upon some special subject in particular connected with spectral appearances.

Now it so happened that Mr. Reuben Gregory, although really a devout believer in spectral appearances, had nothing from his own experience to tell, except a dim and very uncertain story about the ghost of his grandmother, which he thought he once saw, but was not quite sure, and who, he fancied, said something, but he did not know what.

Of course, Mr. Gregory was fully aware that such an unsatisfactory tale of a ghost as this would never do to say anything about to the club, and as day after day became to him a perfect agony to think that the time was coming round when he would have to tell something, he used to walk about like some curious, little, old maniac, muttering to himself,—

"I got nothing to tell—what shall I do?—I must sink my grandmother—I must sink my grandmother."

This was his constant cry, until all of a sudden he thought of an old acquaintance of the name of Jack Anderson, whom he had not seen for a long while, but who in their juvenile days was celebrated for knowing something about everything that could be broached upon any subject whatever.

Reuben Gregory considered that the idea of going to consult Jack Anderson was one of the most lucky and brilliant thoughts that had come across him for many a long day, and as that learned individual lived but a short distance from the city, Reuben made up his mind, when the business of the day should be over, that he would pay him a visit, and state at once candidly the difficulty in which he was placed.

Quite elated now at the prospect of an escape from his troubles, Mr. Gregory, about an hour before sunset, betook himself to the suburban locality where Jack Anderson resided.

"Oh he is my man," said Gregory to himself, as he walked along; "he knows everything and everybody, and as for stories about ghosts, I should not be at all surprised if he is upon the most intimate terms with at least half-a-dozen of them."

It would be but a poor compliment to the natural sagacity of Jack Anderson, if we did not state that he at once saw, by the appearance of Reuben Gregory's countenance, that something hung exceedingly heavy upon his mind.

After the usual compliment had passed, and Reuben was seated in Jack Anderson's snug parlour, with a glass of the most unexceptionable sherry before him, he began to state the object of his visit.

"My old friend," he said, "I am going to confide a great secret to you, and then to ask you a very important question."

"Out with it," said Jack, "and out with it instantly; don't come to me with the ghost of a confidence."

"The what?"

"The ghost of a confidence. I must have the substance, the reality, or nothing at all."

"Well," said Reuben, "if you will believe me you're uttering those words is one of the most wonderful and throughly curious coincidences that ever I heard of. You say something about the ghost of a confidence, and, strange to say, Anderson, the subject that brings me here is concerning ghosts."

"You don't say so," said Anderson, as he poured out another glass. "You don't say so. Have you seen one?"

"Seen one! I rather think I have; but what I want to know is, if you have seen one."

"If I have seen one what a question. Why? I have seen lots—oceans of them."

"I am delighted to hear it, and now I will just tell you how I want you to oblige me."

Reuben Gregory then related the whole particulars concerning the club, and the great difficulty he was in, with regard to having to tell a story when he did not know one."

"Difficulty," said Anderson, "you don't mean to call that a difficulty?"

"Well, I think it looks extremely like one. If I don't know a story about a ghost, how am I to tell one?"

"Invent one, to be sure."

"I invent one! I think I see it. I never invented anything in my life."

"How can you say that, when you know you invented a new chimney-pot, that wouldn't let any of the smoke out, but sent it all down again into the room; you know that well enough, and you talked of getting a patent for it."

"Oh! I said I would, but that I found out that so many other chimney-pots did the same thing without my invention, that I gave it up; but when I said I never invented anything, of course I meant in the way of a story, and that I certainly never did; and now what I want you to do is just this—to tell me something, so that when it comes to my turn to tell something to the club, I may repeat it, and not look like a fool."

"Well my dear fellow, with regard to not looking like a fool, I think that is out of my power to remedy, for certainly you do not look like a second Solomon; but as to telling you something which you can repeat again,—I'll do that with pleasure, provided you think you can recollect it, and not spoil it by omitting some of its most essential particulars, because if you do that, you know, I'd rather not tell you, for I'm well aware how you murder an anecdote."

"I murder an anecdote! Well! I always thought I told one remarkably well."

"Remarkably well! why, gracious Providence, did I not tell you one day the respectable and venerable old joke, of a man going into a tavern and ordering a rump steak which was so long in being brought to him, that he called out to the waiter.—'Holloa there if your steak aint ready my chops are.'"

"Well I know you told me that, and I told it again."

"Yes, you did tell it again with a vengence, but when you came to the gist of the thing, you made the gentleman call out to the waiter?—'Holloa! is that steak ready, because if it aint, I would rather have a chop.'"

"Well, I consider that was the same thing, wasn't it? and I always used to be very much surprised that nobody laughed; and some people used to have the impertinence to say to me—Well, what then? as if that was not the whole of it, and a very funny thing indeed,—but never mind about that, Anderson; you tell me the ghost story. That's what I want to hear, and you may depend I shall not make any mess of it, but tell it capitally."

"Well then, listen," said Jack Anderson, and he gave the table a blow with his fist, that made the glasses jump again, and startled every nerve in Mr. Gregory's composition.

"Don't be so violent, I am listening."

"There was a man who being faint, weary, and tired, once went towards the close of a summer's evening into a road-side public house."

"Yes."

"He seated himself upon a wooden chair, and in a voice which indicated that he wanted something to drink, he ordered a pint of half-and-half."

"Yes."

"Don't say yes every minute, you will drive me distracted. The half-and-half was brought him, and raising it to his lips he drank it at a draught, but finding that with the last drop there was a strange flavour,"—

"Yes."

"Now did not I tell you to be quiet? I beg you won't say yes any more. Finding that there was a strange flavour with it, and being a man of an ill-regulated mind and strong passions, he immediately cut his throat."

"The devil!" said Mr. Gregory, "you don't say so. Do you mean to say cut his throat just because he didn't like the half-and-half? I never heard of such an ass in all my life."

"He did, though; and ever since then, his ghost haunts that old public ouse with a pewter pot in one hand and a sixteen-bladed penknife in the other."

"Yes."

"Well, that's all."

"Don't you think it's rather short?"

"Yes; but it's very surprising, which is the beauty of it; I am quite certain that your friends never heard anything like it before."

"Yes," said Mr. Gregory, "it is surprising, but somehow or another, I don't think that would do. Of course, if you say he cut his throat on account of the half-and-half, I believe he did."

"Perhaps there was a blue-bottle in it, and if I were you when I told the story, I would say so, because it makes it look all the more natural, and you can call it, you know, by some terrific name, such as the 'Mysterious Suicide,' or the 'Demon Blue-bottle,' and, of course, you dress it up in proper language. Why, bless you, in proper hands, that incident would make a volume; look how you could describe how fatigued the man was before he reached the public-house, and how two or

three singular adventures befel him on his progress; and then there ought to come on a storm, and in the midst of it he ought to see the blue-bottle, who afterwards got into the half-and-half, buzzing round his head, and exulting in the idea of the dreadful deed he intended making that man of irregulated passions commit."

"I do see all that," said Mr. Gregory, "but it's out of my power—I couldn't do it; and if you really want to be of any help to me, you will tell me something of a different sort—something longer and serious—that I can recollect all the particulars about."

"Well," said Jack, "as I really wish to get you out of your difficulty, and as I hope that, in course of time, you will take occasion to propose me as a member of your club, I don't mind communicating to you a circumstance that you really can tell, and which I will tell you in all seriousness; so fill up your glass, and lend me your attention."

Reuben Gregory did so, and after a slight pause, during which Jack A derson seemed to be recollecting himself, he commenced as follows:—

In one of the green lanes, not far from Coventry, was situated a gentlem.

No. 22.

seat, long known as the "Bloody Hall," on account of some deeds that occurred there that gave it that appellation, though that was not the only appellative it deserved, for there, on certain nights in the year, no human being could live or sleep in it, the cries for "Mercy" being loud and piercing, and none were there who could tell whence they proceeded.

It was formerly in the occupation of the family of the Lees—a family known for their wealth and power in the county for many generations, but of whose private history little or nothing was known, save the facts which I will now relate, and which were too public to be kept secret after the death of the actors themselves.

Mr. Henry Lee was the only son of his father, of that name, and had to come into a splendid property when he came of age ; his father and mother were both dotingly fond of their son and only child.

He was scarce sixteen years of age, when his father made some overtures, which were mutual, to form an alliance with some family that he was well acquainted with—one whose estates lay contiguous to his own, and who, like himself, had but one child, which child was a daughter.

Nothing could be better for the future prospects of the young people than the possession of a large estate from either of their parents—an immense fortune and unincumbered property.

This was the reason that both parents were so anxious that the young people should by all means have some love for each other, and in default of that to compel them to be united, for to secure the union of the properties was their great object—an object, for the attainment of which, they would individually have acrificed their existences.

There is usually some one grand object in a family, which, if not cordially sought after by all the members, is sure to produce a derangement of family interest, and a split takes place—the seeds of disunion are sown.

Or if one of the family will not consent to something that is desired by the others, he or she is persecuted till health and strength fail them, and hatred takes the place of love.

The father and mother united to their love of their child an ambition to see him the richest man in the circle of their acquaintance, which was very extensive. This marriage project was the darling project of their lives, and, sooner than it should not come about, they would sooner have sacrificed themselves and their son too.

However, they had not any occasion as yet to exert their authority. The marriage could not well be fixed on for three years at least, at which time the son would be nineteen and the lady about eighteen.

About six months after his eighteenth birth-day, his father called Henry into his library, and said to him—

"My dear son, it's time that I should tell you what I dare say you know something about already ; and that is, I have a happiness designed for you—one I am sure you will embrace with gratitude, since it is the growth of years, and much forethought and care on my part."

"I shall be happy to accept of anything you may design for me," said Henry, with something like an equivocation.

"I am sure you will. I have provided you with a wife—a thing most young men make terrible mistakes in, for, though they choose them according to their fancy, they at least find, like a newly-painted stick, all the colours wear off in handling, and where they remain they only pall the senses—beauty soon loses its charms by possession. However, I have something more desirable than that— wealth, my boy, abundance of wealth."

"And I am thankful to you for it," replied the son.

"Aye, but the lady too ; she has great estates and plenty of money. All ~~you~~ have to do is to ask and to have."

"Y~~es~~ ~~I pray!~~"

"~~Ye~~s ; I have paved the way for you. Besides, you are not unknown to the ~~lady~~, nor she to you."

"I am at a loss to understand you."

" Why, the daughter of my friend and neighbour, Sir Francis Godfrey. She is an heiress."

" But decidedly plain."

" Consider ten thousand a year! There are charms for you! Was ever woman so beautiful ?"

" Well, to be sure, if we are to judge of females by wealth and not at all by weight, she must be ten times as beautiful as one with only one thousand a year."

" Exactly."

" Well, sir, I'd rather not take a wife upon those terms."

" What, sir," roared his father, " you will not take a wife of my choosing ! Do you mean to say that? Do you mean to tell me you will be disobedient ?"

" No ; but I don't want a wife."

" By God, sir, ——"

Here the old gentleman's utterance was impeded by the force of his passions, and he fell back in his chair covered with blood. He had burst a blood-vessel.

Immediate assistance was procured, and the old gentleman put to bed, when it was declared that he could not survive another day. Mrs. Lee spent the night by her husband's bed, and there solemnly promised him she would see the marriage performed.

The next day he died. His only thoughts seemed fixed upon that marriage, and he died solemnly enjoining his son to comply.

It was some months before the subject was again broached by his mother, for he was left under her guardianship until he was of age.

But at the end of the six months the same kind of conversation was renewed by his mother, who opened the matter with more tact but with equal determination, and then he declared he had no intention of marrying.

" But Henry," she said, " it is not necessary to have any inclination. What I am doing for you, or endeavouring to do for you, a few years hence, you will thank me for."

" I cannot be otherwise than grateful to you whatever the result may be, since I know your intentions are the best."

" Listen to what I have to propose."

" I am content, mother."

" You must go to Sir Francis Godfrey, and propose yourself as the suitor for Emily Godfrey, and you have no further trouble. You know how to conduct yourself towards a lady."

" Certainly."

" I have sworn to your father that all this should be done, and unless you wish to see your last parent, your mother, descend to a dishonoured grave, you must consent to this marriage ; you must, Henry you must."

" Mother, I cannot! I am already married ! "

The mother sank upon the floor, shrieking out the word " Married !" and then relapsed into a death-like trance, in which she remained for some hours, and when she recovered, she resolutely refused to speak to any one—even her son.

Suddenly however, she arose, and taking a small stiletto from her work-box, she left the room and went in search of her son Henry. She found him alone, and sat down beside him for some moments, and looked at him fixedly without speaking.

" And how are you, mother ?" he said kindly.

" Speak not to me," she said sternly and with some emotion ; " speak not to me, save what I shall demand of you :—did I hear aright, when you said you had married ?"

" You did, mother,"

" Wretched boy ! what could induce you to commit such an act ?"

" Love, mother."

" Cease such trash. What rank in life did she hold ?"

" None—at least that can be boasted of. She is the daughter of an officer, retired only upon his half-pay—that is all she has in the way of fortune."

" Fortune ! " replied his mother, with a bitter sneer ; " rather beggar—but she shall not triumph over me, nor you either."

As she spoke she raised her hand and aimed a furious blow with the stiletto, at his breast; he raised his arm to ward off the blow, but he was too late, it had reached him—he fell senseless and weltering in his own blood, on the floor.

The wretched mother uttered a wild laugh that rang through the house, and brought immediate assistance to them, for it sounded so wild and so unearthly, that they were all alarmed; and their alarm was not diminished when they saw Henry lie weltering in his blood on the floor.

"There! there! there!" she said, pointing to the body; "see—I have done it—I killed him!—yes, I!—his mother, did it! What do you stare and gaze at, fools? Speak—say what are you all stricken dumb at?"

As she spoke she swung out of the room like a fury, with the bloody stiletto in her hand; the attendants all shrunk from her, and she passed through the midst of them, and shut herself up in her own room.

In the mean time many were sent for assistance, and young Henry was carried to his bed, and there left to the care of his medical attendants, who believed his wound mortal.

The story got wind, and it was deemed proper to have Mrs. Lee taken into custody, and officers were sent on purpose to take her and consign her to safe keeping, until the result of her son's state should be known.

But when they came to search for her she was not to be found; she had left the place and gone no one knew whither—all search was vain—she could not be found.

After a time Henry's wounds showed symptoms of healing, but it was months before he could speak to any one, or before he could sit up in his bed, and eight months elapsed before he was able to quit his room; and a month after that he left England for Italy, in hopes that the air of the south would restore his weakened constitution—that it would, in fact, give him a chance of recovering his strength.

*   *   *   *   *   *   *   *

The servants were left in charge of the house, and the place was shut up, save such parts as were required to be open for the servants' accommodation.

On the same night twelvemonths after the deed that had been done, there was heard some wild laughter in the rooms above, just the same as had been uttered by Mrs. Lee when she struck her son.

The servants were terrified; they knew the sound, and it struck upon their senses like the return of the dead to life—it must be the spirit of the unfortunate mother come back to haunt the spot of the attempted matricide.

The laughter was followed by loud screams and wails—calls for mercy and forgiveness—that were petrifying to listen to : not a soul dared stir hand or foot to examine into the cause of this; they all huddled round the fire and dared not move till they, one and all, rushed outside the house a little before day-dawn, and then, after a time, they beheld a figure approaching towards them.

They shrank beneath the trees, and there saw the figure pass them, while they trembled like aspens. The figure approached. It was wan and thin and pale, so worn and attenuated that it seemed more like a thing of another world than this, and the eye was lit up in a wild, unearthly manner.

It flitted by and was not seen after that, and the sounds and cries were gone.

Many were the surmises that were uttered by the servants; all, however, concurred in thinking that it was the apparition, or the spirit of Mrs. Lee, condemned to wander for such a time, and to spend a yearly visit of the like nature for a certain time, until her period of probation should end.

The next year the same thing occurred; and year after year it went on, and people were terrified to hear it, and would not stop in the same house on the nights it came. The figure had often been way-laid, but no one dared speak to it, much less dared they lay hands upon it.

One night, however, as soon as the cries began, one of those whose curiosity was the greatest, set fire to the house in four or five different places, and then retired.

The house burnt rapidly, there being much wood-work about it, and the whole place in five minutes was enveloped in flames, and in half an hour the roof fell in with a tremendous crash, and then, at that moment, a loud and piercing shriek struck upon the ears of the appalled spectators.

The next day the ruins were examined to discover if any lives had been lost, when the body of a female was discovered burnt almost to a cinder; but from certain rings found upon it, Henry Lee, who arrived on that day, identified the body as that of *his mother.*

"I think that will suit very well," said Gregory, "and I can't help feeling greatly obliged to you for detailing it to me."

"You are welcome to it," said Jack Anderson, "but if that don't suit, couldn't you manage one in the comic line?"

"I don't think it would be exactly in accordance with the rules of the club, but I might try."

"True; I'll just give you the incidents, and then you can dress it up yourself, if you think it will do."

"Some years since, an acquaintance of mine was boasting in company one evening of his disbelief in the supernatural. There was an undertaker amongst us, and he and I laid our heads together, for the purpose of giving him a fright, if possible. Well, the undertaker offered to lay him a wager that he would not be courageous enough to visit his workshop the next night and open a coffin there, in which a corpse was then lying. My acquaintance accepted the wager, and we all waited with impatience the coming of the appointed time. A few hours before, I went to the undertaker's and dressed myself in a shroud, intending to play the part of the dead man; and then, until my acquaintance came, I and the undertaker smoked our pipes by the side of the coffin, and made ourselves as comfortable as we could, and enjoying ourselves at the expense of the boaster. Twelve o'clock struck—I jumped into the coffin, the pall was thrown over it, and then my friend was introduced, and the door shut upon him. Summoning up courage, though I could hear him muttering in a tremulous voice, he advanced and raised the lid, and as he did so, I started up in the coffin with a loud shriek. The effect it had upon him was tremendous—he uttered a louder shriek than I did, with one bound darted to the door, opened it, tumbled headlong down the street, and rolled insensible into the gutter. We won our wager, and he never boasted of his nerves again. There, you've had enough for once; mind now, and don't forget your promise to introduce me to the club, for if you do I will relate things of such an astounding character that I am quite confident after them none of the members will be able to sleep in their beds."

"You don't say so!"

"I do though, and I mean it. You shall soon discover that all you have hitherto heard is but tame in comparison with what I shall be able to tell you."

"Then you may make your mind up," said Reuben Gregory, "that I will introduce you to the club. Good night now, it's getting late, and when I tell this tale that you have related to me, I will call upon you and let you know what they all said about it."

CHAPTER IX.

THE FIRE AT THE CHURCH.—THE LAST MEETING OF THE CLUB.—THE DISPERSION. —THE CONCLUSION.

ONCE again had the dark mantle of night been spread over the old church, and the silence of the dead reigned around, and even the light of the stars was withdrawn, for they had shown a tendency to shine in the earlier part of the evening; but now all was dark—so dark, that there was nothing in nature to liken it to. The old church stood up in this still and silent spot; its grim form could scarce be seen at many yards' distance, so dark was the night, and when it was viewed closely and seen it appeared as extensive again as it really was.

Odd corners would appear strange and mysterious, and the steeple could only be partly discerned, leaving it to the imagination to bring to the mind all kinds of resemblances to the most out-of-the-way and even fearful appearances that could well be thought of. It was a strange and fearful time and place; the iron tongue of the clock had long since sounded the last hour preceding midnight, and that dread hour which opens the graves and causes them to give up their dead to haunt the spot of sepulture, and hold converse and fraternise with each other and interchange the communion of spirits.

These were hours and moments when men would fly these places, sacred to the fame of those things and sights men would shrink from, and when no man would venture near.

How many strange reflections rise upon the minds of men when they contemplate such things! A chill feeling creeps over them, and they appear to feel, rather than think of, bad things, they have as yet but heard of. The wonderful naturally attracts the wandering imagination of childhood, and when we are old we cannot divest ourselves of those early impressions which are so impressed upon us.

The hour draws nigh—midnight is at hand! There is the vault to which we have so often introduced our readers, and to which we now once again bring them. The vault is tenantless, save by those emblems of a past generation—those remnants of by-gone days, whose bones now rotted and crumbled in their niches. The silent hour is never so silent as in such a place; no sound—even the ticking of a death-watch—was to be heard, but death himself reigned here.

The vault was dark and silent; it was a common grave, from which nought but noxious vapours were exhaled, and from which no sounds, save the voice of one of the club, was ever heard within those dreary walls, for it was long since even the sound of a funeral service was heard, or even the removal of a coffin, or the addition of a new one.

Hark! the iron tongue of the old church clock strikes the hour so dread to many minds—so awful, so drear, and so fearful. The last stroke had scarcely been struck, the sounds still vibrated strongly from the clock tower or turret, when, from a door in the vault, entered the figure of a man who advanced to the usual place, and was succeeded by another before he had seated himself.

This was repeated till all were present. A candle—one solitary light—illumined but dimly the funeral vault, and the bare walls scarcely received any of the fugitive rays of the miserable flame. The figures one by one seated themselves, with the light in the middle, and a solemn silence was for some moments preserved amongst them, as though some sudden impulse actuated them.

Then the one who entered first said in a deep sombre voice which produced no echo even in that bare place, and which fell dead, as it were, in the vault.

"Again we have met," he said, "and again we must elect our president from amongst us. This little communion amidst the remains of those who were once living and breathing men like ourselves, must be conducted as it has been; and brothers, why should it not?"

"Why should it not, indeed?" said another; "let us proceed to do that which we have hitherto done on every occasion. Methinks the light burns more sombre than usual."

"A noxious vapour arises."

"It matters not, we are of the living and these were once the same, the rank vapours are such as we ourselves must one day exhale; we may as well get used to it by times, they can't hurt such as we—we feel ourselves at home among the dead."

They thus proceeded to check their passions, which, when done, there was a pause of some time, as if they were waiting to allow the past to cease to have any connection with the present.

"Are we all here?" inquired the president.

"All, all," they replied slowly, and in such low audible voices that they seemed unearthly.

"Then, brothers, we have now to ballot for him who shall relate the next incident, and yet I know not why, but an oppression weighs upon my spirits, as though we were not to meet here very often, perhaps some one of our members, perhaps myself, may be numbered among the dead; one of those who have been, should such be my fate, and who can say it will not, those who remain will yet meet and leave my seat empty, so that you will, when you look at it, say that one is gone, and then remember me."

"We will—we will."

"And then you will meet and relate such things as we have been accustomed to hear, and when it comes to my turn, believe that I am looking down—that I am present in spirit as you are in body."

"You may be the last," said another, "to quit these walls, who can say?—who shall predict, with truth, which of us shall leave this vault alive?"

"None—not one amongst us."

"The heartiest amongst us may be laid low and unable to make even a sign. Death spares no man, and we are in the abode of death, and such thoughts are by no means out of place."

"No, no—not out of place, for what can be better than the inquiring into the future? Our destiny is not complete, but it takes the future to do that."

"It does—it does."

"But how long that future may be we know not. I, for one, have a strange sensation at my heart, a sensation for which I can find no name. I feel that some of us may, indeed, never meet again; but be that as it may, we have met here for a specific purpose, and that purpose we will carry out; that is our present purpose to the letter, and let us see who it is that will this night give us that entertainment we seek, and have so often enjoyed."

"Yes, let us ballot—let us cast lots as usual."

"Then let it be so," said the president.

There was a pause, and then the skull was produced, into which, as before, were placed the papers which were to be drawn, until he who was to minister to the entertainment of the rest should be thus chosen, and then the others would listen to the sound of the speaker's voice, and attend to the narrative which he gave, with the utmost eagerness, yet with silence and decorum.

The place was dull and misty; the smell of the vaults was by no means wholesome; the emblems of death and the remnants of mortality formed a feature, by all means in the power of man to make sad, solemn, and awful. There they sat in this sad, solemn state. The lot had fallen upon one of those who had sat silent and motionless, leaning against one of the arches of the vault, looking on the earth with a downcast look.

"The lot has fallen upon you," said the president.

"It has," he replied, and then relapsed into silence. They all remained silent and sat for some time waiting for the beginning of the relation, believing that he was merely collecting the materials in his own mind, for the purpose of doing more justice to the incidents he was about to relate.

"I feel great difficulty," said the one who was chosen, "in performing the duty I have now incurred. I know not the reason, but I have that to say which would chain your attention to my words, but at the same time, I have hardly power to make myself heard."

"In a few minutes more time you may get over this difficulty,—I feel it myself; I know not why, but this is one of our saddest meetings."

"Aye, and, if my mind does not impress an untruth, upon my soul it will be our last—mark me this; and remember my words—I have had a dream."

"A dream!" echoed several.

"Aye; a dream—a dream which, if I rightly interpret, I know indicates a change in our position as a body of individuals—a great change—a very great change. I hope we may never come to any other end than a natural one, and that not before our full course of life has run."

"And then," said the president, "we shall have filled our allotted space, and drop in the fulness of time into those graves that have yawned so many years for us."

"It is too true—we must all die."

"We who meet here are peculiarly well aware of that—we know we must die. All around us are spread the emblems of death. Here, in our very hands, is the skull of one who was once a man like ourselves; what is it now? A dull emblem of mortality."

"Yes, once eyes and brains, now filled the empty cavity into which we place our ballot papers; but come, brother, to your tale: we have talked and conversed to give you time, and to cheer your spirits."

"Ah! well, I may as well make a beginning; I cannot tell, but I do not feel as if I could go through with it; but our rule must not be broken, and not by me. Well, then, but hark! what is that?"

"I heard nothing," said the president.

"Nor I," said another, "nor I."

"I thought I heard some noise above me, but it is merely a fancy: nothing else. It seems to me that we are all subject to saddened spirits; we feel and hear the flitting of a bat, though it were outside the walls of the old church itself. The light burns more dimly than usual—the air seems damper and heavier than heretofore, and I feel a difficulty in breathing, such as I felt not before.

"'Tis fancy—mere fancy—we have been seized by the spirit of fear; it sits heavy upon our souls, and we feel all those things we most dread, and only because our terrors point them out. I am free; however, I feel not that general co-operation of soul. What means it that you all should feel and speak thus?"

"There can be no explanation given for it, suffice it, for the occasion, that it is so; the fact stares us in the face, and we cannot shun it."

"That is true—but come, let us proceed."

"I will no longer delay," said the one who was to relate a series of incidents, "I will begin at once, and it shall be one you will not have heard the like for many a day."

"Proceed then."

"Well, the sexton of Beemington grave-yard was a lone old man. A tall gaunt form—iron-bound in frame, and with features as gaunt and grim as his body; his nose was crooked, and his eyes were crossed; his legs appeared to swing about as though they were not confined by joints, but merely hung upon loops, and they bent and bandied to and fro without any exertion of will in the owner.

"Now, the sexton was so old that none knew how old he was, nor where he lived. Some said in the church-yard, while others said he inhabited, like an ogre, some of the graves he had helped to make. Some said one place, and some said another.

"However, he lived in a vault, mid coffins and rotting palls, where no human eyes ever peered, but where he found means to introduce himself, and here he lived; but it was known to none save himself, for no one knew of the existence of the vault, it having been bricked over.

"Here, all alone, by a solitary lamp he would sit and sleep; he would dream of the future and recall the past; he cared for no one, and, truly, no one cared for him; no one knew him as belonging to his generation, but merely as some relic of the past—of a time that men talked of, and believed once to have been—but nothing more. Nobody sympathized with the morose old sexton.

"Here, however, all among the dead men, he would sit and smoke his solitary pipe to keep away the odour of the dead, and to render the impure air a little less unwholesome than it was; moreover, people used to say that the old sexton smelt of the grave. The very odour of the dead they said clung about him, and few were there who were at all aware of how true it was.

"They little thought that in a small confined space, where lay some dozen or two of corpses all long since mouldered to ashes, whose very bones could not be said to hold together, only some of the harder parts still retained their shape, but not all.

"Here the old sexton would sit and carouse as though he were in a world of spirits. Perhaps those who lay there might once have been his friends—people with whom he did hold communion. They belonged to that age to which he himself belonged, but they were dead and he was living.

"Here he would pass the coldest nights till he fell asleep, and when he awoke he went out into the fresh air to inhale some more wholesome atmosphere.

"Thus he lived for more than thirty years—he was a plague to everybody.

"At night he used to go to a certain house in the village, a public house, and there he used to sit and eat his supper, sip his twopenny, and then in silence he would leave the house, and for that night disappear from human sight, no one could tell whither he went.

"Once, twice, aye often was he followed and watched; he never looked behind, but he always contrived to elude his pursuers. He always disappeared suddenly, and nobody could find any traces of him; how he had disappeared no one knew, nor could they guess, but they often would say that there was no means of finding him on earth—that he had gone below.

"Some insisted that he must be more than mortal, that he would long since have been dead, had he been so; indeed, he was no longer a human being they would say, he was a goblin sexton, and by that name he was known; and some very old men said they remembered him when they were boys, and he was an old man then, but that must have been at least seventy years since.

"Well, it was at length determined to watch the old sexton carefully, and station people in various parts of the church-yard, so that he should be the less able to hide himself.

"He came, and was seen to enter the church vaults by an unfrequented door. Who could follow him? none, not one attempted this. They dare not attempt it—it was impossible—they could not venture down among the dead men—that they dared not do.

"And yet they saw the old sexton light his pipe, which burned brightly, and they saw that after he had disappeared below and then that was gone.

"It was now, it was fully ascertained what sort of an abode the old sexton occupied, and those who had kept the watch determined to return to their comrades and relate all they had seen and heard; accordingly, they returned to the house where they had left them.

"Then came the relation of what they had seen, which caused great consternation, and then a debate, in which it was agreed that it would be better to go and take lights and search the old church over, vaults and all, and by that means they would find out the exact spot, and at length it was agreed that they would do that, and that it was to be at once attempted.

"They got together as many as would go, with lanterns and different weapons of offence and defence, and all marched straight to the old church.

No. 23.

"It was a moonlight night—there was not a cloud to be seen at that moment—but, when they got near the old church, there was a cloud that came up from the vaults, and one which speedily spread itself through the old church, and filled it so that it was not possible for human beings to stop there.

"The church was on fire!"

"The old sexton has set it on fire with his pipe," said one.

"And he now is gathered to his fathers, after many—many years sojourn."

At that moment an awful shriek rent the air, and no one spoke, but each looked his fellow in the face with a look so full of ——

"Brethren," said the president, suddenly interrupting the narrative, "I know not whether it is what we have heard, or a mere fancy, but I have felt a great difference in breathing the atmosphere of this place. It has been coming on this last half hour."

"I think so too," said another; "there is a change."

"It is perceivable by all," said another; "the air grows thick and dry; and I think, too, there is a smell of smoke; see, the light burns dimly."

"It is mere imagination," said one, "mere imagination."

"That is all—that is all; what we have heard naturally fills our minds with these images, and we believe they have become a reality. When, indeed, we shall be able to shake off——"

"Fancy or not—imagination run wild—or be it the pent-up fears engendered by our meeting, suddenly burst loose, I know not; but this I do know, that I am not ashamed to own my fears that we are, somehow or other, beset by dangers. Hark!"

There was a pause; and then a sudden roar burst upon their ears. It was an indistinct sound, and one that they were scarcely able to understand, for it was over head, and they knew not what to make of it; but the smoke now burst upon their senses.

"This is no dream!" said one.

There was a sudden rush to the door, but it was no sooner opened than such a furnace-like heat and smoke came upon them that they were scarce able to shut it again. Then came a pause—an awful pause, during which they glared at each other, and nothing said. It was a moment of intense suffering and fear; no human pen can tell the feelings that pervaded them!

"We are dead men," were the first words that were uttered, and they were uttered by the president. "We are dead men, and must die a horrible death!"

The smoke grew thicker and thicker, but it was slowly; for the smoke had to travel downwards, which is against its general law, and only peculiar circumstances will cause it do so. What was to be done? There was no help; there was no prospect—no possibility of relief.

"God of Heaven! is there no hope?"

"None!" said a deep voice.

"Is there no possibility of escape—none at all? Must we stay here and die like so many rats? Surely, surely, the Eternal cannot have ordained so terrible an end—so fearful, so awful. Wherefore should it be done? Save—save us—save us in our hour of need! We cannot die the death of a rat. Great God! it cannot be that we must be—it must be——"

"There is no impossibility about it," said another; "the fearful truth lies above, as we hear and we can feel, and what more proof would you have of the truth of what we most dread? We are likely to make as fearful an end as any we have related to each other."

"The goblin sexton not excepted."

"No, his time was come; his course was run; but we are many, and but ill-prepared for such an event. We shall die unknown and unlamented."

"Horrible! horrible! horrible!"

The smoke grew thicker and their light grew dimmer, and the long horrified visages glared at each other in the pale and dim light that was now left them.

That night, from some unknown cause, the old church had caught fire. There is no soul to tell the tale living. How it caught fire, none knew—none saw the spark kindle—none saw it smoulder, and then the dark, thick smoke, arose from the burning materials, and gradually spread itself through every permeable portion of the building.

Had the members of this singular club taken warning from their first impulses, they would no doubt have been saved; but they saw not the hand that pointed by their instincts—they felt not the impulse, as such, which should have been to them a warning.

But they heard them not—they heeded them not—or, wanting that quickness which many timid animals possessed, and enable them to fly ere danger becomes unavoidable—they could not fly—they would not show any fear, unless the danger pressed them close indeed.

The fire smouldered and smoked; then, indeed, the spark beamed out—the dull red glow, by a gentle zephyr was wafted into a blaze, which soon took a firm deep hold of the timbers of that pile. It was old and dry. It had seen many ages, and had been built principally of timber. It was a well-fed fire that; the sparks and the flame cracked, and roared, and leaped, with demoniacal glee.

It seemed as though the fire had been directed by the furies, who urged it on to prevent the escape of those who were below. Now it rushed with a furious whirlwind, and then it would suddenly calm, and then the bright red and yellow flame would spring up, sending out smaller flamelets, whose forked tongues shot upwards with large bodies of smoke, which arose and filled the whole body of the church.

It was a grand and awful sight, to those who might have witnessed the destruction of the antique building; its huge fabric stood out on that intensely dark night, a body of light and fire. It was a fearful sight, and the contrast was great between the darkness and silence of the night, and the noise and light to be heard and seen in the church.

The roar of the flames, the splitting, cracking, and falling in all directions, offered something so terrible and so fearful to the mind, that it has never been equalled by anything on earth; there, indeed, was a light spread all through the old church-yard, and all around for many yards. It penetrated the otherwise impenetrable darkness of the night, and lit up the grave stones.

It was a fearful and even a ghastly sight, to see the white and grey tomb stones suddenly standing out in bold relief against the light that was thrown from the burning pile. The very trees wore a blood-red hue, and seemed to weep tears of blood for the tragedy that was going forward, unknown and unnoticed by any human being.

The very graves, dilapidated and broken down as they were, stood out bold in the deep red glare of the fire, for it now seized the whole body of the church, and burst from every window, while the flames shot upwards to the roof and the tower, and licked with their forked tongues every point that could be seized hold of, until it caught the blaze.

Then indeed the black tower, and belfrey, and steeple, shone out plainly in the light, and looked down from the darkness of the upper air with a frowning aspect upon the scene of desolation that was taking place below, and in which it was to become a sharer.

*   *   *   *   *   *   *

But for those below—those whose destiny had led them to such a spot, and at such an hour, and under circumstances which appeared to preclude the possibility of any one rendering them assistance—they heard the sound of the fire, the roaring and rushing; they felt the warmth imparted to their unpleasant and dreadful situation, by the hot air that was introduced through every crevice, and besides was fast becoming vitiated.

There they sat, gazing upon each other in silent horror and mute despair, scarce knowing what to think—they were paralysed, and their thoughts were completely frozen up.

"Cannot we force our way up singly? If we can, it will be better to die in braving such an enemy as fire. We had better perish bravely fighting for our lives than passively sink beneath the stroke of fate, which ought not to be borne."

" It matters not, our struggles with the element will not save us but protract, perhaps shorten our struggles, and makethem more painful."

" I think not ; if we could make a sudden rush up we might reach the door we came in at, and then we should be in the open door ; the fresh air would recover us, but here we must perish.   Come, who will make with me the attempt to save themselves ?   I will make it single-handed, rather than stay cooped up here.   Come, this may be our last hour, and we may as well die as become men, fighting to regain our freedom, who are in fact struggling for life."

" I am with you," said one.

" And I, and I," said several voices, till they all assented ; and they stood up more like spectres than men, and they reeled to and fro like drunkards.

" Now," said he who had got them all together, ready to make the attempt, " now, do you all make a rush after me, and we may chance to find our way out; if I fall, you will pick me up, and roll me out of doors in the open air."

" Yes, yes, we are all ready—all ready."

" Then follow," cried the president ; and at that instant the door was thrown open, and the members were about to rush up the narrow staircase : a volume of flame exhibited itself, and they started back ; at that moment some beams and rubbish fell across the doorway, blocking up the passage and door, at the same time they were compelled to shut the door suddenly, to keep out flame, heat, and smoke.

Now, indeed, they were without hope.   Rafters and beams fell on all sides; the church now gave way, and they were surrounded on all sides.

*   *   *   *   *   *   *

How they terminated their career none could tell.   They were imprisoned in the vault beneath the burning pile ; but whether they perished there by the most miserable of deaths we cannot tell, or whether they received timely and unlooked for assistance is equally beyond our knowledge, and the fulness of time only will reveal the secret, and show if they should ever again appear in some other quarter.

But the old church still burned on—the whole body was one sheet of flame, and a furious flight of sparks flew upwards as the roof fell in with a loud and fearful crash ; then came a body of smoke that for a moment obscured all around and enveloped everything in darkness, but it was soon changed, for a bright and immense flame shot upwards and lasted about a minute, and then the flight of sparks continued long, while a red lurid light shot upwards, and the steeple stood out in bold relief.

Now, indeed, the tower and steeple was the only part standing, and which now began burning furiously ; the clock itself was illuminated—the hand was five minutes to two, nearly two hours since the meeting of the club—the time passed quickly—nothing now remained but the steeple, and even that began to feel the effects of the flame—this was made of wood, and the flames ran up it, and away it flared to the very vane, which pointed where the wind blew from

The clock struck two.   The sounds had scarce died away on the air—scarce had the vibration of the sounds ceased before a loud creaking commenced, and then a rush like a whirlwind, then a shock to the earth was felt, and darkness for a moment reigned around.

The steeple and clock tower had now fallen, but the darkness of the night was succeeded by the light emitted by the burning embers, which had been obscured for a moment by the falling rubbish, but which now continued to burn unheeded till daylight broke upon the scene, and then the flames burnt themselves out.

THE END.